The Omega

Paul Clark

This first edition is published in Great Britain 2024
by Friston Books.

ISBN 9798874086565
Cover art and design by Van Garcia

Friston Books

Contents

Acknowledgements

Dominic's Alpha Course and all his lectures are based on two books by Nicky Gumbel: *Questions of Life: A Practical Introduction to the Christian Faith* and *How to Run the Alpha Course*. I have added, embellished, omitted and made changes for the sake of narrative fluency, but I hope I have captured the essence of Gumbel's message.

You can find detailed source notes on the ideas put forward by Bee in her 'Omega Course' on my website at https://paulclark42.com/omega. In order to keep the story moving, I have removed some details of her arguments from the novel and added them as appendices at the end of the book. The reader can choose whether to read these or ignore them.

Bee's arguments lean heavily on the following books: *A History of God* and *A Short History of Myth* by Karen Armstrong, *The Historical Figure of Jesus* by EP Sanders, *The First Coming* by Thomas Sheenan, *Who Wrote the Bible* by Richard Elliot Friedman, *The Bible Unearthed* by Israel Finkelstein and Neil Asher Silberman, *The Invention of God* by Thomas Römer, *Introduction to the Bible* by Christine Hayes and *God: An Anatomy* by Francesca Stavrakopoulou. There are suggestions for further reading at the end of this book.

All Biblical quotations are taken from THE HOLY BIBLE, NEW INTERNATIONAL VERSION®, NIV® Copyright © 1973, 1978, 1984, 2011 by Biblica, Inc.® Used by permission. All rights reserved worldwide.

All emojis are taken from OpenMoji https://openmoji.org/. For copyright reasons, all the modern hymns are original to this book.

Special thanks to my editor Talia Estavillo, to Nathalie Lodomez for checking my French, and to my daughters Angie and Penny for help with the counselling scenes and Generation Z conventions respectively. Also thanks to Anastasia Parkes for her critique, and to Alan Lomas for helping to recruit people to read an early draft of this book, among them two Anglican clerics. Thanks to them for their kind feedback on a book with which they were bound to disagree.

Thanks above all to my wife for putting up with her husband's obsession with his book.

To the memory of my parents, who did the heavy lifting for me.

Part One

The Fall

Chapter One

Ross didn't wait until he got home. Even as he sat in his instructor's car, in the passenger seat for the first time since his initial lesson, he took a photo of his driving test pass certificate and posted it on Instagram. By the time his instructor pulled up outside his house, it already had 15 likes.

'Well, there you go,' said his instructor. 'Congratulations.'

'Thanks.'

'Don't forget, drive carefully. The next twelve months are the most dangerous. Did you know that? Twenty-one percent of new drivers are involved in an accident in the first year after passing their test. Make sure you aren't one of them.'

'Will do.'

The instructor offered his hand and Ross shook it.

'Thanks for everything.'

'How old's your little brother?'

'Fourteen.'

'Well, tell your dad to give me a call in three years.'

Once inside, he messaged both his parents to tell them the good news. After that, he contacted his friend Raj.

Ross:	I passed 🍾
Raj:	Yeah I saw congrats
	So tomorrow still on?
Ross:	Yes I just have to persuade my mum to let me have her car
Raj:	Dani says she's gonna bring sofie
Ross:	👍
Raj:	She's determined to fix you two up
Ross:	😳

Ross told his brother as soon as he got back from school. He briefly looked up from his phone and pronounced this news awesome. When his mother came home, she gave him a hug and made him tell her all about the test, from the 'show-me-tell-me' questions at the beginning to the route he took, the reverse parking and the uphill start. He told her about how he thought his clutch control might let him down at one stage, but it worked out okay, and about the cyclist who got in his way but he thought he earned bonus points because he was very patient.

His father got home just before dinner. Once he had swapped his suit and tie for jeans and a pullover, Ross repeated everything for him. He waited until they had finished eating to ask the question that had been on his mind ever since he passed his test: 'Mum, will you be using your car tomorrow?'

'Don't know. Haven't seen the weather forecast.'

'I don't think it's going to rain.'

'I'll check in the morning. If it's dry all day, I'll take my bike.'

That was exactly the answer Ross had been waiting for.

'Don't go out of town,' said his father. 'On Saturday, we'll go out, and you can get used to driving fast and dual carriageways and what not. If you like, we can go up to Gatwick so you can try the motorway.'

'Okay. That'd be great.'

'And you have to take the learner plates off and put the P-plates on the car.'

'They're not a legal requirement,' said Ross.

'Put them on. Let other drivers know you're inexperienced.'

'What he means is let other drivers know you're a menace,' his younger brother said.

Ross laughed and looked at his mother, who was fixing him with her sternest stare.

'Oh, all right then.'

They all grinned.

'Remind me after dinner,' said his father, 'and I'll call the insurance and let them know, make sure you're properly covered.'

'Do you need to send your licence off?' his mother asked.

'The test centre's already done it.'

'Make sure you have your pass certificate with you if you take the car out,' said his father.

Ross nodded, but he wasn't thinking about that, or about waiting for Saturday before driving out of town. He had agreed with friends that tomorrow would be a day off from revising for their exams. They would spend the day in Brighton to celebrate him passing his test. And they wouldn't need to take the bus – he would be the designated driver.

After that, it would be time to get down to work. His first exam was just five weeks away.

*

Ross woke up soon after eight, while his parents and his brother were having breakfast. He waited until they had all gone and then popped downstairs to retrieve his mobile. He turned on his VPN so he could get round his parents' internet filter and access the kind of website he would always delete from his browsing history the instant he left it.

He got up half an hour later and made scrambled eggs on toast. When he got to the bathroom, he had a good look in the mirror. He liked what he saw: not just any old 17-year-old but a driver, with brown hair, very short at the back and sides but long and thick on top. He always brushed it forwards, but he had a natural parting on the left that would sneakily assert itself during the day, so he kept a comb in his back pocket to straighten it up again. He hadn't shaved for three days now and his stubble was starting to look good. He would leave it today but would have to shave it off soon. If he let it get too long, it would look scraggy.

Unlike his tall and very muscular friend Raj, Ross couldn't be bothered to go to the gym, but he kept himself lean and fit. He played a lot of football and table tennis, though he had decided to give up both for the rest of the season because he really needed to revise. His coursework had always been a bit last-minute, so he couldn't afford to screw up his exams.

He messaged his friends and set off at 9:45. He was slightly nervous about the journey, but he was also ecstatic at being able to drive by himself at last. His mother's grey Nissan Micra was hardly the sexiest car on the road, but Ross was now part of a very small elite in the first year at college who had passed their test first time.

Sofie lived just two minutes' drive away. Where Ross's house was fairly large and detached, hers was in a row of small terraced houses. She came out as soon as he pulled up. Quite short and slightly plump, Sofie had a round face and wore her hair in a bob. She had gone to a different school from Ross, but since starting college, they had found themselves in the same French class. She had also become his cousin Dani's latest BFF. Ross knew from his mother that Dani's mum didn't entirely approve of Sofie, though he didn't know why. She seemed perfectly okay to him.

She opened the front passenger door. 'Hiya.'

'Hi.'

'Congratulations.'

'Thank you very much.'

'I tell you what – shall I get in the back? If we keep those two apart, you won't be distracted every time you look in the mirror.'

Ross laughed.

It took another 20 minutes to pick up Dani and then Raj, who wasn't ready and kept them waiting. For the next 15 minutes, Ross drove along familiar roads to Polegate junction, where he turned left onto the A27 and headed out of town. He knew this part of the road well enough and had driven along it several times with his father. It was single-carriageway and surprisingly busy, with the traffic moving at around 50 miles per hour. For the most part, the road was quite winding, though there were a couple of straight bits where the traffic speeded up, one just before the Alfriston roundabout and the other between Glynde and the Southerham roundabout.

When they hit the dual carriageway, Ross was able to put his foot down at last. He got into the outside lane and took the car to a little over 65, which made him one of the fastest cars on the road, though three times he had to pull in for speed freaks who tailgated him and flashed their lights.

Raj worked out that, with four of them, it was cheaper to park in the city centre than to go to the Park and Ride and take the bus. Ross drove right down to the seafront, where he turned right and headed for the Churchill Square car park. He felt elated. He had driven all the way to Brighton without a hitch. He was on fire.

They walked to the shingle beach. The tide was out, exposing the sand where the sea came in. Raj took his shoes and socks off, rolled up his trouser legs and paddled in the water. Ross did the same. The sea was freezing cold, but he grinned and motioned Dani and Sofie to join them.

'No way,' said Dani.

She and Sofie walked back up the shingle and sat down.

Ross and Raj hunted for stones to skim across the calm sea. Raj threw first and his stone bounced twice. No such luck for Ross, whose first throw plunged straight into the water.

'Come on, Ross,' said Raj, and sent a stone that bounced three times before it disappeared.

Ross responded with a double bounce. The pattern was set, and Raj bested him with just about every throw. It seemed to Ross that if he threw a three, Raj threw a four. If he managed four bounces, Raj got five.

It was the same when they played table tennis. Ross was the better player: over the season, he had a much better win ratio, but when they played each other, Raj nearly always won.

When they had enough of throwing stones, Ross and Raj picked up their shoes and made their way gingerly up the painful pebbles to where Dani and Sofie were sitting. They sat down, Raj next to Dani and Ross on the far side by Sofie, and began to brush the sand off their feet.

'Hey, Raj,' said Sofie, 'Dani says I should ask if you fancy going for an Indian.'

Raj grinned and shouted, 'No!'

Dani burst out laughing.

'What's wrong with Indian?' said Ross.

'I have Indian every bloody day,' said Raj. 'I am not eating Indian with you lot. It'd be the same as my mum cooks but not as good.'

'His mum's a brilliant cook,' said Dani.

'Don't forget your promise,' said Raj, and Dani laughed again.

She explained the joke to Ross and Sofie: 'I promised him if we get married, he can have chips with everything, like at our gran's.'

Raj suggested fish and chips but Sofie said she knew of a good Buddhist vegetarian restaurant.

Dani agreed. She grinned and fluttered her eyelashes at Raj.

'As long as it's not Indian.'

'It's not,' said Sofie. 'They do bagels and things like that.'

Nobody was particularly hungry, so they decided to spend some time on the pier before lunch.

They made their way up the beach, Raj and Dani in front, Ross and Sofie behind. Dani and Raj had been together since December, almost four months now, and they were still clinging onto each other whenever they had the opportunity.

As he watched them, Ross couldn't help but feel a pang of envy. Not because he fancied Dani – she was his cousin, so that was impossible, even though she was very good looking. She had great cheekbones and was tall and slender, with an ability to make whatever she wore look the height of fashion.

Ross was envious of Raj because he would have loved to have a girlfriend. In fact, he had acquired one soon after the start of his first term at college, a girl called Mollie who he barely noticed until she sidled up to him one evening at a party. They both got quite drunk and ended up leaving the party and finding a dark alleyway.

They exchanged numbers and met up again the next day, after which they were a couple.

But six weeks later, she dumped him. Ross wasn't heartbroken, though he was upset at the way she cut him off, refusing even to look at him. He also felt he had lost his place in the social hierarchy of the college. Only a minority of boys had a steady girlfriend, and he was no longer a member of that exclusive group.

*

At the ticket office on the pier, they realised they had a choice: either unlimited rides and a very cheap lunch at McDonald's, or just three rides and enough money for a decent meal. After much discussion, their taste buds won out.

First stop was the Booster, a giant crane that span an enormous metal pole with four seats at each end. Ross and Sofie were locked into two seats together, with Raj and Dani behind them. The Booster sent them some 40 metres into the air and then stopped while people got on the other end. After that, the spinning began, round and round and upside down. Ross hung on for dear life while Sofie screamed. Once back on solid ground, they all agreed it was brilliant. Ross said nothing about the fact that he had no desire to get back on any time soon.

The next ride was even more terrifying. The Air Race looked like it was made of giant Meccano, with a dozen or more pairs of seats set on rather sad little models of Spitfires. Ross and Sofie sat next to each other once more, and the first 30 seconds were rather tame, spinning round at no great speed. But as the speed of the spin increased, the centrifugal force pushed them out and then round and upside down. Ross enjoyed it much less than he claimed afterwards.

Raj wanted to go back on the Air Race for their final ride, but the girls preferred the dodgems.

'Yeah, let's go on the dodgems,' said Ross. 'They're much cheaper.'

Afterwards, they made their way through the shops and cafes of The Lanes to North Laine, the heart of bohemian Brighton. For a moment, they walked past the vegetarian restaurant, which was situated in a tiny shop between a crystal jeweller's and a second-hand clothes shop. Then Sofie spotted three little outside tables. These were occupied, so they went indoors. It took their eyes a moment to adjust to the comparative gloom and find the last free table.

A vegan pancake snack, two halloumi bagels and a smashed avocado with cashew nuts later, the four of them left and wandered slowly through the narrow alleyways of Brighton's Lanes. They returned to the beach, where Ross enjoyed a short nap. At 3:30, they bought an ice cream and ambled slowly towards the Churchill Square multi-storey car park.

Ross decided to drive via the Lewes by-pass again rather than take the coast road. He had enjoyed putting his foot down on the dual carriageway. He also knew there was a petrol station. He would put five pounds' worth in the tank so his mother didn't get suspicious. She was far more likely to notice the petrol gauge than the milometer.

Driving out of Brighton was no problem: the road was wide and spacious. He got onto the dual carriageway easily enough, and he and Raj sang 'Al-bion! Al-bion!' as they passed the Amex Stadium. He thought about taking the car up to 70, but there was quite a lot of traffic, so for the most part he drove at just under 60 miles per hour.

Getting back onto the road after stopping for petrol proved to be harder than he had anticipated, but everything else seemed to go well until they passed Lewes and hit the single-carriageway road.

Ross found himself behind a Ford Focus, whose driver seemed incapable of going faster than 38 miles per hour, even though for much of the road, the limit was 60. Ross would have been quite happy to go at 50, or even 45, but 38? That was ridiculous. And in the places where the speed limit dropped to 40, the Ford Focus would slow down to 35.

Raj clearly shared Ross's frustration. 'Hey, Grandad,' he said, 'speed up.' After a while, this changed to, 'Come on, Ross. Overtake the old git.'

'I will when I get a chance.'

Dani, sitting in the back of the car, saw things differently. 'It's not worth it. We'll be home soon anyway.'

Overtaking was proving to be very difficult. The road was too bendy, and whenever it straightened out, there always seemed to be traffic coming the other way. In his mirror, Ross could see a queue of cars building up behind him, and his failure to get past the Ford Focus was turning into a major embarrassment.

Twice he indicated that he was about to pull out, and twice he lost his nerve. The cars coming in the opposite direction seemed too close.

But after the Drusillas roundabout, the road opened up. There was a long, straight patch with nothing coming the other way.

'Yay,' said Raj. 'Go!'

Ross grinned. He knew exactly what to do.

He signalled right, shifted down to third gear and began to pull out.

Bang!

Something hit him from behind and almost lifted the rear of his car off the ground.

It span towards the kerb, completely out of control.

He slammed on the brakes.

For an instant, he thought the car might tip over.

The front mounted the grass verge with a loud thump.

He steered between two trees, where a mass of thin branches and very young saplings brought the car juddering to a halt.

He heard an almighty crash somewhere behind him.

'Bloody hell!'

'What was that?'

'Is everyone okay?' It was Dani's voice.

Ross looked at his hands and down at his body. Whatever had just happened, he had survived it. He looked at Raj, who seemed to be all right, and in the mirror at Sofie and Dani. They were obviously shocked, but didn't seem to be injured.

'What the hell just happened?' said Raj.

'I don't know,' said Ross. 'I was just pulling out. I think someone hit us from behind.'

'Why did you drive off the road?' said Raj.

'I couldn't help it.'

'We'd better get out of the car,' said Dani. 'Just in case.'

Ross tried to open his door, but it was locked. He reached for the key and turned everything off. The doors unlocked and the four of them got out, fighting their way through the twigs and saplings that surrounded the car.

It was then that Ross noticed the disaster that had unfolded a short distance past them. A blue Renault Clio had flipped right over and a white Transit van had smashed into it, shunting it further along the road. Ross could make out skid marks and a trail of broken glass.

'Oh my God.'

All the traffic had now stopped, blocked in both directions by the upside-down Renault.

Dani was first to react. She rushed towards the Transit van and Raj followed her. Ross didn't move. He was still trying to process what had just happened.

The Ford Transit had been behind him for ages, he knew that. But where had that Renault come from? And why had it flipped over?

Dani ran round to the far side of the Transit. The driver's door opened and a man in paint-splattered overalls got out. He was tall and quite chubby. A younger man in his 20s got out of the passenger side. Dani spoke to the driver, put an arm round him and led him towards the kerb. He had a red mark on his face and was clearly very shocked. The younger man seemed bewildered but otherwise okay.

Sofie went down to help Dani shepherd the two men off the road. The driver was saying something, but it was a moment before Ross could make it out: 'It just flipped over right in front of me. I couldn't stop.'

Meanwhile Raj had joined two other motorists who were crouching by the upside-down Renault. One of them straightened up, took out his mobile phone and made a call. Raj stood up and brushed his fingers through his hair. He looked back at Ross and walked towards him.

'You all right, mate?' Raj said as he got within earshot.

'What's happened to the driver in that Renault?'

'It don't look good.' He shook his head. 'It really don't look good. She's stuck upside-down in her seat. The airbag's popped out and there's blood. We can't get at her.'

'Is she going to be all right?' Ross asked.

'It don't look good.'

'Has someone called an ambulance?'

'Yeah.'

Ross was still trying to piece the events together in his mind. He had seen the Transit van in his mirror, he was sure of that. But not the blue Renault. He had no memory of it at all.

'Oh God.'

He turned away from Raj, facing the girls and the two men from the Transit van.

'Oh, Jesus, no.'

'What's wrong, Ross?' It was Dani, who came towards him and put a hand on his shoulder.

He had turned white and broken into a sweat. He thought he might vomit at any minute. He walked up to the Transit van driver.

'Did that Renault hit me?'

'Yes. It was overtaking you when you pulled out.'

'Oh, Jesus Christ. No, no, no.' He put his hands up to cradle his head.

'It smashed into you,' said the Transit driver, 'and then it just flipped over right in front of me. I tried to stop but I couldn't.'

Ross shook his head. 'It's not your fault. It's my fault. I didn't look in my mirror before I overtook.'

Raj put a hand on his shoulder. 'You sure about that?'

'Yeah, I would have seen the Renault. It was overtaking me and I pulled out right into its path.'

Raj was silent for a moment. 'Look, be careful what you say. If the police come, you don't want to be telling them that. She was behind you, right? She rammed into you, so it's her fault.'

'No. Oh God. They drill it into you: mirror, signal, manoeuvre. God knows how many times my instructor said that to me. I didn't look in the mirror. It's my fault, Raj. All this is my fault.'

Chapter Two

By now, Ross could hear a siren. It was a police car, coming from the Lewes direction, driving rapidly along the empty lane opposite. It stopped by to the Transit van. Two policemen got out, putting on their caps as they did so. One looked over at Ross's car and the people standing near it, and then both went to crouch down by the Renault.

Ross's heart was racing. He wanted to cry but was determined not to do so in front of the others. He couldn't bear to look and turned away.

'Your mum's car's in a bad way,' said Raj. 'Especially the back, that corner.'

Ross shook his head. 'Screw the car. I'm more worried about the driver of that Renault.'

But then he realised he was going to have to tell his parents. Oh God. His dad had made him promise not to drive out of town.

Oh no. Jesus. He was so screwed.

It would have been better if he had failed his test.

More sirens. It was another police car, this time coming from the other direction. It halted the other side of the Renault and a policeman and policewoman got out. The policeman joined his colleagues near the Renault and the policewoman hurried towards Ross and the others. She was in her 30s, her dark hair tied back.

'Hi,' she said as she drew near. 'Are any of you guys injured?'

Ross's friends all said, 'No.'

She turned to the men from the Transit van. 'What about you?'

'I got smacked in the face when my air bag popped out,' said the driver. 'I'm okay apart from that.'

The younger man shook his head. 'I'm all right.'

'Are you from that Ford Transit?'

'Yes.'

'We'll get you both checked out at A and E.' She turned towards Ross. 'How about you?'

'It was my fault,' he said. 'I didn't look in the mirror.'

She touched his arm and guided him away from the others.

'Okay,' she said. 'Tell me what happened.'

'I pulled out to overtake another car. And the Renault hit me from behind. I hadn't seen it because I didn't look in the mirror. I'm so sorry.'

He started to cry, wiping the tears with his fingers.

'Is this your car, the Micra?'

'It's my mum's.'

'And you were driving it?'

'Yes.'

'And were the others with you in the car?'

'Those three, yes, But not those two. They were in the Transit van.'

Ross began to sob and covered his face with his hands.

The policewoman put her hand on his shoulder. 'Here, have a tissue.'

'Thanks.'

Ross wiped his eyes and blew his nose.

'I'm going to need your details. Have you got your driving licence?'

'It's been sent to DVLC. I only passed my test yesterday.'

'Oh. Are you eighteen?'

'No, I'm seventeen.'

'Ah, right. Okay. I'm not really allowed to ask you any more questions till you've spoken to your parents. First thing, you need to call your mum and tell her what's happened. After that, you need to come with me to the police car to take a breathalyser.'

Ross shook his head, 'I haven't been drinking.'

'It's procedure.'

Ross nodded.

'Second thing, tell your mum we're going to take you to the police station. Not the one in the town centre but the one in Hamlyn Drive. Are you from round here?'

'Yeah, I'm from Old Town.'

'Your mum's going to need to come to the police station, her or your dad, and you're going to need a solicitor. If she hasn't got one, there'll be a duty solicitor there to help you. Okay?'

Ross nodded. He took out his mobile and called his mother.

'Hi, Ross.' She sounded cheerful.

'Hi.'

'Ross, are you okay? Has something happened?'

Ross took a deep breath. 'I'm sorry, Mum, but I took the car to Brighton. There's been a crash.'

'Are you hurt?'

'No, but maybe the driver of the other car is.'

'Oh no.'

'Yeah. I'm with the police. I'm supposed to tell you something but I can't remember.'

The policewoman held out her hand. 'Give me the phone. I'll speak to her.'

*

She escorted Ross to her car, where she took out a breathalyser and made him blow into it.

'Negative.'

He nodded.

She took down his full name, address and date of birth. 'Okay, what's going to happen next is I'm going to arrest you. When we get the chance, we'll take you to the police station. You'll see a doctor or a nurse there and they'll check you out, make sure you're okay. We'll wait for your parents. Your mum says

16

they're going to try and bring a solicitor for you. After that, we'll let you go, and you'll go back and make a statement in a day or two, when you've had time to speak with your solicitor. Do you understand?'

'Yes.'

'Right, here goes: Ross Collins, I'm arresting you on suspicion of driving without due care and attention. You do not have to say anything. But it may harm your defence if you do not mention when questioned something which you later rely on in court. Anything you do say may be given in evidence. Is that clear?'

'Yes.'

Ross struggled to believe that such a thing could actually happen to him.

She took a file out of the glove compartment and, after searching for some time, gave him a leaflet that explained his rights.

'There's another one for minors, but I can't find it. The custody sergeant will give you one at the station.'

'What about my friends? How are they going to get home?'

'We'll take their details, and then they'll have to get someone to come and pick them up.'

'What about my mum's car?'

'It's not going anywhere for a while.'

'Do you need the key?'

'We'll sort that out when we get to the station.'

An ambulance arrived a few minutes later, followed by a fire engine and a third police car. Only then did the policewoman and her partner drive Ross to a police station, which, to Ross's surprise, was located in a small industrial estate on the far side of town.

They took him to a small interview room with no windows.

'Would you like some tea or coffee?'

'No thanks.'

'I'll get you some water,' said the policewoman.

She popped out and came back with a small bottle of cold Buxton water. Ross wasn't feeling thirsty, but he felt obliged to open it and take a sip. She then left, leaving Ross with her partner, a slightly overweight policeman who looked younger than her.

He asked Ross questions about everything and anything other than the accident: where he was studying, which subjects, whether he liked football, which team he supported and what he thought about the new stadium and Chris Hughton, Brighton's manager.

Ross answered most of his questions with just one or two words.

All this was brought to a close when a sergeant came in with Ross's parents. Ross stood up.

His mother hugged him tight. 'Are you okay?'

'I'm all right. Mum, I'm so sorry.'

'You're all right. That's the main thing.'

17

His father put a hand on his shoulder.

'I'm sorry, Dad.'

'It's okay.'

The overweight police officer left and came back with a fourth chair. He departed again and Ross, his parents and the sergeant sat down.

The sergeant introduced himself as the custody officer. 'Don't worry – we're not going to lock you up. I'm just going to go through the paperwork and then we'll let you go home. Your parents tell me your solicitor should be with us fairly soon.'

Ross nodded.

The paperwork was interminable. The custody officer seemed to be quite shocked when Ross said he hadn't been given the leaflet for minors. He produced one and insisted on going through it, explaining everything in great detail.

Half-way through this procedure, Ross's solicitor arrived. Tall and blond with a big nose, he was in his late 40s. He introduced himself as Damian Luscombe, and his accent betrayed a very expensive education. He and the custody officer obviously knew each other.

As he shook hands with Ross, he asked how he was.

'I'm okay.'

'Have you had a medical examination yet?'

'No.'

The solicitor raised an eyebrow at the custody officer.

'The nurse is busy. I'm just going through the paperwork while we wait for her.'

The solicitor nodded. 'Do you think I could have a chair?'

The custody officer went out to get one, after which the paperwork resumed.

Once everything was done, the custody officer left them alone to wait for a medical assessment plus a vulnerabilities assessment by a member of the Youth Offending Team.

'Ross,' said the solicitor. 'Tell me what happened.'

Ross closed his eyes. 'I took the car to Brighton...' He looked at his parents. 'I'm sorry.'

'Why are you sorry.'

'He only passed his test yesterday,' his mother answered. 'We told him not to go out of town yet.'

Ross looked at the floor.

'Carry on, Ross.'

'I was driving back, and I got stuck behind this car that was going really slow. I went to overtake it, but I forgot to look in the mirror. This other car crashed into the back of me. It flipped over and a Transit van smashed into it. I think the other driver might be badly injured.'

'Are you sure you didn't look in the mirror?'

'Yeah. I would've seen it.'

The solicitor nodded. 'Okay, now this is important. What have you told the police?'

'Well, here, nothing. They told me they wouldn't ask me any questions till I'd spoken with you.'

'What about when they arrested you?'

Ross hesitated.

'Did you say anything?'

'I told them it was my fault because I didn't look in the mirror.'

'You actually said that?'

'Yes.'

'In as many words?'

'Yes.'

'Did they ask you a lot of questions?'

'Well, when I said I was only seventeen, she said she wasn't allowed to ask any more questions.'

At that moment, there was a knock on the door. The custody officer came in and asked Ross's solicitor to go out for a word.

Ross and his parents sat in silence.

The solicitor came back. His face was very serious.

He sat down opposite Ross and looked at him and his parents. He then addressed himself to Ross. 'I'm afraid I've got some very bad news for you. The driver of the other car that was involved in the accident...she was pronounced dead at the District General Hospital half an hour ago.'

Chapter Three

Ross's mother cried all the way home. He didn't know what he could say or do. Neither of his parents said anything about him taking the car to Brighton, something he had done in direct contravention of his promise not to do so. He knew they must be angry with him, but they were in supportive mode. He half wished they would let it out and yell at him, tell him he was a stupid bastard and it was all his fault.

Once home, he retreated to his bedroom. He had no idea what to do. Normally, he would be straight on Instagram or WhatsApp, checking out his friends and running three or four conversations simultaneously. He had plenty of messages waiting for him, including from Raj and Dani, asking what happened at the police station.

What was he supposed to say? 'Yay, I'm a killer.' That would be a good status update. It would be the only thing he could say that was true.

He sat on his bed, his head in his hands, reliving the accident. He tried to work out whether he had looked in the mirror. He guessed that it must have taken him four, maximum five seconds to signal, change down into third and pull out. The car that crashed into him must have taken at least five seconds, probably six, to pull out and pass the van behind him.

He would have seen it. He was sure.

He hadn't looked in the mirror.

The accident was his fault.

A woman was dead because of him.

He googled *accident A27*, but nothing came up. He had a Twitter account that he never used. He had long since forgotten his password and needed to reset it, but eventually he got on and found posts asking why the traffic had been disrupted all the way back to Lewes. Several tweets had photos of his mother's battered Nissan Micra, the Ford Transit and the upended Renault Clio.

His mother called him down for dinner. She had prepared a quick meal with pizza and salad. Nobody spoke as they ate. What was there to say?

It was Ross's turn to tidy the kitchen and load the dishwasher. He turned on BBC Radio Sussex as he did so, and at seven o'clock, the news came on. His accident was second item. It said a 43-year-old woman had been killed in an accident involving her blue Renault Clio, a Ford Transit and a grey Nissan Micra with P-plates. The driver of the Nissan had been arrested and was helping police with their enquiries.

So, she was 43 years old? The radio gave no other details of the victim, leaving Ross to wonder about her. Was she married? Did she have children? Were her parents still alive? Maybe he hadn't just ended her life but had also wrecked the lives of the people who loved her.

He turned the radio off and stood leaning on the worktop with his eyes closed. After a moment, he took a deep breath, opened his eyes and put the dishwasher on. He cleaned his mother's favourite carving knife and wiped down the tops. Then he scurried upstairs and shut himself in his room.

Half an hour later, his mother knocked on the door with a cup of tea and a biscuit. She sat on the swivel chair by his desk.

'She was forty-three years old,' said Ross. 'It said on the radio.'

'Yeah. It was on the BBC local news too.'

'Do you think she had children?'

'I don't know. It didn't say.'

They sat in silence for some time.

'Why haven't you yelled at me? For taking the car to Brighton.'

'What good would it do?'

'Aren't you angry with me?'

'I'm just heartbroken. I'm too heartbroken to be angry.'

'Isn't Dad angry?'

'We're on your side, Ross. We love you, and we're always on your side.'

*

He got little sleep that night. His mind raced round and round in a raging torrent.

I've killed someone. Oh, Jesus Christ, I've actually killed someone. How could I do that? That's the worst thing I could ever do.

But it wasn't my fault. It was that idiot in the Ford Focus. Couldn't he go faster? Stupid bastard.

You didn't need to overtake. All you had to do was be patient for a few more minutes.

Oh God, what have I done?

What have I done?

Thanks to bloody Raj. If he hadn't nagged me, I wouldn't have done it. He stressed me out. That's why I didn't look in the mirror.

You can't pin this on Raj. It wasn't him that overtook. It wasn't him that forgot to look in the mirror.

That woman's dead because of you.

Because of me.

What have I done?

She must have seen me indicate. Why didn't she stop overtaking as soon as I indicated?

Don't go blaming her. She didn't forget to look in the mirror.

What about the driver of that Transit? Why was he so close? Why didn't he hit the brakes as soon as he realised something was wrong?

But it's you. It's so simple: mirror, signal, manoeuvre.

Why did you forget?

Why?

If you'd looked in the mirror, there would have been no accident.

But…

It's no good trying to blame anyone else. It's all your fault, you stupid, pathetic wanker.

*

At six the following morning, he crept downstairs to turn on the WiFi and get his mobile (it was a family rule that no IT of any kind was allowed in bedrooms at night). There was no more news about the accident. Ross knew his name would be kept out of press and TV because he was under 18. But social media was another matter. He had several messages from classmates and other friends, some of them checking if he was all right, others asking if it was true he had crashed into a woman's car on the A27. One even asked if he had killed her.

What could he say? Better to say nothing.

He went back downstairs to use the laptop he shared with his brother. He wanted to find as much as he could about the woman he had killed. It didn't take long. Her name was Elizabeth Johnson and she was married with two young children, though he couldn't find anything about their ages. She was assistant manager at a branch of a building society in Brighton.

He opened up Instagram to see if she was there. He found a never-ending scroll of Elizabeth Johnsons. He knew the password his mother used for everything, so he opened her Facebook account and looked there. It was the same. She would probably be on LinkedIn and his father had an account, but Ross couldn't remember his favourite passwords.

If she was 43 years old, then her children were probably younger than him. Maybe early teens. Possibly even younger than that.

He tried to imagine what it must be like to lose your mother so young. His dad was great for all the fun they had with him and all the things he knew. But all his life, if he needed a shoulder to cry on, someone to talk to, he had gone to his mum. And these two young children had just lost that, all because of him. Who would they go to when they needed help? Could their father do that for them?

Ross heard noises upstairs as his father got up, sneezed and went into the bathroom. He shut the laptop down and crept up to his bedroom. He would avoid contact for as long as he could. He had a gruelling day ahead of him. But then again, it would be nowhere near as gruelling as Elizabeth Johnson's family's day.

When he got downstairs, his mother said, 'I got an email to say someone had opened my Facebook account. Was that you?'

'Yeah. Sorry about that. I was looking for Elizabeth Johnson, the woman who died in the accident.'

'Did you find her?'

'No. There's millions of Elizabeth Johnsons.'

She nodded and pointed her finger at him. 'Keep out, okay?'
'Yeah, sorry.'

*

Both of Ross's parents had taken the day off work to accompany him. At 10:30, they took him to his solicitor's office in the elegant, Victorian-style Upperton district near the town centre. The terraced buildings were all three storeys plus basement, painted white with enormous bay windows on the ground and first floors.

Ross's father parked behind the solicitor's office and they walked round to the front. They climbed the steps to the imposing black door, and Ross's mother pressed the bell.

'Hello. Ross Collins for Mr Luscombe.'

The lock buzzed and let them in. The receptionist invited them to sit down on a long sofa, which sagged under their weight. Nobody spoke. Ross looked out of the window. It was a beautiful spring day. His plan had been to revise French vocabulary for a couple of hours and then play on his Xbox until lunch time, after which he and his friend Natalie would test each other via WhatsApp. And then a bit of history revision. He would start with the divine right of kings.

'Oh God,' he thought. 'You really have screwed up this time, haven't you?'

My Luscombe turned up after five minutes, wearing a brown checked suit and a yellow tie that Ross thought clashed horribly.

'Hello there.'

He and his parents stood up and Mr Luscombe shook them all by the hand, starting with Ross. His grip was firm but not crushing.

'Can I offer you tea? Or maybe coffee?'

Ross's father asked for tea with milk no sugar, but Ross and his mother declined. Mr Luscombe passed the order on to the receptionist and invited them upstairs to his office, which had heaps of files and legal books all over the place. Only two of the seats for clients were free, so he removed a pile of papers from another chair, which he offered to Ross's father.

Once they were all settled, with Ross to the right and his parents to the left, Mr Luscombe leaned forwards, elbows on his desk. 'Okay Ross, start at the beginning. Tell me everything that happened.'

Ross recounted the events of his day in Brighton. His solicitor was particularly interested in his route to Brighton, the traffic, the speeds he drove at, what he had eaten and drunk and the nap he had on the beach.

'You didn't have any alcohol?'

'No. They breathalysed me.'

'Yes, I saw that. You didn't smoke any weed or anything like that?'

Ross shook his head. 'No.'

'And how were you feeling when you set off back home?'

Ross shrugged. 'Fine.'

23

'Not tired or anything?'

'No.'

'Nervous?'

'Maybe a tiny bit, but I was more nervous in the morning.'

'Excited?'

'I wouldn't say excited, but I was looking forward to the drive.'

Mr Luscombe interrogated him at length about the journey back, the accident and his conversation with the police. 'It's a shame you said that about it being your fault.'

'But it was my fault.'

'Not a hundred percent.' He rifled through the papers on his desk. 'Here it is: you think you broke rule one hundred and sixty-three of the Highway Code: you tried to overtake without first using your mirrors. Yes?'

Ross nodded.

'But also, Mrs Johnson was taking a big risk, overtaking three cars in one go. And she actually broke the rules.' He picked up a sheet of paper and read from it: 'Rule one hundred and sixty-seven: Do not overtake where you might come into conflict with other road users. For example,...blah blah blah...when a road user is indicating right. You did indicate, didn't you?'

'Yes.'

'How long before?'

'I don't know. A second or two.'

'And she was behind you. She'll have seen you indicate, so she was wrong to go ahead with the attempt to overtake you.'

Ross looked down. He knew what his lawyer was up to – he was trying to get him off. That was his job, after all. That was why his insurance company was paying him. But Ross didn't want to get off. If he had looked in the mirror, Mrs Johnson would still be alive. She deserved justice for that. Her family deserved justice. And his clever-clever lawyer saw it as his job to make sure they didn't get it.

Ross raised his hands to his head and ran his fingers through his hair. He felt a lump in his throat and thought he might burst into tears at any minute.

'Let me tell you what's going to happen,' said his solicitor. 'At two o'clock, you have to make a police statement. There'll be an investigating officer and probably one other. I'll be there plus one of your parents.' He looked at Ross's mother and father. 'I think both would be overkill.'

They glanced at each other. 'I'll go,' said Ross's mother.

"Okay. So, we'll negotiate the wording of your statement. Now there's one thing I want you to say: just say "I don't remember looking in the mirror." Don't say you didn't look. Okay?'

'But I didn't look.'

'It doesn't matter. Make life easy on yourself and just say you don't think you looked or you don't remember looking.'

Ross looked away and nodded.

Whatever.

'It's a very time-consuming process,' said the solicitor. 'Possibly as long as two hours. How's your spelling, Ross?'

Ross shrugged. 'Not bad, I suppose.'

'See how many spelling mistakes you notice on your statement. Most plods have atrocious spelling.'

*

The plods, as Ross's solicitor called them, consisted of a sergeant from the Accident Investigation Unit and the policewoman who arrested him. The sergeant did most of the talking and the policewoman did all the writing. Ross couldn't see much wrong with her spelling.

It was all very informal, almost friendly. The policewoman greeted him with a smile and 'How are you coping?' For the most part, the sergeant's interrogation was gentle but thorough. The only time it became insistent was when he asked whether Ross had looked in his mirror before indicating or pulling out.

'I don't know,' said Ross. 'I don't remember looking in the mirror.'

'You don't know?'

'No.'

The sergeant glared at Ross's solicitor, who gave a little shrug.

'When you spoke with Sandra just after the accident, you said you hadn't looked in the mirror.'

'Sandra?' interjected Ross's solicitor.

'That's me,' said the policewoman. 'Constable Sandra Samuels.'

She looked at Ross and smiled.

'You don't have to answer that question,' Ross's solicitor said.

Ross felt bad enough about agreeing to obfuscate about whether he had looked in his mirror. He wasn't going to lie about what he had said to the policewoman.

'Yes, I did say that.'

'But now you don't remember?'

Ross's solicitor put a hand across Ross to shut him up. 'I don't think you should put too much store by what Ross said then. Any court would judge it to be inadmissible. He was probably in a state of shock. He hadn't spoken to an appropriate adult, never mind a solicitor, and he hadn't even been cautioned.'

'Point taken,' said the sergeant. 'We'll put in the statement that that's what he said then, but looking back, he isn't sure. Okay?'

'Fine, but we'll add that it was very soon after the accident, and he hadn't been cautioned.'

The sergeant nodded. 'Okay. Now, Ross, did you see the car before it hit you?'

'No.'

'You're sure?'

'Yes.'

He made Ross mime his actions after he decided to overtake the Ford Focus and did or didn't look in the mirror: indicate, clutch down, change to third gear, start to pull out, bang as the other car hit him. He timed it using his mobile.

'I make that five point one seconds. Let's do it again.'

Ross re-enacted this twice more. Both times came in at a little under five seconds.

'Okay, so we'll put in the statement that it probably took between four point five and five point five seconds. Is that okay?'

He looked at Ross and his solicitor, who both nodded.

When Ross described the aftermath of the collision, the sergeant said, 'We call it a rotary impact collision: the other car hit your rear offside with her front nearside. This span both cars towards the side of the road. It's really dangerous when it happens at speed. That's why her car flipped over. You'd have flipped over too if you'd been going much faster.'

Ross shuddered.

As his solicitor had predicted, it took more than two hours to complete the statement and get it signed. The policewoman took it out to photocopy for the solicitor. While they were waiting for her, Ross turned to the sergeant.

'Can I ask a question?'

'Yes?'

'Mrs Johnson – how old are her children?'

'She's got a girl who's nine and a boy who's six.'

Ross hung his head.

'I'm really sorry.'

Tears welled up in his eyes. He covered his face with his hands and started to sob. His mother put her arm round his shoulder.

He was still crying when the policewoman came back. She sat down and nobody spoke until Ross had regained control and wiped his eyes and his nose.

'I'll tell you the next steps, Ross,' said the sergeant. 'Maybe Mr Luscombe's already told you. We have lots of witnesses to interview, and our crash investigators have to examine both cars and things like skid marks on the road. Because you're under eighteen, we'll prioritise it, and I think it'll take about two weeks. Then we send a file to the Director of Public Prosecutions. They look at it and they decide what steps to take. They're not quick, I'm afraid. It'll take at least two months, and in a worst-case scenario, we may not hear from them till after the summer.'

Ross nodded.

'So, I'm going to make an appointment for the sixteenth of July. Is eleven in the morning okay for you?'

Ross looked at his mother, who nodded. The solicitor checked the diary on his mobile and agreed.

'Okay. Between now and then, you're free on unconditional bail. Have you got exams coming up?'

'Yes.'

'That'll keep you busy. Keep your mind off things. We'll meet again in July.'

'Can I just have a minute with my client?' said the solicitor.

Once the police had left, he turned to Ross and said, 'I think that went okay. He was bound to want to put what you said to the constable in, but I think we can neutralise it in court.'

Ross lifted his hand slightly and opened his mouth to speak, but then sat back and said nothing.

'Do you think he'll be charged?' Ross's mother asked.

'The DPP's office will only press charges if they're sure of getting a conviction. They've got their targets to meet. I think driving without due care and attention is pretty certain, in which case you can expect to lose your licence and have to take your test again.'

Ross shook his head. 'I'm not going to drive again, not for ten years.'

The solicitor pressed on: 'As I said before, a charge of causing death by careless driving would be much more serious. It's very possible, even though the Renault driver bears at least as much responsibility as you for the accident. I'd say the chances are about sixty-forty.'

Ross shrugged. 'I did cause her death, though, didn't I?'

'You don't want that on your record,' said his solicitor.

Ross didn't see the point in arguing. He was just saying what lawyers always say.

'As I said before, theoretically, that would carry a maximum sentence of five years. But in your case, that's not going to happen. There's a lot of mitigating factors here, starting with your inexperience plus your attitude since the accident. You'd get a rehabilitation order with a community punishment, something like that. So don't go worrying yourself about prison. It's not going to happen.'

Ross gave a slight nod.

'There's nothing you can do between now and July. As the sergeant said, just concentrate on your exams.'

*

Ross spent the next day on his own, with his parents at work and his brother at school. He decided to try once more to find Elizabeth Johnson via social media. Given her age, he thought Facebook would be the best bet, so he opened up his mother's account on the laptop, safe in the knowledge that she wouldn't get another automatic email. There were almost a hundred Elizabeth Johnsons. He was able to eliminate some because they lived in London,

Pennsylvania or wherever, but he had to open up most of their profiles and check them out.

A few had privacy settings that stopped him seeing anything much, apart from profile pictures, most of which looked too young or too old. He dawdled over a few very good-looking Elizabeth Johnsons, but for the most part he was systematic: open, eliminate, move on. His biggest fear was that he might accidentally make a friend request.

It took him 45 minutes to go through all the Elizabeth Johnsons. No luck. Next, he tried Liz Johnson, Beth Johnson and Lizzy Johnson. More than two hours later, he was bored and deflated. He had two more throws of the dice: Lizzie and Libby. He couldn't think of any other variants on the theme of Elizabeth. He decided to go for Lizzie first.

And there she was, fifth one down. He knew at once that it was her. Her profile picture was of a woman with a pleasant, smiling face and long, straight brown hair. She wore a bright red and blue top with thin straps that showed her shoulders. She was sitting in one of the cafes by the seafront, a little blond boy with an ice-cream cone on her knee and the pier in the background.

Ross couldn't help but like her. He thought everything about the picture was warm, friendly and relaxed; she looked so happy and the boy looked so comfortable.

He opened up her profile. Her cover photo was her two children in Disneyland Paris Main Street, with Sleeping Beauty's castle in the background. He scrolled down and read the tributes on the page.

'Auntie Lizzie – I can't believe you have gone. I love you so much and I miss you.'

'I just heard the news. I'm so devastated. You're such a good friend to me. Will miss you loads.'

'Anthony, Jude, Adam, my heart is breaking for you.'

'Still miss the time we had together just before you moved in with Anthony. You were the best flatmate ever. Can't believe I won't see you again. Will miss you babe. xx'

There were other tributes, but Ross didn't read them. He closed his eyes and covered his face with his hands.

What have you done, you stupid, stupid bastard? What have you done?

He sat there for a long time without moving. Eventually, he brought his hands down, opened his eyes and scrolled down to look at Lizzie Johnson's photos, which were mostly pictures of her with her husband and children: trips to the beach, Easter eggs, Christmas dinner with grandparents, Halloween and summer holidays in what looked like Spain or Portugal. Her husband looked a little older than her, quite tall, thin on top with a friendly smile. It was a portrait of the perfect happy family. And he had gone and destroyed it.

*

28

The next day was Saturday, and Ross's family were at home. He avoided them as much as he could and took the laptop upstairs, where he spent more time exploring Lizzie Johnson's Facebook page. Her husband had put a message there: 'Thanks to everyone for your messages of support. It's come as a terrible shock and we are all absolutely heartbroken, as you can imagine. But the children are coping and family and friends have rallied round. We'll get through this. I'll put up details of the funeral as soon as I can.'

Ross clicked the window shut. He had no right to read this. What would her husband think if he knew his wife's killer was spying on his family's private grief?

But then he opened her Facebook profile up again and started to scroll down deeper into her past. He discovered that her birthday was on the 17th of November and, judging by all the good wishes on her timeline, she had plenty of friends.

Looking through her photos, he saw that she had had a big party for her 40th. She had hired what looked like a church hall, and a lot of people had gone. She had also been tagged in several photos with her husband in what looked like ballroom dancing classes, but these seemed to have stopped three or four years ago.

All the photos were full of smiles. Not the fake smiles and pouts so many of his friends put on their Instagram feeds, but real smiles, laughter, excited children.

He got as far back as the birth of her little boy. How could she know that they would have just six years together? Ross felt the pain of a lump in his throat, though he managed to suppress his tears.

He closed the window and promised himself that he would never look at her profile again.

That afternoon, Dani came round with her mother (the younger sister of Ross's mum). Ross allowed himself to be called downstairs, but he found it very hard to join in the conversation, which, for once, was very strained.

Eventually Dani came out with what Ross guessed was the real purpose of her visit. 'The police are coming to our house tomorrow. I have to make a statement. Is there anything you don't want me to say?'

Ross shook his head. 'Tell them everything. That's what I did.'

'Okay.'

'Do you blame yourself?' Dani's mother asked him.

'Yes.'

'Everyone blames themselves,' said Dani. 'That guy driving the decorator's van, he blamed himself.' She hesitated for a moment and then said, 'Raj blames himself because he was nagging you to overtake.'

Ross almost said, 'So he should.' He caught himself just in time and said, 'It wasn't Raj who forgot to look in the mirror.'

'He says he can't face you.'

'Tell him it's not his fault.'

On Sunday afternoon, another visitor came round. Ross heard the doorbell, followed by the sound of his mother and a young woman's voice, though he was unable to make out who she was or what they were saying. After a moment, he heard his mother come up the stairs and knock on his bedroom door.

'Ross, Natalie's here for you.'

'Oh? Okay. I'll be right down.'

Ross and Natalie had been good friends since year nine. She sat next to him in his French classes at college, and they had been planning to help each other out with revision. Ross found Natalie very attractive; she had big eyes and an infectious smile that lit up her face. He had enjoyed a couple of drunken snogs with her, and Dani had told him she was keen to take their friendship further.

But Ross was wary of doing so. When he was going out with Mollie, he had enjoyed her company and became quite fond of her, and he had certainly been keen on the physical aspect of their relationship. But at no stage had he ever fallen in love with her.

She quite obviously sensed this, because when she dumped him, she said, 'It's not me. It's you. You don't love me.' When he said nothing in reply, she said, 'See. You don't even deny it. I'm wasting my time.'

He had taken advantage of Mollie's feelings for him and was determined not to make the same mistake again.

When Ross got downstairs, his mother left him and Natalie alone together in the dining room.

'How are you?'

'I'm okay. I wasn't injured.'

'I don't mean that.' She pointed to her heart.

Ross shrugged. 'Not great, to be honest.'

'We're all worried about you. You're not replying to any of our messages.'

'Yeah, sorry about that.'

'You've got lots of friends, Ross. People care about you.'

He gave a wan smile and they sat in silence for a moment.

'Are you beating yourself up?'

Ross thought for a moment and then said, 'I've been looking at Lizzie Johnson on Facebook.'

'Who's Lizzie Johnson?'

'The woman I killed.'

'You didn't kill her. She crashed into you and died.'

'Yeah, but it was my fault.'

'Only partly.'

'If I'd looked in my mirror, she'd still be alive. It's my fault. You're supposed to look in your mirror before you indicate. Mirror, signal, manoeuvre. That's what they teach you.'

'It doesn't mean you killed her. You made a mistake. You're not a murderer.'

'She's still dead though, isn't she?'

Natalie sighed. Ross noticed tears well up in her eyes.

'You can't keep beating yourself up for ever,' she said.

He said nothing. He wondered just how long he should beat himself up for. Six months? A year? Ten years?

'Have you thought about seeing Kitty?' (Kitty was the Student Counsellor at their college, where all staff were known by their first names.)

'That's what my parents say.'

'So, what do you think?'

'Don't know. I'll think about it.'

*

Raj contacted him that evening.

Raj:	Hey ross
Ross:	It's not a good time man
Raj:	I just thought we should talk
Ross:	I got nothing to say to you
	Last time I listened to you I ended up making the worst mistake of my life

Ross sat staring at his mobile for a long time, but Raj didn't reply. Eventually, Ross closed his eyes and put his mobile down.

'Oh, shit,' he said out loud.

He spent the rest of the evening alone in his room, cursing himself for what he had done and for trying to shift the blame onto his closest friend. He didn't see any way out of this.

Oh God.

What do you do when you have killed someone?

Well, there was one obvious answer: suicide.

Bloody hell!

Where did that thought come from?

But that would be justice, a life for a life. And it would show Lizzie Johnson's family that he genuinely regretted what he had done.

And it would end his pain.

'No,' he said out loud. That wouldn't end his pain. It would just transfer it to his mum and dad. It would be a terrible thing to do.

*

Next morning, he went for a walk, the first time he had been out by himself since the accident. It was a beautiful April day, quite cool but sunny and warm enough to go out without a jacket.

He walked down to the main road and turned right. He continued for half a mile, until he reached the traffic lights, where he turned left and headed downhill towards the town centre. But he couldn't face meeting anyone he knew, so just before he reached the supermarket, he veered off to the right towards the park.

He looked up at the sky, which had very quickly changed to a threatening grey. It was obvious it was going to rain, and he knew he should really go back home. But he needed to go somewhere. He needed to do something. So, he carried on all the way to the park and walked in, past the manor house and through the manor gardens. He headed down the flagstone pathway, passing the tennis courts and the skateboard park with his face pointing the other way.

He rounded the corner and came to the café, with the children's playground behind it and the wide open lawns that led to a small thicket and a football pitch at the far end. He walked past dog walkers and pensioners out for their mid-morning stroll, round the football pitch, and back up the far side of the lawns. It started to rain before he reached the children's playground, where he saw mothers rushing to take their babies and toddlers off the swings and slides and put them in their pushchairs.

He started to run, round behind the tennis courts and through the manor gardens. By the time he reached the main exit, it was really tipping down. He ran across the High Street near the supermarket and headed for St Margaret's Church. He knew there was part of the old parsonage where he could shelter until the worst of it passed.

Just before he got there, he noticed that the main entrance to the church was open. He could go inside.

Why not?

He walked in, glancing at the parish notices and the pictures of aid projects in Africa as he did so. The church was empty, cool and silent; the sound of the rain had disappeared. He walked into the aisle and looked down towards the altar, pulpit and organ. At the far end there was a stained-glass window that featured scenes from the life of Christ. The dark-brown benches smelled of wood polish, dust and leather.

He sat down three rows from the front, right in the middle, near the aisle. It occurred to him to pray. After all, he was in a church. He knelt on the cushion in front of his bench, closed his eyes and put his hands together, probably for the first time since he had been in the scouts.

'Please God,' he prayed out loud. 'I'm sorry. It was my fault. I know it now. I've been trying to find a way blame other people, but I know it was my fault. It was all my fault. I'm so, so sorry. I didn't mean to do it.'

He could hardly breathe, and his face twisted into a silent scream. Tears poured from his eyes and streamed down his cheeks. With his elbows on the hymnbooks on the little shelf in front of him, he buried his head in his hands and howled.

He had been crying like this for some time when he heard a voice behind him.

'Excuse me? Can I be of any help?'

Ross looked round. A vicar standing behind him, quite tall, in his early 30s with glasses and short, dark hair.

'Oh, I'm sorry. I didn't realise there was anyone here.'

'Well, there's always someone here, if you see what I mean.'

Ross gave a little smile and sat up on the bench.

'Would you like to talk about it?' the vicar asked.

'I've done something really terrible.'

The vicar sat on the bench in front of him. 'What have you done?'

'Have you seen that story on the local news, the woman who died in a car crash?'

'Was it a few days ago?'

'Yes.'

The vicar nodded. 'Yes, I think so.'

'That was me. I was the other driver.'

The vicar frowned. 'Do you blame yourself?'

'It was my fault.' Ross looked away from him. 'We were stuck behind a very slow driver, and she was overtaking me. I pulled out to overtake, but I didn't look in my mirror. She slammed into the back of me and her car tipped over. A big Transit van smashed into it and killed her.'

With his fingers, he wiped away the tears that had started to fall again.

'You must feel really bad about it.'

'She's got two children. I killed their mother.'

He wept uncontrollably, hiding his face in his hands.

'Let your tears flow,' said the vicar. 'Sometimes you have to let them out.'

It was a long time before Ross regained control.

The vicar put his hands together, almost touching his lips. 'I wish I could wave a magic wand and ease your pain,' he said. 'But I can't. It's going to be very difficult for you to get through this, very difficult.'

Ross nodded.

'But you've taken the first step. You've acknowledged your responsibility. That's a very important start. If you denied it, if you blamed others, you wouldn't get anywhere. You'd just feel a part of yourself shrivel up and die.'

Ross nodded again, shoulders hunched, eyes looking down. It was true. He had accepted it now. The accident was his fault. Nobody else was to blame.

'You don't have to take this journey alone. God loves you. Jesus loves you.'

'I wish I could believe that.'

'You find it difficult?'

'I've never been religious.'

'You find it difficult to believe?'

'Yes.'

The vicar said nothing. He seemed to be waiting for Ross to speak.

'I suppose my parents didn't bring me up to believe it. My…my dad always says it's all superstitious nonsense.' He cast a quick glance at the vicar and looked down again.

'A lot of people think like that. They think it's a question of objectively weighing up the evidence to see if it's true. But that's not what it's about.'

'No?' Ross brought his eyes up to look at him.

'No. I'm a believer because I made a decision to believe. I made a decision to let God into my life, and he's filled me with his goodness ever since.'

Ross's eyes widened. 'Don't you ever...? Don't you ever have doubts?'

'Sometimes. But I have faith. I made a decision to believe and I stick with it.'

Ross looked away from him. 'I really wish I could believe, but I don't know if I can.'

'You find it hard to make that leap of faith?'

'Yes.'

'Some people do find it hard. Some people, it seems to come naturally.'

Ross nodded.

It was some time before either of them spoke.

'We do a course for people like you,' said the vicar. 'Maybe you've heard of it, it's called the Alpha Course. It's for people who would like to believe but find it hard. We've got a course starting in July. Would you be interested?'

'Yeah, maybe.'

Chapter Four

The meeting with the vicar and the prospect of the Alpha Course cheered Ross up. Perhaps there was hope. Wasn't Christianity all about repentance and redemption? He vaguely remembered something about more joy in heaven over a sinner who repents than…than something, he wasn't quite sure what.

Ross actually managed to do more than half an hour of revision that afternoon before Lizzie Johnson's Facebook page sucked him back in. He looked at all her old profile pictures, right back to the first one. She was much younger and thinner then, her hair dyed with henna. Ross saw how pretty she was, with a nice smile and eyes that seemed to sparkle with life.

A life that he ended.

His mood came crashing down. He closed down her Facebook page, hating himself for stalking her like this. Usually, it was stalkers that turned into killers, but in Lizzie Johnson's case, her killer had become her stalker.

At dinner, his mother asked, 'Have you given the idea of counselling any more thought?'

He put his knife and fork down and raised his hands to the side of his face. 'Just…just…Give me space, will you?'

His mother sighed and glanced at his father, who gave a little shrug.

Ross didn't dare to say that he had found an alternative in the Alpha Course. His father wouldn't approve, and in a sense, that was part of its appeal. It was his solution, not his parents'.

He just had to hang on until July, and then he would find a way through this mess.

But hanging on until then was going to be very difficult, all alone in the house, with revision he couldn't do and Lizzie Johnson's Facebook page calling to him just a few clicks away.

He didn't know how to distract himself from the accident and Lizzie Johnson. Music was no good. Uplifting songs clashed so sharply with his mood, and more downbeat songs, of which he had plenty on his Spotify, just pulled him further down. None of his favourite podcasts spoke to him any more. All the humour, all the optimism, all the energy, it simply jarred.

Messages from friends had mostly dried up, apart from the occasional hello from Dani and Natalie, which he didn't reply to. Raj had gone completely silent.

He continued to stay away from the social media that normally filled up so much of his time. What was he supposed to post? Maybe he could restrict himself to just liking other people's posts: 'Yay – good job. You haven't killed anyone today.'

Even watching porn didn't bring him any joy. It all looked so fake and the dopamine failed to hit. The only thing it aroused in him was self-loathing.

On Tuesday evening, he managed to sit through a whole football match on TV with his father and his brother. They watched Brighton bounce back to draw one-one with Spurs, thanks to a penalty. But it was difficult to concentrate. The game had lost all its power and was reduced to 22 men kicking a ball.

Apart from mealtimes, that was just about all he saw of his parents. He kept out of the living room and turned down all invitations to play table tennis with his father or his brother (they had a table in the attic). He stayed hidden in his room most of the time, pretending to revise, but in reality going over the accident again and again in his mind. If he wasn't being overwhelmed by its horror, he would be consumed with a ferocious anger no longer directed at others but exclusively at himself.

How could he be so stupid?

Why didn't he look in his mirror?

Why?

Idiot, idiot, idiot.

*

Next day, Natalie contacted him and suggested that they test each other on French adjectives. He agreed but on Friday, when it came to time to go round to her house for the test, he ducked out, saying he hadn't been able to revise at all.

Natalie: Well come round here, we can revise together
Ross: No I'd rather not thanks
Natalie: Shall I come to your place?
Ross: It's ok I'll do some revision on my own

Not that he did any. He just sat in his room, his head in his hands, rocking backwards and forwards. Every now and then, unwelcome thoughts of suicide sprang into his head: he lived just an hour's walk from the cliffs at Beachy Head, one of the most popular suicide spots in the world. All he had to do was jump, and all his pain would be gone.

No.

He had no right to kill himself. He had already destroyed one family. There was no way he could do that to his own.

*

The following Monday, he went back to the church at 10:30, in the hope of finding the vicar. He was sitting at the front, speaking in hushed tones with an elderly woman. The vicar spotted Ross, nodded at him and carried on his conversation with the woman. Ross sat at the back, out of earshot.

He wasn't sure what to do while he waited. Normally, he would take out his mobile and play a game or look at Instagram, but it felt sacrilegious to do so in a church.

He fixed his eyes on the enormous stained-glass window at the far end. Overwhelmingly blue and shaped like a Norman arch, it was dominated by a central panel depicting the crucifixion. Another panel had the angel telling the Virgin Mary that she would have God's child. To the right, two panels showed the Three Wise Men presenting their gifts to the infant Jesus, who was in his mother's arms.

The theme of motherhood set Ross off again, and images of Lizzie Johnson and her children flooded his mind.

The vicar interrupted his reverie.

'Hi, Ross.'

'Hello, Father.'

'Call me Nigel. Mind if I join you?'

He sat on the bench in front and turned round.

'How've you been?'

'Not great, if I'm honest.'

'I suppose that's to be expected.'

'Yeah.'

'Have you managed to do any revision?'

'Almost none.'

'So, what have you been up to?'

Ross shrugged. 'Mostly thinking about the accident, really. I...I found her Facebook page, the woman I killed. I know I shouldn't, really, but I've been looking at it.'

'Does it help?'

Ross laughed sardonically. 'No.'

'Have you been able to speak to anyone?'

Ross shook his head.

'Not even your parents?'

'No. They want me to have counselling.'

'What do you think about that?'

'That's not what I need.'

'What do you need?'

'I don't know.'

'Have you thought about praying?'

'I don't know. It wouldn't seem right.'

'God is always there. He'll hear you.'

Ross shrugged.

'You could come here. We have morning worship at nine-twenty every day, Eucharist at nine-forty-five and evening worship at five. It would get you out of the house, and you could meet people. I'm always here for a chat.'

'It wouldn't feel right.'

'What? Because you don't believe.'

'Yeah, maybe after the Alpha Course.'

'That's nearly three months away. What are you going to do between now and then?'

Ross said nothing. He looked away from Nigel, his face in a half-formed scowl.

'Maybe your parents are right and you should try counselling. What's the worst that can happen? It might even help, you never know.'

*

On his way home, Ross called his college and asked how he could contact the student counsellor. They gave him an email address and he sent a short message:

Hi

My name's Ross Collins and I'm a student at the college. I'm having a bit of trouble and wonder if I could fix a time to see you.

Thanks

She got back to him that afternoon and suggested Thursday at 10:30, in her office opposite the college library.

He told his mother soon after she got home.

'Oh, that's good news. I'm sure it will help.'

Ross said nothing, but he was equally sure it wouldn't. What was the point? Just sit there talking, and then be positive, look on the bright side, try to stay upbeat, there's always hope, don't worry, be happy, every cloud has a silver lining.

No it bloody well doesn't.

Could counselling bring Lizzie Johnson back from the dead? Could it wash her blood from his hands?

No.

Okay, he would go through with it, just to prove that it was a complete waste of time. And then he would hang on until the Alpha Course in July. That was his one shot at redemption.

On Thursday, Ross wasn't at all happy about having to go into the college for his appointment. He dreaded the thought of meeting other students, even though he knew hardly anyone would be there. He made sure he arrived at the last minute and hurried through the empty corridors with his head down until he reached Kitty's office.

He knocked, and a woman in her 40s with a petite figure and long, permed hair opened the door.

'Hi, I'm Kitty. Are you Ross?'

'Yes.'

'Come in and have a seat.

The room was small and pokey, with a desk under the windowsill, and four soft, blue-green armless chairs. Ross sat down and Kitty sat opposite him, placing a folder and some papers on her lap. She put on a delicate pair of gold-framed glasses.

'Can we go through some formalities first? Is it Ross Collins?'

'Yes.'

'What's your date of birth?'

'Eleventh of December 2001.'

'So that makes you seventeen?'

'Yes.'

'Which tutor group are you in?'

'Harry Liptrot.'

She nodded and wrote on her papers. Then she took off her glasses and looked at Ross. 'Okay, before we start, I need to tell you that whatever you say will be treated in confidence. I'm not going to gossip to anyone. I won't tell Harry Liptrot or any of your other teachers what you say without your express permission. But I can't promise one hundred percent confidentiality, I'm afraid. If you tell me something I need to share with the Designated Safeguarding Lead, then I have to tell her. Are you okay with that?'

Ross shrugged. 'Yeah, I suppose so.'

'So, you have my email if you need to set up another meeting. I'm here every Tuesday and Thursday in term time. I can't enter into a detailed correspondence with you, but we can meet up as many times as you need.'

Ross nodded.

'So, how can I help?'

'I don't know if you can.'

She nodded. 'Perhaps you're right. Sometimes I can help. Sometimes I can't.'

Ross said nothing.

'Would you like to tell me about the problem that's brought you here?'

Ross shrugged. It was a long time before he said anything. 'Did you hear about the accident on the A27, just over two weeks ago?'

Kitty hesitated. 'Not that I remember.'

'A woman was killed, Lizzie Johnson.'

'That's very sad.'

'She had two children, six and nine years old.' Ross hung his head as he spoke.

A long silence.

'Do you mind if I ask – what's the connection?'

'What do you think?'

'In my job we're trained not to jump to conclusions.'

Nobody spoke for almost a minute, until Ross closed his eyes and said, with a voice just above a whisper. 'I killed her.'

He looked at her. His words didn't seem to have caused her any consternation.

'Don't worry,' he went on, 'I'm not a psycho killer. It was an accident.'

After a moment, Kitty said, 'Would it be right to say that you blame yourself for the accident?'

Ross gave a little laugh. It was all he could do to stop himself saying, 'Top prize in the Brain of Britain award.' He looked down at his feet and said, 'I didn't look in the mirror. You're supposed to look in the mirror before you overtake, but I forgot. She hit the back of my car and flipped over.'

Silence.

'You seem very distressed about it.'

He gave a little shrug and glared at her. 'Well...yes.'

He looked out of the window. It had been sunny when he arrived, but now it was clouding over. He hoped it wouldn't rain before he got home.

It was a long time before either of them spoke again.

'Are you finding it very difficult to talk about it?'

'It wasn't my idea to come here.'

After a moment she said, 'You feel that you're here under duress.'

Ross said nothing.

'Is there something about being here that you don't want?'

'It's your job to make people happy. I don't deserve to be happy.'

It was some time before she spoke. 'I can feel a sense of guilt and self-blame, that you feel you don't deserve to be happy.'

He shook his head. 'This is a waste of time.'

'I'm sorry you feel that. But it's not necessarily my job to help people to be happy. Sometimes people are unhappy for a very good reason. Sometimes I'm just trying to help them find a way to cope.'

He got to his feet. 'I can't do this.'

'Ross, I'd like you to stay, but if you'd rather not speak now, that's fine.'

'Good, because I'd rather not. I'm sorry for wasting your time.'

With that, he left the room without looking at her again.

He had known counselling would never work, and he had been right. The Alpha Course was his only hope, but it was almost three months away. He just hoped he could hold on until then.

Chapter Five

A hundred miles away, in the Cambridge University Library tea room, Bee Ormerod found an empty table by one of the tall windows. She put her tray down and dangled her bag on the back of the chair. She took off her red plastic raincoat and hung it on the same chair, sat down and removed the teacup, saucer, metallic tea pot and milk jug from her tray. She also picked up the side plate with a slice of chocolate brownie and put it in front of her. She knew she shouldn't have bought it but would redeem herself by not touching it until Robbie arrived.

Not that Bee needed to worry about her weight. She was tall and slim with short, spiky hair with blond highlights. She liked to think that her blond highlights and her nose stud were her only vanities. She never wore makeup and was dressed in old skin-tight jeans and a light-blue top she had bought in a charity shop.

She took out her mobile and opened the Guardian app.

Robbie arrived as she was stirring the teabag in her pot. He put a hand on her shoulder and leaned down to exchange a quick kiss on the lips.

'Hi.'

'Hi. Been here long?'

She still found his Edinburgh accent very sexy.

'Nah. Just got here. Have you seen this? Donald Trump's coming to London in July,'

'Ooh, there'll be a big demo.'

'Yeah, why don't we meet up there? And then you can come and...meet the parents!'

Robbie laughed. 'What? Will they be on the demo?'

'No. Well, my dad might, but not my mum. But you can come and meet them after.'

'Yeah, okay. I guess we've reached meet-the-parents stage, haven't we? Do you want anything else from the counter?'

'No thanks. I've got my brownie.'

'Yes, I noticed. If you let me have half, we can pretend we're being good.'

'Deal.'

She watched him as he set off for the counter. She always felt she was punching a little above her weight with Robbie. He was a postgrad student three years older than her, very bright, very athletic and very handsome, with his thick brown hair, mischievous blue eyes and a deep voice that made her want to close her eyes and bathe in its melody.

He returned a few minutes later with a cappuccino and another chocolate brownie.

'I thought we were being good.'

He shrugged. 'We tried.'

41

'Guess what,' she said as he sat down.

'What?'

'My parents have only gone and bought their dream house by the sea.'

'Really? So I won't be meeting them in London?'

'I don't know. They only signed the contract yesterday. I don't know when they're moving.'

'You don't sound very pleased.'

'No. I don't know anyone down there. I was looking forward to spending summer with all my mates in London.'

'You can stay in Cambridge with me.'

'Maybe I will, just to spite them. They're tearing up my roots. I'm losing my whole identity.'

At that moment, there was a loud crash, as a student at the far end of the room dropped her tray. Some students laughed and applauded. Bee and Robbie glanced at each other and grinned.

'I didn't know being a Londoner was so important to you.'

'Yeah, but it's not just that, is it?'

'What?' said Robbie. 'You mean the whole loss of faith thing?'

'Yes. I mean, that's who I am, isn't it? A south London Christian girl. Now I'm supposed to be…what? A south coast atheist?'

'Oh, so you've decided you're an atheist after all?'

'I'm not an atheist. I'm just confused.'

'I'll tell you what you are.'

'What?'

'You're Omega Bee and you're amazing. And I've so got the hots for you.'

They both laughed.

Chapter Six

Ross returned to the church the following Monday. Nigel the vicar seemed to be waiting for him and they sat down together on a pew at the back, speaking quietly so as not to disturb the two elderly women sitting near the front.

'So, how've you been?'

'Not good.'

'Are you managing to do any revision?'

'Not really, no. I just can't concentrate.'

'Yes, I can understand that. What about counselling? Have you given that any more thought?'

'Yeah, I had a session on Thursday.'

'And?'

Ross shook his head. 'It's not for me.'

'No?'

'She was very nice, but it just didn't feel right.' As he spoke, it occurred to Ross that he had been quite rude to Kitty.

'So, what are you going to do now?'

'I'm going to hang on for the Alpha Course, see if that helps.'

'That's not for another three months.'

Ross shrugged.

'You don't want to come to church?'

'It wouldn't feel right.'

Nigel thought for a moment. 'Have you got friends who can help you with your revision?'

'There's one girl in my French class. We were supposed to be study buddies but I haven't…you know.'

'You need something to take your mind off the accident. Why don't you get in touch with this girl and start working together?'

Ross nodded.

'What about the other subjects?'

'I suppose she's doing General Studies too, but I haven't really got any close friends in my other classes.'

'Well, ask her to help with General Studies too.'

'Okay.'

'When's your last exam?'

'Middle of June.'

'So that would leave three or four weeks between then and the Alpha Course. Look, do you fancy a summer job to keep you busy after your exams?'

'Like what?'

'My parents run a hotel near the seafront. They need waiting staff for the summer, for breakfast and dinner. It's quite a fun job. I used to do it when I was your age. What do you think?'

Ross nodded. Maybe he could earn enough to pay his parents back the excess on the legal fees and the damage to his mother's Micra.

'That sounds good.'

'They need two people. Have you got a friend who'd be interested?'

'Yeah, maybe.'

Nigel said he would put in a good word with his mother and promised not to mention the accident. 'Okay, you check with your friend, and I'll see you again next Monday.'

*

When he got home, the answerphone on his parents' landline was blinking. Ross pressed play: 'Hello, Damian Luscombe here from Myers and Pickford. Just ringing to say the police have completed their investigations and sent the file to the Director of Public Prosecutions. Hopefully, we'll hear what they've decided on the sixteenth of July. Until then, we just have to wait, I'm afraid. Do give me a ring if you feel you need to discuss anything.'

Ross scoffed. 'Bloody lawyer.'

He was sure Mr Luscombe would love it if his parents rang for a lengthy consultation at a squillion pounds per hour. 'How nice to hear from you. *Kerching!*'

He was more concerned about the friend he would contact about the job in the hotel. The obvious candidate was Raj, but would he even reply? Maybe he was still angry because he had blamed him for the accident.

Ross:

Raj got back to him at once.

Raj:	Hey ross long time no see where you been
	Wot you been up to
Ross:	Slashing my wrists mostly
Raj:	Really??
Ross:	Metaphorically
Raj:	Don't blame yourself it was her that crashed into you
Ross:	I know I'm not messaging about that
	Do you fancy a job this summer me and you working together
Raj:	What kind of job
Ross:	Waiter in a hotel breakfast & dinner
Raj:	Sorry mate my mornings are all tied up
Ross:	Wot? Sleeping?
Raj:	In a manner of speaking yes
	Dani's mum goes to work at 8:30

44

Dani will text me at 9 to let me know the coast is clear & I'll be round there like a shot to spend the rest of the morning in her bed 😀

Ross laughed at this. He might have guessed.

Raj: If you got any sense you'll spend your mornings doing exactly the same with natalie
         Much better than serving breakfasts to a load of old biddies in some hotel
Ross: Yeah right

Ross closed his eyes and exhaled noisily. That had gone okay. Pity Raj didn't want the job, though. It would have been good to work together.

He wondered if Dani's mum knew she was sleeping with Raj, and how she would react if she found out. For that matter, he had no idea whether his parents knew he had sex with Mollie. His father had mumbled something embarrassing about condoms soon after they became an item, but that was before they had even done it.

That evening at dinner, his father asked him how revision was going.

'Yeah, not bad.'

'Good. These exams do matter, you know. If you want to go to a good university, you need to do well.'

'I know, I know.'

His mother weighed in: 'This is your big opportunity, Ross. Things have been very difficult for you since the accident, but now you've got the chance to get a success under your belt. It'll do you the power of good.'

'I know,' said Ross. 'I'm on it.'

Next morning, he messaged Natalie. She seemed delighted that he was ready to buddy up for French revision. They agreed to look at conditionals, conjunctions and the past historic and meet at her place the following day.

He didn't actually manage to do any revision, but French was his strongest subject, and he was confident that he would be able to keep up with her. For the most part, he turned out to be right, though her conditionals were better than his. They agreed to team up for some more revision together after his history exams.

As they sat at her family's dining table, he told her about his abortive counselling session and the vicar he had met, though he said nothing about the Alpha Course.

'This vicar, he said he could get me a holiday job at his parents' hotel. Waitering. Breakfast and dinner. He said they were looking for two people. Would you be interested?'

'I'd love to join you but I've got a job lined up already. Do you remember? Me and Rachel worked as cleaners at the Westmoreland Hotel last summer. We've arranged to go back this year.'

Ross couldn't think who else to contact, but that evening he got a message from Sofie.

Sofie: Hi Ross. You there?
Ross: Hiya
Sofie: Dani says you're looking for someone to work in a hotel this summer
Ross: Yeah – interested??
Sofie: Definitely. Where is it?
Ross: Not sure it's this guy I know he says his mum has a hotel near the seafront
They need waiters, breakfast and dinner
I asked raj but he said no
Sofie: Probably planning to spend the whole summer shagging Dani
Ross: Right first time
Sofie: 😑
Anyway, count me in

Ross returned to the church the following Monday. He asked the vicar if he was missing out on his May bank holiday because he had promised to meet him.

'No. Bank holidays are actually quite busy for me. Lots of people are freed up to come to church.'

Ross couldn't help noticing that they were the only people there. He explained that he was managing about an hour a day when he was able to forget the accident and do some revision. He and his friend had done a session together, and another friend was interested in working in his parents' hotel.

'What's his name?'

'Sofie.'

'Oh, it's a girl. Is she your girlfriend?'

'No, she's a friend of my cousin.'

'Okay, because my mum won't have boyfriend and girlfriend working together. Says it stops them concentrating.'

'We're just friends.'

'Okay, I'll get my mum to give you a ring to arrange an interview.'

*

The Livingstone Hotel was at the end of a 19th-century Italianate terrace that ran at a right-angle to the seafront. It was set in Harrow Square, which had terraces either side and a wide, open garden in the middle.

Ross and Sofie walked up the steps and into the hotel. The interior was decorated in bright, fresh colours with new-looking leather barrel chairs in the reception area.

Nigel's mother, Mrs Akehurst, was waiting for them. She was in her 50s, tanned, very slender, with a hard-looking face and neat grey hair that had a hint of purple. She greeted Ross and Sofie with a surprisingly firm handshake and led them into the dining hall, where the décor was quite grey and the chairs much older. The tables were round, covered in white tablecloths and set for dinner. Most had four seats but two in the middle of the room had six.

'Sofie, you'd do the tables over here, and Ross, you'd do over there. Breakfast is seven till eight-thirty and dinner's six till eight. You have half an hour at the end of each shift to get the dining room ready for the next meal. After that, you can eat here. How do you feel about early mornings?'

'Not a problem,' said Ross.

Mrs Akehurst raised an eyebrow at Sofie.

'My little siblings wake me up at the crack of dawn every day, so that's fine.'

'How would you get here?'

'I've got a bike,' said Sofie.

'Yeah, me too.'

'Do you live far?'

'In Old Town.'

'Okay. You can leave your bikes round the back.'

She explained that at breakfast, the guests could have tea or coffee with toast, followed by either a cooked breakfast or cereal, porridge or prunes. 'It's not silver service, but place what they order on the table gently. Try and do it from their left, and always serve the lady before the gentleman.'

Ross and Sofie nodded.

'At dinner, they get a choice of two meals. We don't get many vegetarians because most of them are pensioners. The meat or fish is plated up, but the vegetables, potatoes, gravy and what-not aren't. After the main course, there's a choice of two desserts, all served plated up. Then tea or coffee at the end. Think you can do that?'

'Yes,' Ross and Sofie said in unison.

She looked at Ross: 'Black trousers for you, black shoes, polished, white shirt, dark tie.'

He nodded.

'For you,' she looked at Sofie, 'black trousers or preferably skirt, not too short. Black shoes, sensible heels, white blouse. No need for a tie.'

'Yes, that's fine.'

'And no visible tattoos.'

'I haven't got any.'

'Nor have I.'

'Good. You can leave your work clothes here and get changed when you arrive, especially if you're cycling. You work Monday, day off Tuesday, work on Wednesday, Thursday, Friday and Saturday. Saturday's a very busy day because one coach party leaves in the morning and another arrives in the afternoon. Sunday's your second day off, apart from the first week. I'd want you to start on the Sunday so we can train you up.'

They nodded again.

'You're both under eighteen, aren't you?'

'Yes.'

'Hmm…there's probably some ridiculous paperwork I have to do to employ minors. Still, that's my problem, not yours. It's minimum wage, so that's four pound twenty per hour for under-eighteens. You work twenty-two and a half hours per week, so I make that ninety-four pound fifty plus tips. Will this be your only job?'

'Yes.'

'Good. No tax. There might be national insurance but you can probably claim that back next April.'

Ross and Sofie nodded.

'Now, there's just one more thing,' said Mrs Akehurst. 'Nigel assures me you're not boyfriend and girlfriend. Is that right?'

'Yes,' said Ross. 'Yes, as in no, we're not.'

She looked at Sofie.

'We're just friends. I don't fancy him. Sorry, Ross, no offence intended.'

'None taken.'

They both grinned and Mrs Akehurst smiled her first smile of the encounter. 'Good. I've been caught out with that before, waiters too busy making cow eyes at each other. Okay, you seem like nice, smart, respectable young people, and if Nigel likes you, Ross, you can't be that bad. So, yes, shall we go for it?'

'Yes, please.'

'That would be great.'

'Okay, come with me and let's get the paperwork done. Remember I said you'll have to prove you have the right to work in the UK. Did you bring your passports like I asked?'

'Yes,' said Ross.

'I'm afraid I haven't got one,' said Sofie. 'I've brought my birth certificate. Is that okay?'

'Yes, that's fine.'

The paperwork completed, Ross and Sofie waited until they had got outside and walked safely out of sight before they burst out laughing.'

'What a dragon!' said Ross. 'No visible tattoos indeed.'

'I quite like her,' said Sofie. 'She's pretty direct.'

'So are you. "I don't fancy him." Thank you very much for that.'

Sofie blushed bright red. 'Sorry. You are fanciable, honest. Just not my type.'

He pulled a face at her and they laughed.

'One thing,' said Ross, 'I noticed your surname's Manning. Any relation to Simon Manning?'

'Yeah, he's my dad. Do you know him?'

'I've played table tennis against him.'

'Oh, does he still play? Surprised he can stay sober enough to hit the ball.'

Ross wasn't quite sure how to respond to that.

'Did you beat him?'

'I can't remember. His team's called the Old Codgers. They beat us, I remember that, but I can't remember if I beat your dad.'

Sofie grinned. 'Sounds like he beat you.'

*

Sorting out a job for the summer came as a big boost. He had something else he could spend his time on instead of sitting brooding in his bedroom. His parents were delighted when he told them. He didn't mention the vicar but said they had got the job through someone Sofie knew. He told his parents how Mrs Akehurst had made sure they weren't boyfriend and girlfriend before agreeing to take them on.

'I've heard things about Sofie,' said his mother. 'I'm very glad you're not boyfriend and girlfriend.'

'What things?'

'I'm not telling you. Let's just say she's not as sweet and innocent as she looks.'

'You can't say that and then not tell me.'

'Oh yes I can. You'd be much better off with someone like Natalie. She likes you, you know.'

Ross rolled his eyes. 'Don't worry, Mum, me and Sofie isn't going to happen. She told Mrs Akehurst she didn't fancy me.'

'Good.'

Chapter Seven

Dani and Sofie met up at a coffee shop in Old Town next morning. Dani ordered a cappuccino for herself and an Americano for Sofie. 'Do you fancy sharing a cake?'

'Yes but no,' said Sofie. 'I'd better not.'

They took their drinks to a small table by the window.

'So, you're going to be seeing a lot of my cousin this summer?'

'Piss off.'

They both laughed.

'You like him.'

'Yes, I like him.'

'And you said he's fit.'

'He is fit.'

'So?'

'Dani, no. He's just a mate. I'm not going to fall in love with him.'

'He's a lot nicer than your last boyfriend.'

'That's a very low bar.'

'Well, I think you'd make a lovely couple.'

Sofie scowled and looked away. After a moment, she grinned and they both took a sip of their drinks.

'How was he?'

'He seemed perfectly normal.'

'Apparently, his mum's really worried about him. He just sits in his bedroom all day, thinking about the accident.'

'He should have counselling,' said Sofie. 'Presumably Kitty's still around.'

'He had one session with her and walked out after five minutes.'

'You're joking.'

'That's what I heard.'

'Why don't you have a word with him? He might listen to you.'

Dani shook her head. 'Ross? Listen to advice? No way. He's so…Let me give you an example: when we were kids, right, my mum taught us to rollerblade.'

'I didn't know you could rollerblade.'

'Yeah, I'm a demon, man. You ever done it?'

Sofie shook her head.

Dani took another sip and continued. 'Thing is, right, when you start rollerblading, you have to put your feet like this…' she made a V with her hands '…and then, you take tiny steps. That's the key thing: tiny steps. But Ross, he got it into his head that he wanted to take big steps. And the result was, surprise, surprise, he kept falling over. My mum was like, "Tiny steps, Ross, tiny steps." But would he listen? No. In the end my mum refused to teach him any more because she was scared he'd do himself an injury.'

'So, can he rollerblade now?'

'No.'

Sofie put the tips of her index finger and thumb together and made an obscene gesture.

Dani burst out laughing.

*

Ross's improved mood gave way to panic as he realised just how far behind he was with his revision. He had just four days to go before his first exam: Britain 1851-1914. That was a vast syllabus. How on earth was he going to revise everything in just four days?

He decided to concentrate on his favourite bits and hope they came up: Ireland, the Suffragettes and the rise of the Labour Party. His teacher said Gladstone and Disraeli were bound to come up, so he would revise them too.

Unfortunately, planning was much easier than getting down to revision. Tea and coffee, the biscuit tin, Instagram and an afternoon nap conspired to distract him, and the dark cloud of the accident periodically cast its shadow over him, bringing everything to a halt.

Saturday and Sunday were better. His parents were home, and his mother kept him supplied with tea and biscuits. She also made him work in the dining room, where she could keep an eye on him. He revised pretty much all day both days, apart from a couple of hours of TV on Sunday to watch Brighton get thrashed four-nil by Liverpool.

On Monday, he was alone again and found it impossible to get going. Instead, he popped down to the church to see Nigel the vicar.

'Hi, Ross. So, you got the job?'

'Yes. I just came to say thank you.'

'My pleasure. How are things going apart from that?'

'Much better, thanks. I've actually managed to get some revision done.'

'That's good.'

'Yeah, my first exam's tomorrow. I'd better get home and get on with it.'

Except he didn't. He listened to music and had a long nap instead.

His exam started at 1:30 the next afternoon. He cycled to college early and headed for the nearby park, where he loitered for as long as he could. He joined the other students waiting outside the main entrance at the last minute.

'Watch out,' said a familiar voice. 'Here comes Ross. Mind he doesn't crash into you.'

The voice belonged to a student he knew as Pete the Prat, who had asked Dani out in year 11 and made her life a misery for several weeks when she spurned him.

Ross did his best to ignore him. A couple of students laughed but one girl told Pete in no uncertain terms to shut up.

Only one other student spoke to him about his accident, a classmate called Mark. He and Ross had gone to the same secondary school. They had never been part of the same friendship group but they had always got on, and at college, they sat next to each other in history.

'Sorry to hear about your accident, Ross. You all right?'

'Yeah.'

The preliminaries took an eternity: queueing up, proving identity with student cards, despite the fact that the teachers invigilating the exam knew all the students personally, handing in mobiles 'and MP3 players' (this was the cause of much sniggering).

He found the desk with his name, two rows from the front, near the window. The girl at the next desk smiled at him and he smiled back. He only knew her vaguely as she hadn't gone to the same secondary school as him and wasn't in his history class. She was wearing a very short skirt, and he hoped her legs wouldn't be a distraction.

He had to copy the date, centre number, exam number and candidate number onto his answer sheet. Then he endured a lengthy reminder of the rules, followed by an interminable wait for the clock on the wall to register 1:30. He just wanted to get on with it. His heart was racing and his innards were tight.

'Now begin,' Ross's history teacher said at last. 'Read the instructions carefully, and good luck.'

He opened the question paper. The first question was compulsory and was about the Liberals and Labour. Yes, good. The second question had two options, one of which was the Conservatives and Ireland 1886 to 1914. Yes, he could do that. The gods had smiled on him. And Gladstone and Disraeli were nowhere to be seen.

He finished with just over five minutes to go, with his hand in agony and stress hormones coursing through his body. Once the papers had been collected in and his mobile phone retrieved, he made straight for the exit. He had no desire to speak to anyone. He headed for the bike sheds, unlocked his bike and rode home.

*

Having survived one exam with a minimum of revision, Ross was confident he would be able to do the same with the next. And this time, he would have five full days to get ready. Next morning, after a late start, he began to plan. His next exam would be about the build-up to the English Civil War. Before the accident, he had outlined 10 topics, but now he only had time for five, so he chose the divine right of kings, the Duke of Buckingham, puritanism, popular radicalism and Scotland.

He would start after lunch. And, it turned out, after 90 minutes on Angry Birds and Instagram. He managed less than two hours that day. Friday was just as bad, but the weekend, working under his mother's watchful eye, was better. On Saturday, he was glad of an excuse to give Prince Harry and Meghan Markle's wedding a miss, but that evening, he took time out to watch the FA Cup final between two of his least favourite teams: Manchester United and Chelsea.

By Monday, complacency had given way to panic, which dragged his mood down and brought the accident back to the forefront of his thoughts. He spent most of the day despondent, with over an hour stalking Lizzie Johnson, this time on LinkedIn.

He opened a fake account and quickly found her. She had gone to school in Hailsham, about eight miles to the north. There was no mention of any university. Instead, she seemed to have started work in 1996, when she must have been just 18 years old. Her first job was as an admin assistant at a small cosmetics factory in nearby Hampden Park. Five years later, she switched to a building society in town, where she seemed to have stayed for 17 years until she moved to Brighton to take up an assistant manager's position.

Ross couldn't imagine spending 17 years, his entire life to date, in a single job. He imagined how pleased she must have been to get promotion, with more money and more responsibility. What she hadn't known was that after less than two years, it would be her misfortune to encounter an idiot who forgot to look in his mirror, and her daily commute would end up killing her and tearing her family apart.

He couldn't do any revision after that. Instead, he sank deeper and deeper into a quicksand of self-hatred and despair.

*

In the exam room the following day, Ross wanted to kick himself for his failure to revise. He knew he was in big trouble.

The first question was compulsory: 50 minutes on how people chose which side to support in the Civil War, with reference to extracts from contemporary documents. He sat for several minutes with his head in his hands and no idea how was going to answer this.

In the second question, one of the options was the divine right of kings. That was an easy choice, so he did that question first.

But the compulsory question left him stumped. He thought about walking out. He might have done so were it not for the humiliation of having to hang around for 40 minutes to collect his mobile phone. He had no option but to waffle. He wrote an introductory paragraph that repeated the question, followed by two paragraphs of nothing from the opposing points of view and a concluding paragraph that repeated the question again.

This left him with 20 minutes to fill, and the accident wrapped its tentacles around him once more. He thought he had got his life back on track, with exam success to be followed by a summer job that would keep him busy and an Alpha Course that would show him a path to redemption. But now he had fallen at the first hurdle.

What a disaster. He had failed this exam; he was sure of that. And if the other exams went as badly, he might end up having to repeat the year. That would be a massive humiliation.

There is a solution: paracetamol.

The thought popped into his head uninvited.

Just 20 tablets. That will kill you.

But it would be a slow and horrible death, and his mum would be there saying, 'Why did you do it, Ross? Why did you do it?'

How could he answer that?

He remembered watching something on TV about a girl who overdosed on paracetamol and survived, thanks to a liver transplant, but they had to amputate her hands and her feet to save her.

The thought of it sent a shudder through him.

No way.

In any case, suicide wasn't a solution. It was a coward's way out. He had to find a way through this. Just hang on until the Alpha Course. Just hang on.

*

The message sat unanswered on Ross's mobile for hours.

Raj: Hey ross how was your exam today

He didn't know what he was supposed to say. That it was a complete shitshow, to add to the complete shitshow his life had already become. He hadn't told his parents just how bad it had been. He didn't want to admit how little revision he had done.

Eventually, he answered Raj with a single emoji.

Ross: 💩

The answer came back very quickly.

Raj: Yeah i heard
Ross: Wot?? Who told you??
Raj: Dani
        She said suzi told her you spent half the exam just sitting there not writing anything
Ross: Who's suzi??
Raj: She says she was sitting next to you
Ross: Oh her

After a minute, Ross fired off an explanation.

Ross: I revised the wrong bit I couldn't answer one of the questions
Raj: Bummer

Ross: Yeah 🤦

The evening belonged to despondency and dark thoughts about the accident. And as he lay awake that night, the cliffs at Beachy Head came back to stalk him. One quick jump and it would all be over.

No. That would be an evil thing to do.

But it would be quick.

No, no, no. It would be evil.

He felt like Gollum, from *Lord of the Rings*, fighting against himself.

This was one fight he couldn't afford to lose.

*

Next morning, he began to take stock of his situation. He had 12 days before his next exam, but after that, they would come in a rush, with seven exams in nine days.

French was his strongest subject, so he wouldn't revise at all for his language exams and would gamble on his linguistic ability getting him through. The literature questions were another matter. He had hated Albert Camus' novel *L' Étranger* and hadn't thought much of Françoise Sagan's *Bonjour Tristesse*, either. He would have to read up on why people loved these two books so much, so that he could parrot all the reasons why they were intellectual triumphs and not just boring stories about obnoxious people. Each would need a full day's revision, plus maybe a bit of time with Natalie to practise discussing them in French.

The third thing that could come up in this part of the French exam was François Truffaut's film *Les Quatre Cents Coups*. He hoped there would be a question on this as he had loved it. He just needed to watch it one more time and gen up on the themes and which bits were autobiographical.

For General Studies, a day spent dipping into his textbook would do. A lot of it was just general knowledge.

The really difficult test was going to be English literature. He had so much to revise: *Othello, Death of a Salesman, The Nun's Priest's Tale, Emma* and Angela Carter's *Wise Children*. If he gave them a full day each, that would leave him with two free days to plug gaps and do some last-minute revision.

He messaged Natalie:

Ross: Hiya 👋

She replied straight away.

Natalie: Oh hello. How are you?
Ross: Yeah ok thanks
Natalie: I hear you had a bit of a disaster in your history exam
Ross   I can guess who told you
Natalie: You probably can.

Ross: I revised the wrong bit
Natalie: Revised the wrong bit or didn't revise at all?
Ross: Ooh 🐱

Natalie started writing but it was a long time before her reply came through.

Natalie: Sorry!
Ross: I did actually do some revision just the wrong bit
          Anyway i was contacting you about the French language revision
          we were planning to do…
Natalie: Yes?
Ross: I'm bailing out – sorry
Natalie: Well there's a surprise!
Ross: 🐱
          Sorry i got so much english lit I'm gonna have to wing it in French
          lang
Natalie: You'll probably get away with it
          What about French Lit?
Ross: Yeah can we fix a date to go over that together – en francais
Natalie: What about Friday 1st in the afternoon?
Ross: Deal
Natalie: OK. Look, Ross, how about we revise everything together? I come
          round to your place in the afternoon and I do my revision and you
          do yours but we keep each other from getting distracted
          What do you think?
          I'm getting really bored. I think it would be good for both of us

Ross took a while to reply.

Ross: I think I'd do it better on my own - sorry
Natalie: You sure?
Ross: Yeah
Natalie: OK. Let me know if you change your mind.

*

The doorbell rang just after two the following afternoon. Ross opened it and, to his surprise, saw Raj standing there, his backpack dangling on his left shoulder.

'Hello. To what do I owe this pleasure?'

'Revision.'

'Pardon?'

'I've come to do some revision. I won't disturb you. We can go in your dining room. You do your revision and I'll do mine.'

'Whose idea was this?'

'Mine.'

'Not Natalie's?'

Raj grinned. 'She did tell Dani you were being a miserable git.'

'I thought you were revising with Dani.'

'I was. Trouble is, we keep getting distracted. I mean, I am taking biology, but the bits of the biology syllabus that keep distracting us won't come up in the exam.'

Ross laughed.

'Are you going to let me in?'

'I should make a stand for my cousin's honour, you know.'

'Bit late for that, mate.'

Ross let him in and made tea. They went into the dining room where each of them opened up his books and got down to work.

As they revised together over the following days, Ross felt an enormous sense of gratitude towards Raj. He hardly managed any revision in the mornings and evenings, but in the afternoons, he clocked up a good three or four hours. They took short breaks to chat, check their mobiles or make tea or coffee, but for the most part, they simply got on with their separate revision tasks.

But when they spoke, there was one topic they never mentioned: the way Raj had goaded Ross into overtaking and the two-week silence between them after Ross had a go at him over it. Ross wanted to bring it up but didn't know how.

And so the topic sat between them like an ugly goblin, sometimes invisible, sometimes very clear. Ross wondered if Raj saw it too, and whether it would gradually fade away.

On their third day together, he had a question he was able to ask: 'How come Dani's mum doesn't like Sofie?'

'Who says she doesn't?'

'My mum.'

'How does she know?'

'Duh! She's her sister.'

'Oh yeah, I forgot.' Raj scratched his head. 'I don't really know. Dani mentioned it once, but I don't know what's behind it. She didn't tell me.'

'Do you like Sofie?'

'Yeah, she's really nice.'

'That's what I thought.'

'Why? Are you having *thoughts* about her?'

Ross laughed. 'No. Get back to your revision.'

*

It astonished Ross how much of the literature he revised concerned itself with death. He was able to keep dark thoughts at bay while he revised alongside Raj, but in the evenings, thinking about these books would bring them back. The accident and its consequences would overwhelm him and pull him down once more.

Despite its title, *Death of a Salesman* was in fact a tale of a life wasted in a futile pursuit of the American Dream. On the other hand, Angela Carter's *Wise Children*, written when its author knew she was dying of cancer, was an affirmation of life, in particular sex, laughter, music and dance.

This kind of hedonism was the starting point of Françoise Sagan's *Bonjour Tristesse*, but its dramatic climax was an apparent suicide. The central character, Céline, was a girl of Ross's age whose main aim in life was to do as little as possible while monopolising the attention of her dreadful father. She took against her new stepmother Anne and manipulated her father into dumping her. Anne responded by driving off a cliff.

Ross hadn't enjoyed the book, and he hadn't found Anne's death convincing. Now, however, he understood just how easy it was for thoughts of suicide to invade your mind. His thoughts often told him how easy it would be to steal his dad's car keys and drive up to Beachy Head. It would take less than 10 minutes. Then all he had to do was run to the edge of the cliff and jump off. It wouldn't hurt. His biology teacher at school once said that we live half a second behind everything that happens, because it takes our brain that long to process sensations. He would be dead before the pain of impact had time to register.

But then he thought of the anguish Anne's death induced in Céline, and Céline didn't even like her. What would his death do to his parents? There was no way he could do that to them. No way.

He re-read the final chapter of *Bonjour Tristesse* and understood that, just as Céline lost her innocence with Anne's death, he had forever lost his with Lizzie Johnson's.

When he and Natalie practised discussing the book in French, he told her how he felt about his loss of innocence. She shook her head: *'Mais ce n'est pas la même. Céline est une salope manipulatrice. Tu n'es pas comme elle. Tu n'as fait qu'une erreur.'* ('But it's not the same. Céline's a manipulative slut. You're not like her. You just made a mistake.')

'That's a bit sexist, isn't it? Calling her a *salope*.'

Natalie grinned. 'I don't know the French for bitch.'

'I'll google it.'

'Don't bother. I'm not going to say that in the exam, am I?'

When he studied *Othello*, Ross hated the eponymous hero for killing his supposedly unfaithful wife, and he had little sympathy for his remorse once he realised she was innocent. Even now, he couldn't connect with him, but his disdain for Othello helped him understand how he must appear in the eyes of Lizzie Johnson's family. It didn't matter how much remorse he felt; they would always hate him. Even if he followed Othello's example and killed himself, they would have no reason to forgive him.

The bleakest of all the books he revised was Albert Camus' *L'Étranger*. Ross couldn't understand how Meursault, the central character, was seen by some as an existentialist hero. He was appalling: self-centred, vain and a cold-hearted killer. How could he feel no remorse over the Arab he shot? Was he a racist, a psychopath or both?

The book had generated heated discussions in his French class, some of which had spilt over into the breaks. Ross had found it difficult to get behind the surface narrative, but other students felt they understood what Camus was trying to say: that life is random and absurd with no deeper meaning, that the only truth that matters is that we are all going to die and be forgotten. Some of his classmates said they loved Camus for his intellectual honesty. Others hated his message. Most trenchant of all was Sofie, who argued passionately that there had to be more to life than death.

He wondered if the Alpha Course would really be able to supply him with an alternative to the hedonism of Céline and the nihilistic absurdism of Albert Camus. He remembered what Camus had said about religion, that it was 'philosophical suicide', a resort to make-believe in order to wish the harsh realities of life away.

Was that what he was planning to do on the Alpha Course, commit 'philosophical suicide'? His father would certainly think so.

For the first time, Ross began to wonder whether he should go through with it.

'But what else can I do?' he asked himself again and again.

Chapter Eight

'Well?' said Omega Bee's father. 'What do you think?'

They were sitting in an old tea shop not far from the beach.

Bee gave a little shrug. 'It's a nice house.'

'It's a beautiful house.'

'Yes.'

'We could never afford anything like this in London.'

'Yeah, I can see that.'

'Tell her,' said her mother.

Bee looked quizzically at her father.

'With the money we make moving out of London, I can take early retirement.'

'What? Are you going to stop working?'

'No, but I can give up the rat race. I can get part-time work as a long-distance taxi driver. Airport transfers, things like that. Your mum'll find a part-time job down here.'

'You're serious?'

'Yes. We've worked it out, and I know a guy who can give me an opening. We won't need to earn a lot of money, just enough to cover day-to-day expenses.'

'Your dad's been doing fifty to sixty-hour weeks for the last twenty years.'

'But not any more. I've had enough, and now this move'll give me the chance to start living.'

Bee took a sip of her tea and finished off her chocolate brownie (these things were becoming a bit of a habit). She had been planning to discuss her problems at university, the crumbling of her faith and how this was making it increasingly difficult to motivate herself to study for her theology degree. But maybe this wasn't the time. It would only upset her mother. Better to let her parents enjoy the anticipation of their new life in a new home.

'Shall we order some champagne?'

Her father smiled. 'Better not. I've got a long drive back to London.'

Chapter Nine

Ross put his pen down. He couldn't think of anything more to say about Peregrine Hazard, the weirdest character in *Wise Children*. This was his final AS-Level exam, and he had survived, thanks to Raj keeping him company and enabling him to do just about enough revision. His results wouldn't be brilliant, but they would be good enough to get him through to year two of his A-Levels.

He had, however, been dreading the end of his exams. With no more revision to do, he knew how easy it would be to spend the next four days thinking about the accident and stalking Lizzie Johnson. The World Cup would start on Thursday, and Raj wanted him to watch the games with friends, but he wasn't feeling up to it. The last thing he felt able to do was enjoy himself. What was he supposed to say to them? 'Yeah, so I killed this woman, but let's watch the footie and have a good time.'

Four days of depression coming up.

*

'You nervous?'

Sofie shrugged. 'Not like before my exams. What about you?'

'Same.'

They were behind the hotel, locking their bikes together in the corner of the hotel's small car park.

They walked in through the back entrance and followed the corridor to reception, where they met a man who looked like Nigel the vicar but fatter, greyer and almost bald on top.

'Oh hello,' he said, folding his paper copy of the *Daily Telegraph*. 'Are you Ross and Sofie? I'm Mr Akehurst.'

He shook hands with them.

'I'll take you round to the boss,' he said with a grin.

Mrs Akehurst was in the dining room, chatting with two waiters. She introduced Ross and Sofie to them. It turned out that they were a husband and wife from Turkey. They had been working at the hotel while the husband studied for a Master's degree at Sussex University.

'What?' Sofie said to the husband. 'Did you work full-time and do your Master's at the same time?'

The Turkish husband smiled. 'Yes.'

'Wow, that's impressive.'

'Not one day off sick,' said Mrs Akehurst. 'They'll be a hard act to follow when they go home at the end of this week. You two will shadow them until Wednesday, and on Thursday, you'll be on your own. You've got a lot to learn between now and then.'

As Ross observed the Turkish husband at work, he could see how good he was. He was quick and efficient and unfailingly polite and friendly to both the guests and the kitchen staff, including the very grumpy chef.

As the guests came in for breakfast, the waiters had to greet them with a cheery 'Good morning' and ask if they would like tea or coffee, and if they preferred white bread or wholemeal for their toast. When they brought the teapot or coffee pot, they would offer a choice of a cooked breakfast or porridge, prunes or cereal (Ross was astonished how many chose prunes). While the guests were eating, the waiters would bring round the menu for the evening, so they could make their choice.

All the guests were old-age pensioners, mostly in their late 60s or 70s, though some of the older guests were much older and very pallid and shaky. They sat four or six to a table, and perhaps two thirds of them were women. They had come as a coach party from the north of England, and had a programme that would include day trips to Brighton and to Hastings and Rye, as well as half-day excursions to local beauty spots and the gardens at either Sissinghurst, Nymans or Chartwell.

Breakfast finished at nine, and the waiters started to clear everything away, except where latecomers were still eating or chatting over tea and coffee. They stripped the tables, put on new tablecloths and set crockery and cutlery for dinner.

After they finished, they retired to the staffroom, where they were joined by the kitchen staff and a cleaner named Veronika for a full English breakfast. Ross had already eaten before leaving home. Maybe he would just have a couple of oat biscuits tomorrow.

Veronika the cleaner turned out to be Polish (there was another cleaner from Liverpool, but she didn't join them for breakfast). The chef was Albanian and the kitchen porter Latvian.

They asked Ross and Sofie lots of questions.

'I hope you're not boyfriend and girlfriend,' said the kitchen porter.

Everybody laughed.

'No,' said Ross. 'She told Mrs Akehurst she doesn't fancy me.'

'God, I'm never going to live that down,' said Sofie.

After breakfast, almost everyone went outside for a smoke, leaving Ross and Sofie with Veronika.

'How long have you been working here?' Sofie asked.

'Two years now.'

'You must like it.'

'Yes, except there's not much work in winter.' She explained that Martha, the English cleaner, was married to Mrs Akehurst's son, so she had priority when there was only enough work for one cleaner.

'What?' said Ross. 'Is she married to Nigel?'

Veronika laughed. 'Mrs Akehurst got two sons. One is priest, but other one, he is many things but he certainly not priest.'

Ross retired to the male staff toilet to take off his white shirt and tie and put on an old T-shirt. The kitchen porter showed him where to hang his shirt and tie in the chef's changing room. He waited for Sofie, who hung up her skirt and blouse. Just as they were about to leave, Mr Akehurst put his head round the staffroom door.

'Ross? Could you prepare coffee for me and my family? Four of us today.'

The Turkish waitress showed him exactly how they liked their coffee and which crockery and teaspoons to use. Sofie helped him to get everything ready. When he took the coffee in to their private quarters, he saw Mr and Mrs Akehurst, along with Martha, the English cleaner, and the Akehursts' other son Sid. He was tall, with very short hair and tattoos on his arms and neck. Ross thought he looked like a younger, better-looking and much tougher version of Nigel.

Sid, his father and Martha were laughing uproariously. Mrs Akehurst seemed to be suppressing a laugh and trying to disapprove of whatever Sid had just said.

Once Ross had finished serving coffee, he and Sofie made their way to their bicycles.

'So,' said Sofie, 'what did you think?'

'I think it's all right.'

'Yeah. We can do this.'

*

In many ways, Ross found dinner easier than breakfast, as the guests had already decided what to eat. The waiters just had to bring out the vegetables, potatoes and gravy or sauce and then the plated meat and fish. The Turkish waiter showed Ross how to carry three plates, two in one hand and one in the other.

'Tomorrow I'll show you how to carry four.'

The most complex part of the evening shift was drinks, where the waiters had to keep a record of who ordered what. The guests put their room numbers and signed for what they had ordered, which would go onto their bill.

By now, the guests were getting to know the others on their tables, and as the drink flowed, they became chattier and the volume in the dining room increased.

Some of them asked Ross lots of questions.

'Are you a student?'

'Yeah.'

'At university?'

'No, just done my AS-Levels.'

'How did they go?'

'Mostly okay, one disaster.'

'Are you planning to go to university?'

'Yeah.'

'What are you going to study?'

'French. I fancy a year abroad.'

'*Ooh là là!*'

'*Je pense qu' il aime les filles françaises.*'

Ross smiled. He was sure he would like French girls.

*

Next morning, after all the work was done and the staff had finished their cooked breakfast, just as Ross and Sofie were about to leave, Mr Akehurst popped his head round the staffroom door.

'Sofie? Could you prepare coffee for me and my family? Four of us today.'

Ross helped her to get everything ready and waited in the dining room while she took everything in. When she came back, her face was red and flustered.

'You okay?'

'Yeah.'

At that moment, the Akehursts' younger son Sid came in. He looked at Sofie and gestured her to follow him.

They went into the kitchen, leaving the door ajar. They spoke quietly, but Ross was able to make out what they were saying.

'What the hell are you doing here?'

'What does it look like? I'm working.'

'You can't work here.'

'You can't stop me.'

Ross couldn't hear what they said next, but then he heard Sofie say, 'Look, I didn't know you were here, right? I need this job. I need the money,'

'Yeah, well just make sure you behave yourself. And keep your mouth shut.'

Sid came out and glared at Ross as he walked past. It was some time before Sofie came back. She was shaking and her eyes were red and puffy.

'What was all that about?'

She looked away from him and wiped her eyes. 'Me and Sid know each other. We're not exactly best mates.'

Chapter Ten

Omega Bee looked around her. The furniture was all the same. The dining table and the chair she was sitting on were the same. The bed upstairs was hers, just like the wardrobe and the chest of drawers. She had grown up with the two little sofas in the living room. The cooker, the fridge-freezer and the washing machine were theirs, as were all the books in boxes, waiting to be put on the bookshelves. And the same golden retriever was sitting by the French windows, looking out at the rain.

But it didn't feel like home.

Yes, the house was bigger. There was a spare bedroom, a conservatory and a beautiful if somewhat overgrown back garden. And from her parents' bedroom, you could see the sea just a couple of hundred yards away.

But it wasn't home.

She fired up her laptop. She had something very important to do. She needed to find a job.

It wasn't just the money, though that would be useful. A job was the only way to avoid spending the whole summer cooped up with her parents. She didn't know anyone else in town, and the thought of 15 weeks with no social life was unbearable. She didn't need any old job; she needed one that would help her to make some friends her own age.

A Google search had told her she had three basic options: holiday cover in the enormous book warehouse on the edge of town; working as a waiter or cleaner in a hotel near the seafront; or work as an activity leader in one of the town's dozen or more language schools (some of the more disreputable schools might even take her on as a teacher).

She was pretty sure that language schools were her best bet, so she set to work on her CV. When it came to her university studies, she left theology out and just put that she was a BA student at Cambridge.

Chapter Eleven

It was Ross's turn to make the coffee again on Wednesday. Nigel was there too, along with a woman he introduced as his wife.

There was no raucous laughter this time, and Sid was sitting hunched in his chair, almost in a foetal position.

'Hi Ross,' said Nigel. 'How's it going?'

'Good, thanks.'

'Enjoying the work?'

'Yes, thanks.'

On Thursday, Ross and Sofie were on their own, as the Turkish waiters had left, amid hugs and gifts and fulsome praise from Mrs Akehurst, who was clearly very fond of them.

When Mr Akehurst asked Sofie to make coffee, Ross offered to take it in instead.

'Nah, you're all right. I'll do it.'

The two shifts went well. Ross liked the work, and he anticipated that it would keep him busy enough to keep dark thoughts at bay for most of the day. He thought Sofie seemed to enjoy it too, despite the presence of Sid.

*

When Ross and Sofie arrived for their evening shift next day, Sid was in the staffroom playing with his mobile. He seemed to have a bit of a snuffly cold, or maybe hay fever. He said hello to Ross but he and Sofie didn't so much as glance at each other.

Sofie retreated to the toilets to get changed, brush her hair and apply a little lip-gloss and mascara. Ross was already in his black trousers, so all he needed to do was swap his T-shirt for a white shirt and tie. As there were no female staff present, he decided to do so in the staffroom. He turned his back on Sid as he changed his shirt.

'Who do you support, Ross?'

'Brighton.'

'Oh, God. Bloody useless. You think you'll stay up next season?'

'Hope so.'

'Betcha don't.'

Sid had a strong working-class accent, almost Cockney. This surprised Ross, as his parents and his brother were all quite posh.

'Who do you support then?'

'*Ar-se-nal!*' With that, he took out a cigarette, lit it and went out.

Sofie returned a moment later. She looked very smart with her black skirt and white blouse. Her sleeves looked as if they had been folded and ironed so that they ended halfway down her forearm.

'Has someone been smoking?'

'Sid.'

She rolled her eyes. 'What a jerk.'

*

On Saturday morning, Ross and Sofie received almost £80 of tips from the guests, though this fell to £10 each by the time the rest of the staff got their share. The chef told them to expect about £20 per person in future.

They decided to celebrate with an ice cream on the beach. As they walked across the Western Lawns, Ross noticed Sid, his wife Martha and their two little girls in the distance. Ross guessed that the oldest was four or five years old and the youngest about three. Sid and the children were playing a game of 'it'. The littlest one was 'it' and was chasing the other two. Sid eventually allowed himself to be tagged and then chased the children with mock incompetence. Ross could hear their squeals of delight as he failed to catch them.

'How come you know Sid?' he asked Sofie.

'It's a long story.'

She followed this up with a silence that indicated that she had no intention of sharing the details.

The guests changed that day, and by Monday, dinner time was very noisy, with lots of laughter and orders for extra wine and beer. The guests chatted with Ross and Sofie, and lots of the men were eager to share their thoughts about England's chances in the World Cup.

Sid was there again on Wednesday, as Ross changed his shirt for the evening shift.

'You and Sofie going out?'

'No, we're just friends. How come you know her?'

'Why? What she say about me?'

'Nothing, but I saw you talking to her last week.'

Sid shrugged. 'I know her sister. Mind you, she don't talk to her sister no more. Anyway, I was going to give you some advice about women. Whatever you do, don't make my mistake.'

'What's that?'

'Got Martha up the duff, didn't I? God, she wasn't half fit in them days. Not like now. That's what five years and two kids does to a woman.'

Ross wasn't sure what to say.

'You know how you should treat women?' Sid asked.

'How?'

'Find 'em, fuck 'em and forget 'em. I never wanted to be a dad, but I do love my kids, mind you. Love 'em to bits.'

He took out a cigarette, lit it and went outside.

*

That evening, dinner was very easy as England were playing Belgium. Most of the men ate quickly and disappeared to the bar for the match. The majority of women stayed behind. They hung around for a long time but drank much less than the men. Ross was frustrated at being unable to watch the game, though the chef kept a radio commentary on in the kitchen as England went down to a one-nil defeat.

The following afternoon, Sid was in the staffroom again. He asked Ross if he liked Gareth Southgate, the England manager.

'Yeah, I think he's doing a good job.'

'Bloody useless pouf if you ask me.'

As before, he lit his cigarette before walking out, leaving a cloud of smoke behind.

Sofie came back in a moment later.

'Has he been smoking in here again?'

'Yeah,' said Ross. 'He's about as different from Nigel as you can get, isn't he?'

'Have you noticed? If you take the coffee in when Nigel's there, Sid's really quiet.'

'Yeah.'

'He doesn't like him at all.'

'You think so?'

'Definitely.'

Ross liked everyone else at the hotel. The chef could be grumpy during a shift, but he was fun afterwards as he regaled everyone with tales of life under communism in Albania. Veronika the cleaner was very chatty, and she and Sofie seemed to put their heads together and giggle whenever they had the opportunity.

As for Mrs Akehurst, she didn't smile much, but the rest of the staff obviously liked her, so Ross assumed she must be okay.

Other than Sid, the only thing that Ross didn't like about the job was Mr Akehurst's habit of appearing at the end of breakfast and asking him, Sofie, Veronika or the kitchen porter to make coffee for the family. He and Sofie tried gulping their breakfast down quickly and leaving early in an effort to avoid him, but he quickly cottoned on and came round sooner.

'It'd be all right if he put it on a fixed rota,' said Sofie. 'It's so annoying. Just when you think you're free to go: "Sofie? Can you prepare some coffee for my family?"'

'It's not just that,' said Ross. 'I'm a waiter. That's my job. I'm not his bloody servant.'

*

Next morning, just before staff breakfast, Veronika the Polish cleaner indicated to Sofie that she wanted a word in private. They went into the empty dining room.

'Martha, she said me you never look at her when you take coffee in. Why you don't look at her?'

'I wasn't aware of that.'

'Martha is nice person. You should be more friendly to her.'

'Yeah, okay. I will. Thanks, Veronika.'

'And another thing: why Sid don't like Ross?'

'Who says he doesn't?'

'Martha. She just said me.'

'Oh. I don't know.'

'Me too, I don't know. I mean, Ross really nice boy, innit?'

'Yes.'

'I think you like him a lot.'

'We're just friends.'

Veronika laughed. 'That's good because Mrs Akehurst, she sack you if you boyfriend and girlfriend.'

They both laughed.

Sofie told Ross nothing about this conversation.

Chapter Twelve

'Alberta? Hi, I'm Sarah.'

'Hi. Please call me Bee.'

Sarah was in her 40s, sporty-looking with short, wavy hair. She shook Bee's hand and led her from the school's elegant Victorian reception area out to its bright, modern and spacious refectory.

'Sorry to interview you in here. We haven't actually got an office here yet, but I wanted you to see this place because this is where you'd be working.'

They were in Rayfield School, the largest private school in town, with its imposing classrooms and boarding houses nestled round an enormous cricket pitch.

'The school closes down at the end of June,' Sarah explained, 'and we start next day with a hundred and twenty students. On Saturday the eighth, we go up to two hundred and fifty, and we stay more or less at that number throughout July. The last day's the eleventh of August, and we'll be back to about a hundred and twenty by then. The students are aged thirteen to seventeen, mostly from Spain and Italy, but all over the place, really: France, Germany, Russia, China, you name it.'

'Sounds amazing.'

Bee was being interviewed for the post of non-residential activity leader. Sarah explained that it would mostly be afternoon and evening work but all day Saturday and Sunday. This suited Bee perfectly because it would give her an excuse to miss church.

When they came to the part of the interview where Sarah went through Bee's CV, she asked what she was studying.

'It's theology, but I'm not God squad. I won't be going round trying to convert people or anything like that.'

'So why did you decide to do theology?'

'It fascinates me, the whole thing. But don't worry, most of the time I talk about music and movies and the weather and football. Well, maybe not football, but I have to listen to my boyfriend talking about football quite a lot, so I know a fair bit about it.'

Sarah laughed. Bee guessed she had neutralised her biggest worry. There was one more that she saved for later in the interview. She had to go away from Thursday the 12th to Saturday the 14th of July. It was a commitment she couldn't get out of. She didn't mention that it was the anti-Donald Trump demonstration on Friday the 13th.

Sarah shrugged. 'Shouldn't be a problem. Will you be available on the Sunday?'

'Yes.'

'Good, because that's the World Cup Final, and lots of people will be begging for time off.'

Chapter Thirteen

Nigel was always there with his wife on Wednesday and Saturday mornings. And so it was that, on the seventh of July, four days before the Alpha Course was due to begin, Ross encountered him in the family room. On this occasion, there was no sign of Sid, but Martha was there with her children and a face like thunder.

Nigel followed Ross back to the dining room, where Sofie was waiting for him.

'Ross? Just wanted to ask – are you still up for the course on Tuesday?'

'Er…yes.'

'It's six-thirty at St Anselm's church hall. You know where it is, don't you?'

'Yes.'

'And don't have dinner. You'll be fed there.'

'Oh, right, okay. Will you be there?'

'No. It's a friend of mine who's running it. He's called Dominic. You'll like him. And I haven't told him about you-know-what.'

'Thanks.'

Nigel returned to the family quarters.

'What's that all about?' Sofie asked.

Ross blushed slightly. 'When I told Nigel about the accident, he wanted me to pray, but I said I couldn't because I don't really believe in God. He suggested I do the Alpha Course. It's like an introduction to Christianity.'

'Oh, I've heard of that. Sounds really interesting.'

Ross gave a wan smile.

'How long's the course?'

'It's every Tuesday evening. I think it's about ten or twelve weeks.'

'How much is it?'

'It's free.'

'Would you mind if I came too?'

'Really? I was half expecting you to laugh at me.'

'No. I'd be really interested.'

'That's good.'

'Can you ask Nigel if there's room for another?'

'Why don't you ask him?'

'You know him better than me.'

*

Ross slept in very late on Sunday morning (a day off). By the time he had showered and dressed, it was gone 12.

'Oh, hello.' His mother said as he went into the kitchen. 'Back in the land of the living?'

'Yeah.'

'Do you want me to get you some brunch?'

'It's all right. I'll do it.'

'No, let me. What do you fancy? Full English?'

'That would be great. Thanks.'

He drifted into the living room, where his father and his brother were watching the build-up to the England-Sweden game. He picked up his mobile and opened up Instagram.

Almost the first thing he noticed was that his history classmate Mark had replaced his cover picture with a gay pride rainbow flag. He had come out to his parents the previous day and was now coming out to the world.

Ross had never twigged that Mark was gay, but somehow he wasn't at all surprised. He hadn't once liked or commented on anyone's posts since the accident, but he felt he needed to do so here. He tapped on the heart icon and, after thinking for a moment, he wrote, 'Congratulations on coming out Mark. Sending love and support.'

In a sense, he understood how Mark must have felt when he came out to his parents. Today, he would have to come out to his: not as gay but as a potential Christian. He knew his father wouldn't approve.

He waited until dinner time.

'I won't need dinner on Tuesdays.'

'Why's that?'

'I'm going to be doing an evening course.'

'What course is that?'

'Alpha Course.'

'Isn't that sort of…God squad?' his father asked, his hands frozen in the middle of cutting a sausage on his plate.

'I haven't told you this,' said Ross, 'but after the accident, I went to church several times. I met this priest, Nigel. He's been a big help. In fact, it was him who got me the job, not Sofie. His mum owns the hotel. I'm still struggling, but I've got part of the day when I'm too busy to think about the accident. The rest of the time's a nightmare, to be honest. It's all I ever think about.'

His mother reached across and put a hand on his shoulder.

'Nigel, the priest, he said he thought the Alpha Course might help me find a way to deal with it.'

'I hope it helps you, Ross,' said his mother. 'I really do.'

Ross smiled at her and looked across at his father, who still hadn't finished cutting his sausage. He opened his mouth as if to speak and then visibly flinched. Ross was pretty sure his mother had just kicked him under the table.

After a moment, he said, 'I suppose you should give it a try then. See if it helps.'

Part Two

Alpha and Omega

Chapter Fourteen

Bee waited to see how her parents would react. With dinner finished and a cheese platter on the table, she had just told them she was having trouble maintaining her faith, and it was becoming increasingly difficult to motivate herself to continue studying theology.

'Why?' her mother asked. 'You've always been so sure of your faith.'

'It started with Chloe's baby.'

Chloe had been one of her gang of friends in high school. Bee's parents had never really approved of her, and Bee fully understood why. In fact, they hadn't known the half of it. As well as being loud and funny, Chloe was the first in her class to lose her virginity, just as she was the first to smoke cigarettes, drink, smoke weed and dance with MDMA flowing through her veins.

She was also the first to get pregnant.

Just 18 months after leaving college, she gave birth to a beautiful baby boy. But five days later, he tested positive for cystic fibrosis. This meant he would struggle with chest infections all his life. Even if he survived into adulthood, which was by no means certain, he would be unlikely to make it to middle age.

This came as a great shock to Bee. Her recent philosophy of religion module had included a section on theodicy, the study of why God allows terrible things to happen. Bee loved reading up on this. She was especially drawn to the ideas of process theology, an emphasis on 'becoming' rather than 'being', or in John Polkinghorne's memorable phrase, God allowing the universe to make itself. Surely, says Polkinghorne, such an imperfect universe is better than the puppet theatre of a cosmic tyrant.

She had also liked Peter Kreeft's argument that, in giving us free will, God may have created the possibility of evil, but he didn't create evil itself. And free will is necessary, because without it, we cannot have the higher goal of true love.

The tragedy of Chloe's baby shattered all this. Suddenly all these intricate arguments seemed redundant and arcane. Everything she had tried so hard to comprehend felt irrelevant.

But she persevered. She asked her tutor what she could read to help her understand theodicy better, and he sent her right back to the beginning. This took her from the debates of Pelagius and Augustine of Hippo to Leibniz, Immanuel Kant and all the way to modern thinkers John Howard Yoder and Richard Rubinstein.

But nothing seemed to click. Ideas she had once agreed with now seemed full of holes. Books that used to speak to her fell silent. Even Ecclesiastes and Job, her favourite books in the Bible, seemed to have nothing to say.

And then that bitch of a flatmate had to open her mouth.

'The question of why God allows bad things to happen is a non-question. It's no more valid than the question of why Father Christmas doesn't give any presents to the starving children in Africa.'

What a cow.

How dare she humiliate her like that, in front of her other flatmates round their dinner table? It was like saying: 'Your studies are useless. Your belief has no value. Your identity has no meaning. The life of a theologian that you have been dreaming of and working towards, is (as Ecclesiastes would say) meaningless, meaningless, utterly meaningless.'

But what really hurt wasn't the humiliation. It wasn't the friendship betrayed. It wasn't the contempt. It was the nagging feeling that her bitch of a flatmate might be right and she was wasting her time; she might as well be studying Father Christmasology.

Bee said none of this to her parents. She simply said, 'I can't understand how God can allow such a terrible thing to happen to a baby.'

'But Bee,' said her father, 'you've read your Bible. You've read Job. You know we can't understand God. We're nothing next to him. But we have to maintain our faith, no matter how much we suffer.'

'Dad, do you think I don't know that? I've been reading Job and re-reading it, and Ecclesiastes. I know those books like the back of my hand.'

'Then why are you ignoring their message?'

'Because it feels like a cop-out.'

Her father shook his head. 'No. This is the wisdom of the ages.'

Bee had no intention of arguing with him. She had no desire to undermine his faith. She just wanted him to understand why she was losing hers.

'Maybe...' said her mother, 'maybe you need to go back to basics.'

'What do you mean?'

'Well at university you do all these highfalutin things you keep telling us about, all this exegesis and historical-critical what-not. Maybe you need to get back to the basic Christian message.'

She thumped the table with her fists as she said, 'basic Christian message'.

'And how am I supposed to do that?'

'Did you see that notice in the church this morning? There's an Alpha Course starting next week. It's Church of England, but it's better than nothing. Why don't you go on that?'

'Mum, the Alpha Course is basic Christianity for beginners. I'm not a beginner. I've been a Christian all my life. I've done two years of a theology degree. I know the Bible backwards.'

'But maybe you've lost sight of the basics.'

Bee rolled her eyes and looked away from her mother.

'Please, Bee. Please. It's too important. You can't just give up.'

Chapter Fifteen

The following Monday, when Sofie went into the staff ladies' toilet to get changed, Veronika knocked on the door.

'Sofie, can I speak with you?'

'Just a minute.'

Once she was dressed, Sofie opened the door. There was just enough room in the wash-basin area for the two of them.

'I think you need to keep away from Sid.'

'Why?'

'Martha said me that he really fancy you.'

'What?'

'Yeah. She said she had big row with him yesterday. She said when you take coffee in, his eyes follow you, looking your backside and your tits.'

'Oh my God.'

'Yeah.'

'I don't know what to say.'

'You don't want Sid. You got Ross. He's much nicer.'

'Me and Ross are just friends.'

'Yeah, whatever.'

'We are!'

'Whatever.'

Sofie shook her head and Veronika grinned.

'Well, you're right about one thing: I do not want Sid. Thanks for the warning.'

Again, she said nothing to Ross about this conversation.

*

St Anselm's was at the far side of town. They had to take two buses, with a 10-minute wait in the town centre.

'What are you expecting?' Sofie asked, as they took their seats upstairs on the second bus.

'I've got no idea.'

'I hope it's not like these American televangelists, all fire and brimstone and some preacher yelling at everyone.'

Ross smiled. 'Well, Nigel's not like that, is he? As far as I'm concerned, the most important thing is that nobody recognises me.'

'It's nothing to be embarrassed about.'

'No. I mean...you know.'

'Don't worry. I'm sure nobody'll know us from Adam.'

'Well, they'll know *you* from Adam.'

'Ha, ha.'

'Promise me you won't tell anyone.'

'Promise.'

They got off the second bus.

'When was the last time you went to church?' Ross asked.

Sofie was silent for a long time. Eventually, she said, 'A funeral, I think. What about you?'

'Never been. No, I tell a lie, maybe a couple of weddings.'

'Your parents not religious then?'

'My dad's like Richard Dawkins on steroids,' said Ross. 'He hates religion.'

'Really? So he don't like you coming here?'

'No.'

'What about your mum?'

'I don't think she believes in God, but if someone goes to church, she kind of regards it as a badge of merit. Quite weird, really. What about your parents?'

'My dad would only go to church if they had a bar.'

By now, they had arrived. There was a handwritten sign outside the church saying 'Alpha Course' with an arrow pointing to the entrance to the church hall. A tall, red-headed man in his early 30s was standing by the door, greeting new arrivals.

'Hi,' he said as he shook Ross's hand. 'My name's Dominic.' He had the dog-collar of a vicar.

'Hello, I'm Ross and this is Sofie.'

'Come on in and make yourselves at home.'

They went inside, where there were more than 20 other people. They were a very mixed crowd but Ross and Sofie were the youngest.

A woman with shortish blond hair came up to them. 'Hi, I'm Pat.'

Ross and Sofie introduced themselves, and as they did so, Ross noticed that Pat was pregnant. She took them to one of three big round tables, all set out for dinner. Pat sat them between a young woman on Sofie's left and a middle-aged couple on Ross's right.

The young woman was called Bee. She said she was a student.

'Where are you studying?' Sofie asked.

'Cambridge.'

'Oh gosh, very impressive. Is it nice there?'

'It's beautiful. I really love it.'

The couple on Ross's right introduced themselves. The husband had a strong Birmingham accent and a very firm handshake. 'My name's Bob, and yes, I am a builder.'

They all laughed at this. His wife laughed too, but Ross guessed that she must have heard it a thousand times. She was called Alison and worked as a teaching assistant in a primary school.

After 10 minutes, Dominic the vicar clapped his hands and made his announcement: 'Hello everyone. Well, it's really great to see so many people here, and I'd like to thank you all for coming and welcome you to the Alpha

Course. It's going to be a busy eleven weeks, and there's a lot to get through, but I think first of all and most important of all, we need to just relax and get to know each other a little bit. And what better way to do that than for us all to have dinner together.

'Now, before we start, I'd like to introduce myself and the team leaders. I think most of you have met me, my name's Dominic Markham, and I'm the vicar at St Anselm's. Would you like to stand up team leaders?'

Pat, the pregnant woman at Ross and Sofie's table, stood up, as did two others on the other tables, a rather glamorous-looking woman in her 40s and a slightly older man with a tweed jacket and a serious expression.

'Over here we have Pat,' said the vicar.

Pat gave a little wave.

'And this is Andrea.'

A wave from the glamorous woman.

'And Rodney.'

Rodney just nodded. Ross thought he didn't look like the kind of man who would wave without good reason.

A group of women appeared as if from nowhere, armed with very warm plates, jugs of water and apple juice and big bowls and baking trays with vegetables and cottage pie.

Sofie leaned over to Ross. 'It's nice to be waited on.'

'Help yourselves,' said Pat.

The food was delicious: Ross especially liked the thin layer of cheese on top of the cottage pie. He spent most of the meal talking with Bob the Builder and his wife, while Sofie talked with Bee and the woman on the other side of her. Ross was more interested in Bee, but Bob's wife Alison kept bringing him back into their conversation. She told him she had been in floods of tears when she heard on the news that the last boys had finally been brought safely out of that cave in Thailand.

Ross agreed that this was wonderful news. At the same time, he heard Sofie ask Bee what she was studying.

'Theology.'

'Oh gosh. So, what brings you here?'

'A bit of a crisis of faith. My mum suggested it might help to go back to basics.'

As the helpers were clearing up after dessert, a man on the other side of the table asked Bee where modern theology stood on the issue of creationism versus Darwinian evolution.

'It's a big mistake to take the Biblical account literally,' Bee replied. 'For a start there are two completely different creation stories, so how can either of them be the literal truth?'

Ross was surprised. He thought there was only one account of the creation in the Bible: the story of Adam and Eve. He was about to ask Bee what she meant when Dominic stood up and clapped his hands.

'Ladies and gentlemen, if I can perhaps have your attention for a moment. One Biblical passage I love is in Paul's letter to the Ephesians, where he urged them to sing and make music in their hearts to the Lord. That's what I'd like us to do now. So, let me to introduce Tom Bradshaw, who's going to sing for us this evening.'

Tom Bradshaw stood up. An ageing hippy if ever there was one, he had faded jeans and a long, grey-brown ponytail. He strummed his guitar and fine-tuned it. Meanwhile Pat and the other leaders passed round some photocopied lyrics.

'Please feel free to join in,' Pat said to those on her table.

'I'm sure you all know this one,' Tom said into his microphone. 'But maybe you didn't know it's a hymn.'

Amazing grace, how sweet the sound
That saved a wretch like me!
I once was lost but now I'm found
Was blind but now I see.

Sofie sang along. Ross mumbled and mouthed the words a bit, but as a rule he preferred not to sing when he was sober. He noticed that Bee was singing enthusiastically. She had a good voice too.

The next song was more what might be called happy-clappy.

Everything we do, we do in your name
Glory, glory, glory hallelujah.
Everything we have we owe to your love
Glory, glory, glory to the Lord.

Ross thought it buttock-clenchingly naff, but Bee and Pat and one or two others on their table sang and clapped along with gusto. Sofie didn't. One look between her and Ross said it all.

After that Dominic took the microphone.

'Ladies and gentlemen, friends, I'd like to welcome you all to the Alpha Course tonight. I hope that for all of us, these eleven weeks can be a truly uplifting journey. I hope the Alpha Course can bring you where you want to be, can help you find meaning, help you find truth, can help you find forgiveness for all your sins.'

At that point, he seemed to look right into Ross's eyes.

Ross broke off eye contact and looked down. 'He knows about me,' he thought. 'No doubt about it. Nigel must have told him.'

He wondered who else knew. Did Pat know there was a boy on her table who had killed someone? Had she been told to lay it on a bit thick about sin?

But then he told himself not to be so paranoid. Nigel said he wouldn't tell anyone. He wouldn't lie to him about a thing like that.

Even so, for the next few minutes, Ross paid no attention to Dominic. His own personal gargoyle had sunk its teeth into him once more. How foolish he had been to think he could find forgiveness here. Happy-clappy Christians, Jesus loves you, there, there, never mind. And anyway, Lizzie Johnson's in Heaven now, so it's all okay.

*

Bee wasn't enjoying the talk either. She wondered what she was doing there. This was mainstream Christianity for beginners. Bee was no beginner, and she wasn't mainstream either, not since she was five years old and her father told her to stop crying: the story of Noah wasn't really true. God hadn't actually drowned millions of little animals. Noah's Ark was just a story to tell us God loved us, and even if he got cross when we were naughty, he would never hurt us.

She looked around at some of the others on her table. Pat looked beautiful pregnant and had reached the stage when she was starting to glow. Bee imagined that she would be a fantastic mother: kind and loving but firm when she needed to be.

She looked at Nick, the young man who had asked her about creationism. There was something almost military in his bearing. She imagined him as maybe a manager somewhere, and she bet that he didn't take any nonsense from his subordinates.

Opposite Bee were Bob and Alison. She seemed a lot posher than him. Bee wondered if that had always been the case or if she had lived in the south-east a long time and simply lost her accent. Her husband was quite thick-set, but Bee guessed that he must have been athletic-looking as a young builder.

And then there was the young couple, Sofie and Ross. She was very much focused on what Dominic was saying, but he wasn't listening. He looked very stressed about something or other. Bee wondered what it was.

She tried to concentrate on Dominic. He was holding the microphone and sitting on a table. He had cracked a few jokes. The one that got the biggest laugh had been about circumcision, but Bee hadn't been paying attention, so she didn't know what he had said.

He was talking about the meaning of life, quoting with approval the journalist Bernard Levin, who was desperate to know *why* he was born and his fear that if he left it too late, he would never find out. 'Why do I *need* to know why I was born?' he quoted him as saying. 'Because I can't believe it wasn't an accident, and if it wasn't an accident, it must have meaning.'

Bee found it difficult to understand why Bernard Levin could have been so troubled by such a question. Wondering why you were born but refusing to believe it was an accident was a bit like wondering why you are putting on weight but refusing to believe that it has anything to do with all the chocolate brownies you keep eating. If you rule out the correct answer, you are bound to find any question a bit of a puzzle.

As far as Bee was concerned, the answer to the question, 'Why am I here?' was easy: you are here because your father's sperm fertilised your mother's egg. No other reason, end of story.

Dominic spent a long time talking about the meaning of life, the big question: 'Why am I here?' Apparently, Tolstoy and Freddie Mercury were just as desperate to find the meaning of life. Poor Freddie Mercury suffered the same fate as Bernard Levin: he died before he got there. But Tolstoy found the answer in Jesus.

'Well,' Bee thought. 'Dominic would say that, wouldn't he?' Then she told herself not to be so patronising. She would have said the same thing six months ago. In many ways she wished she still believed it.

The next bit of Dominic's talk emphasised something Bee had never believed. He said Christianity was all or nothing. It was either the greatest story ever told, the meaning of life, the universe and everything, or it was a load of old rubbish. It was nothing in between. It most certainly wasn't very nice for those who like that kind of thing.

Bee couldn't help but shake her head at this. Even when she had been secure in her faith, she had never thought that. For her, Christianity was just one of many different paths to God. She was a Christian because she had been born into that particular faith and felt comfortable in it. But she had never taken it literally. She had always thought of Christianity as a path which, as Dominic would rather not say, was very good for those who liked that kind of thing.

*

Ross noticed that there was something else that Bee didn't like: Dominic kept quoting Jesus as saying: 'I am the way and the truth and the life.' Bee looked down and shook her head every time he said this. Ross wondered what was so objectionable about that. What else was any Christian supposed to think? He would have to ask her later.

He found it difficult to concentrate for much of the talk, but then Dominic told the most amazing story, about a Polish Catholic priest by the name of Maximilian Kolbe, who sheltered more than two thousand Jews from the Nazis during the Second World War.

Eventually, the Gestapo got him and he ended up in Auschwitz.

A few months later, one of the men from his barracks disappeared. The Nazis assumed he had escaped (in fact he had drowned in the latrine), so they decided to pick 10 men at random and starve them to death so as to deter future escape attempts.

One man they picked cried out, 'Please don't kill me. I have a wife and children.'

So Father Maximilian stepped forwards and offered himself instead.

The Nazis stripped him and the other nine naked and locked them in a bunker. Father Maximilian led them in prayer and hymn singing and ministered to the others as death from starvation and dehydration

82

approached. He and three others were still alive when the Nazis opened up the bunker two weeks later. They killed them with injections of carbolic acid. It was said that Father Maximilian calmly raised his left arm for them when his turn came.

Dominic explained that Father Maximilian's sacrifice echoed the sacrifice of Jesus, who died for all of us, just as Father Maximilian died to save one of his fellow prisoners. Through the death and resurrection of Christ, all our sins are forgiven, provided we sincerely repent and give ourselves to him.

This cut right through to Ross's reason for being there. Could he really find forgiveness through Jesus? But how could any amount of repentance be enough after what he had done?

*

After the talk, they all stood round drinking tea and coffee. Ross and Sofie went to one side, where they tittered at the happy-clappy hymn and swapped impressions about Dominic and the others on their table.

When the break finished, Pat introduced herself again and asked the others on the table to introduce ourselves and say something about why they were there.

This threw Ross into a panic. What was he supposed to say? That he had accidentally killed someone and was there to find redemption?

The man beside Pat spoke first, and then Alison. Ross was too flustered to listen to what they said. Bob the Builder was harder to ignore, seated right next to Ross as he was.

'I've worked hard all my life, and I've been very successful: a beautiful wife' – he pointed at Alison – 'two splendid children, a successful business, nice house, lots of money, but I've always felt there has to be something more to life than this. I'm here to see if I can find it.'

Then it was his Ross's turn. What to say?

'My name's Ross. I was just going along fine, just finished my AS-Levels. Then something happened that kind of jolted me out of all that. I suddenly need to find answers to some big questions, so that's why I'm here.'

Sofie was next. 'Hi, my name's Sofie. I've got lots of questions, about the meaning of life, really. So, that's why I'm here.'

The next person was Bee: 'Hi, my name's Bee. I'm a student. I've been a very strong Christian all my life, but recently I've been having a lot of doubts. So I'm here to kind of get myself back on the straight and narrow.'

When everyone had introduced themselves, Pat suggested they set up a WhatsApp group in case people wanted to get in touch between sessions. She produced a sheet of paper and sent it round for those who wanted to add their details.

Pat asked how they had found the talk, if there were any thoughts they would like to share. Ross had nothing to say. More than anything, he was relieved that his car crash hadn't come up in the introductions. Sofie kept quiet too, as did Bee, but Ross wasn't the only person who had noticed how uncomfortable Bee was with, 'I am the way and the truth and the life.'

'Why didn't you like that bit?' asked Nick, the young man with a military bearing.

Bee seemed to shift a little uncomfortably in her seat. 'It's in St John's Gospel, Chapter Fourteen, Verse Six. Dominic only said the first half of the verse, the nice bit. The second half isn't nearly as nice.'

'Why?' said Nick. 'What does it say?'

'I am the way and the truth and the life. No-one comes to the Father except through me.'

'What's so bad about that?'

Bee hesitated. She didn't look at anyone as she replied. 'What that verse is saying is that the Christians have all the answers. The Moslems, Hindus, Jews, whatever, they haven't got any answers.' She looked at Nick. 'That verse is the justification for the some of the worst aspects of Christian intolerance: forced conversions, burning heretics, the Inquisition, the lot. There's so much truth and beauty in the New Testament, but not that verse.'

Bee looked down. Nobody spoke.

After what seemed an eternity, Pat said, 'I don't think anyone here's in favour of forced conversions or the Spanish Inquisition. And you can be a Christian and have great respect for Islam and the Jewish faith and Hinduism and Buddhism. But if you believe that Christ is the one and only Son of God, then you have to believe that he's the way and the truth and the life, and as Christians we're dedicated to spreading that truth.'

Everyone looked at Bee. She said nothing, but Ross could see she didn't agree.

*

All the participants had gone. The washing up was done, with everything dried and put away. The chairs were stacked and the tables folded and placed in the store room. Only five chairs remained, in a circle in the middle of the room. Dominic sat on one of them, along with the team leaders Pat, Rodney and Andrea, plus Tom the guitarist.

'Well,' said Dominic. 'Certainly a good turnout. And I thought the dinner was great.'

The others all agreed.

'So, Rodney, this was your first time leading a table. How was it for you?'

'I really enjoyed it. I thought your talk was great, and we had a good discussion on our table, didn't we, Tom?'

Tom nodded.

'Excellent.'

'Yeah, I agree completely,' said Andrea. 'I thought it was a brilliant first session.'

'What about you, Pat?'

Pat shifted in her chair. 'Bit difficult, to be honest. Did you see that young boy Ross? He really wasn't there for half your talk. I thought he was going to burst into tears at one stage.'

'I noticed him,' said Andrea. 'I know that girl he was with, Sofie Manning. I don't think she recognised me, but I certainly recognised her. I never taught her, but she was at Upperton. Problem girl from a problem family.'

Dominic winced slightly. 'Jesus dined with sinners, let's not forget. It sounds like Sofie's exactly the kind of person we should be aiming to help. Perhaps she wants to turn her life around, and we have to do everything we can for her. As for the boy, Ross, he came via Nigel Akehurst at Saint Margaret's. He said he had some kind of personal crisis, but he didn't want to tell me what.'

'Yes,' said Pat, 'he said something about that when we introduced himself.'

'Let's hope we can help him. That's why we're here.'

The others all nodded.

'There's another one in my group,' said Pat. 'The young girl. Not Sofie, but the other one: Bee. I'm a bit worried about her.'

'Why's that?'

'She's studying theology at Cambridge. She says she's here because she's having a crisis of faith.'

'I can understand that,' said Dominic. 'When you study theology, a lot of it's very challenging, especially some of the more liberal theories you encounter. Some people can't cope with it.'

Pat nodded. 'She said some pretty weird things, and she went on about the Spanish Inquisition.'

'Nobody expects the Spanish Inquisition!' said Tom. Everyone apart from Dominic laughed.

'Monty Python,' said Rodney.

'Oh,' said Dominic. ''Before my time, I'm afraid.'

Tom asked Pat if she would like him to join her table to give a bit of support.

'No,' said Dominic. 'You stay with Rodney. If this girl's been studying theology, I think it's better if I keep a special eye on your table and help out if need be.'

Pat smiled. 'Thanks. That would be great.'

Dominic looked round. 'Okay, if that's it, shall we finish with a little prayer? Andrea, why don't you lead us?'

They all closed their eyes and bowed their heads.

'Lord,' said Andrea, 'we thank you for bringing us together tonight to do your work. We thank you for bringing so many people to this place. And we pray that, with your guidance, we can bring these people to truth and light and faith. In the name of Jesus Christ, our Lord, amen.'

'Amen,' the others said in unison.

Chapter Sixteen

After the morning shift next day, Sofie cycled back to Old Town, where she locked her bike outside the Co-op and crossed the road to the coffee shop on the corner.

'Sorry I'm late, babe.'

'No worries.'

'Do you want anything from the counter?'

Dani shook her head. 'I'm okay, thanks.'

Sofie returned a few minutes later with an Americano.

'So,' said Dani, 'how are you?'

'Pretty good.'

'And how's the hospitality industry?'

'It's cool. Quite enjoy it. The money's good. The boss is a bit of a dragon, but in a nice way. There's just one downside – guess who's there.'

'Who?'

Sofie opened her eyes wide and tilted her head. 'Who's the worst person who could possibly be there?'

'I don't know. Katie Hopkins?'

'Sid.'

'What? *The* Sid?'

'The one and only.'

'What's he doing there?'

'His parents only own the place.'

'What? I thought their son was a priest.'

'Yeah. Sid has a brother who's a priest. Not only that, his family are all posh.'

'But you said he had a Cockney accent.'

'Well, he's a fake Cockney, innit? You know he went to private school.'

'Oh, yeah, you said. Have you spoken with him?'

'Only once, just after I started. He goes, "You can't work here." And I'm like, "Piss off. You can't stop me."'

'Good for you, girl. What did he say?'

'Well, what could he say? Nothing.'

Dani narrowed her eyes: 'You're going to keep out of his way, right?'

'Too bloody right.'

They sat back in their chairs and drank a little more coffee. Then Sofie leaned forwards and asked, 'Anyway, how's your summer of lurve going?'

Dani leaned towards her and whispered, 'I've got cystitis.'

'What? Because…?'

'Been overdoing it, yes.'

'Oh no.'

'Raj, right, he's like, "We can do other things." And I'm like, "Yeah, we can play Scrabble." "That's not what I mean." "I know it's not what you mean, but we're playing bloody Scrabble."'

They both laughed.

'Don't tell Ross.'

'Course I won't.'

'How is he?'

'He seems okay. At work, he's just too busy to worry about the accident.'

'From what I hear, as soon as he gets home, he goes and hides in his bedroom.'

'Really?'

'Yeah. Has he said anything about Raj?'

'No. Why?'

'Raj is still worried that he blames him.'

'Didn't they, like, revise together for three weeks?'

'Yes.'

'And they never spoke about it then?'

'Oh, come on. You know what blokes are like. They'd rather give each other wedgies than open up to each other.'

Sofie shook her head. 'They're bloody useless, all of them. Sometimes I wish I was a lezzer, then I could have nothing to do with them.'

They concentrated on their drinks for a few moments.

'So, tell me,' said Dani, 'what's all this about you and Ross going on the Alpha Course?'

'Yeah, we went to the first one last night. It was quite interesting.'

'I understand why Ross is going,' said Dani. 'He's on this mad quest for Christian redemption. But you, I don't get it. What are you doing there?'

Sofie took a sip of her Americano.

'Do you remember I told you about this book we did in French, Albert Camus?'

'Only vaguely.'

'He's this philosopher, right, and he wrote this novel, *L' Étranger,* to get his message across. It was a good novel, yeah, but I really hated his message.'

'What was that?'

'Basically, he says life has no meaning: we're all going to die, and that's that.'

'Very cheerful.'

'Yeah. I know he's wrong, but I don't know what's right. The Alpha Course is about exploring the meaning of life.'

'Sofie, it's not a philosophy course. They're God squad.'

'I know.'

'Promise me you're not going to turn into some born-again religious nutcase.'

Sofie smiled and shook her head. 'That's not going to happen.'

'As for Ross, this isn't what he needs. He needs counselling.'

'This might help.'

Dani shrugged. 'Well, I hope he proves me wrong, but I think he's wasting his time.'

'Do you think I should try and persuade him to give counselling another chance?'

'There's no point. He won't listen. Maybe tell him a little bit about you. Show him that people can get their lives back on track.'

*

That evening, the male guests were very sombre. England had just been knocked out of the World Cup, beaten 2-1 by Croatia. Ross watched the first 90 minutes live at home but had to cycle to work during extra time, and by the time he arrived, the game was over. He wasn't surprised by the result. England had started well and scored first, but by the time Croatia equalised, it had been pretty obvious that they were more likely to win.

Next morning, after the breakfast shift, Ross ended up having to make coffee for the Akehurst family. Sid and Martha were there, along with their children, one on each of Sid's knees.

Sid was in the middle of an anecdote: 'So Tiffany, right, she was wearing that Laura Ashley dress you got her. You know, the one with flowers.'

'Yes,' said Mrs Akehurst.

'And she was standing in front of the flower bed, right? And we couldn't see her at all. Tell Grandma, you were invisible, weren't you?'

The three-year-old grinned. 'I was imbiddible.'

Everyone laughed.

Coffee done, Sofie dragged Ross to the town centre. He was reluctant to go in case they met anyone he knew, but she said she had seen a nice denim jacket in Primark and wanted his opinion.

They parked their bikes near Bankers' Corner and headed towards the Arndale Centre. As they were passing the Waterstones bookshop, they spotted Bee coming out with a rucksack on her shoulder.

'Hiya.'

'Oh hi. Fancy meeting you two here.'

'Bought anything interesting?' Sofie asked.

'Just a trashy novel.'

'Did you enjoy Tuesday night?' Ross asked.

Bee gave a 'so-so' gesture. 'I'm not really sure it's for me.'

'Why not?'

'Well, there's lots of different kinds of Christianity. I've always been at the liberal end. The Alpha Course is towards the conservative end of mainstream.'

'Is this why you don't like the bit about Christianity being the one and only truth?'

'Yes, that and the whole meaning of life thing.'

'What do you mean?' said Sofie.

'All that stuff about finding the meaning of life.'

'But surely,' said Sofie, 'you believe there is a meaning to life, don't you?'

Bee shrugged. 'People have to find meaning in their lives, yes, and religion can help, any religion. But we're talking about human psychology, not something cosmic. Do I believe there's a great big Meaning of Life out there for us to find? No, I'm afraid I don't.'

'What, you think life is meaningless?'

'No. My life means a great deal to me, and to my mum and dad and my boyfriend, and my friends too, I hope. But on a cosmic level? I would have thought the universe as a whole is pretty indifferent.'

'Oh,' said Sofie. Then she asked, 'But you are coming next Tuesday, aren't you?'

'I wasn't planning to, but my mum made me promise to go to at least three sessions. Anyway, can't stop. Got a train to catch. See you Tuesday.'

As they walked away, Sofie turned to Ross. 'That's a bit bleak, innit?'

'What?'

'Bee – she sounds as bad as Albert bloody Camus.'

Ross laughed. 'Maybe she did French for A-Level.'

Meanwhile, Bee was hurrying to the station, astonished by what she had just said. Was that really what she believed? She would certainly never have said such a thing six months ago.

*

Sid was there again before dinner. 'I told you Gareth Southgate was useless.'

'I don't know. He got us to the semi-final.'

'Yeah, but Croatia?'

'They're a good team.'

'Be better if we didn't have a manager who was a pouf.'

Ross wondered if he was this obnoxious with everyone, or if it was just him. He hoped Nigel would keep his mouth shut about the accident. He dreaded to think of the grief Sid would give him if he found out.

When Ross got home that evening, his mother had news for him: 'Mr Luscombe phoned. The date of the inquest has been set for the twenty-sixth of July at two o'clock. We'll go round to Mr Luscombe's at one-fifteen and he'll brief us. He says the inquest is nothing to worry about. It's just a formality at this stage.'

Ross nodded. 'Okay.'

Now he had something else to worry about.

*

On Saturday, Mrs Akehurst came into the dining room after breakfast to collect the tip money from Ross and Sofie.

'Enjoying the work?' she asked.

'Very much,' said Sofie.

'What about you, Ross?'

89

'Yeah, me too.'

'So, I suppose you're starting your second A-Level year in September?'

'Yes.'

'And then university?'

'Yes.'

'Have you decided what you plan to study?'

'Spanish studies,' said Sofie. 'My dream is to have a year in South America.'

'Very nice. What about you, Ross?'

'French.'

'The French are the next, you know.'

'Pardon?'

'Brexit. They call it Frexit. You wait and see. After that, it'll be Italexit.'

'Are you a Brexiteer?' Ross asked.

'You bet.'

'Oh. I assumed you'd be a Remainer, what with all your staff from eastern Europe.'

'Not a bit of it. The EU's made the British go soft. They want immigrants to do all the dirty jobs while they sit on their backsides and claim benefits or study for degrees in stupid subjects like embroidery or surf science.'

'Oh.' Ross was beginning to wish he hadn't asked.

'Are you a Remainer?'

Ross shrugged. He could see Sofie behind Mrs Akehurst biting her lip to stop herself laughing.

'Well, I was only fifteen at the time of the referendum, so I didn't get to vote.'

'Which way would you have voted?'

'Dunno.' At that moment, Sofie ducked into the kitchen and burst out laughing.

'Don't you want your country to be independent?'

'I've always been more interested in whether we'd win the World Cup, to be honest.'

Soon afterwards, it was Ross's turn to make the coffee for the family. As he walked in, he heard Nigel say to Sid, 'I am not a socialist.'

'Maybe not,' said Sid. 'But you're the original bleeding-heart liberal, ain't ya?'

'To that I plead guilty.'

Sid and his father laughed.

'I think that's one-nil to Sid,' said his father.

'More like a consolation goal,' said Sid.

'The Akehursts are all bloody Tories,' Ross told Sofie once he was out of the room.

She shrugged. 'So what?'

'What? Are you a Tory?'

Sofie laughed scornfully. 'You know how much I care about politics?'

She made a cutting gesture with her hand.

Bee came out of the bathroom with a towel wrapped round her. She leaned over the bed and gave Robbie a kiss.

'Wakey-wakey, lazy bones.'

'Why don't you come back to bed?'

'We have to check out at ten.'

'We've got plenty of time. Anyway, they won't mind if we're a bit late.'

'I'm not kissing you again till you've brushed your teeth.'

'But then you'll come back to bed?'

'Maybe.'

Robbie leapt out of bed stark naked and scurried into their hotel room's tiny bathroom.

Bee had to smile. The last couple of days had been wonderful. She had come up to London on Thursday and spent the evening with her old high-school friends. Then on Friday morning, she had met up with half a dozen university friends at King's Cross. Robbie had joined them for a somewhat liquid lunch, after which they had gone to Portland Place to join the huge anti-Donald Trump demonstration, the highlight of which was 'Baby Trump' – an enormous inflatable of Trump in a nappy.

The demonstration over, they went back to King's Cross to see their friends off. Bee and Robbie picked up their rucksacks from left luggage, and then they checked in at the cheapest decent hotel they had been able to find. After a romantic dinner at an Indian restaurant, they retired to bed.

Soon, they would have to go their separate ways: she would head back home, while he went to Cambridge to watch the World Cup Final with friends. On Monday he would come down to meet her parents for the first time.

'You'll be sleeping in the spare room,' she warned him. 'They probably think I'm still a virgin.'

*

Ross had a question he wanted to ask Bee. On Saturday afternoon, lying on his bed between shifts, he created a WhatsApp group with him, Bee and Sofie, whose profile picture wasn't a photograph of herself but the Greek letter omega.

Ross: Hi B
When we were having dinner, I overheard you say that creationism wasn't rational because there are two different creation stories in the bible
What do you mean
I thought there was only one

Bee got back to him almost immediately:

Bee: Hiya I'm on the train at the moment
         Let me have your email and I'll get back to you when I can use
         decent WiFi with my laptop

When Ross checked his mobile first thing on Sunday morning, he had an email from 'omegabee'.

Many Old Testament stories consist of doublets, different versions of the same story that have been woven together so they can be read as one. This is true of the really central stories: the creation, Noah's Ark, Abraham, Isaac, Jacob, Joseph and Moses.

Scholars have had a lot of success in separating out the different versions. Some are quite tricky, but the creation story is easy. The first one is Genesis Chapter One, and the second is Genesis Chapter Two from Verse 4b.

Have a look for yourself and see what you think. The first clue is in the different words the two authors use to refer to God. The second clue is the order of creation, which things are created first, second, third etc. The third is in the different styles the two authors use.

Ross jumped up and went into the kitchen. His father was in his dressing gown making tea and toast for himself and Ross's mother.

'You're up early.'

'Have we got a Bible in the house?'

His father's eyes widened and his top lip curled. 'No. What do you want a Bible for?'

'I want to look something up.'

Ross went back to his room and messaged Sofie. When she didn't reply after 10 minutes, he called her.

'You woke me up.'

'I just got this email from Bee.'

'Ross, this is my day off and you woke me up.'

'I thought your siblings always woke you up early.'

'Yes. And the one day they didn't, you went and woke me up.'

'Sorry. Look, I asked Bee why she said there are two creation stories in the Bible.'

'Yeah, I saw that.'

'Well, she's answered. She told me where to find them in the Bible, but we haven't got one. Have you got one?'

'I'm sure we have.'

'Can I come round? We can look at it together.'

'You can google it.'

'It'd be more fun with you, darling.'

'Oh all right then, Mr Charming. Give me half an hour to get dressed.'

*

Sofie opened the door. Once Ross had kicked off his shoes, she led him into the living room, where a woman he took to be her mother was sitting on the sofa watching *Spidey and His Amazing Friends* with three young children and a cat.

'This is my step-mum Kate. Kate, this is my friend Ross, the one who wakes me up on my day off.'

Kate laughed. 'Hi.'

'Hi, nice to meet you.'

'And these three are my step-siblings, Paula, Lydia and Carl.'

Ross have them a little wave and said, 'Hiya.'

'Say hello,' said Kate, and two out of three duly obliged. The cat eyed Ross warily but didn't move.

Sofie took him through to the dining room, where a half-eaten bowl of porridge, a mug of tea and a Bible were on the table.

'Do you want some tea?'

'No thanks. You eat your porridge while it's still hot.'

Sofie sat down and started to eat.

'Are Paula and Lydia twins?'

'Yeah, but they're not identical.'

'Is your dad here?'

'Nah. Haven't seen him for best part of a year. I live with my step-mum. Bit unusual, innit?'

'Yes.'

'My dad's a useless drunk, and I haven't got a mum. She died when I was nine.'

Sofie's words hit Ross like a punch in the gut. She lost her mother at the age of nine? That was the same as Lizzie Johnson's daughter Jude.

Shit – he needed to say something.

'I'm sorry to hear that, Sofie.'

'Yeah, she got cancer. So, that's why Kate let me stay when she threw my dad out. She's like that, Kate. I really love her.'

Ross's head was spinning. Her father was a drunk? She had said something about that before. Did he take to drink when Sofie's mum died? Maybe he just couldn't cope with the grief.

What about Lizzie Johnson's husband? Would he be able to cope?

Oh God, what have I done?

By now, Sofie had finished off the last of her porridge. 'Now I'll make you a cuppa,' she said. 'And let me have a look at this email while I make it.'

A few minutes later, they sat at the dining table with their tea and a Bible open right at the beginning.

Ross was astonished by Sofie's cheerfulness. She must have been through some really tough times, losing one parent to cancer and the other to drink. But she was always so chirpy and friendly with everyone.

Apart from Sid. She was very good at blanking him.

93

'Are you going to read this or what?' she said.

'Sorry. Miles away.'

They read the opening chapter of Genesis, the first version of the creation story.

The beginning

[1] In the beginning God created the heavens and the earth. [2] Now the earth was formless and empty, darkness was over the surface of the deep, and the Spirit of God was hovering over the waters.

[3] And God said, "Let there be light," and there was light. [4] God saw that the light was good, and he separated the light from the darkness. [5] God called the light "day" and he called the dark "night". And there was evening and there was morning – the first day.

[6] And God said, "Let there be an expanse between the waters to separate water from water." [7] So God made the expanse and separated the water under the expanse from the water above it. And it was so. [8] God called the expanse "sky". And there was evening and there was morning – the second day.

[9] And God said, "Let the water under the sky be gathered to one place, and let dry ground appear." And it was so. [10] God called the dry ground "land" and the gathered waters he called "seas". And God saw that it was good.

[11] Then God said, "Let the land produce vegetation: seed bearing plants and trees on the land that bear fruit with seed in it, according to their various kinds." And it was so. [12] The land produced vegetation: Plants bearing seed according to their kinds and trees bearing fruit with seed in it according to their kinds. And God saw that it was good. [13] And there was evening and there was morning – the third day.

'I don't think I've ever actually read the Bible before,' said Ross.

'God, you're such a heathen.'

'It's not me that's a heathen, it's my dad.'

'So, what do you think? It's good, innit?'

Ross shrugged. 'If you like that kind of thing.'

They read on. It continued in the same manner: the sun, the moon and the stars on the fourth day, fish and birds on the fifth, and then on the sixth day God created wild animals, livestock and man and woman before resting on the seventh day.

'Okay,' said Sofie, 'Ready for Chapter Two?'

Adam and Eve

[4] This is the account of heaven and earth when they were created.

When the LORD God made the heavens – [5] and no shrub of the field had yet appeared on the earth and no plant of the field had yet sprung up, for the LORD God had not sent rain on the earth and there was no man to work the ground, [6] but streams came up from the earth and watered the whole surface of the ground – [7] the LORD God formed the man from the dust of the ground and breathed into his nostrils the breath of life, and the man became a living being.

[8] Now the LORD God had planted a garden in the east, in Eden; and there he put the man he had formed. [9] And the LORD God made all kinds of trees grow out of the ground – trees that were pleasing to the eye and good for food. In the middle of the garden were the tree of life and the tree of the knowledge of good and evil.

'Crikey,' said Sofie. 'This is really different, innit?'
'I bet it was written by a different person.'
They read on. There was a part about all the rivers that flowed from the Garden of Eden and another about not eating from the tree of the knowledge of good and evil.

[18] The LORD God said, "It is not good for the man to be alone. I will make a helper suitable for him."

[19] Now the LORD God had formed out of the ground all the beasts of the field and all the birds of the air. He brought them to the man to see what he would name them; and whatever the man called each living creature, that was its name. [20] So the man gave names to all the livestock, the birds of the air and all the beasts of the field.

But for Adam, no suitable helper was found. [21] So the LORD God caused the man to fall into a deep sleep; and while he was sleeping, he took one of the man's ribs and closed up the place with flesh. [22] Then the LORD God made a woman from the rib he had taken out of the man, and he brought her to the man.

'Sexism!' said Sofie. 'We're made to help you lot.'
'Quite right too.'
She elbowed him in the ribs and they both grinned.
They went back to Bee's three clues.
'It's pretty obvious, innit?' said Sofie. 'Different words for God.'
'Yeah.'
They debated for some time whether there were two different orders of creation. Sofie felt Chapter Two was ambivalent on whether or not God made the animals after he made Adam: 'Look, it says, "The LORD God *had* formed out of the ground all the beasts of the field..." That means maybe he did it before.'
'Yeah, but look. Just before that, it says, "I *will* make a helper suitable for him." so he's already made Adam, and he hasn't made the animals yet.'
'Hmm, yeah, maybe.'
'So let's do what Bee says. Let's write down the different orders.'

Sofie found a pen and an old envelope and they created two lists on the back of it:

Chapter One	Chapter Two
1. The world	1. The heavens
2. Moon and stars	2. Man
3. Vegetation	3. Garden
4. Fish and birds	4. Trees
5. Land animals	5. Animals and birds
6. Man and woman	6. Woman

'Wow,' Ross said when they had finished. 'That's quite a contradiction, isn't it?'

'This is dynamite,' said Sofie. 'How come everybody doesn't know all about this?'

Chapter Seventeen

Sofie replied via email.

Hi B

Ross showed me your email and we've looked at Genesis and we see what you mean: "God" v "the LORD God". Also, animals+Adam+Eve v Adam+animals+Eve. And as you say, the style's completely different.

This is pure dynamite. How long have people known about this? How can anybody take the Bible seriously after this?

Looking forward to your answers,

Sofie (and Ross)

PS – What's with all this Omega business?

Bee sent her answer through not long after lunch. It was Sofie who noticed it first. She messaged Ross, who by now had gone back home, and he checked his email.

Dear Sofie and Ross,

You are correct about the three clues, and you ask two important questions. I will do my best to answer them.

How long have people known that the Bible contradicts itself? For thousands of years. Jews and Christians have always been aware of these contradictions – they would have to be pretty thick not to notice.

How can anybody take the Bible seriously if it contradicts itself? I suppose there are three ways of responding to these contradictions:

1. The Bible does not contradict itself. It is the Word of God and it is literally true.

2. The contradictions are there to remind us not to get hooked on the surface meaning of the text but look for its deeper, spiritual meaning.

3. The Bible was written and compiled by human beings and is therefore just as flawed as the people who wrote and compiled it.

The first response is the refuge of the ignorant, who cannot help it, and the wilfully ignorant, who should know better.

The second response has a very long history, among both Jews and Christians. It is the response of an intelligent, questioning faith, but it does not call into question the divine hand behind the writing of the Bible.

The third response is the response of more liberal Jews and Christians (and atheists too). It stresses the human input into the Bible.

If you follow response (2) or (3), there is no reason why you should not take the Bible very seriously indeed. But you do not take it literally. If you want to take your Bible literally, you have to go for response (1).

Here endeth the lesson.

Best wishes,

Bee

PS – Omega: my name's Bee Ormerod but at school one of my friends called me Bee Omega by mistake and it kind of stuck, except it turned into Omega Bee.

Ross messaged Sofie:

Ross:	Have you read it
Sofie:	Yes
Ross:	What do you think
Sofie:	Well, I guess I'd go for 2, or possibly 3
Ross:	Me too not number 1 that's for your bible belt nutcases isn't it
Sofie:	You could put it like that
	In her first email, she talked about them stitching two different versions of the Bible together. Why did that happen?
Ross:	Why don't we ask her
Sofie:	Do you think she'd mind?
Ross:	We can ask she doesn't have to answer if she doesn't feel like it
Sofie:	OK. Who's going to email her? You or me?
Ross:	My turn

Bee's answer didn't come until after 10 o'clock that night, by which time Ross had descended into his usual evening abyss, made worse by the fact that he was due at the police station next day to find out what he would be charged with.

Sofie messaged him, and he opened up the email, which had a PDF attached. He was delighted to have something that could distract him from his appointment with the police. Bee's email was far too long to read on his mobile, so he went downstairs to get the laptop.

'Don't forget,' said his mother. 'No IT in your bedroom after eleven.'

'Yeah, yeah, yeah.'

Dear Sofie and Ross,

The core of the Old Testament is the Pentateuch, the first five books of the Bible. This starts with the creation and goes on through Adam and Eve, Cain and Abel, Noah's Ark, the Patriarchs, Joseph, Moses and the Exodus from Egypt, the Ten Commandments and finally Moses' death on the eve of the return to the Promised Land.

Jews and Christians always believed Moses wrote these books, but in the 17th century, some sceptics started to question this, among them the English philosopher Hobbes and the Jewish philosopher Spinoza.

They and others pointed out that these books could not have been written by Moses. They contained things like "such and such is the case to this day" and use of words like "here" and "there" that show the books were written within the Holy Land, but Moses died before the Israelites entered the Holy Land. The final book, Deuteronomy, even describes Moses' death and states that there never again arose such a great prophet as him.

What is amazing is not that these sceptics worked this out but that it had taken two thousand years for anyone to point out the blindingly obvious. Unfortunately, the telling of unwelcome truths was not without risk. Spinoza ended up excommunicated by the Jews of Amsterdam for this and other heresies, and in 1697, an 18-year-old Edinburgh student by the name of Thomas Aikenhead was hanged for pretty much the same thing.

When Ross read about Thomas Aikenhead, he had to pause for a few minutes. Aikenhead had been just a year older than him. And they hanged him even though he was far less deserving of punishment than Ross felt himself to be.

Had his mother cried for him? Had his father got him the best lawyer money could buy? Had they begged him to repent?

How must he have felt when he realised they were going to kill him?

And then Ross thought of himself. What was he was facing? He would find out tomorrow morning. His insides knotted up at the thought of it.

His mobile pinged.

He picked it up and looked at it.

Sofie:	What do you think?
	Hello!
	Have you opened her thing yet?
Ross:	Give me a chance haven't finished her email yet.
Sofie:	God you are slow!
Ross:	😜

The debate about whether Moses had written the Pentateuch continued. One of the most important contributions was made by Jean Astruc, physician to the king of France. He noticed two separate strands in Genesis, one that referred to God as Elohim (God) and another that always called him Yahweh (the LORD God in English translations).

The funny thing is that Astruc was arguing for the view that Moses had written the Pentateuch. He thought Moses must have drawn on two different sources to write his text. But Astruc's work ended up being a breakthrough for the anti-Moses side of the argument, who built on what he said to identify first two, then three and finally four separate texts. In 1883, a German scholar named Julius Wellhausen synthesised these findings into a theory that still dominates the subject to this day. We call it the "Documentary Hypothesis". These are the four texts woven together:

The J Text – This refers to God as Yahweh, which begins with a "J" in German. Its author is known as the Yahwist and wrote much of Genesis, Exodus and Numbers (including the second account of the creation).

The E Text – This calls God Elohim until he reveals his name in the burning bush. We call the author the Elohist and find his handiwork in Genesis and Exodus, but it makes brief guest appearances elsewhere.

The D Text – This is Deuteronomy, the fifth book of the Pentateuch. If you read it in Hebrew, it is quite clear that it was written by a separate author.

The P Text – This also calls God Elohim and has a very distinctive style. My tutor at university taught us how to spot a passage from P in less than a week. Most of the really boring bits of the Pentateuch are P, because it concerns itself with the minutiae of law and matters concerned with priests, hence the name "Priestly Writer" for its author. You can find P in Genesis, Exodus and Numbers, but it comes into his own in Leviticus.

Most non-conservative scholars regard Wellhausen's Documentary Hypothesis as a major breakthrough, though there are serious disagreements about things like who the different authors were and when the texts were written.

I have one lecturer who says the Documentary Hypothesis is outdated and J and E are just fragments of lots of different texts. He says it's better to talk about D, P and "not P".

And I have another lecturer who says the Documentary Hypothesis is still the only game in town.

Take your pick!

I'm going to attach Noah's Ark, which I've divided into The Yahwist's and the Priestly Writer's versions. I've copied and pasted from an online Bible, and then divided it from memory, but I may have made one or two mistakes. You can find the proper version in a brilliant book called *Who Wrote the Bible* by Richard Elliot Friedman that explains the whole thing better than I can. Anyway, if you're interested, read through one version, then read the other, and then see how they are stitched together in the Bible.

By the way, I am happy to answer your questions, but when we go to the Alpha Course on Tuesday, please don't tell other people what I've said. I don't want to set myself up as a rival to Dominic and Pat.

With love,

Bee [1]

---

[1] For the reader who is interested, Bee's attachment is included as Appendix One on page 365.

Ross opened Bee's attachment and read the two different versions of the story of Noah. He was glancing through the Bible excerpt that showed how they were woven together when his mobile pinged.

Sofie:	Well?? Wot did U think??
Ross:	Wow pretty amazing really
Sofie:	Yeah. That Priestly writer – he's like the most boring teacher you've ever had but even worse
Ross:	😂
Sofie:	I was half asleep before they even got in the ark
Ross:	Yeah did you notice all the contradictions
Sofie:	You bet. How many pairs of animals?
Ross:	Does he send a raven or a dove
Sofie:	👍
	And how long did the flood last?
Ross:	Did you see how they stitched them together it's like a forgery or a con or something
Sofie:	Maybe it's a compromise
Ross:	How can a compromise be the word of god
Sofie:	☺
	The other question, right, is how can these fundamentalists take the whole thing literally when there's like 2 different versions of everything?
Ross:	Good question

And then Ross remembered Thomas Aikenhead, the young man who had been hanged for his scepticism. He googled him and spent the rest of the evening thinking about him and worrying about the morning. The sense of wonder engendered by Omega Bee hadn't lasted long.

Chapter Eighteen

Ross's mother gave him a lift to work that morning in her Nissan Micra, which by now had been repaired (the insurance company never gave details of either the repairs or the cost). After breakfast, he and Sofie, who was wheeling her bike, walked to the pier, where they waited for his mother. A few minutes later, she pulled up. He said goodbye to Sofie and got into the car. His mother smiled at Sofie and gave her a wave.

'How are you getting on with Sofie?' she asked as they pulled away.

'She's nice. I like her.'

'Don't get too close to her.'

'I don't know why you and Auntie Zoe don't like her.'

'Zoe has her reasons.'

'Has she led Dani astray? I don't think so. Has she got Dani into drugs or anything like that? No. She seems like the same old Dani to me.' (Ross thought it better not to mention how Dani and Raj were spending their mornings.)

'I'm pleased to hear it.'

'You know Sofie's mum died when she was little?'

'No, I didn't know that.'

'Her dad's an alcoholic, and she lives with her stepmother. Did you know that?'

'No.'

'Yeah, so maybe she's been through some tough times. She works hard at the hotel and she's always nice to everyone, so maybe you and Auntie Zoe should give her a chance.'

Ross and his mother didn't speak again for the rest of the journey.

Telling his mother about Sofie and her mum reminded him of what he had done to Lizzie Johnson's daughter. Whatever it was the police decided to charge him with, he deserved it. He was going to plead guilty.

They got to the police station 15 minutes early, unlike his solicitor, who didn't turn up until one minute to 11. They were kept waiting just inside the entrance, where everyone arriving or leaving had to walk past them, glancing at them as they did so. Ross just hoped he wouldn't see anyone he knew.

He felt the tension in his bowels. His whole body was sweating, even though it was cool inside the police station. His mother kept biting her lip, and every now and then, she stood up and looked into the room where all the police officers were, as if to say, 'Come on, what's keeping you?'

At one stage, she said to the solicitor, 'Do you think they keep us waiting on purpose, to soften us up?'

'Unquestionably.'

It was nearly 11:30 when the sergeant who had interviewed Ross came out.

'Ross Collins?'

'Yes.'

'Sorry to keep you waiting. Would you like to come this way?'

He led him into a small interview room. His mother and solicitor followed. The sergeant said they had sent a report to the Director of Public Prosecutions on the 26th of April but hadn't yet received a reply. He extended Ross's bail until the 31st of July and said he hoped they would know the answer then.

And that was it.

Ross had spent weeks spent worrying about this day, plus a night with broken sleep and the best part of an hour almost crapping himself in the police station. And then, two minutes, no news and off you go.

His mother grumbled about it all the way back.

When they got home, Ross's first thought was to see if he could catch up on his sleep. No such luck: he was far too wound up. He had several hours before he needed to go for his evening shift and no idea what to do with himself.

His thoughts turned to the inquest, which would open in just 10 days' time. His solicitor had said the first day would just be a formality, and everything he had googled seemed to say the same thing. No inquest will go ahead until the police have completed their enquiries and any criminal case has reached a verdict.

But the thought of the inquest still made Ross's heart race and caused his innards to tighten, because he knew that Lizzie Barton's husband would be there. How was he going to face him?

His phone pinged and took him out of his thoughts.

Sofie:	Hi Ross
Ross:	Nothing happened!!
Sofie:	??
Ross:	I have to wait till the end of the month
Sofie:	God, that's a bit of an anticlimax
Ross:	You're telling me
Sofie:	Do you fancy doing something together?
Ross:	Maybe tomorrow I'm just too wound up today

He endured a dreadful afternoon alone in his room with his darkest thoughts. He knew he should have done something with Sofie, maybe gone for a walk or something. He couldn't understand why he said no

She came round just before five and, as usual, texted him from outside his house. They cycled down to the seafront together and spent 20 minutes on the beach before reporting for work. He wanted to ask her about her mother's death and how this had affected her, but somehow it didn't feel right. Maybe she wouldn't want to talk about it.

Sid was in the staffroom again, sniffling. As Ross turned his back on him and changed his shirt, he wondered what he would come out with this time. He closed his eyes and braced himself.

'Are you a Remainer, Ross?'

'I didn't vote in the referendum. I was too young. Still am.'

'Yeah but which way would you have voted?'

Ross clenched his jaw.

He turned to face Sid. 'Remain, I suppose.'

'Ha, ha,' said Sid (he was speaking, not laughing). 'You lost. Get over it.'

With that, he left, leaving the stench of his cigarette behind.

Ross shook his head and sat down. He ran his fingers through his hair.

Just then, Sofie came in. 'You okay?'

'Bloody Sid.'

'Thought I could smell smoke. He's just an idiot. Ignore him.'

'I don't get it,' said Ross. 'If he's such a rebel, with all his tattoos and his fake working-class accent, what's he doing hanging round his mother's hotel?'

'Isn't it obvious?' said Sofie. 'He's just a big mummy's boy.'

'You think so?'

'Definitely.'

*

Robbie's train didn't arrive until after 10 o'clock in the evening. There was no point getting an earlier train as Bee wouldn't finish work until 9:30. She picked him up at the station and drove him to her house.

'Are you ready for this?'

'Don't know. Are your mum and dad ready?'

They went inside, where Bee's parents greeted Robbie with warm handshakes. They went into the living room and Bee's father showed great interest in the PhD thesis he was working on. Meanwhile, Bee's mother made some decaffeinated coffee. It was fully 15 minutes before she asked the question Bee had primed him to expect.

'What church are you, Robbie?'

'Church of Scotland.'

'Same as us,' said Bee's father. 'We're Presbyterian.'

'Do you go to church every week?' Bee's mother asked.

'Actually, I've been a naughty boy. I haven't been since Bee came down here at the end of term.'

Bee grinned, and as soon as her parents had gone upstairs to bed, she whispered, 'I never knew you were such a good liar.'

'What?'

'You haven't been to church since the end of term.'

'Well, it's true. I haven't.'

'Yeah, but you've never been to church in your life.'

They both laughed.

'I've been to a wedding.'

'That doesn't count.'

'The statement I made was factually correct.'

'If entirely misleading.'

'In philosophy, this is henceforth known as the Robbie Prisick doctrine: a statement is true if it isn't actually a lie.'

*

Tuesday was Ross and Sofie's day off, and she had persuaded him to go for a long walk out of town, up onto the South Downs and over to the Long Man of Wilmington, a giant chalk figure that had been carved into the hillside hundreds of years ago.

'Alpha Course tonight.'

'Yes,' said Sofie. 'I'm really looking forward to it.'

'What did you think of our little Omega Course?'

'I thought it was amazing. Bee's so knowledgeable, innit?'

Ross shrugged. 'Well, she's doing it at uni. She's supposed to know about it.'

'I think she's brilliant.'

It was a blistering hot day, but fortunately Ross had brought two bucket hats in the bright blue and white of his favourite football team.

'When I was little,' said Sofie, 'we used to take foreign students in our house, before my mum got ill. Once we had this girl from Thailand, and whenever it was sunny, she'd put her umbrella up if she went out. We thought she was so funny.'

Ross laughed. 'I wouldn't mind an umbrella right now.'

'Me too.'

Ross had been given an entry to the question he was dying to ask: 'Was it very tough when your mum died?'

'Yeah. I still miss her, but Kate's fantastic. She's like a mum to me. Maybe I should start calling her "Mum". Do you think she'd like that?'

'Why don't you ask her?'

'Maybe I will.'

'You know the woman I killed...?'

'You didn't kill her, Ross. She crashed into you and died.'

'Yeah, whatever. She had two little children.'

'Yes, I heard. But seriously, Ross, stop saying you killed her.'

'She'd still be alive if I'd looked in my mirror.'

'And she'd still be alive if she hadn't tried to overtake three cars in one go.'

They walked on in silence for several minutes.

'My dad couldn't cope,' said Sofie. 'From what I hear, he'd always liked a drink, but after my mum died, he really hit the bottle.'

Ross's thoughts instantly turned to Lizzie Johnson's husband. Would her death turn him into an alcoholic?

'Kate was my mum's best friend. She was newly divorced with the twins and a little toddler. Maybe she fancied my dad, but from what she says, I think she felt sorry for him more than anything else. Big mistake from her point of view. She thought she could help him stop drinking, but she couldn't.

105

'He was never violent or abusive or anything like that. I think it was her that hit him, if anything. He was just useless. He couldn't hold down a job, and he'd go on these benders. We wouldn't see him for days, and then he'd turn up all sheepish. In the end, she couldn't take it any more and threw him out. I was terrified she'd throw me out too, but she let me stay. I'm so grateful to her for that.'

Ross didn't know what to say. He wanted to give her a hug but was afraid she would think he was making a pass at her.

'Thanks for sharing that,' he said after a moment. 'It kind of puts my problems in perspective.'

'I wouldn't say your problems aren't real. But look at me: I've got through it, thanks to Kate. And thanks to Kitty at college, you know, the student counsellor. She was brilliant. And thanks to Dani too. She's a really good friend.'

*

It took them more than two hours to get to their destination. Hot, thirsty, tired and thoroughly pestered by horse flies and midges, they made their way through a herd of wary bullocks to the crest of the hill that had the Long Man on its flank.

They sat down on the grass. Over in the distance, they could see traffic whizzing along the A27, where the accident had happened. Ross tried to locate the spot where Mrs Johnson had met her end, but it was too far away to make out.

'I know what you're thinking about,' said Sofie.

'Yeah, I suppose you do. It just seems so awful, you know? Just one stupid, stupid mistake and the consequences are so terrible. Just a split second and she's dead. Her family's lives are ruined, my life's blighted, my parents...' Ross stopped speaking. He didn't want to cry in front of Sofie.

'Life can be really cruel, can't it?'

'Oh God, don't we both know it? I just wish I could go back and have those two seconds of my life again. But I can't. It's too late. Now, whatever happens, whatever I do with the rest of my life, when I get to be an old, old man and look back, the biggest thing, the most important thing I'll ever do will be killing Lizzie Johnson.'

'No, you can't say that.'

'Why not? What am I ever going to do that's bigger than that?'

'No, it's not just her life you're going to affect. You have an effect on my life and our friend's lives, and your parents' and your brother's. And one day you'll get married and you'll have an effect on your wife's life and your children. And you'll work, and that'll affect lots of people's lives, and you can do things like volunteer or give money to charity and have a positive effect that way.'

They sat in silence for a moment.

Then Sofie spoke again. 'Your life isn't over. You've made a small mistake...'

'I made a big mistake.'

'No, you made a small mistake but it turned out to have very big consequences. I shouldn't say this, but I actually admire the way you've faced up to it and taken responsibility for it. You could easily go round saying it's her fault or Raj's fault for making you overtake. But you don't, and that's good. Your life isn't over, Ross. You've got so much more to give.'

After a few moments, Ross put his arm round her shoulder. 'Thanks, Sofie.'

She leaned into him and patted his knee.

He brought his arm back down again.

After a moment, Sofie said, 'That's a pub down there, innit?'

'Do you think they'll let us in?'

'We're allowed in. We're just not allowed to drink alcohol, that's all.'

'Come on then. Let's give it a go.'

Ross stood up and pulled her to her feet. They clambered down the hill. To their surprise, the Long Man wasn't carved into the chalk hill at all; it was made of concrete slabs.

'Looks like it's been a bit over-restored,' said Ross.

They got down to the bottom and found a notice asking tourists not to climb on the Long Man for fear of causing erosion.

'Oops!' said Sofie.

'It's a conspiracy. They just don't want us to find out that it's all concrete blocks. But we know the truth.'

Sofie laughed.

They turned their backs on the Long Man and headed down the path towards the village and the pub.

There was a young couple in the distance coming towards them hand in hand. The woman looked familiar, and after a moment, Ross realised it was Bee.

They waved at each other. A few minutes later, their paths crossed.

'Hiya.'

'Hi,' said Bee. 'You two look hot.'

'You could say that. We've walked all the way from Old Town.'

'Wow. Oh, this is my boyfriend. Robbie, Ross and Sofie.'

'Hi.'

'Hello.'

'Ross is quite a Scottish name. Are you part Scottish or something?'

'It's my mum's maiden name. She had a Scottish granddad.'

'Ah, okay. And Bee was telling me you two are on her Alpha Course.'

'Yeah that's right,' said Sofie.

'And you're in touch with the atheist mole.'

Bee laughed and poked him in the ribs.

'We're going for a drink,' said Sofie. 'Would you like to join us?'

Bee looked at Robbie, who nodded. 'Yeah, that'd be cool.'

'We'll just go and have a look at the Long Man first,' said Bee. 'See you in the pub.'

'Okay.'

Ross and Sofie walked on.

'He seems nice,' said Ross.

'He's gorgeous.'

Somewhat to his surprise, Ross didn't like the sound of that.

*

They sat inside, pleased to exchange the hot glare of the sun for indoor gloom. They ordered paninis for lunch plus an alcohol-free lager for Ross and a diet coke for Sofie.

'Do you think they have water?' Sofie asked as they sat down.

'Don't know.'

'Why don't you ask?'

Ross looked away from her and rolled his eyes. He slouched his way to the bar and returned a few moments later with a jug of tap water and two glasses on a tray. They gulped it down.

Bee and Robbie turned up as they were finishing off their paninis. Robbie bought a pint of the local bitter for himself and a glass of tonic water for Bee.

'The Long Man's really great, isn't it?' said Bee.

Sofie and Ross agreed.

'First time I've been here,' said Bee.

'Really?' said Sofie. 'So you're not from round here?'

'No. My parents just moved down from London.'

'Oh.'

'What about you?' Ross asked Robbie. 'Are you a student too?'

'Yes, same college as Bee.'

'Are you doing theology?'

'Oh no. Even more impractical than theology: I'm doing philosophy.'

'I didn't know philosophy was more impractical than theology,' said Sofie.

Bee and Robbie looked at each other and grinned. 'At least I can become a vicar,' said Bee. 'He'll be totally unemployable when he gets his PhD.'

'Would you like to be a vicar?' Sofie asked.

'Not really, but it's better than being a nun.'

Robbie asked Sofie and Ross how they were enjoying the Alpha Course.

'Yeah, it's interesting,' said Ross.

Sofie nodded. 'Funny mix of people. Us two and Bee, we're the only young people there. Everyone else is quite a bit older.'

They entertained Robbie with tales of Dominic's earnestness, the ageing hippy Tom, Bob the Builder and his posh wife, and the awkward questions Nick kept firing at Bee.

'You should come along tonight,' said Sofie.

Robbie grimaced and shook his head. 'Not sure about that.'

108

'He's an unbeliever,' said Bee.

'No, I'm not. I'm an agnostic. You're the unbeliever.'

'I'm just having doubts, that's all.'

'Why are you agnostic?' Ross asked.

'He just likes sitting on the fence,' said Bee.

Robbie smiled. 'No, it's not that. I'd put it like this: there's no evidence for the existence of God…'

'Oh, come on!' said Bee.

'Okay, there's no good evidence...'

Bee rolled her eyes.

'There's just a couple of dodgy philosophical arguments, plus some even more dodgy claims, like miracles and visions and what not. But on the other hand, do you know why the Big Bang happened? I don't, and I don't think anyone else does, either. And if we don't know, then it's a bit arrogant to rule out one hundred percent the idea that some kind of mind might be behind it. But if there is some kind of mind behind it, there's still a very big question of where that mind comes from.'

'Basically,' said Bee, 'he's an atheist with a get-out clause.'

Robbie shrugged.

'What about you?' Sofie asked Bee. 'Why are you having doubts?'

'Theodicy: why God allows terrible things to happen.' She turned to Robbie. 'Tell them what Epicurus said.'

'Is God willing to prevent evil, but not able? Then he's not all-powerful. Is he able, but not willing? Then he's malevolent. Is he both able and willing? Then where does evil come from? Is he neither able nor willing? Then why call him God?'

'Christians and Jews have been wrestling with this question for two thousand years,' said Bee. 'I started to wonder if the answer is in fact very simple: maybe God allows terrible things to happen because he doesn't exist. It's hard to motivate yourself to study theology when you're not sure you still believe in God. I feel like I've wasted the last two years of my life.'

'You haven't wasted them,' said Robbie. 'You wouldn't have met me if you hadn't gone to Cambridge.'

They all laughed at this, but inside Ross cringed. After all, in the worst-case scenario, he might be about to waste a few years of his life. He withdrew from the conversation for a while as the darkness enveloped him again.

When he rejoined it, Bee was entertaining the others with stories of the language school where she was working. 'So many kids get hurt playing football,' she said. 'You wouldn't believe it.'

'I would,' said Ross. 'I play for one of our college teams.'

'What position do you play?' Robbie asked.

'Left wingback.'

Robbie pointed his thumb towards himself. 'Centre forward.'

'What? For the university?'

'I'm not that good. Just our college team.'

Ross and Robbie spent several minutes talking about football. By the time their conversation ran out of steam, Bee and Sofie were speaking about the Bible. Bee was explaining how, for most of history, Jews and Christians had never taken it literally.

At this point, Ross interjected, 'I thought they did take it literally in the old days.'

'No,' said Bee. 'I mean, there was always a debate about how literally to take it, but before the Reformation and the printing press, the Catholic Church had a kind of monopoly on how to interpret it. But when they lost that monopoly, a lot of Protestants started taking it more literally.'

'Tell them about *mythos*,' said Robbie.

'Okay,' said Bee. 'This is one way of looking at it, right. There's two kinds of knowledge, *mythos* and *logos*. *Mythos* is the Greek for story, and obviously we get the word myth from it. From *logos*, we get the word logic. It has lots of different meanings…'

'*Logos* is actually very complex,' said Robbie. 'You could easily spend a whole term just studying *logos*.'

'Yes,' said Bee, 'but I'm just going to use it to contrast with *mythos*. I'm going to use *logos* to mean hard facts, truth, the kind of evidence the police have to look for when they investigate a crime.'

Ross twitched when she mentioned the police. He looked at the others to check they hadn't noticed.

Bee continued: 'We live in a very rational age, and the word myth has almost become a term of abuse. People say, "I don't believe such and such. It's a myth." But you shouldn't ask whether a myth is true. You should only ask what the myth does."

'How do you mean?' said Sofie.

'Myths do four things. Number one, they explain things, like the Biblical myth of the creation.'

'But that's redundant now,' said Ross, 'thanks to science.'

'Exactly,' said Bee. 'Unfortunately, you still get some people who take it literally. More fool them. Okay, second thing, myths teach us things that are easier to learn that way. I guess a good example is The Boy who Cried Wolf. I assume it's a made-up story, but it's a very good way of teaching little children not to play that kind of trick. The way our brains work, it is much more memorable to put it in a story than just to tell a child not to do that.'

'So,' said Sofie, 'is that why Albert Camus put his ideas in a novel, like L' *Étranger*?'

Robbie pointed his finger at her. 'Great example. Great philosopher too.'

'You like him?'

'One of my heroes.'

'I hated his message,' said Sofie. 'So bleak. He's saying life is absurd; it has no meaning.'

'Aye,' said Robbie, 'but he's saying you have to rebel against that. Even though you know life is ultimately absurd, you have to live it to the full because it's all you've got.'

Sofie shook her head. 'There has to be more than that.'

'There's actually a book of the Bible that's not a million miles from what Robbie's saying,' said Bee. 'Ecclesiastes. I absolutely love it. It's about the futility of everything...'

'How can you love that?'

'Because it's saying that despite that, we still have a life to live. We can still love. We can still throw ourselves into everything we do. If you lived forever, anything you did would be meaningless, but if you only have this one short life, everything you do has meaning within the context of that life.'

Sofie frowned.

Robbie leaned towards Ross, 'Much more important than any of this, Albert Camus was a damn fine goalkeeper. He could have gone professional, but he got TB and it ruined his health.'

'The thing you have to remember about Robbie,' said Bee, 'is that, for him, everything comes down to philosophy and football.'

Robbie looked shocked. 'You mean there are other things?'

Everybody laughed.

Sofie pointed at Bee. 'Let's get back to what you were saying. I'm interested.'

'I've forgotten where I was.'

'You were telling us what myths do.'

'Oh yeah. Third thing that myths do, is they provide the basis for rituals, which give life meaning. A very good example is birthdays. From a strictly rational point of view, right, birthdays are meaningless rubbish. What's the difference between someone who's nineteen years and three hundred and sixty-four days and someone who's twenty? Nothing. But celebrating your birthday gives you a framework for your life, a feeling that you're growing up and growing older, that your life is moving to a new phase.'

'Wow,' said Sofie. 'I never thought of it that way.'

'And religious rituals frame our lives and our year. Like christenings, weddings, funerals, Christmas, Easter and what-not.'

'And we have secular rituals too,' said Robbie. 'Graduations, bank holidays, cup finals.'

'See,' said Bee. 'Football again.'

She and Robbie looked at each other and grinned.

Bee continued: 'An interesting example is Genesis One, the first creation story. It's lifted almost verse-by-verse from the *Enuma Elis*, the Babylonian creation myth, which was the centrepiece of the Babylonian new-year ritual. It's quite possible Genesis One was originally used in a ritual, which could mean it was never intended to be taken literally.'

'Really?' said Sofie. 'That is so interesting. So, all these fundamentalists, like, they've completely got the wrong end of the stick.'

'Yeah, completely,' said Bee. 'Okay: fourth and final thing, myths are very important because they bind communities together. A good example is the myth that the English are one community with a common history, language and culture. Pretty dubious when you think about it. How much does a toff in Mayfair have in common with a working-class Geordie? Not a lot, apart from the myths and rituals they share. I mean, one family history has stately homes, the other has workhouses. And when it comes to language, the toff would probably struggle to understand the Geordie.'

'In terms of culture,' said Robbie. 'They'd probably like different sports. The toff would like rugby union. The Geordie would watch football.'

'Yes,' said Bee. 'The Geordie probably has more in common with a working-class Irishman than with the English toff. But the national myth he shares with the toff is incredibly important. Without it, it's harder to have a government that rules by consent. Just look at countries without a proper national myth, like Iraq, or Syria, or Northern Ireland.'

'But this is very interesting,' said Robbie. 'The English and the Scots used to be united by a common myth, you know, Protestantism, industrial revolution, Empire, labour movement, Winston Churchill, Royal Family. But a lot of those things have faded away, especially religion, industry and the labour movement. The Empire's long gone. Even World War Two's fading from living memory. For younger Scots like me, the British myth is losing its power. We're more interested in a purely Scottish national myth. You know, *Braveheart* and all that crap.'

'So what's all this got to do with the Bible?' Ross asked.

'Religious texts are *mythos* in its purest form,' said Bee. 'They do everything myth does. They explain where the religious community came from and why it's important. They teach moral lessons. They're the basis of ritual, and they bind the community together. But they're not *logos*. You should never take them literally. Fundamentally, that's where I disagree with Dominic. He doesn't understand the difference between *mythos* and *logos*.'

*

Bee gave Ross and Sofie a lift home, having extracted from them a promise not to bring up *mythos* and *logos* in that evening's Alpha Course session.

On the way, Sofie asked Bee if her name was short for something else.

Robbie laughed. 'You'll have to tell them your dark secret.'

'My name's Alberta. When I was little, my parents called me Bertie, but when I started school, one of the other kids teased me and said Bertie was a boys' name. So my parents agreed to call me Bee instead.'

'It's quite an unusual name, Alberta.'

'Tell me about it.'

'She has an even darker secret,' said Robbie. 'She still hasn't told me her middle name.'

'What is it?' said Sofie.

'Not telling.'

'I'll ask your parents,' said Robbie.

'Don't you dare.'

'You shouldn't,' said Sofie. 'A woman's entitled to have some mystery.'

'Exactly.'

Ross got out of the car by Sofie's house.

'Thanks for dragging me out today.'

'I didn't know I'd dragged you.'

'You did. I would've just spent the whole day getting depressed and worrying about the inquest if you hadn't.'

'Will you do something for me in return?'

'What?'

'Promise you'll do it, then I'll tell you.'

'What?'

'Promise.'

'Okay, I promise.'

'It's Tara's birthday party a week on Saturday. Promise you'll come.'

He hadn't expected her to say that. He had been in hiding from just about all his friends since the accident.

'Yeah okay, I'll be there.'

Chapter Nineteen

That evening, everybody sat in the same places for dinner. There was no sign of Robbie.

'You left him alone with your parents?' said Sofie.

'Yeah.'

'He's very brave.'

'He's got his thesis to get on with.'

'Get on with or hide behind?'

'Bit of both.'

After a delicious beef stroganoff cooked by the people from one of the other tables, they were treated to two hymns: one traditional (*Glory, glory hallelujah*) and a happy-clappy song that Ross had never heard before.

I take all my hope from Jesus.
He is my strength and my foundation,
He comforts me when times are hard
And brings me jubilation.

After the first verse, it was quite grisly, very much concerned with Jesus' death, his pain, his blood and his corpse, until near the end came his glorious resurrection and a couple of lines that could have been written for Ross:

Now I'm not the prisoner of my sin
His precious blood has freed me.

Ross was hoping that Dominic's talk would be about the Old Testament so that he might get some answers to all the questions Bee had left him with. No such luck. Tonight was all about Jesus.

Dominic started by talking about leaps of faith. Ross remembered what Nigel had said about it not being a question of weighing up the evidence but of making a decision to believe and then God filling your life with his goodness.

But Dominic took a different tack. He started to talk about all the evidence, how the Gospels were written within a generation of Jesus' life, how accurately they had been copied and how reliable our information about Jesus was. He contrasted this with other documents from around the same time: Herodotus, Tacitus, Livy (whatever they were) and Julius Caesar's *Gallic War*. He said we have much more reason to doubt the authenticity of these documents, but nobody doubts it, so we shouldn't doubt the authenticity of the Gospels.

He stressed the fact that Christians don't believe that Jesus was an ordinary man. Jesus had said so himself. He told his disciples that he really was unique.

114

Dominic quoted in full the line that Bee had so hated: 'I am the way and the truth and the life. No-one comes to the Father except through me.' Then he added other quotes in which Jesus said pretty much the same thing:

'I am the bread of life.'

'I am the light of the world. Whoever follows me will never walk in darkness...'

'I am the resurrection and the life. He who believes in me will live.'

'...he who receives me receives the one who sent me.'

'Anyone who has seen me has seen the Father.'

Unfortunately, Ross wasn't paying that much attention. Dominic wasn't the most charismatic speaker he had ever heard and Ross was by now quite bored. He spent some time thinking of questions for Bee, and towards the end of the talk, when Dominic spoke about Jesus sitting in judgement on the world, Ross's thoughts were overwhelmed by the prospect of going on trial himself.

More than anything else, he was terrified of the possibility of prison. He expected it to be full of hard, angry young men who would enjoy the opportunity to make mincemeat of a soft middle-class boy like him. But he couldn't shake off the feeling that he deserved it and it might be the only way he could expiate his guilt.

But wasn't this the alternative to prison, the hope that Jesus could save him from what he had done? He cursed himself for not concentrating on what Dominic had to say.

By now he was talking about Jesus' miracles, standing up and pacing around like an American televangelist. He got very excited when he came to the greatest miracle of them all: the resurrection of Christ crucified.

He said this was the cornerstone of Christianity, and the proof of it was there for all to see: the empty tomb that so baffled those who found it, and, more importantly, the way his followers had behaved afterwards. They had panicked and fled after his crucifixion, and Peter had even renounced Jesus. But after he appeared to them, they had devoted their lives to him and his message, braving persecution and death to do so.

Would they have risked and sacrificed their lives for a lie? Would they have done all this if they hadn't witnessed the resurrection of Jesus Christ with their own eyes?

Dominic said even greater proof of the resurrection lies in the way Jesus can enter our lives today and transform them. He cited case after case of people he had known, drug addicts, criminals, alcoholics and other people who had been saved the day they gave themselves to the living Christ.

Dominic finished by attacking the view that Jesus was a great man but not the Son of God. He said this was impossible. A man who spends three years pumping out the message that he is the Son of God, such a man must be one of three things:

Insane.

Evil and manipulative, the leader of a cult.

115

The Son of God.

We have to choose which of those three things we believe he was. And if we don't believe he was mad or bad, then we have to believe he was the Son of God.

*

Bee was hoping she wouldn't get dragged into the discussion, which turned out to be slow to take off. People seemed reluctant to say very much. Bee thought Alison spoke for several others when she said she felt she had been boxed into a corner by the 'mad, bad or the Son of God' aspect of the talk. 'I see Jesus as an inspiration, I really do, but in this day and age, there are some parts of the New Testament that are very hard to believe.'

'Like what?' asked Pat.

'Well, the miracles, the resurrection, the virgin birth, that sort of thing.'

Pat said she had no problem with these things. 'If Jesus wasn't insane or wicked, then he must have been the Son of God. And if you can believe he was the Son of God walking on this earth, why should it be difficult to believe in things like the miracles and the resurrection?'

Nobody spoke for what seemed an eternity. Then, to Bee's dismay, Nick turned to her and asked, 'When you study theology, do you look at the evidence in the Gospels, like Dominic was talking about?'

'Yes. I did a module on it in year one.'

'And what do you think?'

'What? About what Dominic said?'

'Yes.'

'Well, on the whole I'd go along with most of it.'

'Only most? Not all of it?'

Bee looked at Pat, her eyes pleading with her to move the discussion on to another topic.

No such luck. Dominic was hovering by the table listening in, and he asked Bee which bits she wouldn't go along with.

Bee took a deep breath. 'I suppose I'd be inclined to take the Gospels less literally than you do.'

'Why's that?' Nick asked.

'Well, because of the differences between them.'

'How do you mean?'

Bee felt she had little choice but to go on. 'Well, as you know, Matthew, Mark and Luke are quite similar, but John's very different.'

'Ah,' said Dominic, 'John's Gospel's different because it was actually written by one of the twelve disciples.'

'Yeah but that's the problem,' said Bee. 'Most scholars are pretty doubtful about that.'

'But it says so in the Gospel,' said Dominic.

Bee made to say she didn't think that proved anything, but then she stopped. She had no desire to get into an argument about the authorship of the Gospels.

Nick, however, was clearly keen to keep this discussion going. 'So what are the differences, Bee?'

'Well, most of the material in the Synoptic Gospels – that's Matthew, Mark and Luke – nearly ninety percent of it isn't in John. On a purely factual level, the Synoptic Gospels have Jesus' ministry mostly in Galilee and lasting less than a year. In John it's mostly in Judea and lasts at least three years, possibly even four. Then there are things like in the Synoptic Gospels, chasing the moneylenders from the Temple comes right at the end, just before the crucifixion. John puts it right at the beginning.'

'So who's right?' said Nick. 'John or the other three – what did you call them?'

'The Synoptic Gospels.'

'So which is right?'

Bee looked to Dominic, but he gestured for her to answer.

'Well, that's a big debate among theologians,' she said. 'Most tend to regard the Synoptic Gospels as more accurate historically, but you can make a decent case for the primacy of John.'

'But what do *you* think?'

Bee wished Nick would let it drop, or else contact her online like Sofie and Ross. She glanced at Dominic before she answered. 'I'm with the Synoptic Gospels: Matthew, Mark and Luke.'

'Why?'

'Because they're older.'

'Would you like to say something about when they were written?' Dominic asked.

Bee nodded, pleased to get away from controversial territory. 'The oldest Gospel is Mark, probably written thirty-five to forty years after the crucifixion. Matthew and Luke come next, maybe a decade or two later. Essentially Matthew and Luke tell the same story as Mark, with some differences.'

'Like what?' said Nick.

'Matthew and Luke have more material than Mark. Other than that, in terms of facts, the differences are mostly minor. Sometimes things happen in a different order. Other times, Matthew and Luke are a bit like exaggerated versions of Mark. So, for example, in Mark, Jesus might say something to one person, but in Matthew and Luke he'll say the same thing to a crowd.' Bee looked towards Dominic for a moment, but when he said nothing, she continued: 'A good example of this kind of exaggeration of Mark is when Jesus was arrested. In Mark, one of his followers draws his sword and cuts off the ear of one of the temple guards. Jesus shouts at him and tells him not to resist. In Matthew, Jesus makes a little speech, and in Luke, he touches the guard's ear and heals it.'

'Yes,' said Dominic. 'You have to remember that Matthew and Luke had access to information Mark didn't have.'

'What was that?' Nick wasn't going to let this drop.

'Bee?' Dominic invited her to answer.

'Most scholars think the authors of Matthew and Luke had Mark's Gospel in front of them as they wrote. They also both had another source, and they were combining the two.'

'Like what happened in the Old Testament?' Ross asked.

'Yes, a bit,' said Bee. 'But this time the source is called Q.'

'Sounds like James Bond,' said Nick.

Everybody laughed. Bee was relieved that Nick had distracted everyone from what she had told Ross and Sofie about the Old Testament.

'I'm interested in the contradictions in the story,' said Nick.

'Now I think Bee would agree with me here,' said Dominic. 'Matthew, Mark and Luke drew on various sources. These sources gave them the events of Jesus' life and his teachings. They were like pearls, and Matthew, Mark and Luke provided the narrative thread to string these pearls together in a way we can relate to.'

Bee nodded very conspicuously.

'So are you claiming that all these contradictions don't matter?' asked Nick.

'Not if you're using the Gospels as religious texts,' said Bee. 'If you're using them as a scholar to try and understand the early history of the church, these contradictions do matter. But not if you are reading the Gospels as religious texts.'

'The point is this,' said Dominic, 'the pearls are genuine. Don't let yourself get distracted by the string or the order the different pearls appear in along the necklace. It's the pearls that matter.'

Nick shook his head. 'I'm in the police. When we interrogate someone, we don't just look at the individual bits of his alibi, we look at how the whole thing hangs together. If we can find inconsistencies, then we know he's lying.'

Ross would never know how Dominic answered this point. The revelation that Nick was a policeman induced such alarm in him that he stopped listening.

Did he know who he was?

Did he know what he had done?

Ross's panic plunged him down, down and down again into his pit of hopelessness, guilt and shame.

Chapter Twenty

After the session, Dominic had his usual meeting with the team leaders and Tom.

'That was pretty tough,' said Pat.

'You mean Bee?'

'Yes. I don't know how to handle her. Funny thing is, I don't think she wanted to say anything. That policeman, Nick, he just keeps asking her question after question, and then she comes out with all this stuff. She knows more about it than I do.'

'She does and she doesn't,' said Dominic. 'She knows all the theory, or I should say, all the theories, because a lot of these liberal scholars, they've completely got the wrong end of the stick. But she's lost sight of the basics: the truth of the Bible and the importance of faith.'

Pat nodded. 'Did you notice Ross, the young boy?'

'No?'

'When Nick revealed he was a policeman, Ross almost fell off his chair. I think whatever it is that's stressing him out, he's done something and he's in trouble with the police.'

'You think so?'

'Yes.'

'Nigel Akehurst speaks highly of him,' said Dominic. 'He's got him working at his mum's hotel and he's doing a great job. He said his mum really likes him.'

Tom laughed. 'I know Nigel Akehurst's mum. She's a pretty demanding boss, so if she likes him, he must be all right.'

'Is he at college?' Rodney asked.

'Yes,' said Pat. 'He's just done his AS-Levels.'

'My daughter's at the college. I'll ask her if she knows him. What's his surname?'

'Erm...Collins, I think. Ross Collins.'

'I'll ask her.'

Dominic raised his hands in a 'calm down' gesture. 'I'm not sure it's our business. If Nigel Akehurst had wanted me to know, he would have told me. Ross has come here to find Jesus. That's what we should concentrate on. We're here to help him. It's the same with Bee. She's here because she wants to return to the faith. We have to see her as a lost sheep, not as a threat. Our job is to help people, and the most important weapon in our armoury is Christian love, not gossip about what they may or may not have done in the past.'

*

'Hey, Ross. Is it true you're doing the Alpha Course?'

Ross sighed. He was sure sniffly Sid wasn't asking out of curiosity.

119

'Yes.'

'Why?'

'Why not?'

'Is that why my brother got you a job here? So he could lure you in and convert you?'

Ross took his time tucking his shirt in and tying his tie. He couldn't think of a witty rejoinder, so he said nothing. He got out his mobile and opened the Instagram app. He was sure Sid was gloating.

He was rescued by Sofie's return. Sid lit up and departed.

'You know you're not supposed to smoke in here?' she said after him.

'Don't you tell me what to do, Sofie Manning.'

She turned to Ross. 'What's he said this time?'

'Nigel must have told him we're doing the Alpha Course.'

'He's just a wanker. Don't let him get to you.'

'I just dread to think what he'll say if he finds out…you know.'

'Take it from me, you're a much better person than he'll ever be.' She put a hand on his arm. 'Come on, let's go to work.'

Two days later, it was Ross's turn to take the coffee in for the family. There was no sign of Sid, just his parents and his wife, who was looking very upset.

'I know where he is,' Sofie said later. 'He's been out on the piss and spent the night with some girl. That's why Martha's so angry.'

'You think so?'

'Yeah. Don't forget, I know him. I know what he's like.'

*

After the breakfast shift, they went to the town centre to meet up with Bee. Sofie had suggested Starbucks or Costa Coffee, but Bee had insisted on an independent coffee shop. She chose The Tea and Scones Room, a place near the war memorial famous for its Sussex cream tea. It was all very old English, with old photos of bathing machines and Edwardian ladies walking on the promenade. Ross, Sofie and Bee were the only customers below pension age.

Ross and Sofie ordered tea and shared one scone with jam and cream, but Bee stuck with coffee and a chocolate brownie. She had just seen Robbie off at the station and was wearing the yellow T-shirt of her language school.

'What you up to this afternoon?' Sofie asked.

'Playing basketball with a load of fourteen-year-olds.'

'Sounds good.'

'Sometimes I can't believe I'm getting paid for it. It's an amazing job.'

'I wouldn't say that about waiting,' said Ross. 'But I quite enjoy it.'

'I love the guests,' said Sofie. 'They're just like my grandparents.'

After a few minutes, conversation turned to the Alpha Course.

'Nick gave you quite a grilling,' said Sofie.

Bee rolled her eyes. 'Yeah, you can tell he's a cop.'

'You said you did a module about the historical Jesus?'

'Yeah, really enjoyed it.'

'So, who was the real Jesus?'

'We actually only know three things about him. Number one, he was from Nazareth. Two, he was baptised by John the Baptist. Okay let's make that four or five things. Number three is he was a preacher. Four, he was crucified under Pontius Pilate. And number five, he had a brother called James. That's all we actually know. Everything else is sort of best guess, reconstruction, probably, maybe, etcetera.'

'My dad's got this book, right,' said Ross, pouring himself and Sofie more tea. 'I haven't read it but I've sort of flicked through it. According to this book, Jesus is pure myth and he never even existed.'

'Richard Carrier, *On the Historicity of Jesus*?'

'That's the one.'

'Yeah, I've read that. In academia, these ideas are treated about as seriously as the idea that the moon landings were faked.'

'Really? My dad said it was very convincing.'

'Has he got a background in ancient history?'

'No, he's a quantity surveyor.'

'Well, there you go. The evidence that Jesus existed is pretty solid.'

'My dad's book said there were no contemporary references to him.'

'There aren't. We don't have a single contemporary reference to Spartacus. Not one. Nothing. But nobody uses this to claim that Spartacus never existed.'

'I'm Spartacus,' said Sofie.

'Ha, ha.'

'Sorry. Couldn't resist.'

'The thing is, right,' said Bee, 'we have no contemporary references to ninety-nine point nine percent of the people who lived in the Roman Empire. That doesn't mean they didn't exist. Anything written on parchment or papyrus doesn't last long. The only reason anything at all survives is either because it was buried in fluke conditions that preserved it, or because people copied it by hand again and again every few decades for over a thousand years until paper came along.'

'You sound very passionate about this,' said Sofie.

'I am, because it's such crap. Richard Carrier completely distorts what Paul says about Jesus. And his basic argument's up the wall. He says Jesus is a Jewish take on the dying-and-rising god, which according to him, was all the rage in mystery cults at the time. Except modern researchers into Greco-Roman religion say there were hardly any dying-and-rising gods, if any. The gods that died never came back, and the gods that came back hadn't actually died. Well, if they're right, Carrier's whole theory collapses. And when you get a respected academic like Richard Dawkins promoting this kind of rubbish, that really gets my goat. You know what they say about Dawkins' credentials as a historian?'

'What?'

'He's a good biologist.'

'Okay,' said Ross. 'So, what evidence is there that Jesus existed?'

'Most of it's in the Bible. There's a little bit elsewhere, but it's contested and it's not conclusive.'

'My dad's book says the Bible's not historically reliable.' said Ross.

'Of course it isn't. Not at all. The four gospels, right, they were written decades after the event, and their authors weren't writing history. They were writing *mythos*. They were collecting and editing stories about Jesus to create the myth of Jesus-as-Messiah.'

Ross and Sofie both nodded.

'Take Matthew's gospel: in the author's eyes, the covenant between God and the Christian church mirrors the covenant between God and the Israelites, so he has to make the myth of Jesus mirror the myth of the Moses and Israelites. This is called typology and you see it all over the place in religious literature.'

'How do you mean?' said Sofie.

'Okay, in the Old Testament, the Israelites go down into Egypt – Joseph, right?'

'*Technicolour Dreamcoat* Joseph?'

'That's the one. Then, just before Moses is born, the Pharoah's worried that the Israelites are getting too uppity, so he orders that all Israelite baby boys have to be killed.'

'I've seen the film,' said Ross.

'Yes,' said Bee. 'So the myth of Jesus is like a mirror image of this. Herod orders the massacre of all baby boys in Bethlehem, and Mary and Joseph flee to Egypt to save Jesus. But this is pure myth. Neither of these things actually happened.'

'So the whole thing's made up?' said Sofie.

'Yes. But the thing is, right, if you're writing this myth of Jesus-as-Messiah, you're not going to put anything in that undermines the myth. So if there's something in one of the gospels that undermines the myth, scholars go, "Aha! What's that doing there?" And the conclusion is, they had to put it in because everyone knew it actually happened, so they couldn't leave it out.'

'So,' said Sofie, holding her teacup in front of her, 'you're saying there are things in the gospels that undermine the Jesus myth?'

'Yes, three in particular.' Bee stopped for a moment to finish off the last of her chocolate Brownie. 'Number one: Nazareth. The early church had latched onto a prophecy that the messiah would be born in Bethlehem. But everyone knew Jesus was from Nazareth. So two gospels, Matthew and Luke, they make up stories that have him born in Bethlehem. In Matthew, Mary and Joseph already live in Bethlehem, so Jesus is born there, and then after the flight to Egypt, they go to Nazareth.

'In Luke, Mary and Joseph live in Nazareth but they have to go to Bethlehem for the census, so that's why Jesus is born there. After that, they just present the baby at the Temple and go back home to Nazareth, with no trouble from the authorities.

'Can you see what's happening here? These two gospel writers tie themselves in knots trying to explain away the fact that Jesus came from Nazareth. Why on earth would they do that if Jesus didn't in fact come from Nazareth?'

'So that's proof that Jesus did exist?' said Ross.

'I wouldn't say it's proof, but it is evidence.'

Sofie grinned. 'I was so proud when I was Mary in the nativity play at school. My fifteen minutes of fame. And now you're saying that the whole thing was fiction.'

Bee laughed. 'Not fiction: *mythos.*'

'Fair enough. So, what are the other two embarrassing things?'

'There's more than two. But two more very big ones. The second is the baptism of Jesus. That's really problematic.'

'Why?'

'Because it's inherent in the ritual of baptism that the one doing the baptising is superior to the one being baptised. So John the Baptist is superior to Jesus. Not good. Don't forget, the Baptist's followers were still around as a rival sect. But the thing is, Jesus was the Messiah, the Son of God. John was only a prophet at best. How can he be superior to Jesus?'

'But,' said Sofie, 'didn't John say he wasn't fit to baptise Jesus.'

'Yes,' said Bee. 'Matthew puts that in. But can you see? He's wrestling with a big embarrassment. But he can't leave the baptism out, because everyone knows it happened.'

'So that's evidence that it's a real, historical event?' said Ross.

'Yes. We call it the criterion of embarrassment.'

'What's the third one?'

'The crucifixion.'

'Really?'

'Yeah, massive embarrassment.'

'But Christians make such a big deal of it,' said Ross. 'How's that an embarrassment?'

'Not now,' said Bee. 'But back then it was. First thing, right, the Messiah wasn't supposed to die. He was supposed to swoop down in clouds of glory, send all of Israel's enemies packing, bring history to an end and install himself as God's anointed ruler of the world. So the Christians had a lot of explaining to do if they wanted to convince other Jews that Jesus was in fact the Messiah they'd been waiting for.

'Second, you have to remember that in the Roman Empire, crucifixion was the most shameful and humiliating form of execution possible. It was reserved for slaves, pirates and rebels. Upper-class people could never be crucified. There were no loincloths, by the way. Jesus would have been crucified naked, and typically, the victim's body was left on the cross to rot and get pecked at by crows.

'Even worse, Jews believed that anyone who was crucified would be cursed by God, especially if they were left on the cross overnight, which is what you'd normally expect. Now, there's no way that early Christians would have invented a death like that for Jesus. No way. That's why we can be pretty certain it really happened.'

'So, who was Jesus, the man behind the myth?' asked Sofie.

'Okay,' said Bee. 'Now we move away from almost certain to probably, maybe, possibly. There are different theories, right, so I'm going to tell you what most non-conservative scholars think, but it's not like universally accepted.'

Ross and Sofie both nodded.

'He was basically a peasant. His dad was probably a builder or carpenter, but he could have been the village rabbi. He was almost certainly born in Nazareth, not Bethlehem. He had at least one brother, James. There's no mention of a wife. We don't know if he knew how to read, or what sort of religious education he had.

'John the Baptist baptised him, and sometime after that, he set off on his own ministry, possibly without the Baptist's approval. His basic message was the same: the Kingdom of Heaven is upon us – in other words, the world as we know it is about to end, and you'd better repent quickly if you want God to let you in. But, the tone of Jesus' message seems to have been different. Where John the Baptist was all fire and brimstone, Jesus stressed the positive, the fact that God loves us and wants to forgive us and admit us into his kingdom.

'Jesus believed he had some special part to play in the arrival of God's kingdom, but it's not clear what. Maybe he thought he was the final prophet. Maybe the Son of Man, who ushers in the rule of the Messiah. Or maybe he thought he was the Messiah and he'd shortly become the ruler of the world.'

'Seriously?' said Sofie.

'That's what the Messiah was.'

'That's a bit, well, I don't like to say this about Jesus, but that's insane.'

Bee laughed.

'Oh, one other thing,' she said, 'his message was only for Jews. He wasn't interested in Gentiles at all. And he wasn't particularly original, just a fairly typical first-century Jewish eschatological preacher.'

'What's eschatological?' asked Ross.

'The end of the world is nigh. Shall I tell you what one of my classmates said?'

'What?' Ross and Sofie said in unison.

'She said that if this picture of Jesus is true, then he was one of the most unsuccessful men in history.'

'How'd she work that out?' Sofie asked.

'So, he was a Jew, right? That's a key point.'

Ross and Sofie both nodded.

'And he founds this little Jewish sect, right?' Bee continued. 'Jewish: key point. And he goes round saying, "The end of the world is nigh." Well, spoiler alert, it didn't end. And then he goes and gets himself crucified, a very, very nasty way to die. And then, after his death, his little Jewish sect gets taken over by Gentiles and becomes a separate religion, something he never, ever intended. But even worse than that, this new religion turns round and persecutes Jews for the best part of two thousand years. As Homer Simpson would say: "D'oh!"'

Ross laughed.

'That's really interesting,' said Sofie. 'But I've got two questions for you.'

'What's that?'

'First question: how come you're still a Christian if you believe in your version of Jesus?'

'Well, I'm having a crisis of faith. But what I'd say is that a lot of liberal Christians would have no argument with the picture of Jesus I've just presented.'

'Really?' said Ross.

'Yes. What you have to remember is, they follow the religion Jesus founded, not the historical Jesus.'

'The *mythos*, not the *logos*?' said Sofie.

'Exactly.'

'Okay, second question…presumably Dominic studied the historical Jesus, same as you?'

'Presumably.'

'But he wouldn't agree with what you just said?'

'No.'

'So, how do you know you're right?'

Bee laughed. She sat back and ran her fingers through her spiky hair. 'That's a big question. How can I answer that?' She thought for a moment and then said, 'I know, how about if I tell you the story of how scholars worked it out?'

'That would be interesting.'

'Okay. I'll put it in an email when I have time.'

*

By now, the build-up to the new football season had started. On Saturday, Brighton had a pre-season friendly against AFC Wimbledon, a team from a much lower league. The game went badly, and they lost two-one.

Ross wondered if Sid would be there when he got changed for the evening shift. Sure enough, he came along, sniffly as ever, to gloat about Brighton's defeat. Ross didn't feel this was friendly banter between supporters of different teams. Sid didn't grin as he told him how useless Brighton were: he snarled. Ross had the impression that Sid genuinely didn't like him and was taking any opportunity to get one over on him. He just hoped he could rely on Nigel to keep his mouth shut.

Chapter Twenty-One

On Monday, a very animated Mrs Akehurst spent the first part of the breakfast shift in the kitchen, letting everyone know what she thought about a story in that morning's *Daily Mail*. In Ohio, a man had been sentenced to four months in prison for phoning through a bomb threat in an effort to delay his flight so he didn't miss it.

'Four months?' she said. 'He should have got ten years. They must be pretty soft in Ohio. You know, some states are really tough on crime. They've got this policy: three strikes and you're out. Get arrested third time, doesn't matter what for, and it's life imprisonment without parole. That's what we should have over here.'

Ross and Sofie kept their visits to the kitchen as short as possible, and Ross made sure he didn't make eye contact with Mrs Akehurst. He prayed that Nigel wouldn't tell her about what he had done.

When they got a chance to talk, Ross said to Sofie, 'Didn't realise we were working for a fascist.'

Sofie rolled her eyes and shook her head. 'She might think differently if she knew what I know.'

Ross frowned and looked at her. At that moment, one of the guests raised his hand, and Sofie went to see what he wanted, bringing their conversation to an end.

*

Bee's email came through just before they started the evening shift. Ross and Sofie agreed that they would message each other later that night as soon as they had read it. Ross was glad of the distraction: the inquest was coming up on Thursday, and he knew he would have spent the whole evening worrying about it were it not for this new instalment of the Omega Course.

Hi Sofie and Ross,

Okay, here goes, the email I promised you.

Going back to the early church, it was (wrongly) believed that the four gospels were eyewitness accounts, written decades after the event, so the contradictions between them weren't a big deal. Memories are fallible.

But then people started to see them as holy scripture. And holy scripture is divinely-inspired and therefore without error. So the inconsistencies had to be explained. As usual, a common explanation was that these contradictions are put there to remind us not to get hooked on the surface meaning, but to dig deeper, read between the lines and find the true, spiritual meaning hidden in the text.

But with the printing press and the Reformation, it became more common to take the Bible literally, so people started twisting and turning, their heads spinning round and round, trying to prove that in fact there are no contradictions in the Bible at all. A bit like a game of intellectual Twister.

But then, in 1670, the Jewish philosopher Spinoza (another one of Robbie's heroes) came up with an alternative explanation. Speaking about an Old Testament miracle where the sun stopped in the sky to give the Israelites time to slaughter their enemies, Spinoza said that's impossible: the sun doesn't go round the earth, and if the Bible says this is what happened, then THE BIBLE IS WRONG.

Intellectual earthquake.

In the next century, the historical-critical approach to the Bible was born. Scholars started to treat the Bible like any other historical document and ask: Who wrote this? When? Where? What were they trying to say? What were they influenced by? Why did they write this and not that?

In terms of the Old Testament, this brought us to J, E, P and D etc. In terms of the New Testament, scholars started looking at the gospels and trying to work out what we can learn about their authors and what, if anything, we can learn about Jesus as a historical person.

The most important work in the first wave was done by Germans, liberal Protestant humanists…

Ross stopped and scratched his head. He decided to message Sofie.

Ross: You reading it
Sofie: Yeah
Ross: How can you have a protestant humanist I thought humanists were atheists
Sofie: There's this brilliant thing, right. It's called the internet. There's Google and Wikipedia. You should try them some time
Ross: Have you googled it
Sofie: Just now
Ross: And?
Sofie: 😳 There's Christian humanists all the way back to the Renaissance.
Ross: Oh thanx

…In the 19th century, they looked at the relationship between the four Gospels and worked out that Mark was older than Matthew and Luke. I think I mentioned before that Matthew and Luke often take a story from Mark and expand on it. In Mark, Jesus is more human, more limited, apart from his ability to heal. He sometimes asks his disciples, "What do you think about such-and-such?" In Matthew and Luke that's all edited out. It's implied that Jesus can read their minds, so he never has to ask them what they think.

A man called Christian Hermann Weisse worked out that Matthew and Luke are about 50% from Mark and 25-30% from a different source, which he called Q. Unfortunately, at the time, nobody believed him. Now nearly everyone believes his theory, but I don't think he ever lived to realise he had been vindicated.

Many of these scholars thought the Gospels had distorted Jesus' message. The most important was Adolf von Harnack, who said when Jesus talked about the Kingdom of Heaven, he was not talking about the end of the world but about a time when God would rule our hearts and we would all go round being nice to each other. Basically, he believed Jesus was a liberal Protestant humanist just like him. It's often said that if you go looking for the historical Jesus, you end up finding your own reflection.

(Von Harnack is interesting for another reason – his son was part of the bomb plot that nearly killed Hitler.)

Two things brought this first wave to an end.

One was Albert Schweitzer, a theologian and philosopher. He said Jesus was no mild-mannered liberal. He came up with quote after quote from the Gospels to show that Jesus literally believed the world was about to end: nation rising against nation, earthquakes and famines, stars falling from the sky, the Son of Man coming in the clouds. And Jesus was expecting all this to happen very soon: "The Kingdom of Heaven is upon us...this generation will not pass away until all these things have happened."

The other thing was the First World War.

The next stage started almost as soon as the war was over and was dominated once more by German Protestants, among them Rudolf Bultmann. Bultmann and his colleagues invented a new technique which they called form criticism. With this, they pushed further back to look at the oral traditions of the early church in the decades before Mark and Q were written.

They used the same metaphor of the pearl necklace that Dominic used: the different stories and sayings of Jesus that were handed down were the pearls, and the authors of Mark, Matthew and Luke supplied the narrative string to hold the pearls together.

Bultmann's point was that if you have an oral tradition for 20 to 30 years, it becomes unreliable. There is always the danger that things will get distorted as they go from one person to another.

So they looked at the different pearls (or pericopes, as they called them). Some might be very authentic, pretty near to Jesus' actual words or a good description of something that actually happened. Others not: maybe the early Christians put words in Jesus' mouth, or else they might think, "He can't have said that; he must have said this" and changed his words. Sometimes the early Christians might have exaggerated what happened, or else they conflated the story of Jesus with other Biblical myths or Jewish folklore.

In the end, Bultmann says, the pericopes inevitably end up telling us as much about the early Christians as they do about Jesus himself. We cannot know very much about the historical Jesus, just that he was a preacher who spoke of the love and faith and charity and the dawning of God's eschatological kingdom, and who was crucified for his pains.

And the point is, according to Bultmann, that is all we need to know. It's the Christ of faith that matters, not the historical person of Jesus. It is faith that transforms lives, not scholarly knowledge. It is *mythos* that gives our lives meaning, not *logos*.

Well, that is the theory. That is what I'm still trying to hang on to, but I must admit I'm finding it hard right now.

Here endeth the lesson. I will try to send you the rest of the story tomorrow before Alpha.

With love,

Omega Bee xx

Ross: What did you think
Sofie: B's so brilliant
Ross: I find it quite confusing
Sofie: How come?
Ross: Well like they're all Christians but they don't trust what the bible says
           How can you be a Christian if you don't trust the bible
Sofie: It's mythos and logos innit
Ross: That's what I don't get
Sofie: Why?
Ross: Well I can't explain why I don't get it if I don't get it
Sofie: Well google it then

By now it was nearly 11 o'clock and time to remove all IT from his bedroom, so he took the laptop into the dining room and googled *mythos and logos*.

He found an article about how the Ancient Greeks made a transition from *mythos*-based knowledge derived from their myths and legends to *logos*-based knowledge derived from philosophy. This was apparently one of their civilisation's greatest achievements. There was something about metaphor, but Ross couldn't see anything about Christianity or the Bible.

He scrolled down and found another article that repeated the same argument but said our morals can only come from *mythos*. He wasn't sure he understood why. A third went on to talk about *gnosis* and *episteme*. At this point, Ross gave up. He was having enough trouble dealing with two Greek terms and had no intention of wrestling with two more.

*

He slept badly that night, with fitful dreams about the accident and the inquest. He got up shortly after 10:30 and found a message from Sofie in which she invited herself round to his house so they could read Bee's latest email together.

Ross: I've just got up
Sofie: Lazy git

Ross: I shoulda phoned you first thing to get revenge 😆
        CU about 11

When she arrived, Ross's hair was still wet from the shower.

'Do you want to put the kettle on while I dry my hair?'

'You use a hairdryer?'

He stuck his tongue out and disappeared upstairs. By the time he came back down, Sofie was in the dining room.

'I made you tea. Is that all right?'

'Thanks. Do you want a biscuit?'

'Ooh, yes please.'

He came back with a pack of shortbread fingers and Sofie dunked one in her tea as he fired up his laptop.

'Have you read it?'

'Nah. I was waiting for you. Your house is a bit posher than mine.'

'My dad's on a pretty good salary.'

'What does he do?'

'Quantity surveyor.'

'Oh, I think you said.'

'Have you seen our conservatory?'

'Yeah, I had a sneaky look round when I was waiting for the kettle.'

'We had it built when I was about ten or eleven. I remember, we'd been skiing for the first time that winter…'

'Didn't know you skied.'

'Yeah, every year. You ever done it?'

Sofie laughed and shook her head. 'No chance.'

'Anyway, we had this skiing holiday and then this new conservatory, so I asked him, "Dad, are we middle class?" And he's like, "Yes, I think we probably are."'

'So how come they didn't send you to private school?'

'They're not that rich. Anyway, my dad doesn't approve of private schools. He's quite left-wing.'

'Is that why you don't like Tories?'

Ross shrugged. 'I'm not that interested in politics, to be honest, but there's no way I'd ever vote Tory.'

'Don't think I'll bother voting,' said Sofie. 'Far as I can see, they're all the same. Anyway, enough chit-chat. Shall we get down to work?'

Hi Guys,

Okay, so this is the final part of the search for the historical Jesus…

Rudolf Bultmann thought he had shown its limitations, but he was wrong. In fact, progress accelerated in the following decades.

131

Three reasons for this. First, the Catholic Church got in on the act. Second, Jewish scholars did so too and made a massive contribution in terms of understanding Jesus as a Jew. Third reason: the discovery of new documents, especially the Gospel of St Thomas and the Dead Sea Scrolls. These have given a massive boost to our understanding of early Christianity and the Jewish religious environment that gave birth to it.

One of the most important scholars in this period, and my favourite, is Geza Vermes. His parents were Jewish, but they converted to Catholicism when he was a small child. Unfortunately, that did not save them from the Nazis. Vermes himself only survived the Holocaust because he was hidden in a succession of Catholic seminaries. He grew up to become a priest and a theologian, and he was one of the first to examine the Dead Sea Scrolls. In his 30s, he abandoned Catholicism and went back to being a Jew. In his day, he was widely regarded as the world's greatest living expert on the historical Jesus.

Vermes and the other "post-Bultmann" scholars focused on the pericopes, the "pearls" of the sayings and deeds of Jesus in the Gospels. They had two main disagreements with Bultmann.

First, they say Bultmann exaggerated the extent to which the early Christians were different from Jesus. After all, the church's first leaders had known Jesus personally. They would have wanted to preserve his memory intact as far as they could.

Second, they developed techniques for examining the pericopes to test how authentic they were. They believe they can strip the Gospels back and reveal the *Authentic Gospel of Jesus* (that's the title of one of Vermes' books).

This is how they do it:

Start with only those parts of the Gospels that don't fit comfortably with the message of the early church. This is the criterion of embarrassment that we talked about before.

Next add those bits of Jesus' message that are compatible with the embarrassing bits and are also compatible with the ideas of the early church or contemporary Jewish thought.

Cautiously add other bits that can be found in more than one independent source (e.g. both Mark and Q).

Finally, add any bits that fit in linguistically. Jesus spoke Aramaic but the Gospels were written in Greek, so if the Greek reads like it's been translated from Aramaic, it's more likely to be genuine.

When you have done this, you can go through the Gospels verse by verse, saying which bits are more credible and which bits are less. This cannot take you inside Jesus' head, but we can have a reasonable idea of some of the things he probably said and did.

Oh, forgot to say: there are two more things you need to do:

Be very wary of anything that smacks of typology, patterns that recur in the Bible. (Do you remember? I told you about the massacres of baby boys when both Moses and Jesus were born.)

Final thing: be very wary of anything that is presented as the fulfilment of prophecy. Many events have been inserted into the Gospels in order to retroactively fulfil supposed prophecies in the Old Testament. Some examples:

- The virgin birth. This is the absolute classic case that gives the game away, because the virgin birth was added to the Gospels of Matthew and Luke as a result of a mistranslation.

  In Isaiah 7:14 it says a young woman (Hebrew *almah*) shall give birth to a baby, but in the Greek edition of the Hebrew Bible, the Septuagint, "young woman" is mistranslated as "virgin" (the Hebrew for virgin is *betulah*).

  The myth of the virgin birth and the vast edifice of the cult of the Virgin Mary are built on this very simple mistranslation. (The whole thing is also a total misreading of Isaiah 7:14, but that is another story.)

- Jesus is descended from David – this is put in Matthew and Luke to fulfil several prophecies that were believed to link the Messiah to David's line (e.g. Jeremiah 23:5, Psalms 132:11). The two Gospels give completely incompatible family histories to "prove" that Jesus was descended from David via Joseph, even though they both also say that Joseph wasn't his real father.

- Bethlehem – we talked about that before.

- The three wise men (actually the Bible never said how many there were). This is "predicted" in Isaiah 7:14, so Matthew sticks it in his Gospel. The wise men do not appear in Mark, Luke or John.

So anyway, this is how scholars have come up with today's picture of the historical Jesus. From a Christian point of view, it's a disturbing picture because our *logos* knowledge of the historical person is in conflict with our cherished myth of Christ the Saviour.

It does not make Christianity invalid. Christianity is a superb religion. It can transform people's lives; it can bring hope to the despairing and redemption to the seemingly irredeemable. It can do so much to bring out the best in us as individuals and to bind societies together.

Where I disagree with Dominic and the Alpha Course is their assertion that Christianity rests on a solid base of *logos*. It does not; it rests on a solid base of *mythos*. And I reject their argument that Christianity is THE truth and that other religions are by implication false. They aren't. The *mythos* of Judaism, Islam, Hinduism, Buddhism or whatever can perform the same functions as the *mythos* of Christianity.

But please remember, I don't want you to use what I say to argue with Dominic during the Alpha Course. There is one way in which I do agree with what he's doing. I think it is important to help those who wish to come to Christianity to do so. I might be in danger of losing my religion, but I do not want to take anyone else's religion away from them.

I hope this doesn't all sound terribly confused.

Love,

Bee xx

Sofie finished first. She sat back and waited. When Ross finished, she asked him what he thought.

Ross thought for a moment. 'I googled *mythos* and *logos* last night.'

'And?'

He shrugged. 'To be honest, this whole *mythos* thing: I don't buy it.'

'I do,' said Sofie. 'I was like, soon as she said it, "*Bang!* Yes, I get it."'

'Yeah, but how can you believe in something when you know it's not true?'

'You do it all the time.'

'No, I don't.'

'You do. Every time you read a novel, every time you watch a movie. You know it's made up. You know the characters aren't real, but you feel for them. You worry about them. You're happy when things go right for them, and you're upset when things go badly, and you cry when something beautiful happens.'

'But that's just fiction. It's not the same.'

'Yes it is. You know it's make-believe, but you believe in it. You respond to it as if it's true. It's the same with religion. You can know that Jesus isn't literally the son of God but you can respond to the myth as if it's true, and that can transform your life.'

'So how come Bee can't do it any more?'

'Because that's where she is right now. The myth isn't working for her at the moment. But that doesn't mean it can't work for you.'

Ross shook his head. 'I don't agree. Far as I'm concerned, something's either true or it's not.'

*

It was now the third week in July, and the weather was hot and sunny after a few unsettled days. On Tuesday, Dani persuaded Ross to join her, Raj and Sofie for an afternoon on the beach. Raj and Ross wore boxer trunks, while Dani stripped down to a blue bikini and Sofie wore a multicoloured one-piece swimsuit.

'Come on,' said Raj, 'let's go for a swim.'

They trod gingerly down the shingle beach and entered the water even more cautiously.

'It's bloody freezing,' said Dani.

Raj and Ross waded forwards. Ross sighed loudly as the water reached his private parts.

'On the count of three,' said Raj.

Ross looked at him and nodded.

'One, two, three!'

They dived in, sticking their heads under the water.

Dani looked at Sofie, who nodded, and they did the same. The four of them swam, splashed each other and frantically trod water in the waves.

After a few minutes, Dani swam up to Sofie. 'I've had enough of this. It's too cold.'

Sofie followed her out of the water and they made their way up the painful stones to grab their towels and dry their shivering, goose-pimpled bodies. Then they sat on their towels and began to apply sunscreen.

As she rubbed it into Dani's back, Sofie asked, 'Still playing Scrabble?'

Dani laughed. 'Normal service has been resumed.'

Sofie wagged a finger at her: 'Don't overdo it this time.'

'Yes, ma'am. We do other things, you know, with our clothes on.'

'Like what?'

'We're building a computer.'

'What?'

'Yeah, we got all the parts and now we're putting it together. You should see me with a soldering iron: proper demon, man.'

Sofie burst out laughing. 'Is he turning you into a nerd?'

'Why shouldn't a girl learn a new skill? Anyway, what about you and Ross? You're seeing quite a lot of each other.'

'Yes.'

'And?'

Sofie shrugged. 'We get on very well.'

'And?'

'And what? He's a good mate. We get on well. End of story.'

Sofie sat on her towel and turned her back on Dani, who squirted sunscreen onto her hands and began to apply it to her shoulders.

'You should set your sights higher,' she said.

'Give me a break,' said Sofie. 'In any case, he's got Natalie after him. I don't stand a chance against her.'

'What? Why not?'

'Because she's bloody gorgeous, that's why not.'

Dani shook her head. 'First of all, you're gorgeous too.'

'No, I'm not.'

'Yes, you are. You haven't had much trouble picking up blokes in the past, have you?'

'He just wanted someone young and stupid.'

'And fit. Look at your tits. Better than my little fried eggs.'

Sofie turned round and they looked at each other's breasts.

'You know what?' said Sofie. 'We're still cold.'

They both laughed.

'Anyway,' said Dani. 'He's not interested in Natalie. Doesn't fancy her.'

'You think so?'

'Well, he would have done something by now, wouldn't he?'

Sofie shrugged.

'What about your Christian indoctrination course? How's that going?'

Sofie told her about the sessions and about Omega Bee, her extremely fit Scottish boyfriend and *mythos* and *logos*.

By now, Ross and Raj had come out of the sea to join them. Dani and Sofie handed them their towels and they proceeded to dry themselves, shivering and covered in goose pimples just like the girls had been.

'Sofie's been telling me about Omega Bee and *mythos* and *logos*,' said Dani.

'What?' said Raj.

Sofie and Ross told him about Bee, and Sofie gave a brief explanation of *mythos* and *logos*.

'Oh, yeah, we have that in Hinduism.'

'How do you mean?' said Ross.

'Well, like, you've seen our shrine in our house.'

Ross nodded. 'Yeah.'

'Well, you've seen us, we worship it every morning. The whole family, we do it together. It's really nice, great way to start the day. My family worship five different gods, but we don't believe they actually exist, right. They're just aspects of God.'

'So, do you believe in God?' Sofie asked.

Raj gave a so-so gesture. 'Sort of, but our idea of God's completely different from yours. I mean, your god, he's like one of our gods, with a story and that. For us, right, our God, Atman, it's more like a universal spirit.'

Sofie raised an eyebrow. 'I'd have thought with your politics you'd be a militant atheist.'

Raj shrugged. 'I don't see a connection, really. I mean, I'm totally against the caste system and karma and that. But a lot of Hinduism's really beautiful, even if you don't really believe in it, like…What is it? Lego?'

Ross and Sofie burst out laughing.

'*Logos*,' said Sofie.

'Yeah, you don't have to believe it like that.'

Sofie laughed until tears came to her eyes. 'Raj doesn't believe in Lego!'

*

Ross and Sofie were a lustrous shade of pink when they got to the Alpha Course that evening. The first thing Sofie did was to go up to Bee and take her to one side.

'Thanks for your emails. They were so interesting.'

'Shush.'

'Don't worry,' Sofie said with a grin. 'It can be our little secret.'

After dinner and coffee, Tom Bradshaw tuned his guitar and treated them to two more hymns. Ross only knew the first line of tonight's traditional hymn, so he was mildly curious to read the rest. Having to sing along was a small price to pay.

What a friend we have in Jesus, all our sins and griefs to bear!
What a privilege to carry everything to God in prayer!
O what peace we often forfeit, O what needless pain we bear,
All because we do not carry everything to God in prayer.

'If only it could be so easy,' he thought.
The happy-clappy song was next:

Jesus Christ is my Redeemer
His the blood that set me free
Mine the sin that made him suffer
And nailed him to that fateful tree.

Ross only just managed not to laugh when he saw that last line. It struck him that there was a strong element of sado-masochism in Christianity, so much emphasis on blood and death and suffering. Even the end of the song was a celebration of death and the life to come:

And when the Lord he calls upon me,
And I follow him to that perfect place
By the gate he'll be waiting for me
And I'll see his perfect face.

This hymn put Ross in a foul mood. When Dominic got up to give his talk, Ross wasn't feeling very receptive. But Dominic's talk began to answer the question that the second hymn had put in his mind.

'Why do Christians keep banging on about the death of Jesus?' Dominic asked. 'Most people, after all, we remember them for their lives, but with Jesus we remember him above all for his death.'

The answer lay in sin. We are all sinners. We might not be rapists or murderers (Ross was sure Dominic looked at him as he said the word 'murderers'), but we are all sinners. He quoted Somerset Maugham: 'I do not think I am any better or any worse than most people, but I know that if I wrote down every thought and every deed I have ever done, men would call me a monster of depravity.'

He said sin was a rebellion against God. It pollutes us. We are either full of sin or free from it, just like our driving licence can be either clean or not clean, but never 'fairly clean'.

To Ross's relief, Dominic didn't look at him as he talked about driving licences.

'Sin is an addiction, he said, as bad as any drug. We can so easily be addicted to the sins of anger, jealousy, pride, selfishness, deceitfulness and sexual immorality. We get locked into patterns of sinful behaviour. We become the slaves of sin.'

By now Dominic was very animated. He was pacing up and down, speaking very loudly and giving those who sat near him a liberal spray of his spittle. This was fire and brimstone stuff.

He talked about the penalty of sin. 'It's only natural for us to want the wicked to be punished. It's only natural for us to want justice. And so it is with sin, for the wages of sin is death.'

By now Ross was gripped. Dominic had got right to his reason for being there.

He told them how God loves them so much that he came down to earth in the person of his son Jesus Christ and (by now Dominic was almost shouting) paid the price of our sins for us.

He gave an example from what happened to some Scottish POWs working on the Burma railroad during the Second World War. A Japanese guard noticed that a shovel had gone missing and demanded to know which prisoner had stolen it, presumably in order to sell it to the local population in exchange for food. Nobody answered, and the guard got increasingly hysterical. Eventually he raised his rifle and said he would shoot all the prisoners.

Then one soldier stepped forwards and admitted that he had taken the shovel. The guard attacked him savagely and beat him to death. And then, when the prisoners returned to their camp, they found that there were no missing shovels after all.

This soldier had sacrificed himself for his comrades in just the same way as Jesus sacrificed himself for all of us.

'Have any of you seen *The Passion of the Christ*?' Dominic asked.

Several hands went up.

'I found it unwatchable,' said Dominic. 'It was so graphic, so horrible. But all I had to do was watch a film. Jesus had to suffer that fate. He had to actually go through all that agony, the scourging, the crown of thorns and the crucifixion. Can you imagine? And he did it all for us.

'The wages of sin is death, and Jesus has already paid that price for our sins. So if we believe in him, we don't have to pay again. Jesus is like the judge who fines the prisoner and then writes out a cheque himself to pay the fine. He's like the creditor who pays off his debtor's debts himself. Jesus uses his own blood to wash away the pollution of our sins.'

Dominic gave several examples of people he had known, one an alcoholic, another a drug addict and a third who was a pillar of his local church but had a secret sin of searching out pornography on the internet (Ross looked away from Dominic at this point, his eyes darting from side to side). All of their lives had been transformed when they allowed Jesus into their lives, when they put their faith in him and let his blood wash away their sins.

It was powerful stuff, by far Dominic's best talk to date. And it seemed to Ross to be an answer to some of the questions that had brought him to the Alpha Course in the first place.

*

Bee had heard it all before, and just six months earlier she would have loved every minute of it, because it was a good talk. Dominic was much more animated than usual, speaking loudly and quickly as if he could hardly contain himself. Bee fully understood his fervour. This was the central myth of western Christianity, and what a fantastic myth it was: Jesus the Redeemer, the gift of hope to the hopeless, the promise of light in the middle of our darkest night.

And like any myth, it would crumble into dust the instant it was subjected to the harsh scrutiny of reason, just like a vivid dream that vanishes as soon as you open your eyes.

Because if you analyse it, the myth of Christ the Redeemer is preposterous. If God is all-powerful and all-knowing, as the Christian God is supposed to be, they why on earth would he cook up such a ridiculous scheme?

Bee imagined God speaking to the Archangel Gabriel, telling him about his plan for the new universe he was about to create. 'On the sixth day, I'm going to create these creatures, humans, I'm going to make them in my own image. Except I'll give them the willpower of a tadpole and subject them to all sorts of wicked temptations: anger, pride, gluttony, lust, that kind of thing.'

A confused look appears on the archangel's face, because, of course, he knows none of these sins.

'Take it from me,' says God, 'these are bad things, and humans are going to find it really hard to avoid them. Anyway, let me tell you about the best bit. I'm going to take on human form, and then I'm going to let the humans torture me to death, and then after that, I'll be able to forgive the humans their sins.'

At this, the archangel frowns. 'Sorry, God. Could you just run that last bit by me again?'

The whole thing is absurd. Bee couldn't understand how she could ever have believed it, but she had, in her own way. She had somehow managed to hold two contradictory thoughts in her head at the same time. On the one hand, she had known that, strictly speaking, the idea that Jesus was our Redeemer wasn't historically 'true'. There was no evidence that Jesus had thought of himself in this way. The doctrine had only arisen after his death.

And yet, at the same time, she had been able to 'believe in' the myth, even if she hadn't 'believed' it. She had been able to draw hope and inspiration from it. That myth had been central to who she was. She felt it had made her a better person.

But now, almost suddenly, she had lost it. She had come to think of it as nonsense. She didn't know if she was right in her disbelief. She knew it didn't make her happier, and she had no desire to evangelise on behalf of her new-found lack of faith. But it was painful for her to sit and listen to Dominic. Everything he said stressed her out, and she was dreading the group discussion. She knew that Nick would try to draw her out with more of his questions.

*

At coffee time, Ross avoided Bee. He didn't want to hear what she thought about it. He didn't want her rationalist arguments. He left her to talk with Sofie and Nick while he spoke with Bob the Builder about football and Bob's hopes for his beloved Aston Villa, who had narrowly missed out on promotion to the Premier League last season.

During the discussion round the table, Ross wondered if now was the time to confess his own sin, to tell the others why he was there. He thought about it for a long time, breaking out in a cold sweat as he did so.

What to say? I accidentally killed someone? I caused a crash where this woman died? I was involved in a crash? No, that was a cop-out. I caused a car crash? I forgot to look in my mirror and this woman who was overtaking me...?

He missed most of the discussion, so wrapped up was he in thoughts about his own terrible sin and whether and how to tell everybody. But the moment for confession passed before he found the right words, because the discussion had moved on.

'I live with my girlfriend,' he heard Nick say. 'Are you saying it's a sin if we have sex?'

Silence.

Dominic approached the table and asked Nick to repeat his question.

'I was saying that I live with my girlfriend. Is it a sin for us to have sex?'

Dominic thought for a moment. He clenched his fist in front of his lips.

'The teaching of the Bible's clear. There's nothing wrong with sex. Sex is God's gift to us, and it's something we should celebrate and enjoy. There's even a whole book of the Old Testament, the Song of Songs, which is a celebration of sexual love between a man and a woman. It's actually quite X-rated.'

He put his hands together, as if in prayer. 'But I suppose you're asking the question of where the border lies between the gift of sexual love and the sins of lust and fornication. And the answer to this comes very early in the Bible, in Genesis Chapter Two, Verse Twenty-Four: "For this reason a man will leave his father and mother and be united to his wife, and they will become one flesh."'

'So you're saying it is a sin?'

Dominic hesitated again. 'The church has always taught that marriage is the proper context for sexual love. I accept that it's more complicated than that, particularly these days when divorce is easy and marriage is often nothing more than a piece of paper. Perhaps where a couple have made a real and lasting spiritual commitment to each other, that could be as valid in God's eyes as...as a quick ceremony in a registrar's office.'

'And what about if a man and a woman shack up together and hope it works out?'

Dominic took a deep breath. 'That wouldn't be the path the church would recommend.'

'So the phrase "living in sin" still sums it up for you?'

'We're talking about what the Bible teaches, not what I may or may not think. When you have sex with someone, you become one flesh. This is a lasting commitment; it's not just a bit of fun. The commitment has to come first. Having sex first is like going into a greengrocer's and taking a bite out of an apple without buying it.'

Nick said no more, but from his expression, Ross could see that he was upset by this. Ross looked at Bee. Her face was bright red. She seemed to be about to burst, but she said nothing.

To his surprise, it was Sofie who argued back.

'Surely, the Bible was written a long time ago. In those days, sex before marriage was sinful because it was irresponsible and had unwanted consequences, like babies. These days, people can be responsible and use contraception. It's different.'

'You've raised a very important question,' said Dominic. 'There are liberal Christians who would agree with you, but I'm afraid I'm not one of them. The Bible is God's message to humanity, and that message is eternal. It's not subject to changes in fashion. It's not this week's bulletin or a pick-and-mix menu where you just choose the bits you want.'

'Oh, come on Dominic.' This was Bee, who clearly could contain herself no longer. 'Are you saying you're never selective about which bits of the Bible you follow?'

'No I'm not.'

'How about One Corinthians Fourteen: Thirty-Four to Thirty-Five: "women should remain silent in the churches...If they want to enquire about something, they should ask their own husbands at home; for it is disgraceful for a woman to speak in the church." So if you never select which bits of the Bible you believe, I should shut up, right?'

Bee was almost shaking with anger.

Dominic, on the other hand, remained very calm. 'I think what St Paul is saying is that the leadership of the church should be male. I know that doesn't fit very well with certain aspects of the modern world, but it's not up to us to choose which bits of God's message we want to hear.'

'So is it a sin for men to have long hair?'

For the first time, Dominic looked fazed.

'One Corinthians, Eleven: Fourteen – "if a man has long hair, it is a disgrace to him". Hadn't you better have a word with your guitarist?'

141

The whole room had suddenly gone quiet, and everyone around all the different tables looked at Tom Bradshaw and his ponytail.

Bee seemed to be the only person who hadn't noticed the impact of what she had said. She fired off another question without waiting for Dominic to respond. 'Chapter Six, Verse Nine? "Do you not know the wicked will not inherit the earth...nor homosexual offenders..." Should we take that verse literally? Or was St Paul just reflecting the attitudes of his day?'

'Ah,' said Dominic, 'but don't forget what it says two verses later. "And that is what some of you were. But you were washed, you were sanctified, you were justified in the name of the Lord Jesus Christ and by the Spirit of our God."'

Bee ignored this and pressed on with her attack. 'What about Matthew Twenty-Seven: Twenty-Five? Do you think we should take that literally?'

'That's about all of us,' said Dominic. 'It's got nothing to do with the Jews. Christ's blood is on all our hands. That's the whole point.'

Bee smiled. 'That's a clever answer. You're wrong, but that's a clever answer.' With that she folded her arms, sat back in her chair and said no more.

Ross guessed that everybody desperately wanted to ask what those verses of Matthew said, but somehow nobody dared to.

Chapter Twenty-Two

Bee had parked her mother's light blue Honda Civic near the bus stop, so she walked with Ross and Sofie after the session ended. The sun had just set and streaks of orange and red brightened up the sparse grey clouds above them.

'Oh God, I lost my rag back there,' said Bee. 'I just snapped when he said he never cherry-picks the Bible.'

Sofie laughed. 'Serves him right.'

'I don't think I can go back after this.'

'Oh Bee, no,' said Sofie. 'You can't give up now.'

'It's not for me, and I really don't want to argue with Dominic.'

'I thought you were brilliant,' said Sofie.

'Thank you.'

'What's in Matthew Twenty-Five: Twenty-Seven?' Ross asked.

'Twenty-Seven: Twenty-Five. It's the bit where Pontius Pilate has washed his hands of Jesus' execution. The Jewish crowd shout out: "Let his blood be on us and our children!"'

'Meaning the Jews?' Sofie asked.

'Yes.'

'But Dominic says it means all of us, not just the Jews?'

'That was a good answer,' said Bee. 'He scored a point there. I wanted to hit back with the bit where St John's Gospel says the Jews are the sons of the devil, but I couldn't remember the exact reference.'

'Does it really say that?' Sofie asked.

'Oh yes: John Eight: Forty-Four. I remember the bloody reference now, don't I?'

'Be interesting to see if Tom Bradshaw gets a haircut,' said Sofie.

'Oh God. Do you think he heard what I said?'

'Everybody in the room heard.'

'Oh no. God, that's so embarrassing.'

Sofie laughed, but Ross said nothing. He was too busy checking the football results on his mobile. In their latest pre-season friendly, Brighton had only managed a draw with lowly Charlton Athletic. He knew Sid would be there tomorrow to tell him how useless they were.

His face set in a grimace at the thought of it.

'Do you guys want a lift home?' said Bee as they reached her car.

'No thanks,' said Sofie. 'It's miles out your way.'

'That's not a problem.'

'No thanks. We'll take the bus. Do you fancy meeting up for coffee later this week?'

'That'd be great.'

Next morning, as they waited for the first guests to come down for breakfast, Ross noticed that Sofie had an enormous grin on her face.

'I know what you're thinking about,' said Ross.

'What?'

'Tom Bradshaw's ponytail.'

'No,' she said. 'That was very funny, though. No, this morning, I'm just feeling very, very happy.'

'How come?'

'Last night I asked Kate if I could call her Mum.'

'What did she say?'

'She burst into tears and gave me a hug.'

'Oh, that's brilliant. That's fantastic.'

'Yeah. I'd been thinking about it for ages. It was talking to you that made me do it.'

'Really? Wow. Glad to be of service.'

'Like I said, you can still have a positive impact on peoples' lives.'

They looked at each other and smiled.

*

Bee's mother was fully dressed in the kitchen whisking eggs when Bee came down for breakfast. She was wearing her pyjama trousers and an old sleeveless T-shirt.

'I'm just making some scram on toast for me and your dad. Do you want some?'

'Yes, please.'

Bee took some coffee from the percolator and opened the fridge.

'Your dad's taken the milk.'

'Ah, okay. Shall I get some for you?'

'No ta. Your dad's made a pot of tea.'

Bee went into the dining room, where her father was sitting unshaven in his pyjamas. He briefly glanced up from his iPad and smiled.

'Morning.'

'Hiya.'

She sat down opposite her father and reached over to put milk in her coffee. She took out her mobile and messaged Robbie.

Bee: Morning – how's my sexy philosopher today?
Robbie: Still asleep

Bee laughed.

After a few moments her mother came in with breakfast for Bee and her father, returning after a minute with her own. She sat down next to Bee's father.

'You got in late last night,' she said to Bee.

'Yeah, I went for a walk on the seafront, and then I had a long chat with Robbie.'

'You want to be careful, out on your own late at night.'

Bee chewed a mouthful of her breakfast before she replied. 'I was near the pier. There were loads of people there.'

It was a few moments before Bee's mother asked the question that Bee had been bracing herself for. 'How was the session last night?'

'It was terrible. I got into a big argument with the vicar.'

'What about?'

Bee scratched her head. It had started with a discussion about pre-marital sex. She really didn't want to go there with her parents right now.

'I'm not sure.'

'Well, what was the session about?'

For a moment, Bee genuinely couldn't remember.

'Erm...Oh yes, Jesus dying for our sins.'

'Well,' said her mother, 'that's why he died. Why did you have to argue with him about that?'

'I can't remember what started us arguing. I just remember feeling very upset about it afterwards.'

'You do believe Jesus died for us, don't you?'

Bee spent some time chewing before she answered. 'I don't know, Mum. That's the whole issue.'

'Well, you do believe he was crucified?'

'Yes, of course.'

'I'm glad you believe something. And he knew he was going to be killed.'

'Right at the end, yes. In the last supper.'

'And long before that,' said her mother. 'It's in Mark, soon after he heals the blind man.'

'Mark eight: thirty-one,' her father interjected.

'Yeah, I know,' said Bee. 'Scholars are sceptical about passages like that. Geza Vermes says that passage isn't authentic.'

'What do you mean, not authentic?'

'Jesus probably never said it.'

'So you're saying Jesus didn't know he was going to be killed until the last supper?'

'No. I'm saying it's not clear.'

Her father looked up from his iPad. 'Well, the Baptist's head had been chopped off, so he must have known he was in danger.'

'Yeah, I'll agree with that.' Bee finished off the last of her breakfast, picked up her mobile and messaged Robbie.

Bee: Help! Get me out of here.
Robbie: What's up (or should I say WhatsUpp?)

Bee: Parents

Her mother hadn't finished. 'And all your scholars, do they accept that the passion narrative is authentic?'

Bee put down her mobile and reached for her coffee, holding it in front of her.

'Was Jesus crucified? Yes. By the Romans? Yes. Pontius Pilate? Yes. Were the Temple authorities involved? Yes, probably.'

'What do you mean, probably? It's in all the gospels.'

'Yeah, I know. But there's all kinds of debates about what Jesus would have done that the Temple authorities would want him killed. It's not a hundred percent clear, but, for what it's worth, I think the Temple authorities probably wanted him dead.'

'But Peter witnessed his trial.'

'I'm sorry, Mum, but do you really think it's credible that Peter could sneak into the high priest's house and listen to the trial?'

'Yes.'

'Well, it smacks of narrative device to me.'

'What's that supposed to mean?'

'The only way the narrators can give an account of the trial is to put one of the good guys in there.'

'Rubbish.'

'Oh, come on,' said Bee's father, turning to her mother. 'I remember you saying the same thing to me.'

'That was a very long time ago,' said Bee's mother. 'A very long time ago. Maybe I've matured a bit over the years, learnt to trust God's word. It's a shame you haven't matured more since then.'

Silence.

Bee didn't look at either of her parents. She finished her coffee, ostentatiously checked the time on her mobile, picked up plate and mug and headed into the kitchen.

*

When Ross and Sofie gave the evening menus out at the end of breakfast, the guests had a choice between roast chicken and Thai green curry. Every last one of them opted for roast chicken.

Mrs Akehurst was in the kitchen when Ross went to report to the chef. 'Not a single Thai curry,' he said. 'These guests are a very conservative lot.'

'They're not a very Conservative lot,' said Mrs Akehurst. They're a very Labour lot.'

Ross kept his eyes down and his mouth shut as he retreated to the dining hall.

'You okay?' Sofie whispered.

Ross shrugged.

'You worried about the inquest?'

'Shush.'

'Nobody can hear us.'

'It's not that. It's just Mrs A being a Tory fanatic.'

Sofie laughed.

*

'You really should try a cream tea,' said Sofie. 'It's delicious.'

'I'm happy with my chocolate brownie.'

'Well, have a bit of my scone.'

'Thanks.'

'Do you want some of mine?'

'No ta. I'm just dumping some calories on you.'

They were back at The Tea and Scones Room. Sofie's morning shift was behind her, while Bee was still waiting for the start of her working day.

'No Ross today?'

'He's gone home. He didn't get much sleep last night. He's a bit stressed out.'

'I've noticed that. Something's happened to Ross, hasn't it? Sometimes he gets really stressed.'

'Yeah. I can't tell you what it is, I promised him I wouldn't. But yes, he's having a hard time.'

'Is he going to be all right?'

'Eventually, yeah. Anyway, what about you? What you up to today?'

'Welfare office.'

'What's that?'

'Oh, it's really boring. I have to sit in this office by myself in case any of the kids are sick or hurt themselves playing sports. I'm a first-aid qualified, see, so I have to do first aid, or maybe take them to the doctor's. The worst thing is if I have to take someone to A and E. You're guaranteed a four-hour wait, and that's if you're lucky.'

'So your job isn't all fun, then?'

'This is only really boring bit.'

Sofie changed the subject: 'Were you upset last night, about Tom's hair?'

'Yeah.'

'Sorry I laughed.'

'No worries.'

'No, it was insensitive of me. I'm sorry.'

Bee put her hand on Sofie's arm. 'It's okay. I can see the funny side.'

They both grinned.

'You put up a good fight for the sexual revolution last night,' said Bee.

'Yeah. I mean, do you have to be a prude to be a Christian?'

'Depends what kind of Christian.'

'I'm glad you don't have to,' said Sofie. 'I mean, I have my faults, but I'm not a prude. But you really know your Bible. I mean, it's amazing. You just reel off quotes like that.'

'I grew up with it.'

'Are your parents very religious?'

'Yes. They're completely different, though. My dad's very liberal. I think he'd hate the Alpha Course. My mum's more old-school. She used to be quite liberal but she's got pretty hard-core over the last few years.'

'Do they argue about it?'

Bee shrugged. 'Yeah, sometimes. What about your parents? Are they religious?'

Sofie shrugged. 'My mum died when I was nine.'

'Oh God, Sofie, I'm so sorry.'

'It's okay. I don't mind talking about it. It is very sad, though. My family fell apart. My dad's an alcoholic, and my sister, she's a drug addict.'

'Oh, no.'

'I went through a very bad patch. When I say patch, I mean, like six or seven years. I was a little horror at school.'

'But you're so bright.'

'You think so?'

'Yes.'

Sofie shrugged. 'I always did get good results, but I bet my teachers hated me. I got suspended once, but I always managed to not quite get myself expelled.'

'But that doesn't seem like you.'

'I did some growing up, you know. I've changed. I feel like a different person. And I had a lot of help. My step mum, she put up with a lot of shit, to be honest, but she stuck by me. I live with her now, not my dad.'

'Maybe she loves you.'

'She does, yeah.' Sofie stopped speaking for a moment. Tears welled up in her eyes, and she forced a smile to hold them back. 'And when I started college, I had counselling. That was a big help. And I got a new best friend, Ross's cousin. She's helped me a lot too. She's amazing.'

'Sofie, am I getting in your way, on the Alpha Course?'

'No! Absolutely not.'

'You're sure?'

'One hundred percent. I don't like a lot of what Dominic says. It's very…I don't know. I mean, it's almost like, reactionary, innit? But as soon as you told us about *mythos* and *logos*, I was like, "Yes! I get that."'

'That's good.'

'I'm so full of questions. I want you to tell me everything.'

'What? All in one go?'

They both laughed. Then they sipped their drinks and ate some cake.

'What Dominic said last night, about Jesus dying for our sins, I suppose you'd say that's the *mythos*.'

'Yes.'

'So, what's the *logos*?'

'How do you mean?'

'Why did he die?'

'Well, the simple answer is the authorities wanted him out of the way.'

'Why?'

'You have to remember that there was a fairly small Roman garrison in a city that was full of hundreds of thousands of pilgrims come to celebrate the Passover. They would have been very keen to nip any trouble in the bud.'

'What kind of trouble?'

'Any hint of rebellion, either against Rome or against their Jewish cronies. There's all kinds of debates about what Jesus could have said that would make them want him dead. Maybe he created some kind of disturbance in the Temple. Do you know the story about how he chased the moneychangers out of the Temple?'

Sofie nodded.

'Even if that story's exaggerated, just the threat of a disturbance might be enough to make him a marked man.'

'But this idea that Jesus died for our sins, it's what Christianity's all about, innit?'

'Yeah, that and the resurrection. And they're amazing myths. It means there's always hope, no matter what you've done, there's always hope of redemption.'

Sofie nodded. 'And you don't have to believe it's literally what happened. But you have to believe *in* the myth.'

'Exactly.'

'Do you believe in the myth?'

'That's a good question. I used to, but I'm not sure now.'

'But you never really thought that's what happened, like *logos*?'

'No.'

Sofie thought for a moment. 'I think it's fascinating, you know? How you can have two different ideas, and they contradict, like, but it doesn't matter.'

Bee nodded.

Sofie put her hands in front of her head as she spoke, 'My head's just exploding with questions. I mean, Dominic, right, he's giving me the *mythos*. He thinks it's *logos*, like, but I understand it's *mythos*. But I want to know the *logos* too. I want to know what really happened, so I can...' She waved her hands in front of her. 'Does that sound weird?'

'No.'

'So, what happened? I mean, I get that the resurrection never actually happened. Dead people don't suddenly come back to life, right. But why did the disciples believe it did? I mean, they were convinced, right?'

'That's a big question. I'm not sure I have time to answer it before I go to work. Shall I put it in an email?'

'Oh, that would be so great. Yes, please.'

'Chances are I'll have sod all to do in Welfare. I'll try and write it then.'

'Fantastic.'

'Shall I send it to Ross too?'

'Yeah. I'm sure he'd be interested.'

*

When Ross and Sofie returned for the evening shift, they could hear the laughter coming from the staffroom before they went in. Sid was inside, showing the kitchen porter something on his mobile, and both of them were laughing so much that they had tears in their eyes. The kitchen porter waved at Ross and Sofie, but Sid didn't so much as glance at them.

The presence of the female kitchen porter gave Ross an excuse to get changed in the male staff toilet. He was surprised how messy it was, with lots of what he assumed to be talcum powder on the top by the wash basin and on the floor.

Unfortunately, Sid was still there when he came out, so he had to endure the inevitable comments about how useless Brighton were and how they would definitely go down next season.

Sofie took her time getting changed. Ross suspected that she was keen to avoid Sid. Once she was ready, they went into the dining room and stood waiting for the first guests to arrive.

'One of you naughty girls has been using our toilet.'

'Oh yeah? What'd they do? Leave the seat down? Not pee on the floor?'

'Worse than that. They left bloody talcum powder all over the place.'

Sofie burst out laughing. 'God, Ross, you're so innocent.'

'What?'

'It's not talcum powder. It's bloody cocaine.'

'What? How do you know?'

'Oh, come on. Have you seen anyone here who's always sniffing? It's not hay fever, you know.'

'You mean Sid?'

'Duh!'

At that moment, the first guests walked in, bringing their conversation to an end.

Chapter Twenty-Three

Ross had to finish work 10 minutes early next morning so he and his parents could meet his solicitor before the inquest. Their meeting was very quick, and they then walked the short distance to the court together. The receptionist showed them to a small office that served as a waiting room.

Ross could hardly speak. His mouth was dry and he knew that if he held his hands in front of him, they would visibly shake. More than anything else he was dreading his encounter with Lizzie Johnson's husband. How could he look him in the face? Then again, how could he not do so? Wouldn't it be a dreadful act of cowardice?

Or if he looked him in the eye, would Mr Johnson interpret that as insolence?

What if he had to speak to him? What on earth could he say? Ross had sometimes imagined their conversation like a ridiculous scene straight out of PG Wodehouse: 'I say, old bean. Awfully sorry about your wife, what?'

'Never mind, old chap. These things happen.'

'Rather!'

After 20 minutes of tortuous waiting, a middle-aged woman came in.

'Are you Ross James Collins?'

'Yes.'

'And who's representing you?'

Ross's lawyer stepped forwards. 'I am.'

'Oh, hello Mr Luscombe. I didn't see you there.'

'Hello Mrs Miller.'

'What's your religion, Mr Collins? For the oath.'

'Oh, erm, Church of England I suppose.'

'Very well. I'll come back and take you to your seats in about five minutes.'

Ross turned to his solicitor. 'I thought you said I wouldn't have to give evidence today?'

'You won't. Don't worry.'

It was another 20 minutes before the official came back for them. She led them into the courtroom and to some seats near the back. The sergeant who had interrogated Ross was already there, as were some other official-looking people. He also spotted the driver of the Ford Transit, who was wearing a suit that was too small for him. He was sitting next to a quite elderly woman.

Mrs Miller pointed to the witness chair and told Ross that if he was called, he should go there and stand to take the oath. His solicitor would go with him to advise him, though he wouldn't be allowed to answer questions on his behalf.

She went off and then reappeared, this time with a tall man in his 40s plus an elderly couple and a woman in her late 20s. The tall man looked right at Ross, who broke eye contact and looked down.

He was Lizzie Johnson's husband. Ross had seen his picture on Facebook.

After a moment, Mrs Miller said 'All rise for the coroner.'

They stood up and a rather impressive-looking man in a grey suit appeared. He sat down and Mrs Miller invited the others to do likewise.

'I would like to declare open the inquest into the tragic death of Mrs Elizabeth Marjorie Johnson,' the coroner said. 'The purpose of this inquest is to establish four things: to confirm who has died and when she died, and to establish how she died and the circumstances that led to her death. Perhaps we should start by identifying the interested parties in this case. I understand that the police have investigated it. Would the investigating officer please make himself known to the court?'

The sergeant stood up. 'I'm Sergeant Perry Peters of the Accident Investigation Unit of the Sussex Constabulary. I'm investigating officer in this case.'

'Thank you. And I understand that Mrs Johnson's next of kin is here today. Could you identify yourself to the court, please?'

Lizzie Johnson's husband stood up. 'My name's Anthony Johnson, sir.'

'Thank you, Mr Johnson. May I offer you my deepest condolences?'

'Thank you, sir.'

'Do you have legal representation, Mr Johnson?'

'Yes, sir.'

Mr Johnson's young solicitor stood up and introduced herself.

The coroner then looked at Ross and the driver of the Ford Transit.

'Mrs Johnson was involved in a road traffic accident on the day of her death. If the drivers of the other vehicles involved in that accident are present here today, could they perhaps identify themselves to the court?'

He gestured towards the driver of the Transit van, who stood up.

'My name's Nicholas Demant. I was driving the Ford Transit van.'

'Do you have legal representation, Mr Demant?'

His elderly solicitor stood up and identified herself.

The coroner nodded at Ross, who stood up, quivering, and said in a shaky voice, 'Erm, my name's Ross Collins. I was the driver of the Nissan Micra.'

'Do you have legal representation, Mr Collins?'

'Yes, sir.'

Ross's solicitor, raised a hand, stood up and said his name.

The coroner turned to the police officer. 'Sergeant Peters, I'd be grateful if you could take the stand.'

He went to the witness chair and swore on the Bible to tell the truth, the whole truth and nothing but the truth.

'Sit down, please. Now, Sergeant Peters, for the record, you are the investigating officer in the case of Mrs Elizabeth Marjorie Johnson, are you not?'

'Yes, sir.'

'And you were present when Mr Anthony Johnson identified Mrs Johnson's body. Is that correct?'

'Yes, sir. He identified the body as that of his wife, Mrs Elizabeth Marjorie Johnson.'

'And could you tell the court when this occurred?'

'Approximately seven forty-five on the evening of Wednesday the eleventh of April, twenty-eighteen.'

'Thank you. The post-mortem was carried out on Friday the thirteenth of April. Is that correct?'

'Yes, sir. We received the report from you on Monday the sixteenth.'

'And you had no objection to my releasing Mrs Johnson's body for burial on Wednesday the eighteenth of April?'

'That's correct, sir.'

'Have you now completed your investigation into Mrs Johnson's death?'

'Yes, sir. We believe that we've built up a good picture of what happened.'

'Are any prosecutions pending?'

'We sent a report to the DPP on the twenty-sixth of April, but we haven't yet received a reply.'

'Do you know when you'll receive a reply?'

'I hope by the end of this month, sir.'

'Thank you very much, Sergeant Peters.' The coroner turned to Mr Johnson's solicitor. 'Do you have any questions for Sergeant Peters?'

She stood up. 'No, sir.'

He turned to the elderly solicitor, who stood up to say that she had no questions.

'Mr Luscombe? Do you have any questions for Sergeant Peters?'

'No thank you, sir.'

'Very well. Thank you very much, Sergeant Peters. You may stand down.'

Once the policeman was out of the way, the coroner turned to Mr Johnson's lawyer. 'Does Mr Johnson wish to take the stand?'

She stood up once more to answer. 'No, sir.'

The same question to the van driver's solicitor elicited the same response.

'Does Mr Collins wish to take the stand?'

'Not at this stage, sir.'

And then the question Ross had been dreading, directed at Mr Johnson's lawyer: 'Do you have any questions for Mr Demant or Mr Collins?'

'No, sir. Not at this stage.'

'In that case,' said the coroner, 'I'm minded to adjourn the inquest until such time as the Director of Public Prosecutions has decided whether anyone should face charges over this matter and any court cases have been concluded.'

And that, more or less, was that. Mrs Miller intervened to keep Ross and his parents in the courtroom until the Johnson family were safely out of the way.

153

That was fine by Ross. He had no desire to bump into Mr Johnson in the corridor or anywhere else.

*

When he got home, Ross rushed upstairs to the bathroom and vomited the contents of his stomach into the toilet. It was the first time he had puked up sober for years, and it surprised him just how unpleasant it was. He flushed the toilet, rinsed his mouth with water from the tap and retreated to his bedroom.

A message pinged on his mobile.

Sofie:	How was the inquest?
Ross:	😫
	Actually nothing much happened like my lawyer said
Sofie:	Was her husband there?
Ross:	Yeah and her parents
Sofie:	That sounds tough
	Do you fancy doing something this afternoon?
Ross:	Nah too wound up CU when we cycle down
Sofie:	B says sorry she hasn't sent her email yet
Ross:	Wot email
Sofie:	About the resurrection. I told you last night.
Ross:	Oh yeah I forgot about that I had a lot on my mind

Ross said nothing to Sofie, but he wasn't sure he would read Bee's email when it came. He wasn't convinced that it would be of any help to him.

Soon after, his mother knocked on the door and came in with a glass of cold water.

'You okay?'

Ross sipped the water and shrugged.

'Do you want to call the hotel and tell them you're not well enough to work tonight?'

Ross shook his head. 'I like working. It's the only time I don't think about it. I'm just too busy.'

His mother nodded. 'What about the Alpha Course? Is that helping?'

'I don't know. Sometimes I think yes, and other times I wonder if I'm wasting my time. The last session was quite good, actually. It was about how we can find forgiveness through Jesus.'

'That's good.'

'Why do you say that? You're not a Christian.'

'I don't care whether you become a Christian or not. I just want you to find a way through this.'

They were silent for a moment.

'Do you mind if I ask, are you and Sofie…?'

'What? Going out?'

154

'Yes.'

'No. We're just friends.'

'You've been spending a lot of time with her.'

'Yeah. She's not leading me astray or anything. Why are you and Zoe so against her?'

'I'm sworn to secrecy.'

'What? So you can slag her off generally but not give me any details?'

'Afraid so.'

'She's not had it easy, you know. Her mum died and her dad took to the bottle.'

'You told me.'

'She had a really hard time, but her step-mother's really kind to her, and I think she's in a good place now.'

'You think so?'

'Yes.'

'I hope so, for your sake.'

'What's that supposed to mean?'

His mother didn't reply.

Eventually, Ross said, 'She's making me come out of hiding on Saturday.'

'How's that?'

'She made me promise to go to Tara Wright's birthday party.'

'That's good.'

'I'm dreading it.'

Chapter Twenty-Four

Bee's email about the resurrection didn't arrive until late Friday morning. Sofie messaged Ross as soon as it arrived, but he didn't feel like reading it. He knew what it would say, that the resurrection never really happened and it was just *mythos*. He ignored it that evening and didn't read it between shifts on Saturday. He sensed that Sofie was quite cross with him when he turned up for the dinner shift without having even opened the email.

'You're being very naughty, not doing your homework.'

'I just didn't feel like it.'

'I want to talk about it with someone.'

'I'll try and do it tomorrow.'

They had left their bikes at home that evening, since as soon as work was over, they had to walk to the town centre for a bus that would take them to Tara Wright's 18th birthday party. They got off two stops after the Tesco roundabout and walked 10 minutes to Tara's house. When they arrived, the party was in full swing.

Ross knew exactly what would happen next.

'Hey Ross.'

'Good to see you, mate.'

'Long time no see.'

'Where've you been?'

'How you keeping?'

The best he could manage was 'Hi.'

After a few minutes, he retreated to the kitchen to get some beer for himself and a can of diet coke for Sofie. His cousin Dani joined him.

'Good to see you out and about, Ross.'

'Yeah.'

'Everyone thinks you and Sofie are...'

'Well, we're not. We're just friends.'

'Are you sure that's all Sofie wants?'

'What do you mean?'

'I'm just asking.'

'Look, she doesn't fancy me. She said I'm not her type.'

'Did she?'

'Yes.'

'Oh.'

The living room was getting crowded, with music not quite loud enough to make the neighbours come round and complain. The big question everyone who spoke to Ross wanted to know was how much trouble he was in.

'Well, I'm waiting to see if I get charged with anything. My lawyer says if I get done for driving without due care and attention, I'll probably just get fined and lose my licence.'

'That would be so unfair,' one girl said. 'It's not as if it was your fault.'

'Well, actually it was my fault.'

That shut everyone up for a moment.

One of the boys said, 'So you won't get sent down, then?'

'Theoretically, I could, but my lawyer says it won't happen. He says I'll just get community service.'

Some people were interested to hear about the Alpha Course, even more so when they told them about Omega Bee.

'So, which do you like best?' one friend asked, 'Alpha or Omega?'

'I like both,' said Sofie. 'It's really good to get both points of view.'

'What about you, Ross?'

'I don't know. Sometimes I find it confusing.'

As more guests arrived, the conversation repeated itself again and again.

'Hi, long time no see.'

'Have you been charged yet?'

'I hear you might get sent down.'

Ross was surprised at how far news of his flirtation with the God squad had got. And there was another question that he was asked twice more.

'Are you and Sofie...?'

His answer that they were just good friends was met with scepticism, and one girl told Ross that he was being heartless and unfeeling.

His friend Natalie turned up quite late. She greeted him with a hug, took him to one side and asked how he was coping with the aftermath of the accident. Next time he saw her, she was sitting on the stairs deep in conversation with a boy called Declan, who Ross knew from one of the college football teams.

Mollie, his ex-girlfriend, was there. She hadn't so much as looked at him since the day she dumped him, but tonight she came up to him as he was getting his fourth can of beer from the fridge.

'Hiya.'

'Hi.'

'Really sorry to hear about your accident.'

'Yeah.'

'I hear you're having a hard time.'

He nodded. 'You could say that.'

'You're not a bad person, Ross. Don't be too hard on yourself.'

'Thanks, Mollie. That means a lot coming from you.'

She smiled and gave him a quick hug before hurriedly filling up her wine glass and heading for the living room.

Ross decided to give Mollie a wide berth, so he went into the dining room, which was just as crowded. There he spotted his gay history classmate Mark, who introduced him to his boyfriend Dennis (they were the only out gay couple at the party). Ross knew Dennis from college but had never spoken to him.

157

'I hear you're God squad now,' said Mark.

'I wouldn't go that far. I'm attending the Alpha Course, but they haven't converted me yet.'

'Well, just make sure you don't turn into one of those dreadful homophobic evangelicals.'

'Don't worry about that,' said Ross. He told them about Bee and her Omega Course.

'This Bee sounds a bit more like it,' said Mark. 'Make sure she keeps you on the straight and narrow.'

'I think straight and narrow's the wrong metaphor,' said Dennis. 'More like bent and narrow.'

They all laughed.

Tara, the birthday girl, was very drunk. She had been among those who had headed to the bottom of the garden soon after Ross arrived to smoke a bit of weed. She pinned Ross to the wall by the stairs and gave him the same interrogation as all the others.

Her final question was, 'So, you going out with Sofie now?'

'No, we're just friends.'

'That's good, because in that case she won't mind if you give me a birthday kiss.'

Tara was very fanciable, and normally Ross would have jumped at the chance to wrap himself round her, but he felt very uncomfortable as she began to wrap herself around him. And she stank of tobacco and weed. But all that ceased to matter when their lips and tongues met.

Whoa that was good.

She broke off the kiss and gave him a little peck on the lips.

'Aren't you going to wish me a happy birthday?'

'Happy birthday, Tara.'

'Why, thank you, Ross.'

As she detached herself from him, Ross spotted Sofie looking at him from the living room. She broke off eye contact and turned and walked away in evident disgust. He wanted to follow her but thought he had better wait until his body had calmed down a little.

Two friends from his football team came up to him: 'Hey Ross! Where've you been? Haven't seen you for ages.'

Conversations eventually moved on from his accident and the Alpha Course to more normal topics: who was going out with who, how they thought their exams had gone, the World Cup and the whole Brexit shambles. Raj got into a passionate debate with two Brexiteers. Ross preferred to make them all laugh with tales of his Brexit fanatic of a boss whose staff nearly all came from eastern Europe.

By 11 o'clock, Ross was slumped in the corner of the living room between the sofa and an armchair, watching others dance. The sociability and fun stages of drunkenness were long behind him, and he was now in the depressed-and-wondering-if-he-was-going-to-throw-up phase.

He needed some fresh air, so he went through the kitchen into the back garden. There were half a dozen people outside, smoking cigarettes of varying degrees of legality.

'All right, Ross?'

'Yeah.'

He wandered down to the end of the garden, where he spotted a couple who very definitely needed to get a room. He was astonished when he realised they were Natalie and Declan.

Unable to stay where he was but unwilling to go back to the party, he unbolted the gate and went through it.

*

He found himself in an alleyway just wide enough for a car. He turned right and walked as far as the road, then headed left towards the seafront. The chill night air had woken him up a little, but it had done nothing to lift his mood. By the time he got to the beach, Lizzie Johnson and the accident had once more taken control.

He jumped from the promenade to the shingle beach below and instantly fell over. He swore, picked himself up and staggered to a point just beyond the reach of the waves. The tide was right in, and he sat down, confident that he wouldn't get wet if he fell asleep.

He thought it would be easy to dive in and swim out until he was exhausted. But no, it would be cold and horrible, probably painful too, when he drowned. And what if he swam out and changed his mind, decided he didn't want to die after all, and then was too exhausted to make it back? That would be absolutely terrifying, and a stupid way to die.

Far better to steal his father's car and drive up to Beachy Head. He once saw a thing on TV that said men and women often do it differently. Women tend to sit by the edge and then push themselves off, while men are more likely to take a run up and leap off. And then it would be quick. No more than five seconds.

He closed his eyes and saw the cliff edge, inviting him, calling out to him, offering to ease his pain.

He shook his head.

No.

No.

He had no right to do that. He had to find a way through. He had to take whatever was coming to him. And he had to survive it, get past it and work out how to get on with his life.

But he didn't know how.

Could the Alpha Course really help? And if it could, was it time to stop reading Bee's emails? He wished that he could understand *mythos*, but he couldn't get past the idea that something is either true or false and there is no in-between.

He sat for a long time, watching the lapping of the waves. Then he heard a voice calling his name.

'Ross! Ross!'

It was Sofie. She hadn't spoken to him since she caught him kissing Tara. He knew she must have been upset with him, more than upset if her feelings were what everyone else seemed to think they were.

But there she was, out looking for him.

He stood up and swayed for a moment.

He waved to her. 'Sofie!'

She spotted him and waved back. As she walked up to him, she took out her mobile and called someone. Ross thought he could make out what she said.

'It's okay. I've found him...Yeah, no worries. Thanks for your help. Can you let Nat and Declan know? I haven't got their numbers.'

'Who was that?' Ross asked as she approached.

'Just Dani and Raj. We was a bit worried about you.'

Ross shook his head. 'I'm not going to top myself.'

'I'm pleased to hear it. You okay?'

'You know how it is. I'm okay for a while and then I'm not.'

She stepped forwards and the two of them embraced.

He wanted to kiss her, but somehow it didn't seem right. He didn't feel anything sexual in her embrace, just warmth, comfort and affection.

They sat down on the shingle, shoulder to shoulder.

After a moment, Ross said, 'Did you see Natalie got off with Declan?'

'Yeah, that was a surprise. Raj was worried you'd be upset about it.'

'Not in the least.'

'She's fancied you for a long time.'

'I know.'

'So why didn't you ask her out? You like her, right? She's really pretty, much prettier than me.'

'No, she isn't.'

'Yes, she is.'

'No.'

'You're very sweet, Ross, but you're a terrible liar.'

Ross laughed. 'Well, there's nothing I can say now, is there?'

'No. So just tell me why you never asked her out.'

Ross was silent for a moment. 'When I went out with Mollie, I was never in love with her. But she was in love with me. I was taking advantage of her. I wanted to have a girlfriend. I wanted to have sex. So that's why I went out with her. I felt really guilty about using her, so I promised myself my next girlfriend would be somebody I really loved.'

'God, you are a sweetie.' After a moment, she added, 'Do you want to know what Mollie said about you?'

'What?'

'She told everyone she knew you never loved her, but she also knew you'd never forget her because she took your virginity.'

'What? Did she really say that?'

'Yes.'

'To everyone?'

'Well, to all the girls. Us girls talk about more important things than football, you know.'

Ross laughed.

'Haven't you ever been in love?' Sofie asked.

'Only once, a long time ago.'

'Who was she?'

'I went on a French exchange when I was about fourteen. There was this French girl, Sylvie, and I fell in love with her.'

He stopped speaking.

Sofie nudged him. 'And?'

He gave a little laugh. 'It was the full package. You know, weak at the knees, heart pounding, tongue-tied. And then she did the worst thing she could possibly do.'

'What's that?'

'She said,' Ross put on a French accent, '"I just want us to be friends."'

Sofie laughed. 'Were you heartbroken?'

'Totally devastated.'

'You going to stalk her when you have your year in France?'

Ross laughed. 'Maybe not.'

'Never fallen in love since?'

'No. I mean, I fancy loads of girls, but I haven't fallen in love like that, no. What about you?'

'I fell in love with a complete bastard. Nothing funny there.'

They sat in silence for a long time. It was Ross who spoke next.

'Can I ask you a question?'

'What?'

'It's a bit delicate.'

'Go on then.'

'My aunt Zoe, Dani's mum, she's worried that you might lead Dani astray. How come?'

'Who told you that?'

'My mum. Zoe's her sister.'

It was a long time before Sofie answered.

'When I was fifteen, I went off the rails. I mean, I was no angel anyway, but boy did I go off the rails. I think what was behind it was Kate and my dad, right, their relationship was falling apart. I could see they were going to split up, and I was terrified I was going to lose my whole family, Kate and her little kids, who I love, and be stuck with my useless dad.'

'I started missing school and…I'm not proud of it, right. I caused a lot of problems for some teachers and some of the other girls. One girl in particular, I was really horrible to her. And outside school, you name it, I did it. I was hanging around with my sister. She's four years older than me and she's got her own place. I spent a lot of time in Ziggy's.'

'Ziggy's? How did you get in?'

'My sister was going out with one of the bouncers, so she could get me in. Once you're in, they don't care. I did a lot of drinking. Not just drinking. I was smoking weed, doing coke, the works. I was self-harming. Do you want to see my scars?'

She took out her mobile and shone its torch on the inside of her left elbow. Ross looked and made out a dozen or so short, pink scars, all packed together.

'Wow. I'd never noticed.'

'No. It's mostly faded away.'

'You know, before the accident, I thought people who self-harmed were stupid. Now I understand exactly why people do it.'

'You haven't done it?'

'No.'

'Well don't start. It is bloody stupid. When I'm eighteen, I'm going to get a tattoo along here.' She ran her finger along her left arm, from elbow to wrist. 'It's going to be in beautiful cursive writing, and it'll say, "Whatever doesn't kill you…" Do you know that quote?'

'No.'

'Whatever doesn't kill you makes you stronger.'

'Cool.'

'Yeah.' After a moment, she said, 'Anyway, where was I?'

'Self-harming.'

'Oh, yeah. Kate and my dad, right, they were so busy quarrelling they didn't notice what I was up to. And then I got pregnant.'

'What? At fifteen?'

'I was sixteen by then. It was Kate who noticed. I should call her my mum, innit? It was her what emptied the bin in the bathroom, and she was like: "You haven't had your period. Are you pregnant?" And then, straight away, "You need an abortion." And she sorted it.'

'Wow.'

'Yeah, wow.'

'Was it very traumatic?'

'I don't know if that's the right word. It was a shock. Bloody hell, it was a shock. I'm not one of those people who thinks having an abortion is murdering a baby. I mean, it was about the size of a raisin. But it's not nothing, is it? Sometimes I look at little babies and think…'

'Do you regret it, the abortion?'

'No way. Not in the least. I regret getting myself in a situation where I needed one. And I'm so grateful to Kate for sorting it. Anyway, me and her did a lot of talking. She said the only reason she hadn't thrown my dad out was she didn't want to lose me.'

She stopped speaking and looked away from Ross. After a moment, she wiped tears from her eyes. Ross put his arm round her shoulders and pulled her towards him. They sat with their heads touching.

He wanted to wrap her up and keep her safe. She had lost her mother when she was nine years old, the same as Lizzie Johnson's daughter. Oh God, that was so terrible, so sad. What was her name, that poor little girl? He couldn't remember. Bloody hell. He had killed her mother but he couldn't even remember her name.

Sofie detached herself from Ross and took a tissue from her bag to blow her nose.

'When we changed from school to college,' she said, 'it was just what I needed. It was like a chance to reinvent myself, start again. But I was still screwed up. That's why I had counselling with Kitty. She really is good. You should try her when college opens again.'

'I did. It didn't work for me.'

'So, what will work for you?'

'I'm hoping the Alpha Course will. Does Dani know about your abortion and all that?'

'Yeah, I told her everything.'

'You know what you should do?'

'What?'

'Get Dani to tell her mum about you.'

Sofie burst out laughing. 'What? No way. You think hearing about snorting cocaine and having an abortion will make her like me?'

'She probably knows something about the bad stuff. She needs to know why you went off the rails.'

Sofie said nothing.

'Look, Sofie, you didn't go off the rails because you were stupid. You're not a bad person, are you? From where I'm sitting, you're one of the nicest people I know. You were in a bad place through no fault of your own, and like you said, you've come through it.'

'Thank you, Ross. You really are very sweet.'

'So maybe tell Dani to give her mum some edited highlights.'

'Maybe. I'll think about it.' She glanced at her phone to check the time. 'It's very late. I think we should call it a night.'

'Yeah, the party's probably finished anyway. Good job there's no work tomorrow.'

'And no waking me up early,' said Sofie.

'Promise.'

'Do you want to get a taxi?'

'Nah, let's walk. We'd have to wait ages for a taxi anyway, this time on a Saturday.'

They had a long way to go, made longer by the fact that Ross couldn't walk straight. Sofie put her arm around his waist to steady him, and he put his arm on her shoulder. They made their way along the seafront to the pier, where they cut through the town centre and headed up the hill to Old Town.

It was a long time before either of them spoke.

'Everyone thinks we're going out,' Ross said at length.

'I know.'

'You've been so good to me, Sofie. I wouldn't be able to get through this without you.'

She gave him a squeeze with her arm. 'That's what friends are for.'

Ross felt her answer eliminated the need for his next question. In a sense, he was relieved. It was her friendship he needed now, and somehow, he didn't feel he deserved the happiness that falling in love would bring.

They didn't speak much as they staggered home, though they laughed a lot as Sofie struggled to keep him on his feet.

Sofie wanted to take him to his house, but he insisted on escorting her home. They stood by her garden gate. Ross wrapped his arms around her and they embraced again, staying like that for a long time.

'Are you going to be all right walking home on your own?'

'Yeah. I've sobered up a bit now. Thanks for tonight.'

'Thanks for listening to me.'

'Shall we meet up tomorrow?'

He felt her head nod against his chest. 'I'll message you.'

'Make it afternoon. I don't think I'll be around in the morning.'

Chapter Twenty-Five

Sunday belonged to his hangover: his head, his stomach and his mouth, but most of all his head. He woke up at 6:30, went to the loo and then headed for the kitchen, where he drank two large glasses of water. Once it hit his stomach, the water seemed to churn up all the alcohol and make him feel drunk again. He went back to bed but couldn't sleep, so he decided to make himself some beans on toast, which he was then unable to finish. He curled up on the sofa in front of the TV, where he went back to sleep.

His father woke him up when he came downstairs to make breakfast.

'Thought your generation didn't drink.'

'Ha, ha.'

'Coffee?'

'Yes please.'

It only made Ross feel worse.

'Looks like you had a good night last night.'

'Yeah, not bad.'

'You sounded like a herd of wildebeest when you got home.'

'Did I? Sorry about that.'

'No worries. That's what being seventeen's all about. In my day, we could get away with drinking in pubs.

'Not any more.'

Ross finished his coffee and went back to bed. It took him ages to get back to sleep, and he didn't wake up again until almost midday. He went into the bathroom and confronted himself in the mirror: pale skin, bloodshot eyes, hair all over the place and a mass of stubble.

Once dressed, he checked his mobile. Sofie had messaged him:

Sofie:	Why don't you come round here? Kate's taken the little ones to the beach.
Ross:	I'll get some lunch first see you in a bit
Sofie:	OK CU later.

'You were pretty smashed last night,' Sofie said as she opened her door.

'I know. I just hope I didn't do anything stupid.'

'Don't you remember?'

'Why? What did I do?'

'A little matter of your tongue half way down Tara's throat.'

'Oh God. Don't remind me.'

'So you didn't enjoy it then?'

'Not in the slightest. And it was her tongue down my throat if you really want to know.'

Sofie laughed. 'I believe you. Thousands wouldn't. Anyway, what do you fancy doing?'

'Dunno. I need something to stop me thinking about my appointment at the cop shop on Tuesday.'

'We could read Bee's email together.'

'I thought you'd already read it.'

'I'm very happy to read it again.'

'Yes, why not?'

Sofie turned on Kate's iPad and signed into her own Gmail account.

Dear Sofie and Ross,

This feels like a university assignment. I hope you give me a good grade.

Okay, with the resurrection, we get into deep water, because this is the right at the heart of Christianity. If the resurrection is literally true, then Dominic is right and Christianity really does have something that other religions don't have. If it is not, then Christians may have a superb religious myth, but Christianity isn't necessarily superior to other religions.

Christians put forward three main kinds of evidence for the resurrection story, and I think we need to deal with them one at a time:

1. The story of Jesus' empty tomb
2. Jesus' appearances to his followers after the resurrection.
3. The contrast between the way his followers behaved after the crucifixion and later after the resurrection.

1. THE EMPTY TOMB

The empty tomb is crucial. Essentially, the story in Mark is that Joseph of Arimathea managed to get permission to have Jesus' body buried in a proper tomb rather than just dumped in a common grave for criminals. On Sunday morning, Mary Magdalene and two other women went to anoint his body. When they got to the tomb, they found that Jesus was no longer there.

This is one of the most heavily researched and keenly debated episodes in the whole of ancient history. Probably the only other event that has been so thoroughly combed over is the nativity.

There are all kinds of issues that are still subject to intense debate. One of the most important is whether crucified criminals could be buried in a tomb or whether they would be left to rot on the cross and/or thrown into a common grave. For what it is worth, I lean towards the left to rot/common grave side of the argument, but I also suspect that if somebody had been willing to give a large enough bribe to the right person, they might have found a way to get Jesus buried in a tomb.

One point which gives the story of the empty tomb credibility, by the way, is that the people who discovered it were women. In those days, women were considered unreliable witnesses, so if the early Christians were going to invent a story about an empty tomb, why on earth would they make the witnesses women? Remember the rule of the modern search for the historical Jesus: if something in the Gospels was not comfortable for the early church, it is more likely to be authentic.

So I think it is possible there was an empty tomb, so we have to try to find a way to explain where this story came from. I will list all the possible explanations I can think of below. Maybe you can think of others. I don't think we will ever know which of these explanations is correct, but we can divide them into three categories: "Possible", "Possible but not very likely" and "Yeah, right, pull the other one".

Why not categorise them for yourself as you go through the list?

Two rules of thumb as you do so – one is Occam's Razor: when confronted with different explanations, always go for the simplest one(s). Number two: extraordinary claims require extraordinary evidence.

So here are the possible explanations for the empty tomb:

1. There never was an empty tomb. Somebody made the story up, probably in order to cover up the shame of Jesus' corpse having been left on the cross to rot and then thrown into a common grave with other criminals. The stigma attached to such an end was very real, particularly for Jews, because they believed that if Jesus was left on the cross overnight after his death, he would be cursed by God (Deuteronomy 21:23). Remember that it was standard practice for Roman crucifixions for the body to be left to rot for a long time.
2. Mark's tale of the empty tomb was never meant to be taken literally. Disappearing bodies of heroes and prophets was a common trope in both Greco-Roman and Jewish myth, and it would be understood by Mark's audience as a symbolic way of saying that Jesus was now seated at the right hand of God.
3. Jesus was buried in a tomb, but when the Jewish authorities found out, they removed his body and threw it into a common grave.
4. Same reason, but this time it was the Roman authorities.
5. Jesus was buried in Joseph of Arimathea's family tomb, but when Joseph's relatives found out, they removed the body because they believed the presence of a crucified body desecrated their tomb (see Deuteronomy 21:23 above).
6. Similar to the above, but this time the owners of neighbouring tombs removed the body for the same reason.
7. Jesus was buried in a tomb, but some of his followers removed the body because they were afraid the authorities/Joseph of Arimathea's relatives/the owners of neighbouring tombs were about to remove it.
8. Jesus' followers forgot where the correct tomb was, and the so-called "empty tomb" was simply the wrong tomb. (I know I'm scraping the bottom of the barrel here, but are you seriously going to tell me that this is less likely than reason number 15?)
9. Slightly different: some of Jesus' followers removed the body in order to fake the resurrection. This allegation would later feature in anti-Christian propaganda.

10. Jesus was still alive when he was taken down from the cross.
11. A variation on the theme: Jesus faked his death. (I put these last two in the "Yeah, right, pull the other one" category, but some scholars who should know better seem to take them seriously.)
12. The crucifixion never happened. It was an illusion or someone else was crucified in place of Jesus (this is the Moslem explanation).
13. Aliens came down in a flying saucer and nicked the body.
14. It was a case of spontaneous combustion.
15. Jesus was dead when he was buried, but he came back to life, got up and left.

If you apply Occam's Razor, then surely explanation number 15 has to fall into the "Yeah, right, pull the other one" category. The only thing that can rescue it would be if there was extraordinary evidence to back it up. Conservative Christians say there is; I say there isn't, as you'll see below.

In my view, the explanations that make it into the "Possible" category are numbers 1 to 6. I'd say 7 and 8 are possible but not very likely, and none of the other explanations are credible. And I would also say that this is as near to the historical truth about the empty tomb as we are ever likely to get.

Did you get the same answers?

'What do you think?' asked Sofie.
'Aliens nicked the body, definitely.'
'Ha, ha.'
'Well, she's right, isn't she? I think it's probably number one, or maybe number two.'
'Or someone moved the body.'
'Yeah,' said Ross. 'But I don't get it. How can she be a Christian if this is what she believes?'
'*Mythos* and *logos*.'
Ross shook his head. 'I really don't get that.'
'I know you don't, but she gets it. I get it too.'
'So, are you a Christian now?'
'I don't know yet. First, I want to get all the *mythos* from Dominic and all the *logos* from Bee and see how it works for me.'
Ross frowned. 'I kind of need it to be either true or not true. When I listen to Dominic, sometimes I think, "Yes, this is good," and sometimes…' He shook his head.
'What about what Bee says?'
'Well, she's right, isn't she? But I don't understand how she can believe these things and still be a Christian.'
'Maybe that's because you've got this caricature in your head of what Christianity is. Maybe it's a lot more complex than you think.'
Ross nodded. 'Yeah, maybe.'
'Are you ready for the next bit?'
'Nah.'

'Why not?'

Ross put on a sad face and pointed to his head.

Sofie laughed. 'Serves you right.'

'Thank you very much.'

'Maybe you caught something nasty from that Tara.'

Ross grinned.

'Do you want some paracetamol?'

'No, better not. I had some just before I came out. Look, why don't you just tell me what's in the next bit of the email?'

'Read it yourself, you lazy git.'

'Oh, come on, pretty please.' He put on the saddest of puppy faces. 'Can't you see how much I'm suffering?'

She laughed. 'Oh, all right then. It's really complex.'

'Just a summary.'

Sofie scrolled down on the iPad: 'Okay, so, she looks at what St Paul says in the Bible and the Greek word he uses. She says this doesn't mean people actually saw Jesus, just that he appeared to them.'

'Isn't that the same thing?'

Sofie shook her head. 'It could be a voice or just a general sense of his presence.'

'Oh, right.'

She scrolled further: 'Then there's this long list of people having visions. Some were in the Bible, and she wrote about Islam and loads of different religions, and then people like Joan of Arc. She's so knowledgeable, Bee, don't you think?'

'I bet she just looked on Wikipedia.'

'Oh piss off. I really admire her. If I was a lesbian, I'd fall in love with her.'

'Are you trying to tell me something, Sofie?'

'No!'

'Are you sure?'

She went to hit him, but he evaded her.

'Is this why you don't fancy me?'

She rolled her eyes. 'You're never going to let me forget that, are you?'

'No.'

They looked at each other and grinned.

'Anyway, then she says, "How do you know which of these visions are genuine and which aren't?" She says it's no good saying, "My God's better than your God: the visions in my religion are genuine and all the others are fake." Much better to say they're all hallucinations.'

'Maybe they're all genuine.'

Sofie snorted. 'Yeah, right. Pull the other one.'

Ross shrugged. 'It's a possibility.'

'She mentioned one guy, right, God appeared to him and told him not to eat so much. Do you really think something like that's genuine, or maybe he's just a religious nutcase?'

Ross raised his hands in mock surrender.

Sofie thought for a moment and scrolled further down.

'Oh yeah. She wrote about trances, which cause hallucinations. And how do you cause a trance? Prayer, meditation, chanting, music.'

'Or magic mushrooms.'

'Yeah, she talked about drugs. Then at the end, she comes back to the Bible and she says people's stories of hallucinations of Jesus got mashed up with the story of the empty tomb, and that's how we got the *mythos* of the resurrection.'[2]

'You should be a teacher.'

Sofie burst out laughing. 'That would be ironic: little horror in secondary school ends up being a teacher.'

'You'd be good.'

'Flattery will get you nowhere. I'm not summarising part three for you. Read it yourself.'

'I will. Promise. But not today.'

'So, what do you fancy doing?'

'Have you got FIFA or anything like that?'

'We've got an old Nintendo. It's got Super Mario.'

'Wow. I haven't played that for ages.'

'So, you're too hungover to read an email but not too hungover to play Super Mario?'

'Yep.'

For a moment, Sofie looked very stern. Then she smiled. 'Come on then.'

She led him into the living room. She was wearing yoga pants, which enabled Ross to admire her backside as she fished the Nintendo out from behind the TV and plugged it in. He liked her back and shoulders too, and the way a little bit of neck peeped out from under her bob. He thought how nice it would be to snuggle up behind her, kiss that neck and bring his hands up to caress her ample breasts.

And then he told himself not to be stupid. This was his friend, his very good friend. And she had said in as many words that she didn't fancy him. But just at that moment, he found himself wishing that she did.

---

[2] For the reader who is interested, the second part of Bee's email is included as Appendix Two on page 372.

Chapter Twenty-Six

When Ross woke up on Monday, his nerves were frayed. One more day until he found out what he was going to be charged with. Thank God for his job, which kept him busy and provided a welcome distraction. But he knew he would have to deal with Sid before the evening shift. On Saturday, Brighton had barely managed a draw against Birmingham, another team from a lower league. He dearly wished Brighton could actually win a game or two.

That would get Sid off his back.

On Tuesday morning, both of Ross's parents went to the police station with him. When his solicitor came, a constable showed them into a small interview room. The constable had to bring in two extra chairs so that they could all sit, leaving another chair for the more senior officer who would join them. Ross was happy that they were out of the reception area. He had enough to worry about without the fear that Nick might walk past and recognise him.

The solicitor leaned forwards and looked at Ross. 'It looks like you're going to be charged today. The question is, will it be careless driving or causing death by careless driving? After they charge you, they'll ask if you'd like to make a statement under caution. All you need to do is say that you've already made a statement under caution on the twelfth of April – don't worry if you forget the date – and you have nothing to add at this stage.'

'Okay.'

Ross could almost hear his heart pumping; his hands were sweaty and his mouth was dry.

After a wait that seemed to go on for ever, the custody officer Ross had met on the day of his arrest came in.

Ross stood up.

'Hello,' said the custody officer. 'Please sit down.'

He sat at the desk, placing a file of papers on the desk in front of him.

'Can I just confirm your identity? What's your full name?'

'Date of birth?'

'Address?'

'And postcode?'

'Do you have any ID?'

'I've got a debit card and my student card from college.'

'Can I just check your student card? Thank you.'

He looked at Ross's parents. 'Could you say who you are?'

'We're his parents,' said Ross's father.

'Could I have your full names?'

'And is it the same address?'

'And Mr Luscombe, presumably you're representing Ross?'

'Yes.'

'Can you remind me – which firm are you?'

'Myers and Pickford.'

'Ah, yes.'

The preliminaries completed, the custody officer turned to Ross.

'Okay, Ross, I'm going to read out the charge…Ross James Collins, you are charged with causing death by careless driving, under Section 2B of the Road Traffic Act, 1988. The charge is that on the eleventh of April twenty-eighteen, by attempting to overtake a car without first looking in your rear mirror, you caused the accident in which Mrs Elizabeth Marjorie Johnson died. Do you understand what I'm saying?'

'Yes.'

'Do you want to say anything about the charge that was just read to you? If you keep quiet now about any fact or matter in your defence and you reveal this fact or matter in your defence only at your trial, the judge may be less likely to believe you. This may have a bad effect on your case in court. Therefore, it may be better for you to mention such fact or matter now. If you wish to do so, what you say will be written down, read back to you for any mistakes to be corrected and then signed by you.'

Ross looked at his solicitor. 'I can't remember what I'm supposed to say.'

Mr Luscombe spoke for him: 'My client has already made a statement under caution on the twelfth of April. He doesn't wish to add anything at this stage.'

'That's fine. Okay, Ross, I'm giving you unconditional police bail. That means you are free to go, with no restrictions. You are to attend the Youth Court on Monday the seventeenth of September, twenty-eighteen. The court will inform you of the exact time of your hearing, and they will let you know if there are any delays. Do you understand?'

'Yes.'

'Okay. Now I'm going to give you this charge sheet, which has details of the charges against you. Your solicitor will go through it with you.'

He handed Ross a sheet of paper and asked Ross to sign that he had heard and understood the charges against him. His solicitor countersigned as an appropriate adult.

The custody officer then left Ross with his parents and his solicitor.

They were silent.

The solicitor read the charge sheet and passed it to Ross's parents, who read it. Ross's mother passed it to him. He tried to read it but gave up after the first paragraph.

'You okay, hon?' his mother asked.

Ross shrugged. 'Well, it's not unexpected, is it?'

'No, I'm afraid not,' said his solicitor. 'First thing to say is that, although in theory the maximum sentence is five years, that simply isn't going to happen in your case. There are so many mitigating circumstances: your age, your inexperience and the way you behaved after the accident. If you're found guilty, you'll almost certainly lose your licence for two years, and you'll have to take your test again when you get it back. You'll probably be fined, and you'll probably have a community service order, maybe fifty hours or something like that.'

Ross nodded. He had heard all this before.

'If you're found guilty, you'll have a criminal record, but once your driving disqualification is over, it will count as spent, so you won't have to tell potential employers or landlords about it. It won't appear on standard criminal record checks but will appear on enhanced, I'm afraid.'

Ross nodded.

'Now,' said the solicitor, 'we're going to have to give careful consideration about whether you're going to plead guilty or not guilty.'

'I'm pleading guilty.'

'Perhaps. We have to think about it carefully.'

'I am guilty,' said Ross, 'so I'm going to plead guilty.'

'Hold on,' said Ross's father. 'Let's just hear what Mr Luscombe has to say.'

Ross looked at his solicitor. 'I know it's your job to get me off, and that's fine. But I have to live with what I did. I didn't look in my mirror, and because of that, a woman's dead. Two children have lost their mother, a man's lost his wife and two old people have lost their daughter. Can you imagine how awful that is for them? I have to live with that, and part of that is I have to put my hands up, admit what I did and face the consequences. That's what I intend to do.'

Everyone was silent for a moment.

'All right,' said the solicitor. 'We'll discuss it again nearer the time.'

*

They met at the bus stop. Sofie asked him how he was feeling.

'Has it ever happened to you?' said Ross. 'The thing you've been dreading finally happens. And then, when it does, and you're still standing, you actually feel better than before. That's how I feel now.'

'That's good.'

'So, what do you think we're in for tonight? More fireworks between Dominic and Bee?'

'Do you think Bee'll be there?' said Sofie. 'She only promised her mum she'd go to three sessions.'

'Hmm. We shall see. And I wonder if Tom's still got his ponytail.'

*

The first thing Bee noticed was Tom Bradshaw's short back and sides. His ponytail was no more. She thought she had better say something, so she walked up to him, at the far end of the hall, where he was speaking with Rodney and an elderly woman from his table.

'Tom? Have you got a minute?'

'Hi, Bee.'

They stepped to one side.

'I just want to say I'm really sorry, what I said last week. I didn't mean to have a go at you.'

'Don't worry about it. You were right. I hadn't realised.'

'I'm sorry if I embarrassed you.'

'It's all right, Bee. I was a bit surprised, but I'm not angry at all.'

'You're very kind. Thank you.'

'It's my pleasure. Thank you for pointing it out to me.'

Bee retreated to where Sofie and Ross were chatting with Nick.

'You okay?' Sofie asked.

'Yeah.'

'Was he all right about it?'

'Yeah. He said he was grateful to me for pointing it out.'

'Well, for my part,' said Nick, 'I'm still living in sin.'

They all laughed.

*

After dinner, when Tom got his guitar out, he said, 'As you can see, I've had a word with my manager in the sky, and we've decided that I need to change my image.'

Everyone laughed.

'Same old songs, mind you.'

The Lord's my shepherd, I'll not want;
He makes me down to lie
In pastures green; he leadeth me
The quiet waters by

This week's happy-clappy song was surprisingly sombre. In fact, the tune was slow, nobody clapped and the whole thing seemed rather mournful. Ross wondered if it reflected Tom's mood now that the ponytail that must have defined him for most of his adult life had been chopped off.

Oh Lord we are all sinners
In our hearts and in our deeds
We're weak and we are foolish
And we forget our real needs.
We sin against our neighbours
And sin against your word
And yet you're always there for us
Our prayers are always heard.

Then Dominic began his talk: 'How can I be sure of my faith?'

He talked about himself. His parents had been very religious and had taken him to church every Sunday, but as a teenager, he had gone through a rebellious phase. He had found church boring, and he had wanted all the things that clean-living Christians seemed to shun. In particular, he was very keen to get as much drink, cigarettes and girls as he possibly could.

What he didn't realise was that Christianity isn't about going to Church and listening to boring sermons. It isn't about mouthing the words of prayers and hymns that mean nothing to you. It isn't even about being a goody-goody who doesn't get drunk, doesn't smoke and stays a virgin until he gets married.

Christianity is about your relationship with the living God, a God who loves you and wants the best for you. He quoted St Paul: '"...if anyone is in Christ, he is a new creation; the old has gone, the new has come!" This means that when you become a Christian, you become a new person. You're literally born again. Where there was despair, there's now hope. Where there was anger, there's now forgiveness. Where there was emptiness, there's now meaning.'

Dominic was in full excited preacher mode, but what he was saying had Ross transfixed.

'Someone once asked the psychoanalyst Carl Gustav Jung whether he believed in God. He answered: "I will never say I *believe* in God. I *know*." This is what it's like to be a Christian. You don't have to believe. You know. This is what it says in John's first letter: "you who believe in the name of the Son of God...may know that you have eternal life."'

Dominic broke off and calmed down. He told them about one of the great joys of his work as a vicar, conducting weddings. He spoke about the photographers who come to record these beautiful days and how they place their cameras on a tripod to keep them steady.

'So it is with our faith. Our faith rests on three pillars, just as a camera tripod rests on three legs. The first of these is the Word of God, the second is the work of Jesus and the third is the witness of the Holy Spirit.'

By 'Word of God' Dominic meant the Bible.

As far as Ross was concerned, this broke Dominic's spell. How could it do otherwise? Bee had convinced him that the Bible was the word of people, not God, and was far from infallible. Ross looked at Bee. It was impossible to tell what she was thinking. Her face was completely impassive.

She caught him looking at her and they both smiled.

He looked away and glanced at Sofie. She was leaning forwards, interested, following Dominic's every word. He guessed that she must be filtering it all through this *mythos*/*logos* distinction that he really didn't get.

Dominic seemed to go on and on about the Bible. Ross tried his best to concentrate, but he wasn't very successful, and before long, he was sinking, drowning once more in thoughts about the accident.

After a while, he noticed that Dominic was reciting a list of art galleries. This seemed such a peculiar thing to do that it captured Ross's attention pulled him back up. He was talking about a Pre-Raphaelite painting of Jesus standing at the door to our life, waiting for us to let him in. 'Jesus will always be there. But he will never force that door open. It's up to us to choose whether we want to let him into our lives.'

But once we open that door, Jesus promises he will never leave us, and Dominic quoted passages from the Bible that proved this.

And then he talked about the resurrection: 'The resurrection isn't just a reversal of Christ's defeat on the cross. It's his victory. It shows us he's alive and with us today, in all his power and glory. And it's his promise for the future. Death isn't the end; there's the glorious life to come. History isn't meaningless, it's not a cycle of the same old thing again and again. It has movement; it has direction. History is heading towards a glorious climax.'

Now Dominic was speaking louder and faster. 'One day Jesus will return, and he will establish a new heaven and a new earth. That's the promise contained in Revelation Twenty-One: One. When Jesus returns, those who live or die in Christ will be with him forever. That's Paul's promise in his First letter to the Thessalonians.

'There will be no more lamentation because there will be no more pain and no more suffering. There will be no more temptation because there will be no more sin. There will be no more hatred and there will be no more separation from loved ones. Then we will see Jesus face-to-face. This is Paul's promise in One Corinthians Thirteen: Twelve. And we will be given glorious and painless resurrection bodies – One Corinthians Fifteen.

'We will be transformed into the moral likeness of Jesus Christ himself – One John Three: Two. Heaven will be a place of intense joy and delight that goes on forever. As St Paul said: "No eye has seen, no ear has heard, no mind has conceived what God has prepared for those who love him."

'As CS Lewis put it in the *Chronicles of Narnia*: all our life on this earth with all its trials and tribulations is just the cover and the title page. With the return of Jesus Christ, we will begin at last Chapter One of the Great Story which no-one on earth has read and which goes on for ever and ever, and in which every chapter will be better than the chapter before.'

Ross frowned. He wasn't sure if he could believe this. It all sounded too good to be true. What was it Sofie said? You don't have to believe it: you just have to respond as if it's true. He shook his head. What did that even mean?

*

Bee was finding the whole thing difficult too. What had she been thinking, imagining that this kind of old-fashioned Christianity could revive her dying faith? She had never believed in the Second Coming of Christ, and she hadn't believed in the survival of the individual after death since she was a young teenager. She had always preferred the Buddhist concept of Nirvana, in which the individual soul is absorbed into the wider cosmos.

Now Dominic was back to the theme of Jesus the Redeemer, the perfect man who lived the perfect life and paid the price for all our sins. It occurred to Bee that maybe there was nothing wrong with what Dominic was doing. He was selling a metaphor, a myth, a fiction that contains the deeper truth of God's love. And how do you sell it if you don't dress it up as the truth? How are you going to convert anyone if you can only say, 'This isn't actually true, but why don't we pretend it is and see what happens?' That was hardly going to inspire anyone.

Bee glanced at Sofie, who was sitting forwards, so attentive. She was filled with admiration for the way she had grasped the ideas of a liberal faith so quickly, the way she had been able to take the mainstream Christianity of the Alpha Course and her own semi-atheist arguments and find a middle path between them. She had been astonished when Sofie described herself as a 'little horror' at school. She should have been an ideal pupil, Bee was sure of that: bright, eager, attentive. But her childhood had been blighted by the death of her mother and the havoc it had created in her family. Thinking of it brought a lump to Bee's throat, and she was reminded of Chloe's baby and the question that had wrecked her faith: how can a loving God allow this to happen?

She glanced at Ross. He wasn't listening to Dominic. He was clearly lost in his personal crisis, whatever it was. Bee wondered if she had ruined the Alpha Course for him, if she had prevented him from finding solace in Christianity. He certainly needed to find it somewhere, and Bee worried that if he couldn't find it in religion, there was always the danger that he might find it in something destructive like a bottle or a needle.

The final part of Dominic's talk was about 'The Witness of the Spirit' – the way that God will transform our lives if we turn our backs on sin and let him in. 'Become a Christian, and you'll experience love, joy, peace, patience, kindness, goodness, faithfulness, gentleness and self-control. You'll become a better person, not overnight but over time. Your relationship with friends and family will improve, and you'll live in hope and certainty, the hope and certainty of eternal life.'

'I remember one parishioner I had when I first became a vicar, a lady in her sixties. She told me she had downed a bottle of vodka every day for the last thirty years. We prayed together every week and asked the Holy Spirit to fill her with its love. And it did. She stopped drinking, just like that. She said the Holy Spirit had taken away her pain and she no longer needed to self-medicate with vodka.

'I do a lot of work at the Galaxy Centre. Do you know it? It's in Maze Hill Road. The patients have had their lives absolutely wrecked by hard drugs: heroin, cocaine, crystal meth, you name it. My job's to help those who want Jesus to be part of their rehabilitation. And I can honestly say, the people who quit drugs and stay off – that's the key, stay off – they're the ones who let the Holy Spirit into their lives.

'There are three people who come to my church every week, I met them at the Galaxy Centre. They've never looked back since they let the Holy Spirit into their lives. I could name so many people, deeply troubled and unhappy people whose lives have been transformed by the Holy Spirit.'

Bee was sure it was all true, but she knew she could go to a mosque or a Buddhist temple or even a gathering of Scientologists and find exactly the same thing: people whose lives had improved immeasurably the moment they embraced a completely different kind of faith. And not only religion: there were others whose experience was the same after they joined Greenpeace or became a mother, a nurse, a teacher, a marathon runner, a freemason, a member of this or that political party or a season ticket holder at their local football club.

What these people found wasn't God or Jesus, but meaning, a sense of their place in the world, a feeling that they were a part of something bigger and better than just themselves. For her, religion was an excellent and generally benign way for people to find meaning in their lives. But it wasn't the only way, and it didn't suit everyone. It was, as Dominic would never admit, just good for those who liked that kind of thing.

*

The discussion around their table centred on life after death. The group seemed to be divided between a few who were sceptical about the whole idea and a majority who thought there must be something, though most weren't sure exactly what. Pat pushed the idea that we know what to expect after death because the Bible has told us.

Ross followed the discussion but didn't say anything. Neither did Bee; even when Nick tried to draw her out, she managed not to say very much: 'Put me down as a "don't know". I guess we'll all find out one day. Or maybe we won't because if there isn't any life after death, we'll never know because we'll be dead.'

This made some people laugh, but it seemed to annoy Pat, who said it was odd that someone who had spent years studying theology at university should be so quick to dismiss what it said in the Bible.

Bee didn't respond.

Sofie stepped in. 'Have you read Philip Pullman's books: *His Dark Materials*?'

Bee was the only other person there who had read them. Ross remembered that Dani had tried to get him to read *Northern Lights* just after he had finished one of the longer Harry Potter books, but at the time he had told her he was 'Harry Pottered-out' and wasn't in the mood for any more fantasy novels.

'I think it's in the third book, *The Amber Spyglass*,' said Sofie, 'they go to the land of the dead, and they make it so that when people die, they have to give a true account of themselves before their spirits can be freed. And I just think that's such a brilliant idea. It's not like we should take it literally or anything like that, but it's such a good idea that we should live our life as if we'll have to give an account of ourselves at the end of it. And then if we've had a good life, then...then we don't need to be afraid of death. But if we've screwed up...'

With that, she stopped speaking, her face a picture of horror. She glanced at Ross and then down at the table.

Ross didn't understand what was wrong.

Pat stepped in: 'I don't think it's right to take some ideas from here, some from there and come up with your own personal version of what the afterlife might be like. From a Christian perspective, the answers are all there in the Bible, and that's where we need to look.'

Ross could see that Sofie wasn't listening. Tears were welling up in her eyes. He was about to ask her if she was okay when she got up and half ran out of the room.

Everybody stopped to watch her go. Then Ross felt a jolt on his left shin.

It was Bee. She had kicked him.

He looked at her.

She motioned with her head and mouthed the words, 'Go on.'

Still confused, Ross got up and followed Sofie outside. He felt the eyes of everybody in the room upon him as he did so.

She was at the far end of the car park with her back to him. Was she crying?

Ross walked up to her. 'Sofie? Are you okay?'

She turned round. Her face was flush with tears. 'I'm sorry Ross. I didn't mean it.'

'Didn't mean what?'

'What I said.'

Ross tried to remember. She had been talking about death and giving an account of yourself, and having nothing to fear if you had lived a good life. But if you've screwed up...

'It's okay, and anyway, I have screwed up, haven't I? I've screwed up big time, and Lizzie Johnson's dead because of me. That's why I'm here, isn't it? To try and find a way through it.'

'I'm sorry.'

'Don't apologise. It's okay.'

'You're not the only one who screwed up. I screwed up big time too.'

'You never killed anyone.'

'Well,' said Sofie, 'that's a matter of debate, innit?'

'What?'

'Little matter of my abortion.'

'Yeah, but...'

'I bet there's people in there who'd say I murdered my baby.'

'Oh, come on.'

'And don't you go telling them.'

'Course I wouldn't.'

She reached out and touched Ross's arm. 'Sorry. I know you wouldn't. But seriously Ross, you never killed nobody. Her car hit yours and she died.'

'Yeah, whatever.'

'I've done some pretty horrible things, you know. Not just my abortion. I took my problems out on other people. There was one girl, I gave her a really hard time. I mean, I can have counselling and I can forgive myself, but I don't know how she feels about it.'

'Is she in college?'

'No, I think she studies in Lewes.'

'You could find her and apologise to her.'

'I talked about that with Kitty. I wrote letters apologising to her and two teachers, but in the end, I didn't post them. I decided I didn't have the right to pester them and ask them to forgive me. I can only try to forgive myself.'

'I thought you already had.'

'Yeah, but it's not like, "I forgive myself," click, finished.'

'Don't I know it?'

She smiled at him as she wiped away her tears with her fingers. The intimacy between them aroused him, and he was almost overwhelmed with an urge to kiss her. But he held back. He thought it would be very wrong to make a pass at her when she was vulnerable like this, and in any case, he had no reason to believe she would welcome it.

'Haven't you got any tissues?' he asked.

'In my bag, in there.'

'You can use my handkerchief if you like. It's clean.'

He fished in his pocket and handed it to her. She wiped her eyes with it and blew her nose.

'Sorry about that,' she said, and they both smiled. 'I'll give it back to you washed and ironed.'

'No worries.'

After a moment, he asked her if she wanted to go back in or just go straight home.

'I have to go in. My bag's in there.'

'Okay.'

'Just stay with me for a minute.'

'Sure.'

'And you know what? I was thinking, the Christian version's much better than Philip Pullman's.'

'What?'

'In the Christian version, it doesn't matter how much you've screwed up, if you become a Christian, you can have a new start with all your sins forgiven.'

'Come on Sofie, when I see you upset like this, do you know how much I care about Christianity versus Philip Pullman?'

She smiled. 'That's very kind of you.'

'Well I mean it.'

Once again, he felt the stirrings of arousal. She looked so pretty, so sad. He wanted to put his arms around her, to tell her she was safe with him. He wanted to kiss her, to feel her lips and her tongue against his.

But no. It would be wrong. It would be a betrayal of their friendship. He would be taking advantage of her, like he had taken advantage of Mollie, but far, far worse.

*

'What happened with Sofie?'

'I don't know,' said Pat. She was sitting with Dominic and the other team leaders after the session. 'It was quite weird. She was talking about this book she read, where there was this version of the afterlife where you have to give an account of yourself. And she said if you've messed up, that's that and it's too late. Then she looked at Ross and burst into tears.'

'I know what that's all about,' said Rodney.

'You do?'

'My youngest, Suzi, she knows them both. She's not a big fan of Sofie but she likes Ross, says he's really nice. Apparently, he was involved in a car crash just after Easter. The other driver was killed.'

'Oh dear,' said Pat.

'She says it's really affected Ross. He blames himself and he's turned into a bit of a hermit. He totally messed up his exams, and she thinks he's in trouble with the law too.'

'That explains a lot,' said Pat. 'Poor boy.'

'We keep this between ourselves,' said Dominic. 'Nigel Akehurst didn't want us to know, and I can see why. We mustn't let it affect how we treat Ross. We don't let him know that we know. It wouldn't be fair. A lot of people come looking for faith because they have a crisis in their lives, and Ross is the same. It's our job to help him find hope and redemption in Jesus.'

Chapter Twenty-Seven

Bee opened the back of her father's Volvo Estate and Nobby, their golden retriever, hesitated for a moment before jumping out. At 10 years old, he was still healthy, but he had long since given up chasing balls or sticks and would be content just to walk with Bee and her father.

Her mother had just started her new job as bookkeeper at a printer's, working two days a week in their office behind the station. Bee and her father had driven to Abbot's Wood, some 20 minutes away from their new home. It was too hot to go for a long walk in the sun, but the shade provided by the trees would keep them relatively cool.

Once her father had bought a parking ticket and placed it on the dashboard, they set off through the woods with Nobby in tow.

'Have you spoken to Chloe recently?'

'No, not for a while, actually.'

'Didn't you see her when you were in London?'

Bee shook her head.

'You should get in touch with her. She'll need her friends to stick by her.'

'I never thought I'd see the day when one of my parents encouraged me to keep in touch with Chloe.'

'I always liked her, but she wasn't what you'd call a good girl, was she?'

Bee laughed. 'Definitely not.'

'So, was it just her baby that led to your crisis of faith?'

'No, I think there were other things too, but that was like the catalyst.'

'What other things?'

They stopped for a moment. Nobby had fallen behind to rummage in some long grass by the path.

'Come on, boy.'

He trotted up to them and was rewarded with a pat on his back from Bee's father.

'Good boy.'

'We had this series of lectures on the monotheistic revolution. It was really amazing. I think they were the best lectures I've had in my whole course.'

'Yes?'

'What he was saying was that monotheism isn't just polytheism but with only one God instead of lots of gods. It's something totally new, totally different.'

'Well, yes.'

'In polytheistic religions, you always have mythology, the story of how the gods came to be. In the Bible, there's none of that. At the start of the Bible, God just is. There's no origin story for God.'

'Interesting. I hadn't thought of that.'

'Apparently, the story of how the gods came to be is a very important part of pagan religions. That's because there's something in the background that's greater than the gods. They might be immortal, but they're limited. And they have no power over the thing in the background that was there before them. In Greek religion, it's the Fates. In other religions, it can be darkness, or water, or spirit, like Atman in some versions of Hinduism. Our lecturer called it the metadivine realm, something more powerful than the gods. But the important thing about the metadivine is that it's indifferent. It doesn't care about us. So, the Ancient Greeks would pray to one of the gods, but they'd never pray to the Fates. There was no point. The Fates didn't care.'

'Yes,' said her father. 'I can understand that.'

'He said polytheism, paganism, is more intellectually coherent than monotheism. In polytheism, if something terrible happens, it might be because one of the gods is having a bad day and takes it out on you. Or it might just be the Fates. There's no problem of evil in polytheism. The gods aren't particularly nice, and the metadivine realm is indifferent to suffering. But as soon as you have monotheism, you have the problem of evil. If God is all-powerful, all-knowing and all-good, how can he allow evil and suffering? Our lecturer said monotheism is inherently unstable because of the problem of evil.'

They had come to a narrow part of the path.

'You go first,' said Bee's father.

'Thanks. Come on, Nobby. Good boy.'

'But aren't there books in the Bible that specifically answer this question?'

'What?' said Bee. 'You mean Job and Ecclesiastes?'

'Yes.'

'I'd say those are books that wrestle with it. I don't think they answer it. I mean: what's the message of Job? "What do you know? You're just a human. Stop complaining and trust God." And the message of Ecclesiastes? "Yeah, life's unfair and then you're going to die. Not much you can do about it, so get over it and enjoy the good bits."'

Bee's father gave a little laugh. 'I think there's a bit more to it than that.'

'Yeah, okay.'

'The Book of Job is brilliant,' said her father. 'It's satire, isn't it? It attacks the whole idea of divine justice. It's telling us we have to be righteous, not in expectation of reward, because there might not be a reward. We have to be righteous for righteousness' sake. Even in the face of suffering that feels like divine injustice. Isn't that a marvellous message?'

'Yes.'

'And these awful people in America, with their Prosperity Gospel that says, "You're rich because you deserve to be rich," and by implication, people are poor because they deserve to be poor, I just want to hit them over the head with the Book of Job.'

Bee laughed.

'And isn't it better to live in a world where God leaves us free to make our own choices than in some kind of divine dystopia where he's this control freak who keeps intervening all the time and we're just puppets?'

'I know that argument, Dad. But what about where suffering's baked in? Like, have you seen that video about Nazca booby siblicide? They always lay two eggs, and then the stronger of the two siblings always pecks the weaker one to death? How can that be good?'

'I agree the problem of evil's really difficult,' said her father. 'I don't think we'll ever find a complete answer.'

'Well there is an answer, isn't there? Maybe God allows all these terrible things to happen because he isn't really there.'

'And look where that leads,' said her father. 'It takes you to existential nihilism, absurdism, Albert Camus. And then, before you know it, you arrive at dreadful people like Nietzsche and Ayn Rand.'

'Or humanism. Isn't that an alternative?'

'Humanism's just a bastard child of Christianity. It's incomplete. It has a God-shaped hole at its core.'

Bee wanted to say that maybe a child can outgrow its parents but thought better of it.

They walked on in silence for some time.

'There was another thing,' said Bee. 'These lectures on monotheism, it was like they pulled the rug from under my feet in a completely different way.'

'How do you mean?'

'I'm not sure I believe in *mythos* any more.'

They had reached a fork in the path.

'Which way?' said Bee.

'Let's go left. Stay out of the sun.'

'Okay.'

'So, why don't you believe in *mythos*?'

'It's not that I don't believe in it. But I don't think it's a good explanation of what you find in the Bible.'

'How come?'

'It's complex. I've always believed…well, you taught me not to take the Bible literally. You have to dig into it, read between the lines, find the analogy, try to see what it's really saying.'

'Yes,' said her father.

'Okay. And we know, right, that the Ancient Israelites didn't just suddenly become monotheistic. They went through a henotheistic phase. They believed there were other gods, but they only worshipped one.'

'Yahweh.'

'Yes, and it was only later that they become monotheistic.'

Bee's father nodded. 'And there are bits of the Bible with echoes of this polytheistic past.'

'Yeah, well, that's the point,' said Bee. 'What my lecturer said, and the archaeological record backs this up, is that monotheism came much later than we used to think. The Ancient Israelites were always polytheistic. Proper monotheism didn't develop until much later.'

'Really?'

'What this means is that J, E, and D, plus lots of psalms and even P weren't written by monotheists. They were written by polytheists. It's not a case of the Pentateuch having a few very ancient verses that are relics of a polytheistic past. The whole thing's saturated with it. Our lecturer went through verse after verse of the Old Testament showing us what he meant. When it refers to the council of the heavens, it doesn't mean God and the angels, it means the council of the gods. When it talks about God's face, or his hands, or his breath, it's not an analogy. It literally means Yahweh's face, his hands, his breath. The translations we use tend to smooth this away, but if you go back to the original Hebrew, or to the Septuagint, it's staring you in the face.'

'Yes, okay,' said Bee's father. 'Let's say your lecturer's right, why does that undermine your faith?'

'What he says is that when monotheists took over, they were stuck with these holy texts that were basically polytheistic. So they started to say, "Ah, yes, don't take them literally. Read them allegorically. They're *mythos*, not *logos*."'

'What does that matter?'

'It's saying that the early books of the Bible weren't written as *mythos*. They were written to be taken literally.'

'So?'

'So the allegorical meanings that we love so much aren't part of the original text. They were imposed on the text later.'

'I don't see why that matters,' said Bee's father. 'The Bible isn't the Word of God. The Bible shows us how the Jews and Christians found God. Look, the Jews have got the Hebrew Bible, and then they've got the Midrash and the Talmud, commentaries on the Bible. Maybe the Bible isn't the important bit. It's just the starting point. The really important thing is the Midrash and the Talmud.

'It's the same in Islam. They've got the Koran and the Hadith, and then they've got the Sunna, five different schools of interpretation. Maybe it's the Sunna that's most important. And with Christianity, the Bible's what kicked the whole thing off, but what really matters is two thousand years of theological discussion and debate. This is what fundamentalists and evangelicals get wrong: religious truth isn't something written in stone. It's a process. It's the attempt to get closer to God, something that never ends.'

'Yeah, I know Dad. I know that, and I'm trying to hang on to it.'

She wanted to say that she had a voice in her head that kept saying maybe it was all a waste of time, because God wasn't really there. But she said nothing. Instead, she turned round to see what the dog was up to.

185

*

Sofie's first question as they locked their bikes up before the Thursday evening shift was the same question she had asked before every shift since Sunday: 'Well? Have you finished reading it yet?'

'No. I was too busy cleaning my bike up.'

'Ooh – looks very shiny.'

'Yeah, my new brake blocks are a bit noisy, though.'

'I noticed. But hurry up and finish, will you? I want to talk about it.'

'You can just tell me what's in it.'

'Not this time. You have to read it.'

To Ross's surprise, Sid was in the staffroom. He couldn't think why, since Brighton hadn't played since Saturday. When Sofie went off to get changed, Sid asked Ross, 'You planning to go to university?'

Ross wondered what barbed comment Sid had lined up for him.

'Yeah.'

'What you gonna study?'

'French.'

What d'you wanna learn French for?'

'You get to have a year in France.'

'Urgh. Why do you wanna go there? It's full of frogs.'

Ross shrugged. 'Yeah, but there's some very nice frogettes as well.'

'Frogettes?'

'French girls.'

'Wouldn't want to kiss them. They all stink of garlic.'

*

Next morning, as the last guests were finishing their breakfasts, Ross and Sofie heard a commotion in the kitchen. They looked at each other, and Ross went to see what was happening.

Inside, the chef was waving his arms about.

'You can't bring in kitchen,' he was saying. 'Take it out. Take it out.'

At that point, Ross noticed Sid, who was holding a young herring gull in his arms. One of its wings was clearly broken.

'Have you got a box I can put it in?'

'Yes,' said the chef. 'I find you box, but first you must take it out kitchen.'

'Sid!' it was Sofie's voice, coming from behind Ross, 'Bring it in the staffroom.'

She opened the door leading to the staffroom and Sid took the injured bird in. The chef was still waving his arms around.

Ross and the kitchen porter followed Sid into the staffroom. The gull was conscious, but made no sound and no effort to escape from Sid's embrace.

Sofie appeared a moment later with a large cardboard box. She placed it on the staff-room table.

'Put it in here.'

She held the box open while Sid gently put the bird inside, then together, the two of them wove the top of the box together to keep it closed.

'What happened?' Sofie asked.

'Got hit by a car. Didn't even stop. Just drove off.'

'Bastard.'

'Yeah.'

Sid took out his mobile. 'There's a bird sanctuary in Hampden Park,' he said. 'I took a pigeon there once.'

After a moment, he found it on Google and called. 'Hi. I've got an injured seagull. Got hit by a car. Can I bring it round?...Yeah, okay. Be about twenty minutes, half an hour...Bye.'

He ended the call, and he and Sofie looked at each other and smiled.

'Thanks for your help, Sofie.'

She put a hand on his arm and nodded. 'How you going to get it round there?'

'I'll use my dad's car.'

'Oh? So you got your licence back then?'

He grinned. 'Yeah, quite a while ago.'

As they made their way to the car park to unlock their bikes, Ross said, 'You and Sid are very friendly all of a sudden.'

She stopped and looked at him. 'He might be a wanker but he's not a total bastard.'

'No?'

'No.'

She turned her head away from Ross, who let the subject drop.

That evening, the kitchen porter told Ross and Sofie that the seagull had been too badly injured, and the owner of the bird sanctuary had taken it to a vet to be put down. Apparently, Sid had been very upset by this.

*

Three days later was Sunday, Ross and Sofie's day off. Ross knew that she would spend the day with her maternal grandparents in Croydon. He got up late and went downstairs in his pyjama trousers and a T-shirt. He made himself a cup of coffee and two slices of toast with peanut butter for breakfast. Sofie had been nagging him for days, so it was time to read the rest of Bee's email about the resurrection. He took the laptop into the dining room and opened it up.

He scrolled past the parts about the empty tomb and Jesus' alleged appearances to his disciples and finally reached the bit he wanted.

3. THE WAY JESUS' FOLLOWERS BEHAVED AFTER THE CRUCIFIXION AND THEN LATER AFTER THE RESURRECTION.

Does this give us extraordinary evidence for the extraordinary claim of the resurrection?

Christians often point out the contrast between the panic that gripped the disciples when Jesus was arrested and the heroism they would later show in spreading the faith in the face of persecution. The heroism and the persecution seem to have been very real, by the way. According to tradition, Stephen would eventually be stoned to death, James, the brother of Jesus, stoned and clubbed, Matthias stoned and beheaded, Mark dragged to pieces, Andrew crucified, Peter crucified upside-down and Matthew and Paul put to the sword.

Christians see the apostles' heroism as evidence that they were serious about their belief in the resurrection they had "witnessed". I'd be the first to agree. No doubt about it. They were very serious indeed. However, we have no reason to believe this heroism extended to all Jesus' followers. Some may have simply drifted away.

In any case, this devotion doesn't prove the resurrection actually happened. Nor does it prove that Jesus was the Messiah. Let me give you another example of a Jewish Messiah whose followers' devotion to him survived in extraordinary circumstances.

In 1665, in Jerusalem, a charismatic preacher named Shabbetai Zevi announced that he was the Messiah and the End of Days had arrived. He attracted enormous support, possibly more than any of the Jewish Messiahs that history has thrown up – almost certainly more than Jesus in his lifetime. There was a massive outpouring of eschatological ecstasy among Jews throughout the Ottoman Empire, and Shabbetai's cult spread as far as Jewish communities in Poland, Holland and England.

Within the Ottoman Empire, Jewish prophets emerged, reporting visions of their new Messiah seated upon his throne. Many Jews took the brave step of publicly praying for the welfare of Shabbetai rather than the welfare of the Sultan, and economic activity by Jews all but ceased throughout the Empire.

Hardly surprising then that when Shabbetai went up to Constantinople, the authorities wasted no time in arresting him. He was dragged before the Sultan, who gave him a straight choice: either you convert to Islam or you die.

And what did Shabbetai do?

He capitulated and became a Moslem.

Not surprisingly, much of his following fell away at once, but many remained loyal. His impact on their lives had been so profound that they refused to see his apostasy as a betrayal. Instead they somehow managed to find arguments that proclaimed Shabbetai's capitulation to be an example of his dedication: he had joined the forces of darkness in an effort to combat them from within.

After his death, two hundred families in Greece and Turkey followed his example and publicly converted to Islam while at the same time secretly remaining Jewish. These semi-clandestine communities of *Dönmeh* are still with us today, and in Turkey there are probably about 100,000 of them, possibly many more.

So, if a Jewish Messiah can maintain a substantial following even after converting to Islam, what's so astonishing about the story of a Messiah whose followers believed that his execution wasn't the end? Yes, Jesus' followers panicked when the unimaginable happened and their leader was arrested and killed, but then some of them rallied, fortified by those who spoke about their "experiences" of the resurrection.

Some will find the story of Jesus' disciples a very inspiring story. Fair enough. But does it constitute extraordinary evidence that can convince us of the extraordinary claim that Jesus came back from the dead?

I don't think so.

This does not invalidate Christianity. There are plenty of Christians who do not believe the resurrection was an actual physical event, my dad among them. What he says is that the actual resurrection may not be real, but the early Christians' reaction to it was. He thinks if there is a God with a revelation to make, that is how he would do it, through real, specific, imperfect, temporally-bound lives. This revelation would always be partial so that our own reactions and insights become part of the story.

Ross read and re-read the final paragraph. He didn't understand it. Why would God choose to reveal himself in an imperfect way so that people spent thousands of years slaughtering each other over how to interpret it?

Ross: I've read it!!! 🍾
Sofie: Hiya. I'm in my grandad's car
         Congratulations
         What did you think?
Ross: Amazing story about that Jewish guy
Sofie: Yeah.
Ross: That bit about her dad I seriously don't get it
Sofie: 😳
         For God's sake, Ross. That was the best bit
Ross: You and your bloody mythos and logos
Sofie: Gotta go. Speak later

At that moment, Ross's father came into the dining room.
'Oh, hello. Didn't know you were up.'
'Yeah, been up a while.'
'Do you want some tea?'
'I've just had coffee, thanks.'
'What's that you're reading?'
'It's an email from one of the girls on the Alpha Course.'
'Oh, I'd better leave you to it.'
'No, you'd approve. It's all about how the resurrection never actually happened. It's very good. Just the last part's a bit weird. She says it doesn't

189

matter that the resurrection never happened. What matters is how the disciples thought it did. I don't get that.'

'Sounds a bit like the Seekers.'

'Who?'

'Hold on a sec.'

Ross's father went to the bookshelves that covered the whole wall at the end of the dining room. He retrieved an old orange-and-purple paperback and put it on the table in front of Ross.

He picked it up. The title was *When Prophecy Fails*.

'What's it about?'

'It's about the Seekers, this mad UFO cult in the 1950s, in America. They thought the world was about to be destroyed in a massive tsunami. They thought these aliens would come down and rescue them, but everyone else would drown. And then, when it didn't happen, they didn't say, "Oops, our mistake. We must have been wrong." Instead, they doubled down and said the world only survived thanks to their prayers.'

Ross scratched his head. 'Maybe the early Christians were the same,' he said. 'They thought the world was about to end and Jesus would be revealed as God's Messiah. But when he got crucified instead, they were like, "Yes, well, that was always part of the plan. And he'll be back very soon, and this time the world really will end."'

'If he existed at all,' said Ross's father.

Ross said nothing. He re-read the final paragraph of Bee's email. He still didn't understand it. Wasn't this idea of a 'partial' revelation just a rationalisation of the fact that the early Christians had been plain, old-fashioned wrong about Jesus?

He couldn't see the point in becoming a Christian if Christianity wasn't actually true. That meant he was wasting his time on the Alpha Course. And if he was wasting his time, he might as well stop going.

He had gone in search of redemption but instead had found truth. But how could truth help him when he had killed someone?

The thought struck him with all the impact of a blow to his chest. For a moment he could hardly breathe. He thought he might burst into tears at any minute, so he closed down his laptop and retreated to his room.

Chapter Twenty- Eight

That afternoon, Ross's mother dragged him to the supermarket to help with the shopping. They had nearly finished and were half-way down the personal hygiene aisle when he saw a couple wheel their trolley round in front of them.

The man was Nick, the policeman on the Alpha Course, and the woman with him was Sandra Samuels, the officer who arrested Ross. Nick smiled and gave Ross a cheery wave. He nudged Sandra, who looked up and clearly recognised him at once.

They stopped their trolleys to say hello.

'Hi.'

'Hi.'

'Sandra, this is Ross from my Alpha Course. Ross, my partner Sandra.'

'Yeah, we've kind of met.'

'Oh?'

'Yes,' said Sandra. 'Hello. Hello Mrs Collins.'

Ross's mother obviously hadn't recognised Sandra up to that point. She looked quite pretty in civvies, with her face made up and her long hair loose on her shoulders.

'Oh,' said Ross's mother. 'Hello.'

Nick turned to Sandra in confusion.

'I told you about him,' she said. 'The boy in the accident near Alfriston.'

'Oh God,' said Nick. 'I didn't realise.'

'Yeah well,' said Ross, 'it's not your fault.'

His mother addressed Sandra. 'This is a bit embarrassing for you, isn't it?'

'I suppose so.'

'We'd better be on our way.'

'Yes. Sorry.'

They all mumbled their goodbyes.

'Christ!' Ross said to his mother. 'What a nightmare.'

They decided to give the rest of the supermarket a miss and head for the checkout. Just then Ross heard Nick's voice behind him.

'Ross! Ross!'

He and his mother turned round and Nick came up to them.

'I'm really sorry about that. I had no idea.'

Ross shook his head. 'It's not your fault.'

'Look, whatever you do, don't let it put you off going on the Alpha Course. I promise I won't tell anyone.'

Ross said nothing. He didn't want to tell Nick he had already decided not to attend any more sessions.

Nick said, 'I remember what you said on the first night. You said something had happened that had shaken you up. Well you need to keep going, don't you? If you can't face me on Tuesday, just send a message on WhatsApp and I won't turn up again.'

'Thanks, but I'm not going to do that.'

'Look, for what it's worth, and this is just between you and me, Sandra told me about your accident. She said she felt sorry for you because you just made the kind of mistake every new driver makes, and she told me she had a lot of respect for the way you never tried to bullshit your way out of it. What I'm trying to say is...I don't think badly of you.'

Ross nodded his head, but he was unable to say anything in reply.

'I'll see you on Tuesday, okay?'

Ross nodded.

His mother spoke instead of him. 'Thank you very much. I really appreciate what you've just done. You're a true Christian, sir.'

She and Ross joined the queue at the checkout.

'Look, I can't handle this.'

'I'll see you in the car, okay?'

She gave Ross her keys and he half ran out of the supermarket. He managed to keep his composure until he got into her Nissan Micra, but as soon as he shut the door, he howled his grief and thumped his forehead on the dashboard.

He had calmed down a little by the time his mother joined him. He just about managed to help her bring the shopping into the house, but then he had to go upstairs and shut himself in his room.

His mother waited about an hour before knocking on the door and coming in with a cup of tea.

'You okay?'

Ross shrugged.

She nodded and sat down on his bed.

'People are going to find out.'

'Yeah, I know.'

'Well, there's something else you should know. I'm proud of you, and I'm proud of the way you've taken responsibility for your mistake. A lot of people wouldn't have done that.'

*

His mother's encouraging words notwithstanding, the next few hours were very bleak. There was no way he could go back to the Alpha Course after this. Not that he would have gone back anyway. Except now it would feel like he was chickening out. But he wasn't chickening out. He had already decided not to go back.

He was moping in his bedroom when Sofie messaged him just after nine.

Sofie:	Hiya
Ross:	Hi how was your day
Sofie:	Really great.
	What about you?
Ross:	Pretty crap actually
	I bumped into nick in the supermarket guess who his girlfriend is
Sofie:	Who?
Ross:	Only the cop who arrested me

She audio called him straight away.

'Hi.'

'Oh my God, Ross. Are you okay?'

'I'm still standing.'

'Did she recognise you?'

'Yeah, course.' He gave an account of what had happened.

'My train's just pulling in. I'll come round.'

'I'm all right.'

'No. I'll come round. See you in about forty minutes.'

Less than 25 minutes later, she rang the doorbell. Ross wanted to get to the door before his parents. No such luck. He heard the door open just as he got to the top of the stairs. He stepped back to stay out of sight.

'Oh, hello.' It was his mother's voice, and he didn't think it was the friendliest greeting he had ever heard.

'Ross just told me what happened.'

His mother hesitated and then said, 'Yeah. You'd better come in.'

'Is he in his room?'

'I'll call him down. Ross! Sofie's here.'

He reached back and fiddled with his bedroom door handle to make it sound like he was opening the door. 'Okay. Just coming.'

'Hi.'

'Hi.'

He pointed to the dining room. 'We can go in here.'

Sofie kicked her trainers off and he followed her in and shut the door behind him. They sat down at the table.

'Were you very upset?'

'Yeah.'

'I bet you were. God, the perils of living in a small town.'

Ross gave a thin smile.

'But you're still going on Tuesday, innit?'

'Well, that's the thing. I'd already decided to give it up, the Alpha Course.'

'Ross, you can't go into hiding every time someone finds out. When we go back to college, everyone will know.'

'No, it's not that. This morning, before I went to the supermarket, I already decided to stop going.'

'What? Why?'

'Bee's email.'

'And?'

'Well, she's right, isn't she? About the resurrection. It never happened.'

'Yeah, but not literally, no.'

'I know what you're going to say: "It's *mythos*."'

'Exactly.'

'But, Sofie, you know what I think about *mythos*. It doesn't work for me.'

Silence.

'So you're really not going on Tuesday?'

'No. Sorry to desert you.'

'You're sure it's not because of Nick?'

'Promise.'

'So, what *are* you going to do?'

'What do you mean?'

Sofie's eyes fixed themselves on his. 'You didn't start the Alpha Course because of a sudden interest in theology, right? You need redemption. That's why you went.'

He broke off eye contact.

'So, what are you going to do?'

'I don't know.'

'Well, you have to do something, Ross. If not the Alpha Course, what?'

'Like I say, I don't know.'

'Well, why don't you have counselling again?'

'I've tried that. It didn't work.'

'Well give it another chance.' She was beginning to raise her voice.

'No.' It was a couple of seconds before he could find the right words. 'It's not for me. It wouldn't work.'

She grabbed hold of his arm and he looked at her. 'Ross,' she said. By now she was almost shouting. 'You need help. If you want to give up the Alpha Course, fine. But then you need something else. If not counselling, what? What are you going to do?'

'I don't know.'

'You know what happens to people who need help and don't get it?' Her voice was loud and angry. 'They end up like my dad. Or my bloody sister. Have I told you about her? She spends half her life smashed out of her head on bloody cocaine.'

He looked away from her.

'Ross, I'm your friend and I love you, and I do what I can for you. But I'm out of my depth. You need proper help. If you can't find it in Jesus, fine. But you've got to find it somewhere else. What else is there apart from counselling?'

She let go of his arm and looked away.

They sat in silence for a very long time, not looking at each other.

Eventually, she said, 'I'm sorry. I didn't mean to shout at you.'

'It's okay.'

'I'd better go.'

'I'll walk you home.'

'You don't need to. It's not far.'

'It's dark. I'll walk you home.'

'Thanks.'

While Sofie was putting her trainers back on, he popped his head round the living room door to let his parents know where he was going. His brother had earphones on and was grinning at something on his mobile, but it was obvious from the looks on his parents' faces that they had heard something.

He and Sofie didn't speak as they walked to her house. They stopped by the gate, and Sofie said, 'Will you think about what I said?'

'Yes. Maybe I'll have a word with Nigel tomorrow.'

'Good idea. See you usual time in the morning.'

'Look forward to it.'

She opened her arms. 'Hug?'

'Hug.'

When he got home, he went into the kitchen to get himself a glass of water. His mother came in with that 'very concerned' look on her face.

'You okay?'

'I'm fine.'

'You okay with Sofie?'

'We're cool.'

*

Sofie apologised once more for shouting when they met up to cycle down next morning.

'Don't worry about it. You were being a good friend. Not sure what my parents made of it though.'

'Oh no. Tell me they didn't hear me.'

Ross gave a little nod.

'Was I swearing?'

'Yes, but only the B-word.'

'Oh God. Your mum doesn't like me anyway.'

'It's not that she doesn't like you. She's just a bit wary. Dani's mum must have said something. Have you told Dani to give her some edited highlights?'

'Not yet, no.'

'Well, you should.'

Once the shift was over and he had made coffee for the Akehurst family, Ross cycled to Nigel's church in Old Town. He parked his bike outside the church grounds and walked in. Nigel was there, talking to a man who looked like an electrician or a plumber. He spotted Ross and gave a little wave. A couple of minutes later, he joined him on a pew near the back.

'Hi, Ross. Fancy seeing you here. How's things?'

'Up and down really.'

'I suppose that's to be expected.'

'Yeah. To be honest, the best time's when I'm busy at the hotel. I haven't got time to think about the accident. But, you know, late at night, when I'm alone in my room, that can be pretty grim.'

Nigel nodded. 'I'm glad the job's helping.'

'I'm very grateful to you.'

'My mum is too. She says you and Sofie are a find.'

Ross smiled.

'What about the Alpha Course? Is that helping?'

'That's what I came to talk about. It's very interesting. Sometimes it's very good, and sometimes...sometimes I just don't find it convincing.'

'Really?'

'Yeah, well, the thing is, right, I've got this friend. She's studying theology at university, and she says none of it's literally true. She says it's all *mythos*. Have you come across that concept before?'

Nigel gave a little laugh. 'I have to admit, I'm not a fan of theology. I graduated in social work, and it was only after I'd been working for a couple of years that I felt a calling. When you're doing social work for the local authority, you have to keep your faith out of it, but I could see how much faith could help a lot of the people I was working with. So that's why I decided to change tack. I had to do a postgrad diploma in theology. I didn't really enjoy it, to be honest. But once I started work, I knew I'd made the right decision.'

'Why didn't you enjoy it?'

'Ah, it's so arcane. There are so many different points of view, so many debates. *Mythos* was part of that. And what's the other one?'

'*Logos*?'

'*Logos*, that's it. See – you know more than me. And there's all these debates about whether you take the Bible literally, and if so, which bits, because it does contradict itself all over the place. But the thing is, the Bible isn't one book. It's an anthology. Some of it's theological, some devotional, some of it's songs, and there's a collection of proverbs. There's some history, not always a hundred percent accurate. Then there's biography, philosophy, prophecy. There are letters, and some of them are probably forgeries. At least one book is satire, possibly two. And there's even a book of erotic poetry.

'So I think the question of *mythos* and *logos*, whether you should take the Bible literally, for me that question's redundant. How can you take satire literally? Or philosophy? What does it even mean to take erotic poetry literally? All of this kind of thing is approaching the Bible from the wrong angle.'

'So, what's the right angle?' asked Ross.

'What can the Bible do for you? How can it change your life? How can it inspire you? Now, I wouldn't recommend you start at page one and read it all the way to the end. The Bible's really difficult to understand. That's why we have Bible study groups, so we can give people guidance and they can discuss it together.'

Ross was silent for a long time. Then he said, 'My friend was talking to me about the historical Jesus. She says he's very different from the Jesus in the Bible.'

'Yes, we had to study that. The thing is, you get ten theologians and you ask them about the historical Jesus, you'll get ten different answers. There'll be one who says he never existed at all, another who says he was a revolutionary socialist, another who says he was a Jewish nationalist. You'll get one who says the picture in Mark is the most accurate, and then you get another who says no, John was written by an eyewitness. And it goes on and on like that. And I'd say the same about this as I say about the Bible. They're approaching the question from the wrong end.

'The question is, how can Jesus transform your life? Because I know he transformed mine. It's about a leap of faith, opening the door to Jesus. And when you give yourself to him, then everything follows. Then you understand, and you'll never be the same again. That's what happened to me, and it could happen to you. But you have to let it happen. It's not about theological disputes. The bedrock of Christianity is that leap of faith.'

'She talked about the resurrection and whether or not it really happened. But I suppose you'd say that's the wrong question. It's more a question of what the risen Christ can do for us.'

'Now you're getting there.'

'Thanks Nigel. That's very interesting. You've given me a lot to think about.'

*

As they got ready to start the evening shift, Ross told Sofie her about his conversation with Nigel.

'I used to think all Christians believed the same thing, but they don't, do they?'

'Evidently not. Have you thought any more about what you want to do?'

'I'm going to carry on the Alpha Course.'

'Oh, I'm so glad.'

'But I'm going to give up the Omega Course. It was kind of pulling me this way and that, and I'd rather keep it simple.'

'Fair enough. I'll carry on with both.'

'You like to get both points of view.'

'Yeah, but it's not just that. I think Bee's great. She's the best teacher I've ever had.'

*

Bee had arrived expecting the worst, but in fact it had been fun. They were a nice bunch, every age from Sofie, who was just 17, to Alison in her 50s. And they all agreed that the best thing of all was that none of the men from their table had turned up to help with cooking that night's dinner, unreconstructed male chauvinists that they were. They would only have got in the way. (Ross had told Sofie that he was hiding from Nick.)

It was also good to spend more time with Sofie, who had just told the others she and Ross would get their AS-Level results in just over three weeks' time.

'Are you nervous?'

'A bit, but my coursework was pretty good so I should be okay provided I haven't completely screwed up my exams. Touch wood.'

'Are you planning to go to university?' Alison asked.

'Yeah, I hope so.'

'What are you going to do study?'

'Spanish Studies.'

'Oh?' said Bee. 'So, will you get to spend a year in Spain?'

'I'm hoping for South America.'

'Wow. That'd be awesome.'

'What about Ross?' asked Pat. 'What's he going to do?'

'French. His dream is to spend a year in Paris, drinking red wine and chasing French girls.'

Everybody laughed.

'How do you feel about him chasing French girls?' Alison asked.

Sofie shrugged. 'We're not going out. We're just friends.'

Pat gave Sofie a quizzical look.

While the dinner was cooking, Sofie and Bee went for a walk round the local housing estate.

'Thanks for your long email, Bee. It was really amazing.'

'My pleasure.'

'Must have taken you ages to write.'

'Actually, I enjoyed writing it. It helped me clarify my thoughts.'

'Yeah?'

'Have you ever had the experience where you don't know what you really think till you say it?'

'I know what you mean.'

'Well, it's a bit like that when I write you my emails. I mean, six months ago I would never have written what I'm writing now. But now I write it and I look at it and I think, "Yes, that's what I really do think now."'

'But you know what?' said Sofie. 'You're not putting me off the Alpha Course at all.'

'I'm glad. That's not my intention.'

'I've tried to put what I think in an email to you, but I just can't find the words.'

'Like what?'

Sofie hesitated. 'Okay, I'll give you an analogy, see if it makes sense. It's like, you're walking in a forest, right, and suddenly you come across this stream. It's too wide to jump across, so you have to find some way to get over it. You walk along by the stream for a while, and you see this log, where a big branch has fallen from a tree.

'So, you can use the log to get across the stream, right? And then that's it; you carry on walking, but you don't take the log with you.' Sofie looked at Bee. 'I know this doesn't make any sense, but...but that's what the Alpha Course is to me. It's the log, and you need it...I mean, I don't want to sound stupid or pretentious, but you need that log to get across towards some kind of spiritual awakening or something. Does this make any sense to you?'

'A lot of people think exactly the same as you.'

'They do?'

'Yes, my dad for starters. He hasn't left Christianity behind, but I doubt if he thinks any of it's true, not in a literal sense. Apart from God; he does believe in God.'

'What about you? Do you still believe in God?'

Bee shrugged. 'I'm finding it really hard at the moment. There's so many arguments I used to believe in, but now I just look at them and think they're just so flimsy. But that's because I've changed. The arguments haven't changed, and I think it's brilliant if you're on a spiritual journey, I really do.'

'I'm not there yet. It's like...it's like I've found the log, and I'm wondering whether I should use it, or whether maybe I'd be better off looking for something else or maybe even just staying where I am on this side of the stream.'

'Well don't let me stop you using it.'

'Don't worry about that.'

'To be quite honest,' said Bee, 'I've been feeling really guilty.'

'What for?'

'For offloading my spiritual crisis on you and Ross.'

'Don't worry about that. I'm really grateful to you. I wouldn't be where I am now without you. You taught me about *mythos* and *logos*. There's no way Dominic would ever have made a Christian of me, but maybe you and him together just might.'

'That would be ironic, wouldn't it? To pass my faith on to you just as I lose it myself.'

'But maybe you don't need that faith any more.'

'Oh God, I *do*, Sofie. I've spent the last two years of my life studying theology. What good's a degree in theology if you don't believe in God?'

'It's still a degree though, innit?'

'That's what Robbie says.'

They walked along in silence for a moment. Bee asked: 'What about Ross? Does he think the same as you?'

'No. Actually, I should tell you, he's dropping out of the Omega Course.'

Bee laughed. 'I didn't know I was running an Omega Course. Is he still doing Alpha?'

'Yeah. I think, the thing is, he just wants the *mythos*. He doesn't want the *logos*. He said he found it confusing, having both.'

'Fair enough.'

'He doesn't get *mythos*.'

'Most people don't. Dominic doesn't get it.'

'Ross really wants to believe but he's not sure if he can.'

'Is he still really stressed out?'

'Sometimes, yeah.'

'You know what I think?'

'What?'

'It's a good job he's got you.'

Sofie smiled and blushed a little.

They turned back towards the church hall. After a moment, Bee said, 'Sofie, can I ask you a personal question?'

'What?'

'Are you in love with Ross?'

Sofie hesitated a moment and then said, 'Yes.'

'Does he love you?'

'I don't know. He likes me, but I don't know if he'll ever fall in love with me.'

'Don't you need to find out?'

'It wouldn't be right to put any pressure on him. Not now. He needs me to be his friend. I'm the only one he can talk to.'

'What about your needs?'

'Yeah, well if you love someone, maybe sometimes you have to put his needs first.'

Chapter Twenty-Nine

Ross got to the church hall a little late. Nick was waiting for him outside the entrance and greeted him with a handshake.

'Hi, Ross. I'm so glad you're here.'

'Hi.' Ross didn't know what else he could say.

Everyone was already eating their chicken casserole when they went in. Sofie gave Ross a cross face as she put food on the plate she had saved for him.

'Sorry. The bus was late.'

'All right. I won't shout at you. This time.'

'Phew!'

Ross thought the chicken casserole was nice, but not as good as his mother's. Not that he dared to say as much. Sofie told him the recipe was Alison's and that she had cut all the onions.

'What onions?'

'I know. They've disappeared, but I cut loads.'

Tom Bradshaw's haircut looked a little less severe after another week's growth, and tonight's traditional hymn was more upbeat.

Breathe on me, breath of God,
Fill me with life anew,
That I may love what Thou dost love,
And do what Thou wouldst do.

The modern song was more cheerful too, and it was clearly one of Bee's favourites.

There is hope in Jesus,
There is hope for all of us.
As long as Jesus lives inside us
There is hope for all.

Sofie asked Bee if she liked this song because it was more metaphorical. It didn't speak about Jesus being literally alive but just 'alive inside us'.

'No, I just like the tune.'

*

Dominic started by reminding everyone of the weekend away that was coming up from the evening of Friday the 24th to the morning of Sunday the 26th of August. As the following week was bank holiday weekend, there wouldn't be a session on Tuesday the 28th. He said the weekend away was the most important part of the Alpha Course and he hoped everyone would be able to join them.

Ross hadn't yet mentioned it to his parents. This was going to be awkward, as they had booked a cottage in the Lake District for that week. He resolved to tell them as soon as he got home.

'Tonight's session is all about the Bible,' said Dominic. 'Believe it or not, I came to the Bible reluctantly. My parents are very strong Christians, and they brought me up as a Christian, and I'm very grateful to them for that. But I have to admit, I didn't really get the Bible. I enjoyed singing hymns, but I always found the Bible readings in church services pretty boring. Sorry, that's not true. I found them excruciatingly boring.'

Several people laughed. Ross smiled, and he noticed that Bee nodded her head at this.

But when he was 17 or 18 years old, the vicar asked him to read a passage from Paul's First Letter to the Corinthians at evensong.

'I was a bit reluctant. Believe it or not, in those days I was very shy and didn't like the idea of standing up and speaking to a church full of people. I deliberately didn't even look at the passage until it was time to read it out. But then as I started to read, I was astonished by the power and the beauty of St Paul's words. Let me read a little bit of it to you. Perhaps you'll see what I mean.

'"If I speak with the tongues of men and of angels, but have not love, I am only a resounding gong, or a clanging cymbal. If I have the gift of prophecy, and can fathom all mysteries, and all knowledge, and if I have all faith that can move mountains, but I have not love, I am nothing. If I give all I possess to the poor and surrender my body to the flames, but have not love, I gain nothing.

'"Love is patient, love is kind. It does not envy, it is not proud. It is not rude, it is not self-seeking, it is not easily angered, it keeps no record of wrongs. Love does not delight in evil but rejoices with the truth. It always protects, always trusts, always hopes, always perseveres."'

Dominic read with great emotion, and he communicated it well, because Ross felt it too. This was tremendous stuff, no doubt about it.

'"Love never fails. But where there are prophecies, they will cease; where there are tongues, they will be stilled; where there is knowledge, it will pass away. For we know in part and we prophesy in part, but when perfection comes, the imperfect disappears. When I was a child, I talked like a child, I thought like a child, I reasoned like a child. When I became a man, I put childish ways behind me. Now we see but a poor reflection as in a mirror; then we shall see face to face. Now I know in part; then I shall know fully, even as I am fully known.

'"And now these three remain: faith, hope and love. But the greatest of these is love."'

Dominic told the audience how he had almost cried as he read this passage out. He had never realised the Bible could have such power. He had never realised the Bible could fill his soul the way St Paul filled it that day.

He had gone home from church eager, desperate even, to read more. He spent the rest of the day curled up on his bed, thumbing through his parents' copy of the King James Bible. This was the beginning of the greatest love affair of his life – he was sure his wife would forgive him for saying this – his love affair with the Word of God, the Bible.

He spoke about how the Bible is and has always been the best-selling of all bestsellers, the most powerful book in history, high explosive, the meeting-point between man and the living God. Jesus said, 'Man does not live on bread alone, but on every word that comes from the mouth of God.'

Dominic told stories about Christians smuggling Bibles into Russia during the communist era.

'Why were these people so willing to risk so much to bring Bibles into the country? Why were the communists so afraid of this one book? Because it is the Word of God. It is like the purest mountain stream pouring forth for us to drink. It is there for all of us, cool and clear. It can satisfy all our thirsts as no other water can, for it is through the Bible that God has revealed himself to us.

'The only way we can know God is through his revelation. He revealed himself to us in the person of Jesus Christ our Lord, and it is through the study of the Bible that we can see him. Yes, we can see God through the wonders of the world he has created, through prayer, dreams, prophecies, through the works of the Holy Spirit, but the Bible is there forever. Yes, it is the work of human beings, but every word of it is 'God-breathed'. It is perfect and does not err.

'Yes, there are difficulties in the Bible. There are apparent contradictions, some of which are difficult to resolve, but this shouldn't surprise us. The Bible was written over a period of 1,500 years by at least 40 authors. But these apparent contradictions can all be resolved. For example, it can be difficult to square the love God has for all his creation with all the suffering in the world. But every Christian believes in God's love and seeks an understanding of suffering within the framework of that love.'

All this time, Ross had been carried along by Dominic's words, but at this point it was as if he had run into a brick wall. What did that mean: to believe in God's love and to seek an understanding of our suffering within the framework of that love?

So God had allowed him to make a stupid mistake the first time he had ever driven any distance on his own. And God had allowed this mistake to lead to the death of an innocent woman, ruining the lives of her parents, her husband and her children. God had allowed all this, but you have to understand the fact that he allowed all this within the framework of his love for us.

Ross wanted to scream. This was ridiculous. What kind of love was *that*? It wasn't love. It was neglect. God could so easily have intervened. He could have made the accident just a little bump. He could have made sure Mrs Johnson's car didn't flip over. That would have been enough. It would have given Ross the fright of his life, and he would most definitely have looked in his mirror next time he overtook someone.

Why did he have to let her die? It made no sense at all.

*

Bee felt her posture stiffen and her innards tighten as Dominic's talk progressed. It wasn't anything Dominic said as such. She thought it was a good talk even though she didn't agree with it. She didn't think the Bible was 'God-breathed', even though she loved it, and the passage Dominic read out was one of her favourites.

What stressed Bee out was the question that she knew was on its way from Nick: did she agree with Dominic's talk? Maybe she should go up to him during the coffee break and let him ask his question then. Yes, that was a good idea. That way she could get it out of the way before the group discussion, and then she wouldn't find herself in opposition to Dominic yet again.

She sat back in her chair, confident and relaxed now. She glanced round at the others in her group. Everyone was leaning forwards, attentive. Then suddenly, she saw the change that came over Ross. In an instant, Dominic lost him. He stopped listening and his private agony washed over him.

Bee wondered what it was. She hoped that whatever it was that was preventing him from finding comfort in religion, it wasn't all her 'Omega Course'. And she hoped that he could rise above his problems and find love with Sofie. They would make a beautiful couple.

*

'I know what you're going to ask,' Bee said, almost in a whisper, as she and Nick took their coffee.

'What?'

'You're going to ask if I agree with Dominic's talk.'

Nick laughed. 'How did you guess?'

'Feminine intuition.'

'So, did you agree?'

'If I answer you now, promise you won't ask me again in the group discussion.'

'Yeah, okay.'

'Well the answer is: not really.'

'You surprise me. So, what's the difference between you and Dominic?'

Bee motioned Nick to one side, to make sure nobody else could hear her.

'I love the Bible. Some parts of it are just so beautiful, so powerful, so full of wisdom. There are some passages that really get me: St Paul on love – the bit Dominic read out, the Sermon on the Mount, some parts of Jonah, Ecclesiastes and the Song of Songs, the Book of Job. I just love these things.'

'But?'

'But there are other things that get me too, in exactly the same way. Like in *The Merchant of Venice*, the bit about the quality of mercy. Or Sinead O'Connor

204

singing *Thank You for Hearing Me*, or WH Auden's *Funeral Blues*. Or that scene in *Groundhog Day* when Bill Murray finally understands – have you seen it?'

'I know what you mean.'

'So do I think the Bible is brilliant? Yes, some of it. Some bits are awful, but some bits are so fantastic.'

'And do you think it's divinely inspired? I don't suppose you do, do you?'

'No, I don't suppose I do. But please don't tell Dominic.'

'Don't tell Dominic what?'

Bee turned round to see Dominic, a quizzical expression on his face.

*

The fireworks passed Ross by. The accident had swallowed him once more, and he paid no attention to the passionate debate that raged on their table, Bee and Sofie on one side, Dominic and Pat on the other.

Sofie said it had been the best session yet, she had learnt so much. She talked of nothing else on the two buses she and Ross took home. He had never seen her so absorbed. Usually she would be very sensitive to his mood, but the discussion on the Bible had left her too fired up to think of him.

He felt angry with her. Couldn't she see how the accident had sunk its teeth into him yet again? It was like a pit-bull terrier; it didn't just bite but held him in its jaws and wouldn't let go.

Chapter Thirty

Next morning, Veronika motioned Bee to one side just before staff breakfast. They went to a corner of the empty dining room to talk. 'Guess what Martha tell me yesterday.'

'What?'

'On Monday night, somebody stolen five hundred pound from safe.'

'What? You're joking.'

'No. Martha, she tell me.'

'Bloody hell. Have the police been?'

'Well, that's it. Mrs A, she said not to call police.'

'Really?'

'Mr A, he was very angry, he wanted to call police, but she said, "No, no police." I no idea why.'

Sofie made as if to say something but stopped herself. After a moment, she said, 'Yeah, I wonder why.'

She told Ross nothing about this conversation.

*

The first thing Bee noticed was the absence of Ross. He really had dropped out of the Omega Course, so much so that he no longer wanted to meet the course leader for a coffee.

'No cake today?' she said, as Sofie sat down with her Americano.

'No, I've just had a big breakfast.'

'And no Ross?'

Sofie grinned. 'I told him we'd be talking Omega Course, and I think he got the hint.'

'How is he? He looked pretty stressed last night.'

'He was fine this morning.'

'That's good.'

'You know, I really enjoyed the discussion last night.'

'Did you? I was desperate not to get sucked into it again.'

'No?'

'Have you seen *Godfather Three*?'

Sofie shook her head.

'There's this great line...' Bee spoke with a deep voice in an approximation of a New York accent: '"Just when I thought I was out, they pull me back in." That's how I felt last night.'

'Well, I thought you were great.'

'Thank you.'

'There's one thing you said, right. You said, "The Bible isn't the Word of God. It's the story of how Christians and Jews found God." Tell me more about that.'

'I was quoting my dad.'

'So, is that what he thinks?'

'It's what I thought until recently. Now I'm not so sure.'

Sofie thought for a moment. 'So, tell me what your dad thinks.'

'Okay, let's put it this way…The idea of God, just one God, it's about two thousand five hundred years old, something like that. And the ones who came up with it were the Jews. There'd been sort of semi-monotheistic ideas in other civilisations: China, India, Greece, Persia, Egypt, but the first people who really went all the way were the Jews. So, for the sake of argument, let's say God exists, and he's the ultimate reason why the universe is as it is. Right?'

Sofie nodded.

'But it's pretty weird, right. Think about the Jews two thousand five hundred years ago. I mean, what did they know? They didn't know the sun was a star or that stars were suns. They knew nothing about galaxies, black holes, the Big Bang. They didn't have the first idea how old the universe is or how big it is. They didn't even know the earth goes round the sun. They'd never looked down a microscope, and they knew nothing about cells, bacteria, sperms and eggs or DNA, never mind molecules and atoms. And yet these people, who knew almost nothing about the nature of the world, they somehow worked out what the ultimate cause was. It's like they found the answer to why before they had the first clue about what, when or how.'

'Sounds pretty implausible, innit?'

'Yeah. I mean, think of the police investigating a murder. First thing they do, right, is find out exactly what happened before they can even start to look at who or why.'

'Yes.'

'So,' said Bee, 'the question is, how do you explain it? How do you explain the fact that the Jews worked it out? The only possible explanation is that God was reaching out to them, revealing himself to them, wanting them to believe. Yeah?'

'Yeah.'

'Only thing is, right, he didn't do a very good job. I mean, his message isn't very clear. Do you know how many Christian denominations there are, each with its own particular take on the message? Thousands. Literally thousands. But if God had revealed his message in a clear way, there'd only be one religion and one denomination, because everything would be completely clear.

'But if God is perfect, the only explanation is that he didn't want his revelation to be clear. He wanted us to have to make an effort to understand him. He thought it was better to make us think rather than spoon-feed us, even if we end up making mistakes.'

Sofie took a sip of her coffee. Bee followed suit and finished off the last of her chocolate brownie.

'It's actually a very nice outlook,' she said. 'If you take this attitude, you're not saying, "My denomination's right and all the other denominations are wrong." You're saying Moslems, Jews, Hindus and what have you, they're engaged in the same quest as us, and we can learn from them.'

'And what about atheists?'

'My dad would say an atheist philosopher's engaged in the same search for meaning, yes. He's really serious about his Christianity, mind you. He loves going to church. He loves the Bible. He loves being part of a tradition that's two thousand years old. He thinks that's really important. He loves the fact that the Lord's Prayer is exactly the same prayer that the son of a carpenter taught his followers all those years ago. But does he believe that what it says in the Bible is literally true? No, not at all.'

'That's really interesting,' said Sofie. 'But you know what? When you were explaining it, you sound like you don't believe it any more.'

'I don't know. Sometimes I do; sometimes I don't.'

'So, when did your crisis of faith start? Was there one thing that, like, set it off?'

Bee told Sofie about Chloe's baby.

'Oh, God. That's so sad.'

'Yeah.'

'But it doesn't mean God doesn't exist.'

'No, of course not.'

'My best friend, right, her boyfriend's a Hindu. He says for them, God's more of a universal spirit. Maybe it's not a personal God, not something that intervenes directly.'

'Maybe he's right.'

They were silent for a moment. Sofie drank some more of her coffee and Bee finished hers.

'I'm so...' Sofie raised her hands and shook them beside her head as she spoke. 'I'm just so full of questions.'

'Like what?'

'Everything. It's like I'm just...hungry. I want to know about Christianity, and Hinduism too. Dominic's giving me the Christian *mythos*, which is great. But I need to know the *logos* too.'

'You should do a degree in theology.'

Sofie shook her head. 'No, I'm not going to miss my year in South America for anything.'

They both smiled.

'One thing I want to know,' said Sofie, 'especially after the last session with Dominic: where did the Bible come from?'

'That's a very long story.'

'Yeah, I suppose it is.'

'Shall I put it in an email?'

'Ooh, that would be great. If it's not too much trouble.'

'I'll enjoy writing it. Shall I send it to Ross too?'

Sofie shook her head. 'Better not. He wants to concentrate on Alpha.'

*

Later that afternoon, as he was eating pot noodles for his lunch, Ross opened up Instagram on his mobile and scrolled down to see what was new.

His gay classmate Mark, whose feed had become very political since he came out, had put up a link from the Scottish Sunday Herald. Ross clicked on it and read the article, which was about some high school pupils in Angus who had started an online petition calling on their school to sever ties with the school chaplain over his homophobic remarks.

Mark had posted a link to the petition, so Ross clicked on it and signed it. He also gave the link a like. He remembered Bee mentioning something about homophobia in the Bible, so he decided to google it and see what came up.

He found a Wikipedia article entitled 'The Bible and Homosexuality'. It looked very long, and Ross had no intention of reading the whole thing. He scrolled past the first two paragraphs and came to a headline that said, 'Leviticus 18 and 20'. He read the first quotation:

Do not have sexual relations with a man as one does with a woman; that is detestable.

The next quotation was far worse:

If a man lies with a man as with a woman, they have both committed an abomination. They must surely be put to death; their blood is upon them.

'Wow,' Ross said out loud. No wonder there were homophobic priests. He remembered what Mark had said to him last time they met: 'I hope you're not going to become one of these dreadful evangelicals.'

Ross:	Hello – you there??
Sofie:	Yes.
Ross:	I just been reading a bit of the bible
	Do you want a quotation
Sofie:	Go on then
Ross:	If a man lies with a man as with a woman, they have both committed an abomination. They must surely be put to death
Sofie:	That's a bit grim. Is that really in the Bible?
Ross:	Yeah do you think dominic takes that bit literally
Sofie:	That's why I prefer Bee's version of Christianity
	She's gonna send me an email about where the Bible came from. I can forward it if you like
Ross:	Nah think I'll give the latest instalment of mythos and logos a miss
Sofie:	😜

Sid was lying in wait for him before the evening shift, sniffing loudly when Ross and Sofie arrived (he and Sofie actually exchanged a perfunctory greeting). Ross wondered what he had dreamed up for him this time. He found out as soon as Sofie went to get changed.

'You a virgin, Ross?'

Ross sighed. If he said, 'Mind your own business,' as he wanted to, then Sid would conclude that he was a virgin. He felt he had no option but to answer the question.

'No.'

'How many girls you had?'

'That's for me to know and you to wonder.'

'Ha, ha. That means only one. What was she, some girl you met out of town who none of your mates have ever heard of?'

'No, she was my girlfriend at college, if you must know.'

'You haven't had Sofie yet, then?'

'We're just friends.'

'She ain't no virgin, that's a fact. Right little slapper, from what I hear.'

'Sid, can we just leave it? She'll be back in a minute.'

He took out a cigarette, lit it and departed.

The football season proper started that Saturday. Brighton played Watford, hardly the strongest team in the league, and lost two-nil. Their performance was woeful and Ross knew for certain that Sid would be waiting for him when he went back to work.

And so it proved: 'I see your lot lost again.'

'Yeah.'

'Serves 'em right.'

'What do you mean, serves them right?'

'Well, being so politically correct.'

'Sorry, I'm not with you.'

'Having a black manager. Don't get me wrong, I absolutely love some of the black players out there: Wrighty, Thierry Henri, Viera. But you don't want a black manager.'

'Why ever not?'

Sid tapped his forehead with his finger but said nothing.

'What? Are you saying black people are thick?'

'You said it, mate, not me.'

'So Barack Obama hasn't got a brain?'

Sid lit his cigarette and shrugged. 'Exception that proves the rule,' he said over his shoulder as he departed.

Ross was still quivering when Sofie came back. 'Do you know what that bastard just said to me?'

He gave an account of their conversation and Sofie shook her head.

'Racist bastard. Shall I tell you what Veronika told me the other day?'

210

'What?'

'She said Martha nearly split up with Sid.'

'What? Why?'

'Apparently she went shopping and left him to look after the kids, and when she got back, there was cocaine all over the coffee table and he was out of his brain.'

'Wow.'

'Yeah. She told him, "If you ever take drugs in front of the kids again, I'll leave you and I'll take the kids with me."'

'Bloody hell.'

'Not only that, she said she'd stop him having any access till he cleaned himself up. And he said, "If you take my kids away from me, I'll kill myself."'

'Jesus, that is serious. Do you think he would?'

Sofie laughed. 'Him? Kill himself? Nah, he's just a wanker.'

'But not a complete bastard.'

'What?'

'That's what you said the other day.'

Sofie shrugged.

'So, apart from rescuing the occasional seagull, what stops him being a complete bastard?'

'We better go in. The first guests will be down in a bit.'

Chapter Thirty-One

Bee's father drove them home from church. As her parents went upstairs to change out of their Sunday best, Bee put the kettle on. Once it had boiled, she made tea for herself and her mother and a mug of weak coffee for her father. She put her parents' drinks in the living room and took her own upstairs.

Bee: 👋

Robbie: Hey babes. How ya doin?

Bee: I am so fed up, and it's only one day since my job finished.

Robbie: Fed up or hung over?

Bee: Bit of both. Good night last night. But church this morning was like having my teeth pulled.

Robbie: Can't find the hug emoji. Consider yourself cyber-hugged.

Bee: Thanx

Robbie: So, what are you going to do now you're unemployed?

Bee: Dunno. I might try and get another job, but it wouldn't be as much fun as a language school.

Robbie: You could always come and see your boyfriend in Cambridge…

Bee: I might do that.

Robbie: You know I'm going to Edinburgh on the 18th? Why don't you come and meet the parents!!! 🙀

Bee: Hmm. Maybe. Trouble is I've got this bloody Alpha Course my mum insists on me going to.

Robbie: You can miss one week.

Bee: Okay let's do it.
Talking about Alpha – Sofie wants me to write her a history of the Bible.

Robbie: You'll make an atheist of her yet.

Bee: It'll give me something to do, I suppose. I'm so bored.

She spent a long time thinking about her email for Sofie. She wasn't sure where to start. She opened up a Word document, typed a first paragraph and deleted it. She tried again and typed three whole paragraphs before deleting them.

'Okay,' she said out loud. 'Let's try a different tack.'

You cannot understand who wrote the Bible if you do not know the story of the Ancient Israelites and how they became the Jews, so I am going to have to tell you that story and then the story of how the Bible came to be written.

Yes – that was a good start. Next she typed out a six-sentence summary of 'historical' parts of the Old Testament, from the creation through Noah,

Abraham, Joseph and Moses to the conquest of the Promised Land, David, Solomon, the fall of Israel and Judah and the Babylonian exile.

OK, let's go back to the first bit, the ancient myths, from the creation to Noah's Ark and the Tower of Babel. Sophisticated Jews and Christians have long known that you should not take these bits any more literally than we would take the stories of Zeus, Prometheus and what have you. They are myths, brilliant myths, but no more than that.

She frowned and shook her head. How could people still take these myths literally? Was there something wrong with *mythos*? Why didn't it work the way it was supposed to? Maybe only a certain kind of person gets the difference between *mythos* and *logos*. Do some people, even most people, always take myths literally and either believe them or reject them?

*

While Bee was musing over the Old Testament, Ross was lying in bed. It was his day off and he was wondering whether to get up. The accident had once more sunk its claws into him, and he was worried about Alpha and whether he could really make that leap of faith Nigel had talked about. Because if he couldn't, what hope was there? There was no way he would try counselling again, which meant Alpha really mattered.

He was also feeling irritated with Sofie. He didn't like the way she clammed up when he asked her about Sid. He had been so open with her, more open than with anyone else, but she wasn't reciprocating.

At that moment, his mobile pinged. It was Sofie.

Maybe he should pretend he hadn't seen it.

His mobile pinged again.

Sofie:	You up yet??
	My mum's taking the little ones to the beach after lunch.
	I can either go with them or you can come round and play on my Nintendo.

After a moment's hesitation, he typed out a reply.

Ross:	Congratulations
Sofie:	Wot?
Ross:	You remembered not to call her kate
Sofie:	☺
Ross:	Why don't you come here I got an Xbox
Sofie:	Your mum doesn't like me. You come here

They spent more than half an hour on Sofie's Nintendo, but Ross couldn't get into it and lost every game. At Sofie's suggestion, they abandoned it and went for a walk up on the Downs. The route from her house took them up a long, straight road, through what had been a 1930s council estate, past a housing development from the 1960s and up through some woods that led to a steep hill. They climbed to the top and sat down to get their breath back. They had a great view of the town and the whole sweep of the bay as far as Bexhill, St Leonards and Hastings.

'Looks amazing, innit?' said Sofie.

'Yeah.'

She leaned into him with a bump. 'How you doing?'

He shrugged. 'Bit low this morning, if I'm honest.'

'What? About *it*?'

'Yeah.'

'Do you still think about it all the time?'

'When I'm not busy, yeah.' After a moment, he said, 'I was a bit cross with you, too.'

'Me? Why? What have I done?'

'Because you never answer me when I ask you about Sid.'

'What? So I have to tell you everything?'

'I thought we were friends.'

'We are friends.'

'Well, friends tell each other stuff, don't they?'

'What? Like you and Raj revise together for three weeks and never discuss the accident even once?'

'Who told you that?'

'Dani.'

Ross laughed.

'You know he still blames himself for nagging you to overtake.'

'Wasn't him that forgot to look in the mirror.'

'So, you don't blame him?'

'No.'

'Not even a little bit.'

Ross gave a little shrug.

'You two need to talk.'

'What am I supposed to say? "I hereby forgive you for nagging me."'

'You should just say, "Sofie says you worry that I blame you for nagging me to overtake." And then just take it from there.'

'Yeah, maybe.'

'Anyway, what is it you want me to tell you?'

'Whatever you think it appropriate to share with your friend who's sitting next to you.'

Sofie brought her knees up to her chest and hugged her legs. After a moment, she said, 'My sister dropped out of college before her A-Levels. She got a job in the book warehouse, and she moved out soon after that. I used to go round and stay with her at weekends. We was quite close in them days.'

She paused for a long time before she continued.

214

'After about a year, she got this new boyfriend, Jake. I think I told you, he's a bouncer at Ziggy's.'

'Yeah.'

'He was what you'd call a bad influence. It wasn't long before he had her doing all sorts: skunk, coke, shrooms, speed, dingers, you name it. He never gave her crack or heroin, mind. He wasn't that stupid.'

'Did they get you doing it too?'

'Yeah. Not as much as what Amy did. I only done weed and coke. I had a dinger, but only once. Jake and some of his mates were real bastards. They thought it was really funny to get me stoned. Sid protected me, unlike my sister, it has to be said. He told me it was okay to do a bit of weed and coke, but he wouldn't let me do too much, and he stopped me doing anything else. He wasn't there that time I had a dinger, and he had a right go at the guy who gave it me when he found out.'

'So that's why he's not a complete bastard.'

'One of the reasons, yeah.' After a moment, she said, 'I saw him stop a fight more than once. People like him because they know he can handle himself, but he don't throw his weight around. If there's trouble, right, he can smooth it down, get everyone laughing. And he is funny.' She started to laugh. 'One time, he got hold of some white popping candy. He crushed it into powder and told Jake it was coke. So Jake snorted it.' She stopped speaking and laughed until tears came to her eyes.

Ross smiled.

'You ever done drugs?' Sofie asked.

'Only weed, maybe four or five times. First time, right, it was at this party in year ten. These two guys crashed the party and sold us little bits of dope wrapped in silver foil. But nobody had any cigarette papers, so we couldn't make any joints. So we decided to swallow it. But Raj, right, he forgot to take the silver foil off before he ate his.'

They both laughed. 'Typical Raj,' said Sofie. 'Presumably it came out the other end.'

'Presumably.'

'Did you like it?'

'What? Raj's poo?'

'No, stupid, the dope.'

'It didn't really do anything, except I had some pretty weird dreams that night.'

'What about the other times?'

Ross shrugged. 'It was all right, I suppose. I prefer lager. I don't like smoking, and anyway, I don't like where your money goes if you buy illegal stuff.'

'Well, I know exactly where it goes: Sid and Jake and their lowlife mates.'

'What? Sid's a dealer?'

'Yeah. Officially, he makes his money on eBay. He says he buys stuff from idiots who don't know what it's worth, and then he sells it to other idiots who don't know how worthless it is. But he makes most of his money selling drugs.'

'Jesus.' Ross shook his head. 'Presumably his law-and-order Tory mother doesn't know.'

'I think she knows he has an expensive drug habit, but maybe she don't know he's a dealer. And don't you go telling her.'

'And you say he's not a complete bastard?'

'He's not,' said Sofie. 'Far as he's concerned, all he's doing is giving people what they want. He don't sell nothing he don't take himself, and especially, he don't sell the really hard stuff like smack or crack.'

'Yeah, but go along the chain and you're financing some really nasty people.'

Sofie shrugged. 'Maybe. But you've seen him with his kids. He adores them, and they really love him. Have you noticed, it's always his knee they sit on, not Martha's?'

'Yeah, I have noticed that.'

'I know he's so macho, and he's horrible to you and that. And all his drugs, and chasing after skirt, but underneath it all, there's a decent person in there struggling to get out.'

'You really think so?'

'Yeah. He's just screwed up.'

'How do you mean?'

'He's got this perfect brother, innit? And he can't compete with him. It's like he's desperate for his mother to love him, but he doesn't see how she can love him as much as she loves Nigel. So he pushes and pushes against her, daring her to reject him. But she never does, and that's how he knows she loves him.'

'Bloody hell. That's deep. Where do you get all that?'

'Erm, AS-Level psychology, hoping for a grade A, if you don't mind.'

'Oh, right. I didn't realise I was sitting next to the next Sigmund Freud.'

They sat in silence for several minutes. Eventually Sofie stretched out her legs.

Ross asked, 'You really think that's true about Sid? You know, Nigel and his mum and that.'

'Yes. When I started doing psychology, it was like I was studying the story of my life. Untreated trauma leading to substance abuse? Well, that's my dad and my sister, innit? Traumatised children unable to regulate their behaviour? Well, that was me, classic case. We done things like attachment theory, sibling rivalry, adult sibling envy. And then, when I found out Sid had this brother who's a priest, that's when everything just fell into place. I mean, I bet Nigel really is the apple of his mother's eye.'

'So, is that why he's got all them tattoos?'

'Bingo.'

'And his fake working-class accent?'

'He did go to private school, but he got thrown out. So he ended up at Upperton. He probably had to change his accent pronto if he wanted to get in with the cool kids.'

'So, did you know him at Upperton?'

'Don't be daft. He's more than ten years older than us.'

After a moment, Ross asked, 'So, when did you fall out with him?'

It was several seconds before she answered. 'When I got pregnant. I went round to my sister's flat and screamed at her. I slapped her too.'

'Why?'

Another long pause. 'I blamed her. My boyfriend was always moaning about using condoms. Said he couldn't feel anything. So I asked Amy, my sister, and she said it was safe just after my period.' She scoffed. 'So I let him, and guess what, it bloody well wasn't safe.'

'Oh, right.'

'Sid and Jake were there, so I screamed at them too.' She laughed. 'I slapped Sid as well. I didn't half slap them.'

'How did they react?'

'They threw me out and shut the door. I was outside for about twenty minutes, screaming and hammering on the door.'

'Wow.'

'Never seen any of them since, not till I saw Sid at the hotel. I haven't spoken to my sister all this time, and she's never tried to contact me. Not once.'

Her voice cracked a little as she spoke.

*

Bee stopped typing and picked up her mobile to give herself a break. She spent several minutes scrolling through her Instagram feed and posted some photos of the previous night's end-of-summer party with her language-school friends. Working there was the best thing about coming to live on the south coast. That and getting to know Sofie.

She put down her mobile and re-read the latest section of her 'assignment'. It was about the Patriarchs: Abraham, Jacob, Joseph, Moses and Joshua. She had written about how historians and archaeologists used to assume they were real historical figures. They descended on Egypt and Palestine in search of evidence for them, but despite some early false leads, they didn't find any.

Instead, once they learned to read hieroglyphics, they built up a detailed, year-by-year history of Egypt.

Among other things, they found Egyptian sources that told the intriguing story of the Hyksos, a Semitic people whose story seemed to mirror the Israelite Exodus. The Hyksos settled in Egypt in large numbers, much like Jacob and his sons. They established themselves as rulers of northern Egypt (a bit like Joseph?), but eventually the Egyptians rose up and drove them out.

So is this the Exodus story from the Egyptian point of view? On the face of it, it looks very similar.

But the dates, the numbers and the details just don't fit. Archaeologists eventually had to admit they found couldn't find anything that backed up the story of the Exodus as told in the Bible.

Bee stopped reading and thought about how strange it was that the story of Moses had resonated down the centuries, an inspiration for opponents of slavery and victims of colonisation and racism.

In one sense, this wasn't surprising. It was, after all, a tale of liberation from oppression. But at the same time, the God of the Exodus was a monster. He deliberately manufactured a crisis in order to show everyone how great he was. It was God that hardened the Pharoah's heart and prevented him from letting the Israelites go. And then he punished the whole Egyptian nation by killing all their first-born sons.

Bee understood how such a myth might seem normal in a world where kings would routinely stamp on their subjects to show who was boss, but how can it still be appropriate in a world where the massacre of innocent civilians is a crime against humanity?

Almost all historians think there is probably a kernel of truth in the story of the Exodus: some of the ancestors of some of the Israelites must have settled in Egypt for a time and then either left or been driven out. Perhaps there is a connection with the Hyksos. Maybe there really were leaders called Moses and Aaron, but we will probably never know because the true story is lost in the mists of time.

Whatever the case, we should not take the Biblical account of the Exodus any more literally than the tales of King Arthur and the Knights of the Round Table. The Exodus is a national myth of the Israelites and the Jews, just as King Arthur is a national myth of the English and the Welsh. We are talking about *mythos* here, not history.

Bee worried that she had written too much about Moses. Did she really need to tell Sofie not to take the Bible literally? Hadn't she already worked that out? But then again, she had asked for a full dose of *logos*, so that was what she was going to get.

Next, she had written about the Israelite conquest of Canaan, the most evil part of the Old Testament, a tale of ethnic cleansing and genocide. Only trouble is, none of it was true. The Israelites hadn't invaded Canaan, they had emerged from within it.

Invasions and mass migrations leave tell-tale signs in the archaeological record: different ways of making pottery, houses built differently, weapons and tools made to a different design, that sort of thing. There is none of that here. The Israelites are themselves Canaanites, and they have emerged from within Canaanite society

Bee was happy with this. It would do. But now, she needed a break, and Nobby needed a walk.

*

Next day, as he arrived for the evening shift, Ross couldn't help but grin at the absence of Sid. Arsenal had been thrashed by Manchester City the previous day, and Ross was confident that this would guarantee him a few days' peace.

He smiled at the thought of Sofie slapping Sid. He wished he could have seen it. But then again, it must have been an awful time for her. She must have been really scared to find herself pregnant. And she lost her sister as a result of what happened. Nothing to laugh about, really.

It occurred to him that Sid might have told Sofie's sister that he had seen her. Would this represent an opportunity for her to put out feelers and see if there was any chance of a reconciliation? Perhaps he should ask her.

He waited until they were unlocking their bikes at the end of the shift.

'You know you said yesterday about your sister...'

'Yeah.' Sofie's tone was very flat.

'Does it upset you that you've lost touch with her?'

Sofie let her bike lean against the wall and folded her arms.

'I'll tell you what upsets me.'

'What?'

'That my stupid sister fell in with a bunch of cokeheads. That she was so out of her brain, she thought it was okay to treat a fifteen-year-old like an adult and encourage her to get coked out too. That she was happy for her little sister, who wasn't even legal, to sleep with one of her boyfriend's mates, who was nearly twice as old as her. That's what upsets me,' said Sofie. 'I know what you're going to suggest. You're going to say maybe I should get Sid to put us back in touch. Is that right?'

'I just thought, perhaps...'

'Well don't, right. You concentrate on your problems and leave me to deal with mine.'

Ross raised his hands as if in surrender. 'Sorry.'

She took her bike and cycled off without waiting for him.

'Wow!' Ross said out loud. He shook his head and shuddered.

219

Chapter Thirty-Two

Bee sat back. She had finished the first half of her 'assignment'. She would read through the last bit one more time, paste it into an email and then send it.

Another interesting thing is that at first, the Israelites did not worship Yahweh. Archaeologists can guess which gods a community worshipped by the names they gave people and places. With the Israelites, the clue is in the name they gave themselves: IsraEL. They worshipped the same gods as the rest of Canaan, a pantheon headed by a god called El.

There is strong evidence to suggest that Yahweh did not arrive among the Israelites until around 1000 BCE, possibly brought by a tribe that migrated north into Canaan. Yahweh was a god of storms and war, and he was now incorporated into the pantheons of several nations in the region.

It is likely that Yahweh became a royal or national god of the Israelites under one of their early kings, possibly David. The Bible describes the process in the Song of Moses, a very ancient poem inserted into Deuteronomy, "When the **Most High** gave the nations their inheritance, when he separated the sons of man, he set the boundaries of the peoples according to the number of the **sons of Israel**. For **the LORD's** portion is his people; Jacob is the allotment of his inheritance."

Unfortunately, this translation obscures as much as it reveals. Today, many scholars think that it should really say this: "When **El** gave the nations their inheritance, when he separated the sons of man, he set the boundaries of the peoples according to the number of the **gods**. For **Yahweh's** portion is his people; Jacob is the allotment of his inheritance."

It was not a case of God selecting the Israelites as his chosen people. It was El, the king of the gods, who allocated the Israelites to Yahweh.

Bee gave herself a double thumbs up here. Her university syllabus didn't cover the origins of the cult of Yahweh, but she had researched it herself out of pure curiosity. And it turned out to be useful, after all.

The next part talked about how the myths of different communities of Israelites had coalesced into a single national myth. As she read it, she remembered one of her first dates with Robbie, back in February. They went to see *Joseph and the Amazing Technicolour Dreamcoat* at the Cambridge Arts Theatre. They chose a cheap weekday matinee, and the theatre was full of school parties.

During the interval, Bee asked Robbie what he thought of it.

'On one level, it's really good,' he said. 'It's clever, it's witty. The actors are good, and some of the songs are good.'

'But?'

'But on another level, I'm a bit queasy about it. I mean, I'm assuming none of this stuff actually happened. But these schoolkids, I'm worried that they're going to walk out of here thinking it's a true story.'

Bee then spoke about *mythos* and *logos*. Robbie said he had come across these concepts in his philosophy courses, but he had never understood how *mythos* could still be relevant in a contemporary religious context. They spent the rest of the day talking about it. That date could so easily have been a disaster, but it ended up bringing them closer.

She looked out of the window and sighed. It was starting to get dark. She had spent the best part of two days on this. Time to finish reading through it and give Robbie a call.

In Israel, Yahweh was often worshipped as a fertility god and was strongly associated with the Exodus. There is also evidence of two new factors: one is conflict between those who worshipped Yahweh as a bull and those who did not (we see echoes of this in the story of Moses, Aaron and the golden calf). The other is an intransigent Yahwism that wanted to suppress the worship of the Canaanite bull god Baal.

In Judah, his statues tended to depict him more as a kingly figure, one to whom human sacrifices were sometimes made in times of crisis.

It was common in those days for royal/national gods to take over the functions of other gods, and Yahweh began to do the same, encroaching on both El, the king of the gods, and Shemesh, the sun god. Among other things, he acquired El's wife, the mother goddess Asherah.

So here we have the situation in the two Israelite kingdoms before the catastrophic events of 722 and 586 BCE that destroyed both kingdoms and led to the transformation of Yahweh from a typical pagan god to the transcendent one only God of Judaism and Christianity.

But you will have to wait for the next part of my assignment for that. I will try to send it tomorrow. I hope you have enjoyed this part.[3]

*

Ross: 🖐

It was more than 20 minutes before Sofie replied.

Sofie:	Hiya.
Ross:	Am I forgiven
Sofie:	😔
Ross:	🙏
Sofie:	Oh all right then, on 1 condition
Ross:	What's that

---

[3] For the reader who is interested, Bee's full email is included as Appendix Three on page 376.

Sofie:	You forgive me for being a stroppy little cow
Ross:	🤝
Sofie:	I know you were trying to help, Ross, but I'm just not ready to go there
Ross:	I understand sorry
Sofie:	BTW B's sent me a brilliant email about where the Bible came from Do you wanna see it?

Ross replied with a GIF of Steve Carell yelling, 'No, God please no!' In return, Sofie sent a GIF of American Big Brother contestant Elissa Slater spitting out her drink as she bursts out laughing.

*

Bee woke up at seven. She had a busy day ahead of her, a job to finish. She quickly showered and went downstairs to make coffee and grab a bowl of granola before her parents got up. This would be a working breakfast. She couldn't wait to get started.

She began with a potted history of the Israelites/Jews, and their precarious existence in the shadow of powerful empires: Assyrians, Babylonians, Persians, Greeks and, finally, Romans.

Next, she wrote about how J, E, P and D came to be written. She said the first was probably E, written in the northern kingdom of Israel not long before its destruction by Assyria.

After the fall of Israel, a mass of refugees flooded into Judah. The resulting population explosion triggered an economic and social revolution. Jerusalem grew 15-fold and many other villages expanded into towns…

And with this social and economic revolution came a religious revolution…intransigent Yahwists sparked off a great national-religious movement that called for the unification of all Israelites and the exclusive worship of Yahweh. They didn't believe Yahweh was the only god: merely that the Israelites had a covenant with him in which they promised to worship no other gods. This Yahweh-only faction was something new and different with no real parallels in the other countries of the region, apart from briefly in Egypt some 600 years earlier.

The next text to be written was J, another Yahweh-only manifesto, in this case written by priests from the Jerusalem temple, who insisted that theirs was the only temple where sacrifices could be made to Yahweh.

Bee's 'assignment' spoke about the debate over the date of the D text. For over 200 years, most scholars had dated it to 640 BCE, when the Yahweh-only faction briefly seized power under the boy-king Josiah. But Bee favoured the view of recent scholars who dated D to after the catastrophe of 586 BCE.

The Babylonians had already successfully invaded Judah once, 19 years earlier.

(They) placed a new king, Zadekiah, on the throne, expecting him to be docile. But he rebelled, and in doing so, he doomed himself and his people. The Babylonians marched back into Judah, laid siege to Jerusalem and rampaged through the countryside bringing fire, destruction and death.

In desperation, Zadekiah and his army broke out of the city and fled east. But the Babylonians captured him near Jericho. The Bible tells us the exemplary punishment they meted out to him: "They killed the sons of Zadekiah before his eyes. Then they put out his eyes, bound him with bronze shackles and took him to Babylon."

...The catastrophe was total. Jerusalem was in ruins, the Temple, supposedly the only place where Yahweh could be worshipped, had been destroyed. Every single city in Judah had been burned to the ground. The royal family, the nobility and the priesthood had either been deported or killed or had fled, and much of the countryside had been depopulated.

How could the survivors account for such a calamity?

The traditional explanation would be that Marduk, the Babylonian national god, was stronger than Yahweh, and that was all there was to it.

But some Yahweh-only ideologues put forward an alternative explanation. The destruction of Israel and Judah had not come about because Yahweh was weak. Far from it: Yahweh himself had visited this devastation upon his own people, as a punishment for breaking their covenant in which they promised to worship only him. Yahweh had used the Assyrians and Babylonians to punish Israel and Judah.

One faction...produced a history that put this explanation in writing. This is the Deuteronomistic History, a collection of books that goes from Deuteronomy (the D text, more or less) through the books of Joshua, Judges, 1 Samuel, 2 Samuel, 1 Kings and 2 Kings.

...Every leader is judged good or wicked to the extent that he follows the Yahweh-only, Jerusalem-only, no-mixing-with-foreigners rules. The bigoted, the narrow-minded and the fanatical are hailed as good; the liberal, the cosmopolitan, the pragmatic and the tolerant are condemned as wicked.

This is the dark secret at the heart of the Judeo-Christian tradition. The authors of these key holy texts were not the good guys. They were not pragmatists or cautious conservatives. They were not gentle liberals or far-sighted reformers.

They were fanatics. They were the Robespierre, the Lenin, the Ayatollah Khomeini of their day, fierce ideologues for whom toleration and diversity were dirty words.

Bee frowned as she read the last three paragraphs. Was that fair? Why was she writing like a militant atheist? What was she trying to do? Derail Sofie's spiritual journey? It made her feel dirty. She had no right to inflict her own spiritual crisis on her.

And in any case, all that stuff about 'the dark secret of the Judeo-Christian tradition' was only the case for the prosecution. There was also a case for the defence. Maybe the prophets and the Deuteronomist had been narrow-minded, but isn't that to judge them by the standards of our age rather than theirs?

Somebody once said that you shouldn't judge a religion by its origins. All religions start out with absurdity, but that's not what counts. What matters is what a religion's devotees make of it.

And just look at what they have created in this case: the beautiful and gentle Jewish faith. Was the author of the Book of Ecclesiastes narrow-minded? Was the author of Jonah intolerant? Or what about Saadya Gaon, or Maimonides? Or the great Hebrew poet and philosopher Solomon Ibn Gabirol, was he a narrow-minded bigot? Or Rabbi Lionel Blue, for heaven's sake?

The other great legacy of the Israelite prophets is Christianity. Bee might have been confused about so many things, but there was one thing she most definitely knew: Bartolomé de las Casas wasn't narrow-minded or intolerant. Nor were William Wilberforce, John Brown, Martin Luther King or Archbishop Oscar Romero. Or Archbishop Desmond Tutu, for that matter. The only thing these great men were intolerant of was injustice.

And wasn't that another tradition the Old Testament prophets have handed down to us, a tradition of speaking the truth to power, of being unafraid to cry out against injustice? Is it a coincidence that democracy and human rights have flowered in those societies imbued with the Judeo-Christian ethos? Is it a coincidence that so many great radicals and reformers down the ages have drawn their inspiration from their Christian faith? Is it a coincidence that secular humanism emerged in the Christian West, not in other societies?

But Bee had said none of this.

She hesitated for a moment and then deleted those three paragraphs.

*

Tuesday was a day off, so Ross didn't wake up until almost 10 o'clock. He went downstairs to retrieve his mobile. He smiled broadly when he saw the message from Sofie that was waiting for him.

Sofie:	Fancy doing anything today?
Ross:	Good morning yes Xbox
Sofie:	Oh, you're there! You just got up you lazy git?
Ross:	No been running a half-marathon
Sofie:	Yeah, right
Ross:	So how about it Xbox my parents are at work no sign of my little brother
Sofie:	Yeah, okay

By the time Sofie came round, Ross had set up the Xbox on the TV and put two controllers on the coffee table in front of the sofa.

'Fancy a cuppa?'

'Yes, please. Tea for me.'

'Okay, I'll put the kettle on. You can choose the game on the Xbox if you like.'

When Ross brought two mugs of tea in, he could see that Sofie hadn't touched the Xbox. She was standing near the fireplace.

'What are these trophies?'

On the bookshelves to the right of the fireplace, there were half a dozen silver cups and several medals.

'Table tennis.'

'Are they yours?'

'Mostly my dad's, but that one's mine, near your elbow.'

Sofie picked it up and read it: '"Old Town Young Player of the Year 2017." Ooh, very impressive.'

Ross smiled and puffed out his chest.

'Dani says you can never beat Raj.'

'I can't. I'm a better player than him but I can't beat him.'

'How come?'

'My best shot's my serve. I can disguise the side spin so my opponent doesn't know which way it's going, so I win a lot of points on my serve. But Raj, right, he's played me so many times, he's worked it out.'

'Where'd you learn to play?'

'Here, at home. We've got a table in the loft.'

'Seriously?'

'Yeah. It's like a dormer bedroom but we use it for table tennis.'

'Well, sod your Xbox. Let's go and play table tennis. I want to see your deadly serve.'

'I warn you, it is deadly.'

As they went upstairs, Sofie asked, 'What about your mum? Does she play?'

'Yeah, not in the league and that, but she's pretty good. She's very competitive. She lets my little brother win but she hates it if I beat her.'

*

Bee's 'assignment' went on to talk about the Persian invasion that freed the Jews, as they were now known, from their Babylonian exile. The Persians needed collaborators to help them rule their vast empire, which stretched from India to the frontiers of Greece. So they allowed the Jews to return home and restore their temple in Jerusalem.

She said the P document was probably composed around this time.

The Priestly Writer knew all about J and E. He was not writing a text to complement them but to replace them. He did not like J and E's idea of Yahweh as a merciful god. In his view Yahweh is not merciful; he is just. If you commit a sin, you should not rely on Yahweh's mercy; you should go to the Temple in Jerusalem and make an appropriate sacrifice.

As she read this, it struck Bee just how polytheistic the idea of sacrifice is. You are literally feeding the gods when you give them a burnt offering. But in a monotheistic context, it was utterly bizarre. Have you committed a sin and offended God? Never mind: kill an animal and he will forgive you. Need a favour from God? Kill an animal and he will hear your prayer.

Why?

It made no sense.

She thought about how Christians often imagine that sacrifice plays no part in their religion. But it is right at the heart of it, since they believe that Jesus was sacrificed to atone for our sins. And this wasn't any old sacrifice, it was a human sacrifice.

'Their' religion? That was what Bee had just said to herself. Shouldn't it be 'our' religion? Or had her faith finally evaporated? Was she now an atheist? And if so, what did she believe in?

If there is no God, what is there?

Nothing?

Absurdism?

Existential nihilism?

She had discussed this often enough with Robbie. He liked to say that God may be dead, but that doesn't mean we don't miss him. She had always disagreed: God was still alive, more distant than we might like, perhaps simply some kind of universal spirit like Sofie's Hindu friend had spoken of, but still something we could reach for and hope to connect with.

But what if she now thought the same as Robbie?

Where did that leave her?

*

The table wasn't green or blue but varnished MDF without a line down the middle.

'Is it a bit small?' Sofie asked.

'God, some people are never satisfied.'

Sofie laughed. 'Okay. It's a lovely table. What size is it?'

'Eight foot by four foot six.'

'Which means?'

'It's a foot short and six inches too narrow.'

'So, I was right.'

She walked to the far end and picked up the red bat that was lying there. To Ross's surprise, she held it Chinese penhold style. He picked up the bat at his end and sent an easy serve over.

She smashed it.

'Yay! One-love.'

Ross laughed. He picked another ball out of the box and did one of his disguised side-spin serves. It hit Sofie's bat and went flying way to the left.

'One all.'

'That was your thing?'

'Yes. Didn't know you could play.'

'Yeah, my dad taught me. Quite a while ago, mind you. Haven't played for ages.'

'Nor have I.'

They warmed up for a few minutes and then Sofie threw the ball across the net to challenge him to a game.

'You have to do your best but you're not allowed to do your demon serve.'

'Okay.'

Ross won first serve and the game began. Sofie celebrated every point she won and blamed most of the points she lost on the short table, but Ross won 11-6.

They changed ends.

'So,' said Sofie, 'from now on, you have to give me five points head start. That should make it interesting.'

*

But the Jewish religion was changing. The Deuteronomistic History claimed that it was Yahweh himself who had used the Babylonians to punish Judah. This indicated that Yahweh was a very powerful god indeed, one whose power extended over other nations.

This was the gateway to a massive revolution in Jewish theology, the development of monotheism, the idea that there is just one God, a perfect being who is who is all-knowing and all-powerful. Monotheism is not just polytheism minus all the other gods. It is something new and completely different.

So, let's look at some of the most important differences between monotheism and polytheism.

Polytheistic religions have mythology, the story of how the gods came to be. In the Bible, all this has disappeared. There is no origin story of God. He just is.

Polytheistic gods need names to distinguish them from each other. God doesn't. And so within Judaism there developed the doctrine that God's name must never be pronounced. Most Christian Bibles dispense with his name altogether, replacing "Yahweh" with "the LORD".

Polytheistic gods have a body. God does not. The Old Testament is peppered with references to God's face, head, hands, feet, torso and even (smoothed out by copyists and translators) his genitals. Jews and Christians learned to read all these references to his body allegorically, but we should not forget that they were originally written to be taken literally.

And if God no longer has a body, then he must not be portrayed in a statue. Overt references to statues of Yahweh disappeared from the Jews' holy texts. However, this did not stop their enemies recording the capture of

Jerusalem Temple statues on the stone steles that commemorated their victories.

Polytheistic gods are not particularly nice. They are vain and prone to spiteful and vindictive behaviour if you do not show them due respect. God, on the other hand, is a perfect being.

Here, Jews and Christians have a real problem, because, in the words of Richard Dawkins, the God of the Old Testament is "jealous and proud of it; a petty, unjust, unforgiving control-freak; a vindictive, bloodthirsty ethnic cleanser; a misogynistic, homophobic, racist, infanticidal, genocidal, filicidal, pestilential, megalomaniacal, sadomasochistic, capriciously malevolent bully."

In other words, he behaves like a typical polytheistic god.

Unfortunately, the worst kind of Jew and Christian see this version of God as an example to follow. But for thousands of years, the best Jews and Christians have seen this aspect of the Bible as purely allegorical, as *mythos*, not something to be taken literally at all. And certainly not something to be imitated.

The most intellectually rigorous Jews and Christians see this aspect of the Old Testament for what it is, a remnant of its polytheistic origins.

Monotheism has a big problem with evil. Why does an all-powerful and perfectly good God allow terrible things to happen? Polytheism has no such problem. The gods can be horrible, and in any case, their powers are limited.

One explanation for evil and suffering is to say that God is not evil but just. He allows terrible things to happen to us because he is punishing us for our sins. But, as Ecclesiastes (the best book in the Bible by far) points out: "In this meaningless life of mine I have seen both of these: the righteous perishing in their righteousness, and the wicked living long in their wickedness." There is often precious little sign of divine justice here on earth.

And so the idea of divine justice in the afterlife develops. The deserving shall enjoy everlasting bliss in Heaven while the wicked simply perish (what the first Christians probably believed) or suffer eternal torment in Hell (later Christian doctrine).

It had often occurred to Bee that those who believe in an everlasting afterlife hadn't thought it through. Eternity is a very long time, trillions and trillions of years. So, unless those in heaven were hooked up to some sort of eternal dopamine drip feed, wouldn't they just get bored? Surely no life could be so joyous that it wouldn't turn into the worst kind of curse after the first trillion years.

So, if the reward promised by Christianity had no appeal for her, Bee wondered why she should continue to think of herself as a Christian. Hadn't the time come to let it go?

Another solution to the problem of evil is to give God an antagonist. Satan is a very minor character in most of the Old Testament. He is a provocateur, a member of the council of the gods who acts on Yahweh's behalf. But, perhaps influenced by Zoroastrianism, he evolves into God's enemy, eventually becoming almost his equal in terms of power, and he is projected back into the early texts so that, for Christians, the snake in the Garden of Eden becomes a manifestation of Satan.

But Satan cannot be God's equal, which means that, ultimately, God must triumph over him. This leads to eschatology, a belief in end times and a final, devastating war between good and evil that culminates in the arrival of the Kingdom of Heaven on earth.

Among some Jews, such eschatological beliefs combined with a yearning for liberation from their foreign overlords. The end times would not only entail the defeat of Satan but also the return of a Davidic king anointed by God to lead the Jews to ultimate victory over the Gentile nations.

The Hebrew word for this anointed king is, of course, Messiah.

Bee closed her eyes and rested her head in her hands over her laptop keyboard. It had never occurred to her before that almost the whole of Christianity was a response to the problem of evil. Eschatology, the Messiah, Satan, sin, Heaven, Hell and Christ's atoning sacrifice: it was all part of the search for an answer to the central conundrum at the heart of monotheism. How can an all-powerful, all-knowing, all-good and loving God allow suffering?

But the whole thing was futile. If God was all-knowing and all-powerful, surely there was only one possible answer to the problem of evil: he was neither all-good nor loving. He was indifferent, like the Greek Fates (Bee refused to believe that God could actually be malevolent).

And if God was indifferent, why worship him? It made no more sense than a Greek praying to the Fates.

The only other solution to the problem of evil was that God didn't exist.

Whichever of these two solutions was correct, an indifferent God or a non-existent God, she could no longer see any point in calling herself a Christian.

She felt as if the foundation stone of everything she had ever believed had just crumbled. Her faith had been tottering for months, and now, with the foundations gone, it came crashing to the ground.

But if she was no longer a Christian, what was she?

Who was she?

At that moment, she had no idea.

She only knew that the identity she had spent the last 20 years constructing had disintegrated. She was no longer the person she had spent her whole life becoming.

Chapter Thirty-Three

Bee didn't know what to do. She stared at her laptop and after a moment folded it shut. She needed some fresh air. She went downstairs and poked her head out of the kitchen door. Her parents were in the back garden, digging up some osmanthus bushes that had seen better days.

'I'm just popping out.'

'Okay,' said her mother. 'I'll do lunch for about one-thirty. Is that okay?'

'Yes, that's fine.'

Bee glanced at her Apple watch. It was just gone 12. She went round to the front of the house, put on her trainers and headed for the seafront. She walked along King Edward's Parade, towards the town centre, but as she did so, she saw the Beachy Head bus approach. A quick sprint got her to the bus stop in time and she stuck out an arm.

She hopped on, paid and went upstairs to the open-top deck, sitting on the left, near the front. The bus wound its way uphill, away from the seafront, until it turned left towards the top of the cliffs.

She got off near the Beachy Head Pub, crossed the road and walked to the highest point, which was more than 160 metres above sea level. It was a beautiful sunny day, without a cloud in the sky. The sea glimmered purest blue, and through the haze, she could see Hastings and all the way to Dungeness to the east, and as far as Brighton, Worthing, Bognor Regis and Selsey to the west. Far out to sea, the enormous Rampion wind farm was as clear as she had ever seen it, a massive investment in a better future.

It seemed strange to her that such a beautiful place could be a popular suicide spot. She couldn't understand how anyone could end their lives there. The magnificent view lifted her spirits. She felt glad to be alive, to feel the sun and the wind on her face. This was a place to live, to cherish life, not a place to end it.

She had things to do. She had an email to send to Sofie. There was no point taking the bus back. It would go a roundabout route and drop her off at the pier, over a mile from her house.

She set off on foot. It was quite a long way, but it was all downhill and the views looking east were amazing. When she got back, she gulped down a big glass of water and headed back to her room, where she opened up her laptop and started to read the rest of the final instalment of the Omega Course.

She said the redactors who stitched J, E, P and D together were monotheists, working sometime between the 400s and 200s BCE. The D text more or less survives as Deuteronomy, but people no longer had any incentive to copy J, E or P, and so they disappeared as the parchment and papyrus they were written on became illegible, lost for over 2,000 years until generations of scholars uncovered them.

None of this detracts from the Bible. It just means you should read the Bible as what it is. It is *mythos*, and as such, it can teach you a lot and broaden your horizons. Just don't take it literally, because if you do, you might become like Dominic, a decent man whose faith lifts him up and makes him a better person, apart from the reactionary ideas that infect his mind because he finds them in the Bible.

Don't let what I have said get in the way of your own spiritual journey. There are plenty of devout Christians who would agree with everything I have written in my "Omega Course" and it does not stop them being Christians. So please, please, please, don't let me stop you. I have seen for myself what a wonderful thing religious faith can be and it would be something I would regret forever if I prevented you from experiencing it for yourself.

With love and affection,

Omega Bee xx

She thought the final paragraphs weren't honest. If she thought of Sofie as a friend, it would be better to tell her the truth and let her know that she wouldn't be attending any more sessions of the Alpha Course. So she inserted two more paragraphs after 'because he finds them in the Bible.'

I am going to sign off now. I have enjoyed writing for you, because it has helped me clarify a lot of things in my own mind. It has helped me realise something I haven't been able to face up to before.

I now know that I really have lost my faith. I am not a Christian any more. I am an atheist.

There it is; I have said it. I am an atheist. It is not something I want to be. It means I have wasted two years of my life studying a subject I don't believe in. I am two thirds of the way through a degree that feels a bit embarrassing, and I have spent all these years dreaming of a career I no longer want.

'Oh dear,' she thought. 'That sounds really depressing.'

But just then, her mother called her downstairs for lunch. No time to change it. She highlighted everything, copied and pasted it into an email and sent it spinning into cyberspace.[4]

Her mother had prepared a lunch of Dr Oetker's mozzarella pizza with garlic bread and salad. They closed their eyes as her father said grace, and then they all tucked in.

They had almost finished when Bee's mother said, 'It's Alpha Course tonight, isn't it? So you won't be needing dinner.'

Bee braced herself and said, 'I'm thinking of not bothering tonight.'

---

[4] For the reader who is interested, Bee's entire second email about the origins of the Bible is included as Appendix Four on page 383.

'Why?'

'It's not for me, Mum. I really don't enjoy it.'

'But it's important. You have to hang onto your faith.'

'I haven't got any faith left, Mum.'

There.

She had said it.

'What do you mean?'

'What I just said. I haven't got any faith left. I don't believe any more.'

'No, Bee. No. You don't mean that.'

'I do.'

'That's not possible.'

Bee's father spoke: 'I thought you were just having doubts.'

'I was. And the doubts have won.'

Silence. Nobody spoke. Nobody ate.

'But why?'

'Dad, you know why. We've talked about it.'

'You mean Chloe's baby?'

'It's not just that. Everything...' She held her hands up in front of her. 'Everything just seems to tell me that it's not true, any of it.'

'Not literally true, no,' said her father.

Bee ran her fingers through her hair.

'I know all that. I know about analogy and *mythos* and finding the spiritual meaning. But it just feels like a wild goose chase because there's nothing there.'

'There are lots of good reasons to believe in God.'

'I know,' said Bee. 'I know all the arguments backwards: the five ways, ontological, teleological, design, beauty, morality. I know them all, and I know all the arguments against. And just now, all the arguments for believing are no longer speaking to me. And all the arguments against make sense.'

'That's a change in you,' said her father. 'The arguments haven't changed.'

'I know.'

'But if not God, what?'

'I don't know.'

'Well, you must have an answer.'

'Must I? Isn't it enough to say that I don't know what the answer is, but this answer doesn't work for me any more?'

'But the alternative to God is despair, nothingness, existential nihilism, absurdism.'

'Dad, I'm not trying to convince you. I'm just saying this is how I feel.'

Her father fell silent.

'Bee,' said her mother, 'the most important thing I ever did for you wasn't to give you life. It was to give you the chance of eternal life. You can't throw that away.'

Bee closed her eyes and shook her head. 'I don't believe in eternal life.'

'Please don't say that. If you reject God, there are consequences.'

'That's what you say, Mum, but I disagree.'

'That's not acceptable.'

'I have the right to my own opinion.'

'The law might give you that right, but God doesn't. If you turn your back on him, there are consequences.'

Bee closed her eyes and kept her mouth shut.

Her mother said, 'It cuts me like a knife to hear you speak like this. It's bad enough that your brother's stopped going to church, but at least he still believes. I just can't bear the thought of you throwing it all away like this.'

Bee said nothing. She picked up her last slice of pizza and took a bite, but she hardly noticed its taste at all. Her heart was racing and adrenaline and cortisol were raging through her body.

'Please Bee. Don't give up.' Her mother was close to tears. 'Give the Alpha Course one more try.'

'It won't do any good.'

'Please, for me. Just one more.'

Bee knew exactly what would happen. On Sunday it would be, 'Give church one more chance' and next Tuesday it would be the same with the Alpha Course. She needed to stand up for herself.

'Mum, no.'

*

Ross and Sofie didn't stop playing until 1:50. They had the window open and the fan on, but even so, both of them ended up soaked in sweat. After a slow start, Sofie was now winning by nine games to six. Ross complained that her head start was too big, and Sofie accused him of cheating by deploying his banned serve on at least three occasions.

They went downstairs and worked together to prepare fried egg and baked beans on toast. After lunch, they played Sonic Mania and Pro Evolution Soccer until 3:30, when Sofie said she wanted to go home to read Bee's latest email before tonight's Alpha Course.

'I could stay here if you fancy reading it together.'

Ross shook his head.

Just before she left, she put her hand on Ross's upper arm.

'I really enjoyed today.'

'Yeah, me too.'

They stood looking into each other's eyes for a moment.

'See you at the bus stop.'

'See you.'

Ross stood by the door and watched her until she disappeared round the corner. He closed the door, went into the living room and sat down. He closed his eyes and smiled his biggest smile for months.

Chapter Thirty-Four

Sofie was already at the bus stop when Ross got there. He went up to her and stood right in front of her. He thought he had never seen her face so radiant.

'Hiya.'

'Hi. So, did you read Bee's email?'

'Yeah.'

'Was it good?'

'Brilliant. You should read it.'

He shook his head. 'Look, I know what it says, "The Bible's not literally true and it's all *mythos*."'

Sofie laughed.

'See, I don't need to read it.'

'She said something else as well.'

'What?'

'She's an atheist.'

'Well, knock me down with a feather.'

'It's the first time she's actually said it.'

'So, I don't suppose we'll see her tonight.'

'No.'

'Pity.'

'Yeah, I'll miss her.'

*

As he listened to Dominic's sermon, it occurred to Ross that the accident no longer dominated his thoughts as it had. Every other session he had been to, Dominic had said something that would set him off and push him deep into a dark tunnel.

But there was none of that tonight. He was finding it very difficult to sit still and concentrate. He was wondering what he was doing there – no, he knew the answer to that one. He was there in search of redemption. He was hoping to hear something, anything, that would allow him to make that leap of faith that Nigel had spoken of. But he wasn't sure that Dominic was capable of giving him that something.

He glanced at Sofie. She was giving Dominic her full attention, enjoying it, lapping it up, somehow managing to reconcile Alpha and Omega. It made no sense to Ross.

And there was one other thing that he didn't get: after what Sofie had said about her being an atheist, what on earth was Bee doing there?

*

Bee was asking herself the same question and cursing herself for allowing her mother to browbeat her into doing her bidding yet again.

As she listened to Dominic, it occurred to her what a big thing it was to lose her religion. Christianity wasn't just a set of beliefs. It was much more than that. Ever since she was a young girl, if you had asked Bee who she was, what she was, she had always known what she would answer. She was a Christian. She believed in God. She followed Jesus Christ. She read the Bible.

She didn't just read it; she immersed herself in it. She bathed in its words. She learnt whole passages off by heart. She and her father used to have fun quizzing each other, one with the Bible open, the other doing the washing up.

'Okay,' the one with the Bible would say. 'What about this bit? "So I commend the enjoyment of life, because there is nothing better for a person under the sun than to eat and drink and be glad."'

One point if you could identify the book – Ecclesiastes. That was easy.

Two points if you could also name the chapter – Chapter Eight. That was hard.

Three points if you knew the verse – Verse Fifteen. That was very hard, very hard indeed.

'What about this one? "At that time men will see the Son of Man coming in clouds with great power and glory. And he will send his angels and gather his elect from the four winds, from the ends of the earth to the ends of the heavens." Book?'

'Mark?'

'Correct. Chapter?'

'Hmm...difficult. Thirteen?'

'Well done.'

'Verse?'

'Oh dear. Twenty-six?'

'Ha, ha, got you. Trick question. Twenty-six and twenty-seven.'

'Cheat!'

By the time she was 16 or 17, Bee was more than able to hold her own. And after a couple of terms at university, she was getting better than him. She knew he was proud of her, but he also became competitive, so she would sometimes get things wrong or ask for a clue to spare his feelings, or else she would only ask him relatively easy passages.

And for Bee, Christianity hadn't just been a belief and an identity. It was also what she did. It was what she studied. It was what she was planning to do for a living. She was going to be a great theologian. She would teach in seminaries; she would write books and articles; she would be a guest lecturer and a keynote speaker at conferences, plus perhaps the occasional interview on TV or the radio when they wanted the voice of a liberal Christian on some moral issue. And her passport to this life was to be a first-class degree, followed eventually by a PhD that would make her reputation as a thinker and a theologian.

But now, she knew the final year of her BA would be no labour of love. It would be a grind. And when people asked her what she had studied at university, she would be embarrassed that they would think she was God squad, which she no longer was.

Robbie told her it didn't matter. She could still do a post-grad degree in Bible Studies. You get professors in theology departments who are atheists.

But they were different. They had an excellent command of Hebrew and Ancient Greek. Her lowest marks were in Hebrew, Greek and Arabic. She wasn't someone who could do original research like them. She wanted to theorise, to synthesise, to build on the work of others.

'You could be an RE teacher. You'd be good at it.'

Yes, maybe. She had loved Religious Education at school, but she thought RE teachers had a tough job, teaching a subject that lots of kids considered 'soft' and unimportant.

She was the girl who had her future planned out. She had known where she was going and how to get there. She had been focused and determined, one of the top students in her cohort. But now she would drift through her third year, an undergraduate with no idea what she was going to do with the rest of her life. She just hoped Robbie would consider the new aimless Bee as amazing as the driven Bee he had fallen in love with.

She felt very upset by her mother's reaction, but it was hardly a surprise. She knew it would be a long time before she came to terms with having an atheist daughter. Her father would accept it, but Bee had seen the sadness in his eyes at the dissolution of the close spiritual union they had shared.

And her mother thought the Alpha Course would help. How wrong she was. Dominic's whole argument was an appeal to reason. He was claiming that good old-fashioned historical and logical truth 'proved' Christianity. This was never going to work with Bee. She could out-*logos* Dominic any day, and his sermons just provoked her.

Was this what made her dump her spiritual crisis on Sofie and Ross?

She looked over at them. Sofie was listening intently, taking it in, weighing it up. As for Ross, he wasn't listening to Dominic. He was bored.

But then Bee realised that bored was all he was. He wasn't in crisis. He wasn't thinking about whatever it was that kept taking him over, dragging him down into an abyss. Perhaps he had had good news? Maybe things weren't as bad as he had thought?

Ross noticed Bee looking at him, and they exchanged a smile.

Bee looked at Dominic and tried to concentrate on what he was saying. None of it was new to her; she could easily have written the whole lecture herself. It was about prayer, the importance of praying, how to pray, why to pray (ACTS – adoration, confession, thanksgiving and supplication, as every good Sunday-school girl knew).

He had gone through the Lord's Prayer line by line, and he finished up talking about when to pray – all the time basically.

But Bee knew that anyway.

She wondered how many hours of her life had been spent in prayer. Probably an average of half an hour every day since the age of 13. She spent some time doing mental arithmetic and concluded that, allowing for time to eat, sleep and so forth, she must have spent more than 100 days of her life praying to God. On her knees, hands together, eyes closed, the real thing.

What a waste of time.

*

It was the coffee break. Ross and Sofie made straight for Bee.

'Hello,' said Ross. 'We weren't expecting to see you here.'

'Yeah, I know. My mum twisted my arm.'

'Again?' said Sofie.

'Yes. Today at lunch, I told my parents I really had lost my faith. I think she'd have taken it better if I'd come out as a lesbian.'

'Was she upset?'

'Very.'

'Oh dear.' Sofie touched her arm.

'Yeah, so I promised her I'd come tonight. Just tonight.'

'Well, we're glad to see you,' said Sofie. 'I don't think the Alpha Course would be bearable if we hadn't had your Omega Course to correct it.'

'I'm not trying to sabotage Dominic.'

'Don't worry,' said Sofie. 'I really like hearing two different points of view. Honestly, your emails have been really helpful.'

By now they had reached the head of the queue for tea and coffee, and so they broke off to get their drinks and then moved to one side to carry on their conversation.

'There's one thing I don't get,' said Sofie. 'You said things like Noah's Ark were just myths and we shouldn't believe they were true at all.'

'Myths can be full of truth.'

'Yeah, all right. What I mean is - literally true. But I saw this thing on TV, right, and it said Noah's Ark was based on folk memories of a real flood, when sea levels rose and the Black Sea was flooded. And then refugees from the Black Sea moved to the Middle East and became the ancestors of the Israelites.'

'You get all kinds of theories like this,' said Bee. 'It's just speculation. Yes, sea levels rose after the Ice Age. Yes, the Black Sea was flooded. Yes, there were probably refugees, and yes, some of them may have settled in the fertile crescent. But that doesn't prove anything. It's just one possibility among many.'

'But where did the story come from?' said Ross, 'It had to come from somewhere?'

'Well, it's a very old Mesopotamian myth, we know that. It could be a folk memory of a terrible flood. Maybe there was a farmer who used a boat to save his livestock, or someone who even saved a few wild animals. Who knows? Shall I tell you my dad's theory?'

'What?'

'When I was a little girl, the story of Noah made me cry. I couldn't understand why God had drowned all the little animals. It wasn't their fault that the people were wicked.'

'Ah,' said Sofie. 'That's so cute.'

'So, I suppose that was my introduction to liberal theology. My dad told me it was just a story. So I said the same as you, "Yes, but where does it come from? It has to come from somewhere." So my dad told me this story.

'"Thousands of years ago, the farmers had all brought the harvest in. Their children had been helping them too, because in those days there wasn't any school. They had a party to celebrate the harvest, and then it was time for the children to go to bed. But the children were all excited, and they didn't want to. They said they'd only go to bed if Uncle Zak told them a story. Uncle Zak was the best storyteller in the family and the children all loved his stories.

'"So the children all gathered round the fire, and Zak racked his brains and came up with a new story for them. He told them how the gods were fed up with people because they were too noisy and kept them awake at night. So they decided to make a giant flood that would sweep all the people away so that they could get some sleep. But there was one god who had a friend called Zipsudra, and he told him to build a giant boat so him and his family would be safe."'

'Zipsudra?' said Sofie. 'Not Noah?'

'That was his name in one of the older versions of the myth. So, anyway, "Zipsudra built his boat, and then he gathered animals from all over the world so they would be safe too. Everyone thought he was nuts, but he just carried on until his boat was full.

'"Then came the flood etcetera, etcetera, and some of the gods were angry when they realised Zipsudra and his family had survived. But Zipsudra's friend smoothed things over, and the gods agreed that they wouldn't do it again as long as the people promised to go to sleep at night instead of making lots of noise and keeping the gods awake."

'Anyway, this is the important bit: "The children loved that story, especially the bit about the animals, and they made Zak tell it to them night after night. Then when they grew up, they told it to their children, who told it to their children and so on. Within a few generations, everybody had forgotten that Zak had made it up, and people began to think it must really have happened."'

'And is that how you think the story started?' Ross asked.

'I've got no idea. But that's the point. Nobody knows how these stories first started, Noah, Abraham, Jason and the Golden Fleece, Beowulf. Is there any truth in them or were they simply made up? We have no way of knowing. But my dad's idea is just as likely as all this stuff about the Black Sea flood.'

238

The group discussion was fairly lively. It started off with everyone talking about how much they prayed. Bee came out on top by a long way, though she did admit that she hadn't prayed much in the last few months.

'Why have you stopped praying?' Nick asked.

'Well, that's why I'm here. A bit of a spiritual crisis.'

Everyone agreed that they were better at supplication than at adoration, confession or thanksgiving.

'It's a bit like my kids,' said Alison. 'When they come up to you with that "Mummy, you know I love you" look in their eyes, you know they want something.'

'Yes,' said Pat. 'That's what it must be like for God. "Oh, so-and-so's praying again. I wonder what he wants." There's nothing wrong with wanting something or asking God for it, but we mustn't forget the A, the C and the T: adoration, confession, thanksgiving.'

'Do you really think God answers our prayers?' asked Bob the Builder.

'Definitely,' said Pat.

'How can you be so sure?'

'Because I know he answers mine.'

'What kind of thing?'

'Lots of things, all the time. Little things.'

'Like what?'

'Well, a couple of weeks ago, me and my husband had a bit of a row. I was quite upset, and I asked God to let me see my husband's point of view. And he did, and I understood.'

'You should have asked God to make your husband see your point of view,' said Alison.

Everybody laughed.

Pat said, 'The funny thing is, he did. He saw my point of view.'

'Yes, okay,' said Bob, 'but sometimes it seems pretty silly to me. Like sometimes footballers, when they have to take a penalty or something, Brazilian or Spanish players, they sometimes cross themselves and say a little prayer.'

'Yes?'

'Yeah but why should God care? Why should he care which team wins?'

'But maybe the players aren't asking God to help them score. Maybe they're just asking him to be with them at that moment.'

Bob shook his head. 'Have you ever played football, Pat? They're asking him to help them score, no doubt about it.'

Everyone laughed again.

'Yes, but it's more complex than that,' said Nick.

'How do you mean?'

'Well, you say God answered your prayer and let you see your husband's point of view...'

'Yes.'

'That's really nice, and that's a great thing for you to ask, yeah? But it's quite a small thing. What about all the really big prayers he never answers?'

'Like what?'

'Well, like do you remember the genocide in Rwanda? There was that church where all those Tutsis went to get shelter, and there were the Hutu mobs outside, all armed with machetes and clubs. So weren't the people in there praying? I bet they were. But God didn't save them. It's the same with the Jews in Auschwitz. Where was God when they prayed to him?'

Pat thought for a moment before she answered. 'I know questions like this are very difficult, but I think it's a really big mistake for us to believe we can understand God. I mean, we're this tiny speck in a vast universe, and God is so incomprehensibly awesome. I think that's a word that is over-used a lot these days, but in God's case, well, God is awesome.'

'Yes?'

Nick seemed to be waiting for more, but that was Pat's answer to his question.

He turned to Bee: 'Do you study this at university?'

Bee shifted uncomfortably in her seat. 'Yes.'

'So what do you think?'

'As Pat says, it's a very complex issue. There are lots of different answers, but I don't think any one of them has fully solved the problem.'

'For example?'

Before Bee could answer, Pat said, 'I don't think we really need your kind of answers here.'

Silence.

Bee looked at Pat incredulously. 'Sorry. What did you say?'

'I said I don't think we need your kind of answers round here.'

The whole room had gone quiet, even the other tables.

'What's that supposed to mean?'

'Exactly what it says. I heard you talking just now. You've been sending emails to Ross and Sofie, haven't you?'

'So what if I have?'

'You've been deliberately undermining the Alpha Course.'

'No I haven't.'

'So what have you been doing?'

Sofie spoke: 'That's really unfair, Pat. We've asked Bee questions and she's answered them.'

'And she's given you an Omega Course to "correct" the Alpha Course.'

'No.'

'Yes she has. I heard you say it.'

'That was just a joke.'

'But she's lost her faith and she's deliberately undermining our efforts to bring you to faith.'

Bee shook her head, 'That's not what it's about.'

Pat was not to be silenced. 'I think it's very selfish of you. Some people actually need faith, you know.'

'I never said they didn't.'

'No, you just try to undermine it. Look at Ross. Can't you see how much trouble he's in?'

Ross looked up, startled.

'What do you mean?' said Bee.

'Tell her, Ross,' said Pat. 'Tell her why you're here.'

Ross looked at the others on the table, acutely aware that the whole room was waiting for him to answer.

Nick intervened. 'Ross, you don't have to say anything. It's not their business.'

Pat jabbed her finger at Ross. 'Tell her why you're here.'

He hesitated for a moment. Then he looked at the table in front of him as he spoke. 'I...I was driving my mum's car, coming back from Brighton. There was this other car in front of me, really slow. I went to overtake it, and I didn't look in my mirror. Another car was overtaking me, and it crashed into me. The other car flipped over and a Transit van smashed into it.' He closed his eyes and took a deep breath. 'The other driver died.'

He looked at Bee.

'That's why I'm here.'

Bee covered her mouth with her hand. 'Oh my God, Ross, I'm so sorry.'

Chapter Thirty-Five

There was complete silence. Nobody spoke, either around Pat's table or around the other two. Ross could sense a roomful of eyes, all staring at him. He looked down at the table, his face burning, his whole body coursing with adrenalin. He had no idea what he could do now. He couldn't leave, he knew that. He had to stay where he was, see this through, but he had no idea how he was supposed to do it. He didn't even know where he could look.

Look at Sofie. That was all he could do. Her eyes would be safe.

They were welling with tears, looking straight at him. She gave a thin smile, a slight nod of the head. And she mouthed three words, with just the merest hint of a whisper: 'Well done, Ross.'

Then Alison spoke up, 'Pat,' she said, 'when Dominic spoke about the four different types of prayer...I can't quite remember them.'

'ACTS,' said Pat. 'Adoration, confession, thanksgiving and supplication.'

'What about contemplation? Isn't that a type of prayer too?'

The conversation started around the other tables too, but it was all very strained, like the polite conversation of friends who have just had a massive row but haven't yet reconciled their differences.

Ross didn't listen to any of it. He just sat staring down at the table, willing the time to pass, willing Dominic to bring that dreadful evening to an end and allow him to escape.

But the end, when it finally came, was just as bad. So many people coming up to him to offer support.

'See you next week, Ross.'

'We're all your friends, Ross.'

'Bye, Ross, see you next Tuesday.'

Just about the only person who didn't say anything was Bee.

Eventually, Ross and Sofie disentangled themselves from all his well-wishers and headed out. There were usually two other people from the course who took the same bus, so he and Sofie decided to walk to the next stop so they could be alone.

Sofie said nothing. She just held his arm and walked beside him. When they got to the bus stop, she put her hand on his arm.

'You okay?'

He sighed deeply. 'Yeah, I'm okay. I'm always feeling so sorry for myself, but I'm probably in a better state than Elizabeth Johnson's husband. Or her children.'

'Can I give you a hug?'

He nodded and they put their arms around each other. After a moment, he felt himself becoming aroused, so he broke off their embrace and stepped back a little. 'Thanks, Sofie.'

She shook her head. 'I haven't done anything.'

'Yes you have. You're always there for me.'

'That's what friends are for.'

The bus came a few minutes later and they got on. The others from the Alpha Course were on board. Ross and Sofie gave them a quick nod and went upstairs.

*

Pat was in tears. 'I'm sorry. When I heard them talking about Bee's Omega Course to correct the Alpha Course, it just made me so angry. I'm sorry, Dominic. I should have consulted you. I'm sorry.'

'Yes, well, we are where we are.'

Pat wiped her eyes and her nose. 'Do you think I humiliated him?'

'Well, you did put him in a very difficult position.'

'I thought he handled it very well,' said Tom.

'That policeman,' said Andrea, 'what's his name? Neil?'

'Nick,' said Dominic.

'He was very angry.'

Dominic nodded. 'Yes. He must have known all about it, being in the police.'

'Bee was very upset,' said Tom.

Pat bowed her head. 'I'm so sorry. I didn't mean to ruin it for everyone.'

'Pat, perhaps you should lead us in tonight's prayer,' said Dominic. 'And we have to pray that they all come back: Ross, Sofie, Bee and Nick. There's a lot at stake here, for all of them.'

*

Next morning, Bee had some news for her parents: 'I'm going to Cambridge on the nine-thirty-nine train.'

'Oh,' said her mother. 'I thought you said you were going to meet Robbie on the Scotland train on Saturday.'

'Yeah, I changed my mind. I'm going today.'

'But where will you stay?'

Bee shrugged. 'With Robbie of course.'

She avoided eye contact with her mother, who seemed to have been stunned into silence. 'Yes, mother,' she wanted to say, 'I'll be sleeping in his bed. I'm a big girl now.'

It was her father who spoke next. 'I'll give you a lift to the station.'

'Thanks, Dad. I'd better go and pack.'

*

The revelation of his sins came as a massive setback to Ross. He went into crisis mode once more and spent all his free time the next day crushed by the accident and its consequences. He had no idea how he could find redemption. He wouldn't find it in religion, but he didn't know what else he could do.

243

He thought about making some great sacrifice to show his remorse, like going to Africa or India and devoting 10 years of his life to serving the destitute. But he remembered a story his mother sometimes told him. She had once worked as a psychiatric nurse, out of a desire, she said, to save the world. It hadn't taken her long to realise that she wasn't suited to the job, and she gave it up after less than a year. 'There are three kinds of people who become psychiatric nurses,' she liked to say. 'The angels, like me, who want to save the world, the little Hitlers, who enjoy bossing the patients about, and the pragmatists, who just see it as a job. And of these three kinds, the only ones who are any good are the pragmatists.'

Wouldn't it be the same for him if he went off to the poorest corner of the world and inflicted his inner conflicts on the people there?

What was the point?

If those people needed help, they needed it from a professional, from someone who just got on with the job, not from him.

For the first time in more than two weeks, the cliffs at Beachy Head called out to him. But he dismissed them quickly. The only way he could think of redeeming his guilt was to allow himself to be judged and to accept whatever punishment the courts chose to give him. And that would be the hardest thing he had ever done in his life. He knew his lawyer might want him to plead not guilty and wriggle out of it, and his parents would put pressure on him to do the same. They nearly always managed to get him to do what they wanted.

But not this time.

This time he was going to be strong.

This time he was going to do the right thing.

*

Sitting in the train, Bee sent an email to Ross and Sofie in which she apologised for blocking their path to the church. She said she had no right to dump her own spiritual crisis on them and that she had decided to give up the Alpha Course. It wasn't going to do her any good, and she didn't want to get in the way of others who would benefit from it.

Ross's reply came just before she got to London, a short message saying she had done nothing wrong and it was very unfair of Pat to have a go at her.

Sofie sent a longer email, which arrived while Bee was waiting for the Cambridge train at King's Cross. She said how much she had appreciated Bee's wisdom and her friendship. She understood why she wanted to break off contact for the time being, but she hoped they would be able to renew their friendship at a later date.

Bee didn't reply to Ross. To Sofie she said:

Dear Sofie,

Thanks for your lovely email. It means a lot to me. Let me know how Ross gets on and I'm sure we'll meet again.

Wishing you everything you wish for yourself,
Bee xx

Robbie was waiting for her when she finally came out of the station at Cambridge. She flung her arms round him and burst into tears.

Part Three

The Tongues of Angels

Chapter Thirty-Six

For most of Ross's friends, the central event of the summer was that Thursday, the day they got their AS-Level results. Ross had almost forgotten that it was imminent, so wrapped up was he in his unmasking, but when he woke up on Thursday morning, he could feel his innards tighten as he thought about the day ahead.

He and Sofie had arranged an extra day off, to free themselves up. They would meet Raj, Dani and some other friends at the college at 10:30. When Ross arrived, he found Raj and Dani intertwined on the lawns in front of the college.

'How did you do guys?'

Raj detached himself from Dani. 'An A and three Bs.'

'And you?'

'Better than him,' said Dani. 'Two As and two Bs.'

'That's it,' said Raj. 'Rub it in.'

'You bet I will.'

Ross left them and went to get his results. The woman in reception checked his name and then handed him an envelope. He walked away and tore it open.

English Literature	B
French	A
General Studies	B
History	C

Ross could hardly believe it. French, he wasn't that surprised, but a B in general studies? No way. And a B in English lit? But most astonishing of all was his history result. He almost burst out laughing. How on earth did he manage a C? He must have done brilliantly in the first exam, because the second was a disaster.

He took a photo of his results slip and sent it to his parents, before going outside to act as gooseberry to Raj and Dani until the others arrived.

Natalie was next to turn up with her boyfriend Declan, and predictably enough, she had four As. She grinned broadly as she showed them her results.

'I don't think it was ever in doubt,' said Ross.

'Your history was, though, wasn't it?'

'Yeah, I can't believe it.'

Sofie came soon afterwards, obviously delighted with her three As and a B.

'Did you get A in psychology?'

'Yeah.'

'Bloody genius, this girl,' said Ross. 'The next Sigmund Freud, no doubt about it.'

Sofie narrowed her eyes and shook her head at him.

He caught her eye and nodded.

The last of their friends arrived and got their grades 40 minutes later. All but two were pleased with their results. One of the disappointed students said she didn't feel like celebrating and went home. The rest headed to Natalie's house for an alcohol-fuelled barbecue in the garden.

Later that afternoon, when Raj got into a heated argument with two others about the merits of Labour leader Jeremy Corbyn, Dani and Sofie slipped away and found some shade under an apple tree at the bottom of the garden. They sat cross-legged on the brown grass and Dani, a little unsteadily, placed her wine glass so it wouldn't fall over. Sofie plonked her can of diet coke next to it.

'Haven't had much chance to talk. How are you, babe?'

'I'm good. You?'

Dani nodded. 'Yeah, very good. And congratulations on getting three As.'

'Congratulations to you, too.'

'Yeah, I got better grades than Raj. That's what matters.'

'You two finished your computer yet?'

'Yeah, ages ago. Now we're learning advanced coding together.'

'What?' said Sofie. 'You? Advanced coding?'

'And why not? I'm really into it now, man. We're going to make an app.'

'What kind of app?'

'For sharing Indian recipes.'

'Seriously?'

'Yeah.'

'So your summer of lurve turned out to be a summer of computing?'

Dani leaned forwards and grinned. 'My physical needs are still being met.'

'I'm glad to hear it.'

'Until Saturday, anyway.'

'Why? What's happening on Saturday?'

'I'm going to Spain with my dad and his new, new girlfriend.'

'Another one? He's a naughty boy, innit?'

'Yeah, he says to me one time, "I feel so guilty about not being there for you." And I'm like, "Yeah, well, you shouldn't have left, should you?"'

'What did he say to that?'

'Well, I didn't actually say it, but I thought it.'

'Have you met her before, his new girlfriend?'

'Only once. She seems okay. I usually get on all right with his girlfriends.'

'She got any kids?'

'Yeah, one thirteen-year-old boy.'

'That'll be fun for you.'

Dani shrugged. 'He seems a nice kid.'

'You like everybody.'

Dani laughed sardonically. 'I can think of one or two exceptions.'

They picked up their drinks and took a sip.

'You ever been to Spain?' Dani asked.

Sofie shook her head. 'I've only been abroad once. We went to Disneyland after my mum's first round of chemo. I haven't had a holiday since I was, like, twelve.'

'Seriously?'

'Yeah. If my dad gets any money, he just pisses it away. Kate – I call her Mum now, by the way – she never has any money. Her ex takes the little ones away on holiday, but not me.'

'So, what do you do?'

'Me and Kate, my mum, we treat ourselves to an ice cream on the beach.'

They were silent for a moment, then Sofie asked, 'Is Raj going?'

'No. Not invited.'

'Poor thing. What's he going to do?'

Dani sat up straight and put on the voice of a haughty headmistress: 'He shall have to look after his own needs.'

They both laughed at this.

'What you should do, right, is give him a box of tissues. Gift-wrap it and say, "A little something for while I'm away."'

At this, the two of them fell about laughing, and Dani kicked over both of their drinks.

*

Bee and Robbie lay on their backs on the grass in the middle of Parker's Piece, the large, flat grassy park just outside the city centre. Robbie had his bush hat on his face. His Scottish complexion could only take so much sun.

Bee rolled over to face him and propped her head on her hand.

'Can I ask you a question?'

'Aye.'

'When we first started going out, did it bother you that I was a Christian?'

'No.'

'Why not?'

'Number one, because it didn't bother you that I wasn't. I mean, if you'd been trying to convert me, that would have been an issue.'

'And number two?'

'Because I fancied you so much. It was lust at first sight.'

Bee grinned. 'Not love?'

'No, definitely lust. Love came later.'

She lifted up his hat, leaned forwards and kissed him. Then she gently placed his hat back on his face.

She said, 'I remember once, you said you really liked me because I was so sorted – I really knew what I wanted and where I was going.'

'Aye.'

'Was that a turn-on?'

'One of many, yes.'

'What were the others?'

'Your face and your body, basically.' After a moment, he added, 'Okay, so I'm shallow.'

'Will you still love me now that I'm lost and have no idea what I'm going to do with my life?'

He lifted his hat, raised his head and looked her up and down.

'Same face, same body. I think we'll be all right, babes, as long as you don't go mad with the chocolate brownies.'

She poked him in the stomach and they both laughed.

'Anyway,' he said, 'it's your nature to be driven. You've just got to find your next project and there'll be no stopping you.'

*

Ross got home just after five and headed upstairs to sleep it off. His brother was sent to wake him for dinner, but all he could get out of him was a grunt. He didn't come downstairs until almost 8:30.

His father laughed when he saw him. His mother did her best to disapprove, but even she seemed to see the funny side. She microwaved his dinner, and asked about his friends' results. She was particularly pleased about Natalie. 'She deserves to do well. Such a lovely girl.'

'Her boyfriend Declan did quite well too. I think he got three As.'

His mother's face fell. 'I didn't know she had a boyfriend.'

'Yeah, they were together at Tara's party.'

'You missed out there. She obviously got fed up with waiting for you to make a move.'

Ross rolled his eyes.

*

Next day, Bee and Robbie cycled to Ely. Their route took them along quiet country roads through Swaffham Prior, past Burwell, through Soham and along the River Great Ouse. They planned to have lunch in Ely and visit the cathedral before cycling back via Haddenham and Willingham.

It was a beautiful sunny day, with a gentle breeze behind them.

'We better enjoy this wind while we can,' said Robbie when they stopped for a rest and a drink. 'It'll be against us on the way back.'

Ely Cathedral came into view long before they reached the city. They stopped and Bee handed her mobile to Robbie, who took a photo of her plus bike with the cathedral in the background. She sent it to her parents.

'Do you ever wonder how the hell they built these things back in those days?' said Robbie.

'Yeah. Amazing, isn't it?'

They locked their bikes together at the station and had lunch in a vegan café on Fore Hill. After that, they went to the cathedral, where Bee made a five-pound donation. She worried that they were a little under-dressed (Robbie

250

was in Lycra cycling gear and she was wearing shorts and a sleeveless T-shirt), but nobody seemed to mind.

After they had done the tourist bit, Bee said, 'I want to spend some time here. Do you mind?'

'Shall I wait for you outside?'

'I might be a little while.'

'No worries. Did you see that tea room on the High Street? The one next to the big shoe shop. I'll wait for you there.'

'Thanks.'

'I'll save you a chocolate brownie.'

She sat in the middle of the nave and closed her eyes for a sensory meditation, concentrating first on the sounds around her: the hushed voices, the quiet footsteps, the echoes. Next, she spent time noticing what she could feel, the ground beneath her feet, the cushion under her bottom, the hard, wooden seat against her back, her clothes, the stickiness of her body, the chill air against her arms, legs and face.

She opened her eyes and examined the view, the magnificent pillars beside her, the amazing wooden ceiling with images of the Old and New Testament, and the rood screen in front that led through to the choir and the high altar.

She loved this place. She realised at that moment that she could still love Christianity even as she placed herself outside it. Not the Christianity of evangelicals and fundamentalists who thought unbelievers would all go to Hell. She had always hated that mindset. But the faith that had inspired the anti-slavery and anti-apartheid movements, that lifted people up and made them help others, she loved that. And the faith that offered comfort for the bereaved and the possibility of redemption for even the worst offenders – wasn't that something beautiful?

Her train of thought led her to Ross. Perhaps Robbie was right, and she shouldn't feel guilty about getting in the way of his journey towards Christianity. He was a big boy and was perfectly capable of hearing two different points of view and deciding between them.

She got up and left the cathedral, blinking as she walked out into the bright sunlight. It took just two minutes to find the café where Robbie was waiting for her.

He looked up from his mobile. 'Hi.'

'Hi.'

'How you doing?'

'I'm really good thanks. Really good.'

'Great. Unfortunately, I've got some bad news for you.'

'What?'

'I ate your chocolate brownie.'

*

On Saturday morning, Bee found herself in Robbie's parents' bungalow in Liberton, a residential suburb to the south of Edinburgh. She was sitting at the breakfast table, chatting with Robbie's mother when he came into the kitchen, his hair still wet from the shower. They had gone up to Edinburgh the previous day.

'There's some coffee in the pot,' said Robbie's mother.

'Lovely. You stay there, I'll get it.'

He got a mug from the cupboard and poured some coffee. He helped himself to milk from the fridge and put a teaspoonful of sugar in. As was his wont, he only gave it a token stir. He had told Bee he liked his coffee to get sweeter and sweeter as he got to the bottom of the cup.

'Bee was telling me how she got kicked off the Alpha Course.'

Robbie grinned. 'Yeah, they finally nailed the atheist mole.'

'It was the most embarrassing moment of my life.'

'I can believe it,' said Robbie's mother. 'And I bet it was pretty grim for that boy who crashed his car, too, singling him out like that.'

'Yes. I felt so sorry for him.'

'How did your parents react?'

'They don't actually know all the details. But my mum...' Bee shook her head. 'She's worried about me. She thinks they won't let me in at the Pearly Gates.'

'Oh, I didn't know she was that religious.'

Bee widened her eyes and nodded.

'Does she think you'll go to Hell?'

'She's not quite that bad.'

'Well,' said Robbie's mother, 'if you get locked out of Heaven, you'll have plenty of company: me and Robbie and his dad for starters.'

'She thinks Robbie's a regular churchgoer.'

'What?'

'That's what he told her.'

'I did not. She asked me if I went to church regularly, and I said I hadn't been since the end of term. And that is factually correct.'

Robbie's mother burst out laughing. 'That is so typical of you, Robbie. So typical.'

After breakfast, Bee and Robbie took the bus to South Bridge, from where they walked up to the High Street and headed for Edinburgh Castle. The plan was to walk down from there, along the Royal Mile to Holyrood House. After that, they would climb up Arthur's Seat to see its spectacular views of the city and the Firth of Forth.

As they walked up the High Street, near the statue of Adam Smith, Bee asked: 'It that St Giles' Cathedral?'

'Aye.'

'Oh, let's go in there. I want to see the statue of John Knox.'

They went inside, where Bee made her usual five-pound donation. The statue was in the nave, not far from the entrance. Knox was a forbidding figure, almost two and a half metres tall, made of bronze that had long since turned black. He was wearing the robes of a 16th-century preacher and had a long, ragged beard that reached down to his chest.

'He looks a nice fellah,' said Robbie. 'Reminds me of Ayatollah Khomeini.'

Bee gave a little laugh.

'So why did you want to see this?'

'If I'd been a boy, my parents were going to name me after him.'

'What? John Knox Ormerod?'

'Yep.'

'Well, I'm glad you're a girl.'

'So am I. Shall I tell you my darkest secret?'

'What's that?'

'My middle name.'

'Ah, the big reveal.'

'Yes. Promise you won't laugh.'

'Promise.'

'Knoxley.'

'Oh my God. That's dreadful.'

'I know.'

They both laughed.

'So how come they called you Alberta Knoxley, not Joan Knoxley or Jane Knoxley or something like that?'

'I was born on Saint Alberta of Agen's day.'

'You should change your name by deed poll.'

'What? Omega Bee Ormerod?'

'Yeah. Better still, Bee Omega Ormerod, then your initials would spell "Boo!"'

*

That afternoon, Brighton had their best result of the season so far, a three-two victory over Manchester United. Ross knew he would be safe from Sid for the rest of the week.

The Alpha Course was another matter. He was dreading the next session, when he and his accident would be the centre of attention. He told Sofie that he was thinking of giving it up.

She insisted he had no choice but to go: 'You mustn't hide. People are going to find out. You have to live with that. This is a big test and you need to pass it.'

He didn't finally make up his mind until the last minute. He ended up tossing a coin: 'Heads I go; tails I stay at home.'

It came down tails. That felt wrong.

'Best out of three.'

He tossed again and it landed tails up once more.
'Oh, sod it.'
He messaged Sofie, who got back to him straight away.

Sofie: Well?
Ross: I'm coming
Sofie: 🍾

So, there he was again, in the church hall. The prelude was mortifying: everybody coming up to him and shaking him by the hand or embracing him, telling him how pleased they were to see him, how he had done the right thing to come back. Ross knew they all meant well, but he hated it. He hated the fact that his accident now defined him in their eyes. That was who he was: the boy who had killed a woman in a traffic accident.

He also found it very hard to smile at Pat and shake her hand. He still felt very angry with her for humiliating him in order to get at Bee.

And it saddened him that the member of the group he and Sofie liked most wasn't there. There was no sign of Bee. The Omega Course was now over and, as his father might put it, he had been surrendered to the church for indoctrination. Even Bee, whose own faith had evaporated, had been complicit in this handing over.

This time dinner was followed by a hymn that Ross had never heard before.

Father, Father,
Lord of all the angels
Forgive my sins
And my foolish pride.

The second hymn kept to the same theme:

Oh Lord God, I know I have let you down
So full of sin and foolishness
Over all these years, I have nourished my pride
Please grace me with your mercy
And forgive the wickedness I've tried to hide.

And then Dominic began: 'I have to confess, running the Alpha Course can sometimes be a bit nerve-racking. Believe it or not, the message that Jesus brought isn't an easy one. It's controversial. It tells us things that we may not want to hear. Jesus said it himself, in Matthew Ten: Thirty-Four, "Do not suppose that I have come to bring peace to the earth. I did not come to bring peace, but a sword."

'So it's our job, as Christians, as missionaries, because that's what we are, it's our job to spread the word of God in such a way as to bring people to Jesus, not to scare them away. And at the end of every session, me, Pat, Andrea,

Rodney and Tom, we worry that we might have got it wrong. We worry that we might have said something that upsets somebody, that drives them away. And that worry doesn't go away until the next session when we look anxiously to see if the person concerned turns up.'

Ross could see what was coming and he didn't like the sound of it.

'Well, last week was a difficult session for some of us. Angry words were exchanged, and things that people might legitimately not have wanted everyone else to know were brought out into the open.'

Ross felt his ears and his face prickle. He looked down at the table in front of him, avoiding eye contact with everyone.

'Pat, Andrea, Rodney, Tom and me, we prayed together after the last session. We prayed to God, asking him for his guidance, asking him to wash away our pride and yes, I'll say it, we asked him to wash away our anger with Bee. And we prayed for Ross and we prayed for Bee, and we asked the Lord to bring them back to us.

'Ross, it's good to see you tonight. I'm so glad you're here. And Bee, wherever you are, we're missing you tonight. We wish you were here. Jesus loves you, Bee, and he'll always be there for you, waiting for you to come back to him.'

Ross wondered if Dominic was really missing Bee. He doubted it. More likely he was glad to see the back of her, glad to be able to lead his Alpha Course without someone else in the room who knew more than he did.

Dominic's theme for tonight was all the difficult choices we have to make in life: relationships, whether to get married, whether to bring children into the world, what job to have, how to spend our money etcetera, etcetera. And when we are faced with really big decisions, like who to marry, we really need God's help. Because God has promised to guide those who walk with him.

Dominic had a string of quotes from the Bible to prove his point. And then, he lost Ross completely by saying, 'God has a plan for our lives.'

Ross felt like screaming. So was this God's plan? For him to cause an accident? For him to kill an innocent woman? For him to rob two children of their mother?

And then presumably to attend the Alpha Course and come to Jesus?

But just as suddenly, Dominic reached out and pulled Ross back in: 'The reason we make mistakes is because we don't ask God what we should do. We think about what *we* want. We don't stop to ask, "Is this what God wants me to do?"'

Ross thought of himself stuck behind that Ford Focus, frustrated at going so slowly, embarrassed at not being able to get past it, egged on by Raj, not wanting to look stupid in front of Sofie and Dani.

Oh God, what an idiot. Maybe Dominic was right. After all, it wasn't God who had pulled out without looking in the mirror; it was him. It wasn't God who had killed Lizzie Johnson; it was him.

If he had been a Christian, he could have asked the simple question: does God want me to overtake that car?

To ask the question would have been to answer it, and he would have stayed calm behind the Ford Focus. Lizzie Johnson would have gone home and cooked dinner for her husband and children, and maybe fallen asleep in front of the TV, and this would have been one of the happiest summers of his life.

How Ross wished he could believe.

How he wished he had been a believer that day.

What a difference it would have made.

He tuned in again. Dominic was cherry-picking the Bible once more, finding quotes that showed how God guides us through his word.

'You shall not commit adultery.'

'Give everyone what you owe him: If you owe taxes, pay taxes.'

He said God has told us that we can only marry Christians: 'Do not be yoked together with unbelievers. For what do righteousness and wickedness have in common?'

This came as a shock to Ross. What if a Christian fell in love with a Buddhist, a Moslem, a Jew or an atheist? Would they have to convert them or split up? Evidently Dominic thought so.

He talked about serious study of the Bible. 'It's amazing how you find that almost any page you open speaks to you almost directly about the problems you are facing in your life at that particular moment. Let me give you an example. Tom? Would you like to tell your story?'

Tom Bradshaw stood up, his head still haunted by the loss of his ponytail.

'When I was young, I dreamed of being a rock star. I used to go to concerts and festivals all over the place. Maybe some of you can remember my heroes from those days: Jeff Beck, Jimmy Page and, more than anyone else, Richie Blackmore. I desperately wanted to be like them.

'I started off playing air guitar in my bedroom, but then I got a real guitar. I learned a few chords and I was off. Me and a couple of mates at school, we started a band, and we had a few gigs here and there, mostly pubs and birthday parties. We thought we were brilliant, but I don't suppose we were.

'Well, then I went to North Staffordshire Polytechnic. It's a university now, but in those days, it was a humble Poly. I was doing graphic design, and I joined another band there when their lead guitarist quit. This band was much better, and we had lots more gigs, again mostly in pubs and student unions. We sent off loads of demo tapes. Usually, the record companies didn't even reply. One person who did was John Peel - do you remember John Peel from Radio One?'

Several people nodded.

'Well, he sent us this really nice letter, but he never played our tape on the radio. Even so, we thought success was just around the corner. But it never quite seemed to happen. Then at the end of my second year at the Poly, I got really bad exam results. I mean really terrible. I'd been spending all my time rehearsing and playing gigs.' Tom paused. 'There was a bit of rock-and-roll lifestyle involved too, if I'm quite honest: drink and girls and...exotic cigarettes.'

A ripple of laughter spread around the room.

'Anyway, I had to re-take my exams at the end of the summer. I needed good results or I'd get thrown out of the Poly. Well, my friends in the band, they wanted us to spend the summer together, you know, rehearsing, doing gigs and that. And it was a real dilemma for me. I mean I really wanted to go with them. It was what I wanted, to be a rock star.

'But, I mean, I wasn't stupid. I knew that the chances of making it big were one in a million. I knew I couldn't afford to get thrown out of the Poly. So I was torn; I really didn't know what to do. Then one day, my parents left their Bible on the sofa. They were very strong believers, but I wasn't in those days. It didn't really go with the rock and roll lifestyle.'

Tom picked up a Bible. He opened it at a bookmarked page.

'So I was just sitting there. I think I probably had the TV on, and I was just flicking through the Bible, and then I saw this. It's in Proverbs, Chapter Twenty-Eight, Verse Nineteen: "He who works his land will have abundant food, but the one who chases fantasies will have his fill of poverty."

'Well that was my answer, there and then. I knew what I had to do, and I phoned my mates and I told them, "Sorry, I've got to spend the summer working for my re-sits." Because I had a heck of a lot of catching up to do. So that's what I did, and I got good grades, and I've never regretted it, and now I'm a very successful graphic designer, thank you very much.

'And my mates? They got another guitarist, who was probably better than me, and they had a rock and roll summer, but they never got a recording contract, and they all ended up as engineers and middle managers and what have you.

'And I've always considered the moment I looked at that Bible to be the most important moment of my life. God showed me what he wanted me to do, and I did it, and I let him into my life, and I stopped chasing fantasies and gave up the rock and roll lifestyle. I hung onto the pony tail until Bee pointed out that that wasn't part of God's plan for me either.'

Tom sat down and Dominic resumed, talking about the many different ways God guides us, such as the Bible, dreams and visitations, and about how God speaks to us when we pray to him.

Then he spent a long time talking about how we should let God guide us in our choice of marriage partner: they have to be spiritually compatible (a Christian, in other words), personally compatible and physically compatible.

As he spoke, Ross found himself looking at Sofie and thinking about how compatible she was in every way. She might end up a Christian after the Alpha Course and he might not, but Ross couldn't see that as an issue.

And personal compatibility? Sofie had turned out to be the best friend he had ever had. As for physical compatibility, well she was lovely. She was never going to be a movie star or Britain's Top Model, but then again, nor was he. But her eyes and her smile, they were beautiful.

At that moment, he felt as if a great weight had just landed on his shoulders. He knew she loved him as a friend; she had said so. But she could never love him the way he loved her. She had made that very clear. He wasn't her type.

Chapter Thirty-Seven

Just before Ross and Sofie left at the end of the session, Pat rushed to grab them. 'Just checking – you are coming to the weekend seminar, aren't you?'

Ross's parents hadn't been pleased when he told them about this, as they had booked a cottage in the Lake District and were due to leave on Saturday. His father talked about having to delay their departure until Sunday and missing a whole day of their holiday. He calmed down when Ross found out that he could get a train ticket to Windermere for less than £40 with his student card.

So Ross would depart for the weekend away on Friday, get back to town early on Sunday afternoon and then almost immediately leave for Windermere.

'Yes,' he said to Pat. 'We're both going.'

'Great. Have you got transport?'

'Erm, no.'

Pat turned to Alison. 'I say, Alison? You and Bob are going by car, aren't you?'

'Yes.'

'Have you got space for Ross and Sofie?'

'Yes, it'll be a pleasure.'

Alison arranged to pick them up from their homes at seven on Friday evening.

'Oh, one more thing,' said Pat. 'There's a voluntary contribution of fifty-five pounds per person. Is that okay?'

Sofie and Ross nodded. They both had plenty of money.

'Good. Oh, and bring your own towels.'

'You know what annoyed me?' said Ross, as they waited at the bus stop.

'What?'

'Right at the beginning, where Dominic said how much he wished Bee was there. What a hypocrite. I bet he was glad to see the back of her.'

'I don't think he was being hypocritical. I mean, yeah, part of him would have been glad she wasn't there. But this is where Christianity brings out the best in people, because they have to love their enemies, innit? So I think Dominic was being honest.'

'He's a hypocrite.'

'No, he's not. This is where Christianity challenges you. It makes you a better person.'

'Oh yeah?'

'Yes.'

*

Thursday was their last day at work. At the end of the evening shift, the rest of the staff (including the cleaners, who only worked mornings) came in to say goodbye. Mrs Akehurst made a little speech thanking Ross and Sofie for their hard work and saying how much she hoped they would come back next year. She gave them cards signed by everyone and a £20 Boots gift voucher for Sofie and a WH Smith voucher for Ross.

Afterwards, Mrs Akehurst took them into her office for a quick chat.

'I'll send your P45 and your share of the tips next week. You'll get some statutory holiday pay too. I work it out as ninety-nine pounds and sixty-four pence.'

'Ooh that's great,' said Sofie.

'I really meant what I said. You're both lovely people and I really do hope you come back next year.'

'Thank you.'

'I'm sure we will,' said Sofie.

Ross was tempted to add, 'If you promise to keep Sid on a leash.'

Next morning, Ross went to see Nigel at his church once more. He found him by the entrance, pinning notices on his notice board.

'Hello.'

'Hi.'

'Is it the weekend thing this weekend?'

'Yeah. We're going off tonight.'

Nigel finished the last of his notices and stepped back to look at them. 'Shall we go inside?'

They sat down on a pew near the entrance.

'What brings you here today?'

'You talked about a leap of faith, but I don't know how to do it.'

'Maybe you're trying too hard.'

'Maybe.'

Nigel thought for a moment and said, 'Have you ever lain in bed at night and you just can't sleep?'

'Tell me about it.'

'And the harder you try, the more difficult it is. And that's because you're going about it the wrong way. You don't get to sleep by trying. You just lie still and let your mind wander, and sleep comes to you.'

Ross nodded.

'I remember when it happened to me,' said Nigel. 'It was in my final year at university. I'd been a Christian all my life – my parents are very Christian, as you know. But it wasn't something I thought about very much. It was just part of life, like brushing your teeth. I hadn't been to church for several weeks, and I'd been playing Frisbee with some friends in this park a mile or so from the campus. It was the middle of the afternoon, but it was getting really dark, and we could see fork lightning in the distance, so we decided to call it a day before it rained.

'Our route took us past my church, so I thought I'd pop in. I said goodbye to my mates and went and sat in the pews. I felt really calm, and very happy. I wasn't praying or anything. I was just being in the moment, enjoying the sense of peace that you get in a beautiful church. And then it happened. I didn't make it happen. It just happened. It was really powerful, and beautiful. It was perfect. That's the word I'd use to describe it: perfect. Absolutely perfect, the most perfect moment of my life, something really profound. It was the Holy Spirit, and it filled me and changed my life. That's when I made my leap of faith. That's when I stopped going through the motions and became a real Christian.'

After a moment, Ross said, 'Actually, there's one or two things that have put me off a bit.'

'How's that?'

'I've got this friend who recently came out as gay. He put a thing on Instagram about this really homophobic priest in Scotland.'

'Yes,' said Nigel, 'you do get that. What I'd say is the same as I said last time. These people are coming at it from the wrong angle. They're like the Pharisees, fixated on the rules. That's not what Christianity's about. It's about using faith to lift yourself, to become a better person, closer to God. And the way you do that is to become more kind and loving, not less. You know there are plenty of gay and lesbian clergy out there? And they're campaigning hard so gay marriages can be blessed in C of E churches. It hasn't happened yet, but it will, eventually. Don't let the dinosaurs put you off.'

'No.'

'And don't try too hard. Maybe "leap of faith" is the wrong metaphor. You don't have to leap. You just have to open yourself to change. Let the Holy Spirit do the work.'

'Thanks, Nigel. That's really helpful.'

Chapter Thirty-Eight

That evening, Bob and Alison picked them up in their Citroen Picasso. The Alpha weekend would take place at Northfields Hall in Kent, an hour's drive away.

Bob and Alison asked lots of questions about Omega Bee and her emails. Sofie and Ross told them about J, E, D and P, *mythos* and *logos*, Bee's spiritual crisis and the differences between her take on Christianity and Dominic's. Sofie said she still felt angry about the way Pat had chased her away from the Alpha Course.

'Yes, I felt very sorry for her when that happened,' said Alison. 'Pat was out of order there, especially the way she used your situation, Ross.'

She asked him how much trouble he was in, and he gave a matter-of-fact account of his upcoming court case. To his surprise, he didn't mind talking to Alison and Bob about it. He remembered Alison's efforts to change the subject when it had all come out, and he was grateful to her for that.

'You shouldn't be too hard on yourself,' said Bob. 'You show me a driver who says he's never forgotten to look in his mirror and I'll show you a liar.'

'Has the Alpha Course helped you cope with it all?' asked Alison.

'It's difficult to say. There's been a few times when Dominic said something that really clicks. I mean really clicks. And then there are other times when he says something that puts me off. There's this priest in Old Town, Nigel, he's the one who recommended the Alpha Course to me. He says it's all about opening yourself to change, and then it kind of happens by itself and it all makes sense.'

'Do you think you'll become a Christian?'

'I don't know. I really want to, but at the moment, I'm not sure if I'm ready yet.'

'I can understand that. How about you, Sofie?'

'I don't know. I'm intrigued, and I've always thought there probably is a God. I'm closer to Bee's kind of Christianity than Dominic's. It's like I've dipped my toes in the pool but I'm not quite sure if I want to jump in. What about you two?'

Alison thought for a moment before she answered. 'I'm not sure. Bob's enjoyed it more than me, haven't you? I do believe in God and I think Christianity's a wonderful thing. I mean, the Church and the Salvation Army, people like that, they do such good work, don't they? And if they weren't there to do it, I think a lot of these things just wouldn't get done. But I'm not sure it's for me. There's so many things that just get in the way, like the miracles and having to believe everything it says in the Bible. I mean, Bee was very good at rubbishing that, wasn't she? She made mincemeat of Dominic sometimes.'

Bob piped up, 'Like when she said about Tom's pony tail.'

'She was so embarrassed about that,' said Sofie.

'I bet she was.'

They arrived at Northfields Hall at 8:10, when it was just beginning to get dark. The Hall was a large 18th-century mansion set in an enormous garden that had clearly seen better days. It was teeming with wild rabbits and the flower beds were full of weeds.

Dominic, Pat and the other team leaders were there to meet them. Rodney led Ross up to the top floor and along creaky, labyrinthine corridors to his room in what had once been the servants' quarters.

'I'm afraid it's all rather basic,' he said as he opened the door.

The bedroom furniture showed what he meant: a single bed that sagged as he sat on it, a wobbly wardrobe from the 1960s or 70s and a hideous dark brown chest of drawers.

'The showers are down that way. There's no privacy, I'm afraid, and they take quite some time to warm up. Have you brought your own towel?'

'Yes.'

*

They had a late supper in the dining hall, a huge, high-ceilinged room that must once have been the kitchen. It had an enormous fireplace with grills and ovens, plus a tall dumb waiter in the corner.

There wasn't a session that evening. Everyone just sat around chatting, some about religion and the Alpha Course but most about everyday topics. Nick found an old table-tennis table in what had once been the servant's hall, and he and Ross, Sofie and Bob, who turned out to be a very good player, spent over an hour on that. Ross won every game he played, deploying his deceptive serve whenever he was in danger of losing.

He got up early next morning so that he could have his shower before anyone else was up. Once dressed, he texted Sofie, who said she would meet him for breakfast in half an hour. He lay on his bed and closed his eyes for just a few minutes while he waited. It was the best part of an hour before he opened them again.

Sofie was still there, finishing her coffee and chatting with Alison, Bob and another woman from their table. Sofie pretended to be annoyed with Ross, who helped himself to some Cheerios and a croissant.

At half past nine, Pat came in and suggested they make their way to the room where the meeting would be held. It was a long room with a low ceiling and Georgian doors, three lots of old tables in the middle and 17th and 18th-century family portraits around the edges of the room.

'I love this place,' said Sofie. 'It's amazing.'

Dominic suggested they mix up the usual groups, so Ross and Sofie joined Rodney's table along with Nick and half a dozen others they barely knew. Ross was happy to get away from Pat.

'It's usually a very good session, this,' said Rodney, as everyone sat down.

Tom Bradshaw got out his guitar. Ross had never heard his traditional hymn.

Holy, holy, holy! Lord God Almighty!
Early in the morning our song shall rise to Thee;
Holy, holy, holy, merciful and mighty!
God in three Persons, blessed Trinity!

The happy-clappy song followed:

Holy Spirit, truth of our Lord,
Draw my soul unto your Word;
Fill me with your true desire;
Burn my ego in your fire.
Holy Spirit, joy of our Lord,
Gladden my heart with your Word;
Say what only you can say to me,
Bring me your tranquillity

Dominic's talk was about the third part of the Holy Trinity of Father, Son and Holy Ghost, or as Dominic called it, the Holy Spirit.

His theme was how the Holy Spirit, or the Spirit of God, poured into people and transformed their lives. This chimed with what Nigel had said about his religious experience, but what Dominic seemed to be saying was that the Holy Spirit was a separate person, just as Jesus was separate from God. He quoted passages from the Bible to show that the Holy Spirit thinks, speaks, acts and has emotions just like a person. And this person, this Holy Spirit, is what comes to people and transforms their lives.

For a while, Ross found this confusing, but then he remembered what Nigel had said about sleep coming to you, as if sleep were some kind of magical creature that crept up on you and changed your mental state.

But that was just a metaphor.

And so was the idea of the Holy Spirit as a separate person.

Dominic thought it was real, because it said so in the Bible. But Ross knew it wasn't. Finally, he understood what *mythos* was all about: extended metaphors. For the first time, he understood what Sofie meant about not believing something was literally true but responding to it as if it was.

All he had to do was open himself up to change and let it happen.

Dominic began to tell a story about a close friend of his, who fell in love with a woman who wasn't a believing Christian. He tried to convert her but was getting nowhere. Then, one night in despair, he prayed for her to be filled with the Holy Spirit. That prayer, according to Dominic, transformed her life. The next time his friend saw her, she radiated joy and told him she had found Jesus. She still radiated joy to this day.

264

Next came the tale of the Reverend EJH Nash, a nondescript insurance clerk who became a kind of super-preacher when he was filled with the Holy Spirit and, if Dominic was to be believed, converted just about everyone he ever met.

Ross was sceptical about this. It seemed to him that according to Dominic's speeches, more and more people were becoming Christians all the time, a veritable avalanche of conversions. If things carried on like this, they would soon have to build lots more churches because all the existing ones would be full to bursting.

But Ross knew it wasn't like that. He knew of two churches near where he lived that had closed down. One had been turned into houses, and the other demolished and replaced by sheltered accommodation for old people. So, if there really were as many converts as Dominic claimed, there must be even more people who dropped out.

He wondered how many of these conversions were in fact temporary: people just going through a religious phase that they soon tired of.

But none of this mattered. Ross was used to Dominic's doubtful anecdotes, his dodgy optimism and the way he cherry-picked quotations from the Bible. That was just *mythos*. What mattered was the truth that lay behind it. All he had to do was get out of the way and let it happen. At last, he understood. At last, he was ready.

*

Ross and Sofie took their coffee and found a space where they could talk alone.

'What did you think of that?'

'A bit confusing, really,' said Sofie. 'I mean, it's like they're saying the Holy Spirit is a completely separate person. Where did that come from?'

'But it makes total sense.'

'Really?'

'Yes. Do you remember? I told you what Nigel said about trying to get to sleep: what you really have to do is let sleep come to you.'

'Yes.'

'So, I've been so desperate to make a leap of faith. But Nigel said that's the wrong metaphor. It's not me that makes a leap. It's the Holy Spirit that pours itself into me. Maybe that's a better metaphor.'

'Metaphor? As in *mythos*?'

'Exactly.'

'What? You finally get *mythos*?'

'Yes.'

'Hallelujah!' said Sofie. 'Praise the Lord!'

They both laughed.

'I've been trying too hard,' said Ross. 'I've got to stop trying and just let it happen.'

'So, from now on we're going to get this new, chilled-out Ross.'

He laughed. 'Yes. Perhaps I shouldn't be drinking coffee.'

'They've got decaf.'

He leaned towards Sofie and whispered. 'What I really need's a bit of weed. That'd chill me out. You haven't brought any, have you?'

She laughed. 'Better not. Nick would have to arrest you.'

*

Nigel joined his wife Helen, his parents, Sid, Martha and their children in the family room at the hotel.

'Sorry I'm late,' he said as his mother poured him some coffee.

'Helen was just telling us about Ross and his accident,' said Mr Akehurst.

'Ah,' said Nigel, looking askance at his wife. 'I was kind of keeping that confidential.'

Helen blushed bright red.

'Do you know if he's in a lot of trouble?' said Mrs Akehurst.

'I don't know,' said Nigel. 'We didn't discuss that.'

'Has it affected him badly?'

'Yes. Very.'

'He never showed it here.'

'No, he said working here helped him. He was too busy to think about it.'

'So, is that why he did the Alpha Course?'

'Yes. I kind of jumped the gun a bit there. It wasn't very professional of me to suggest the Alpha Course straight away. Fortunately, I think it has helped him.'

'That's good.'

'I never liked him,' said Sid. 'I always knew there was something dodgy about him.'

'I like him,' said his mother. 'And I think you should be a bit more charitable. It's not as if your own driving record is spotless.'

'Yeah, but I never killed anyone, did I?'

*

There was no discussion after coffee. They went straight into Dominic's next talk. This time, his theme was how people came to God. He quoted the line Bee had hated so much: 'I am the way and the truth and the life. No-one comes to the Father except through me.'

'The only way that people can come to God is through our Lord Jesus Christ and through the intervention of the Holy Spirit. And what does that mean? It means you letting the Holy Spirit into your life, letting it pour itself into your soul. And if that happens, when that happens, boy, will you *know* it. If and when it happens to you, you'll experience it as a rebirth, a rebirth of the spirit.

'Now you might say, "What do I want to be born again for? I've already been born once. Isn't that enough?"'

Up until that moment, Dominic's words reflected Nigel's insight about the need to let it happen rather than attempt to force it, but Ross didn't like the phrase 'born again'. To him it spoke of loud-mouthed American televangelists, right-wing, gun-toting fundamentalists. It was hard to square these connotations with Dominic's genial tone. He wished he would stick to talking about spiritual rebirth. The connotations of that were better.

After a moment, Ross tuned back in. By now, Dominic was getting quite excited: 'The moment you come to Jesus is the greatest moment of your life. It's the moment the barrier between you and God is lifted, the moment the Holy Spirit fills you. That's the moment Jesus Christ takes all your sins and cancels them: "...tread all our sins underfoot and hurl all our iniquities into the depths of the sea."

'That's what happens when you come to Jesus, when you truly come to him, when you open your door to him, when you open your heart to the Holy Spirit. Whatever you've done, whatever terrible sins you have committed, when you're born again, the slate is wiped clean. Only Jesus Christ can do this for you, for he is the way and the life and no man comes to God but through him.'

This time, mention of sin didn't fling Ross back into his usual abyss of dark thoughts. Instead, he felt genuinely excited.

That was why he was here.

That was what he had come for: transformation, rebirth, a new start.

All he had to do was let go and allow it to happen.

*

During the group discussion, Rodney kept wanting to bring everyone back to the Holy Spirit but, largely because of Nick, it got bogged down in a discussion of sin. Nick didn't think much of the wiping clean of slates.

'I mean, are you really serious? No matter what sins you've committed, all you have to do is give yourself to Jesus and your slate'll be wiped clean?'

'Yes,' said Rodney. 'That's what it says in the Bible.'

'Even paedophiles and rapists? Even murderers? There's some very nasty people out there.'

'That's the marvellous thing,' said Rodney. 'Jesus has paid the price of all our sins. All we have to do is believe in him.'

'And the slate is wiped clean?'

'Yes. I'm not talking about in the eyes of the law, but in the eyes of God, yes.'

'Okay,' said Nick. 'Let's take an example. One of my friends in the police, he used to work in north London. He told me once about this case he worked on. There was this Pakistani newsagent who had a lot of trouble with some local yobs. They were harassing him and his family. They broke his shop window twice and there was lots of racist graffiti.

'One evening there were four of them outside his shop, just making a nuisance of themselves. He decided to go outside and talk to them. His wife begged him not to, but he went outside and said, "Hey, come on lads. What do you think you're doing?" Well, you know what happened? They beat him up, and then one of them stabbed him and killed him.'

Ross breathed in sharply.

'That's terrible,' said one of the women on the table.

Others nodded their agreement.

'So,' said Nick, 'are you telling me that all that little thug who stabbed him has to do is believe in Jesus and his slate will be wiped clean?'

'Look,' said Rodney, 'don't imagine it would be easy. He'd have to confront his guilt. He'd have to repent, I mean, really repent. But ultimately yes, if he was born again in Jesus, if he let the Holy Spirit into his life, then his slate would be wiped clean. I'm talking about in the eyes of God. In the eyes of the law, he would still have to serve his sentence.'

Sofie chipped in: 'I think this is one of the best things about Christianity. No-one's beyond redemption. No matter what you've done, you can still be redeemed. Isn't that a beautiful message?'

'But some people *are* beyond redemption,' said Nick.

'No, they're not,' chorused Sofie and Rodney.

'Yes, they are. I deal with them. Most of the crooks I come across aren't beyond redemption, I'll grant you. Some of them are kids who've never had a chance, you know, they've had a really bad start in life. These kids I feel sorry for. They're not bad kids. Me and one of my colleagues, we sometimes take them camping, outward-bound courses, that kind of thing, trying to instil some self-belief into them, give them the confidence to try and make it in the system.

'Lots of other crooks are just idiots. They're such losers, you wouldn't believe it. Those people *can* be redeemed. A slap on the wrist and a good probation officer who keeps them under control and helps them to turn their life around. That can work. And maybe a dose of old-time religion wouldn't do them any harm.

'But there are some real psychos out there. I've met quite a few. Complete psychopaths, not a shred of conscience. Not only do they not have a conscience, they aren't capable of suddenly growing one. It's part of their brain that just doesn't work. Whether it's due to lack of love in infancy or just their genes, I don't know, but these people exist and they're irredeemable.'

'Nobody's irredeemable,' said Rodney.

'Psychopaths are,' said Nick. 'You know there've been all sort of programmes in prison to try and rehabilitate them, and you know what happens? The programmes end up making them worse. They just learn how to fake having a conscience, and that makes them even more dangerous.'

Another member of the group put up his hand. His name was Steve and he worked as a chef in one of the seafront hotels. He was tall and quite fat. Ross was never sure if his hair was blond or if it had gone white.

'Can I ask a question?'

'Yes, of course,' said Rodney.

'Okay, this kid who stabbed the shopkeeper, let's say he isn't a psychopath, but he's a very nasty piece of work, a habitual criminal, spends most of his life in and out of prison. Then, just before he dies, his conscience takes over and he genuinely repents. He goes to church and he becomes a true Christian just before he dies. So he gets his slate wiped clean, yes?'

'Yes,' said Rodney.

'Okay. Now you know it says in the Bible that you can only come to God through Jesus?'

'Yes.'

'Well, the Pakistani shopkeeper who got killed: he would have been a Moslem, right?'

Everyone nodded.

'Okay,' said Steve. 'Now let's imagine him. Let's say he was a really nice guy. You know, family man, devoted husband, kind and loving father, always cheerful and friendly with his customers. Not a saint, you know, he had his moments of pride and sloth and gluttony, just like the rest of us, and he wasn't above the occasional lustful thought. But on the whole, he was a very nice guy.'

Dominic was hovering by the table. 'I can see where you're going with this.'

'You probably can.'

'Yes,' said Dominic. 'The Moslem's slate wouldn't be wiped clean when he died, but the man who killed him, his slate would be wiped clean.'

Steve raised an eyebrow. 'Is that really what you believe?'

Dominic thought for a moment, and then he said, 'It's what it says in the Bible, in John, Chapter Fourteen, Verse Six: "I am the way and the truth and the life. No-one comes to the Father except through me."'

'So the Moslem's slate can't be wiped clean?'

'It kind of goes against the *Zeitgeist*, doesn't it?' said Dominic. 'The modern world is dominated by this relativist view that every culture is equal, that all the different religions are the same. Well, that may be politically correct these days, but it's not what the Bible tells us. As Christians, we believe that Jesus is the resurrected Son of God and that the only path to God is through him.'

'So what are other religions?' said Sofie. 'Paths to Hell?'

'No,' said Dominic. 'Other religions are a part of man's striving for God, and we have to respect that. Other religions can and do take people part of the way towards God, but only one religion can complete the journey. Only one religion can actually bring people all the way. Jesus is the way and the truth and the life. No-one comes to the Father except through him.'

*

After lunch, they had a respite from study. Ross and Sofie spent the afternoon walking in the nearby Forest Way Country Park with Bob and Alison.

'How are you two enjoying the weekend?' asked Bob.

'It's okay,' said Sofie. 'But I'm finding all this stuff about the Holy Spirit a bit confusing.'

'Really?' said Bob. 'For me, it's like I get it for the first time. I really understand what Dominic's on about.'

'You do?'

'Yes. I've felt the Holy Spirit before, when I was younger. I didn't know what it was at the time, but when I listen to Dominic, it's like *Ping!* That's what I felt all those years ago.'

'How do you mean?'

'The first time was on Christmas Eve, when me and Alison were engaged. We'd been to midnight mass and we were walking home. It was a beautiful evening, crisp and cold and a cloudless sky with a bright moon shining down. And I just felt so perfect, absolutely amazingly perfect. The evening was perfect. The service had been perfect. The cold was perfect. And Alison, oh she was just so perfect.'

Alison laughed. 'It was the Ansells bitter.'

'I hadn't had a drop, well not for about three hours.'

'Ninety minutes, more like.'

'And you're sure it was the Holy Spirit?' said Sofie.

'Oh yes, no doubt about it. I had the same sort of thing three or four times when I was young. It's an amazingly powerful experience. I've realised that ever since then, I've been trying too hard. I've been trying to recapture that feeling, trying to understand, trying to see. But it's not a question of us reaching out. It's a question of just letting it happen. If we let it happen, let the Holy Spirit do the reaching out, then that's all it needs. We don't need to do anything. We just have to get out of the way and let the Holy Spirit do the work. Does that make sense?'

'Yes,' said Ross, 'that's exactly what Nigel said. He had the same experience. And he said the same thing about getting out of the way and just letting it happen. It's like I'm starting to understand, you know, for the first time.'

'I'm not sure I get it,' said Alison.

'Me neither,' said Sofie. 'And it's not just that. We had this discussion on our table, right. It really put me off.'

'What was that?' Alison asked.

'Well Nick told us about this case where this guy murdered a Pakistani shopkeeper. And you know Steve, right? He asked if the murderer converts to Christianity, would he go to Heaven? And Dominic says yes. And then Steve asks if the Pakistani shopkeeper, even if he was a really nice guy, he wouldn't go to Heaven because he's a Moslem. And Dominic's like, "Yes, exactly, because that's what it says in the Bible." And I just thought no, that's so wrong.'

'I'm with you there,' said Alison. 'I really want to believe, but when Dominic comes out with things like that, it just gets in the way.'

Ross interjected. 'If there's one thing Bee taught us, it's that there are Christians who don't think like that. You can accept Dominic's message about the Holy Spirit without going along with everything he says.'

'That's a good point, Ross,' said Bob. 'A very good point.'

They walked on further, and after a while, Ross and Sofie found themselves some way behind Alison and Bob.

'I've never seen you this keen.'

'Yeah,' said Ross. 'I feel like I'm turning a corner. Something's happening. I can't wait till the next session.'

*

They got back to Northfields Hall at 4:30, to be greeted with tea and scones, after which it was down to business, starting as ever with two hymns.

When I survey the wondrous cross
On which the Prince of Glory died,
My richest gain I count but loss
And pour contempt on all my pride
Forbid it, Lord, that I should boast
Save in the death of Christ, my God
All the vain things that charm me most
I sacrifice them to his blood

After this, the happy-clappy song came as something of a relief, once they had got past the rather grisly first line:

From the mountain where our dear Lord died
To the deepest valley of the sea,
From Jesus' arms always open wide
His love flows direct to me.

Ross sang and clapped as never before.

Dominic's theme was the Holy Spirit again. Now he was talking about how you can be filled with it. He said some people believe but aren't filled with the Spirit, like a boiler with only the pilot light working – very different from a boiler that is all fired up.

He quoted examples from the Bible: Samaritan converts after hearing Peter and Paul, Paul himself once the scales had fallen from his eyes, and a group of Gentiles upon hearing Peter.

Ross could sense Dominic's passion. Everything else in the room had disappeared. There was just Dominic and the power of his words.

'The Holy Spirit is like a storm-force wind blowing away the cobwebs. It's like a raging fire that rips through the barriers we've erected. It's an overwhelming experience of the love of God. When we're filled with the Holy Spirit, it's as if God himself, the creator and sustainer of the whole universe, God himself stops to pick us up and pour his love into us.

271

'This is such a mind-blowing experience, to be filled with God's love. It makes you want to shout it from the highest hill. It makes you want to spread the word, to tell everybody that you've been filled with the Holy Spirit.'

Ross's heart was racing.

'Very often those who are filled with the Holy Spirit receive a new language. We call it speaking in tongues. Suddenly you can speak a new language you've never spoken before. It can be a human tongue or a tongue of angels. Last year a man did it in my church. Suddenly he stood up in the middle of a service and shouted, "Prosit! Prosit!" It wasn't until weeks later that we learnt that "Prosit" is Swedish for "God bless you." That man is here today. Rodney, please show yourself to us.'

Rodney stood up.

'That's the day that Rodney was filled with the Holy Spirit, the day he was born again.'

Rodney nodded and sat down.

Ross felt a fire burning within him. He could hardly contain it.

Just then, Bob the Builder stood up. Dominic gave him an approving look.

Ross stood up too. He looked into Dominic's eyes and they both smiled.

Bob looked behind him and saw Ross. Then, in a quiet, almost hushed voice, he said, 'Blob brig dib dib nash.'

Silence.

'Blob brig dib dib nash. Spling thorp ferding ferding nash.'

Alison tugged at his arm.

Bob looked utterly bemused, as if he had no idea what he was saying or why he was saying it. 'Blob brig dib nash. Sperding sperding sperding nash. Flobbing flibid airgun ferding ferding nash.'

Alison pulled him again. 'Sit down, Bob!'

'No,' said Dominic. 'Let him speak.'

Bob looked pleadingly at Dominic. 'I don't know what I'm saying.'

'You have the gift of speaking in tongues.'

For what seemed an eternity, everyone looked at Bob, but he just stood there, an expression of bewilderment on his face, and said nothing more. Alison tugged at his arm again and he sat down.

Ross sat down too.

For a moment there was hushed silence. Then Dominic started to declaim. 'And these signs will accompany those who believe. In Christ's name, they will drive out demons, they will speak in new tongues. For they heard them speaking in tongues and praising God. All of them were filled with the Holy Spirit and began to speak in other tongues as the spirit enabled them.

'To one there is given through the Spirit the message of wisdom, to another knowledge, to another faith, to another gifts of healing, to another miraculous powers, to another prophecy and to another speaking in different kinds of tongues. For anyone who speaks in a tongue does not speak to men but to God. Indeed, no-one understands him; he utters mysteries with his spirit.'

Ross felt utterly deflated, as if a spell had been broken. He had no idea what he had just witnessed, but he knew that it wasn't some great mystery of the spirit. Bob wasn't speaking the tongues of angels. It was pure gibberish.

Chapter Thirty-Nine

As soon as they could, Ross and Sofie went into the garden to talk alone. 'It nearly happened,' said Ross. 'I was so close, you know. I was that close.' He held up his hand, his finger and thumb half a centimetre apart.

'I saw.'

He gave an enormous Gallic shrug and then sighed and slapped his hands against his thighs.

'What just happened?' said Ross.

'I honestly don't know.'

'That's the weirdest thing I ever saw.'

'Yeah, really disturbing.'

'Too right,' said Ross. 'I feel…I don't know what I feel. Dominic said about receiving a new language. I mean, "Blob dib blib blob?" That's not some kind of language. That's just nonsense. Baby talk.'

'But at the same time, it was very powerful.'

'I know. I'm just totally weirded out.'

'Did it put you off?'

'You bet. I might not be the sharpest tool in the box, but I do have a bullshit detector.'

'You're a pretty sharp tool, Ross. You got a C in history, remember?'

He laughed.

'I was there,' he said. 'It was about to happen, and then, bloody Bob.'

'Are you upset?'

'I don't know. I don't know if I should be upset or relieved.'

*

Ross passed the rest of the weekend in something of a daze. Saturday evening was devoted to a game of charades made difficult by the fact that *double entendres* were banned. The next morning, Dominic gave a final talk, for the most part a plea for Christian kindness and virtue, with a little section on Christian sexual morality, or, to Ross's mind, Christian prudishness.

By now his enthusiasm had completely vanished. He wondered what he was doing there, whether he was wasting his time. And if so, had he been wasting his time all these weeks?

What the hell was that about, speaking in tongues?

'Blib blob blib blob.'

It was barking mad. And very, very weird, the weirdest thing he had ever seen. Did they really think it was some kind of miracle? Really?

Maybe his dad was right and religion was just bullshit. All of it. And if it was, how was he supposed to find redemption?

What a waste of time.

Bob and Alison agreed to take him to Haywards Heath in good time for the last train to Windermere. He was grateful to them, but the journey was very uncomfortable, sitting behind Bob, who was filled with enthusiasm about his conversion experience.

'It was the most amazing day of my life,' he said again and again. 'I really felt it. It was the Holy Spirit. It just reached down and filled me. Incredible.'

Ross and Sofie exchanged glances but said nothing. From the pained expression Ross saw on her face, Alison was finding the whole thing very difficult indeed.

When they stopped in Haywards Heath, Sofie accompanied Ross into the station.

'You going to be all right in the car with Bob?' said Ross.

'It's only an hour. It's Alison I feel sorry for.'

'Yeah, I know what you mean. I'd better go.'

'Have a great holiday.'

'Have a good week.'

She touched his arm. 'Message me when you get there.'

'Will do.'

It was a long journey to the Lake District, with multiple changes: train to London, underground from Victoria to Euston, train to Manchester, a bus replacement service from Manchester to Lancaster, where Ross caught another train, and finally a juddery local train from Oxenholme to Windermere, where Ross's father picked him up and took him to their cottage in the village of Ambleside.

His mother made him tea and toast and brought it into the living room.

'So, tell me about your weekend.'

Ross chewed his toast. 'It was weird. I mean, so weird. This guy Bob, he had a conversion experience. He suddenly stood up in the middle of the session and started spouting gibberish: "Blib blib, blibberty blob. Blerding blerding blob."'

'That is just such crap,' said his father.

'Mind your language,' said Ross's mother.

Ross's younger brother looked at her, bemused. 'Is "crap" swearing?'

'Yes,' said Ross, 'it means poo-poo.'

'Oh.'

'What happened to your friend *is* crap,' said Ross's father. 'I'll prove it to you. Give me a few minutes.'

He went to fetch his iPad and used AirPlay to mirror its screen on the TV in the corner of the room. Then he googled *Derren Brown Messiah*, which took him to a TV programme recorded several years earlier in which the illusionist and atheist Derren Brown had travelled incognito to the USA and posed as an evangelical preacher.

Ross's father scrolled forwards until 10 minutes and 40 seconds into the programme.

'Here it is.'

Brown started with footage of church services, both traditional and happy-clappy, leading up to footage of American evangelical preachers performing supposed miracles. The programme then showed Brown in Greenwich Village addressing an audience of 20 sceptics.

Within minutes, just by holding out his hand, he converted one of them from atheism to a position where she understood the 'inner hug' that her grandmother had always received when she prayed. She now said she felt open to the idea of God.

Half the audience walked out at this point. Brown called out a volunteer from those who remained, a self-declared atheist. Moments later, the volunteer spontaneously fell back into Brown's arms, just as a Christian had done in the previous footage of an evangelical service. Within minutes, Brown was able to do pretty much the same thing with all but one of his audience, somehow making them fall back into their seats.

Where only one had said she believed in God, Brown had now turned all but one into believers. An evangelical preacher who had witnessed the whole thing declared himself impressed.

Ross's father then called up another video on YouTube: *Derren Brown 'instant conversion' (explained) by mystrybox*. The narrator had some knowledge of the hypnotist's art and explained how, even though the sequences in the programme were heavily edited, Brown's performance had all the hallmarks of a stage hypnotist's act.

For Ross, these videos came as a revelation. Did that explain why he had come so close to being converted himself? Something similar to stage hypnotism?

When he was able to extricate himself from his family, he went into his bedroom and messaged Sofie. He told her about the videos his father had shown him and sent her the links.

He got little sleep that night. His heart was racing and found it difficult to lie still. Had he been wasting his time for the last two months? How could he find redemption in Alpha if they didn't know the difference between stage hypnotism and a miracle?

It wasn't just that. He didn't like the way Dominic took the Bible literally. And all that stuff about the resurrection, Bee had shown that it was just nonsense.

But Nigel said that didn't matter. It was coming at everything from the wrong angle. Whenever he spoke with Nigel, he understood what he was saying, but now he wasn't sure he did. He wished he could speak to him now, tell him about Bob and see what he thought.

Nigel had an encounter with the Holy Spirit too, and that wasn't stage hypnotism. He had been on his own, just sitting in a church. So, what was that? Was it real or was it some weird bullshit, like what happened to Bob?

His train of thought took him to Sofie. She knew how to believe in something even when she knew it wasn't really true. For a few hours, he had thought he could too, but now he felt that he had lost it again.

He smiled as he remembered her. In his mind's eye, he saw her smile, her eyes. He saw her in the hotel with her black skirt and white blouse: quick, efficient, cheerful and friendly. He owed her so much. She was the best friend he had ever had. And now he had gone and fallen in love with her.

Idiot.

*

The next morning, they drove to Grasmere and spent an hour walking round the village and down to the lake. After that, they put their boots on and set off to climb High Raise. It was warm and a mix of sunny and cloudy, with no rain expected. There was a slight breeze by the lake, which got stronger and cooler the higher they got, but the effort of the climb kept them hot.

Ross felt energised by the walk. The views changed as they ascended, and when they were high enough to see both Lake Grasmere and Lake Windermere, he turned round again and again to look at them. Near the summit, his father pointed out Morecambe Bay to the south and the three peaks to the south-east, more than 30 miles away. Ross thought it was the most amazing view he had ever seen.

It was the first time since the accident that he had been able to enjoy himself with his family. The last four months had been a constant battle to keep his mind off the accident, but today, with fresh air, mountain views and a strenuous walk, he felt able to cope. The accident was still there, in the background, but it didn't dominate in the same way as before.

*

'Hi, babe.'

'Hiya,' said Sofie. 'Nice sun tan.'

'Thank you very much,' said Dani.

'Was it hot?'

'Wow, yeah. Had a really great time.'

'That's good. Can I get you anything?'

Dani grimaced and nodded her head from side to side.

'Get us one of them little tubs of ice cream.'

'Strawberry?'

'Please. And treat yourself too, Sofie. It's a bank holiday.'

'Yeah, why not?'

They were in the coffee shop on the corner opposite the Old Town Co-op. Sofie returned a few minutes later with an Americano and two tubs of strawberry ice cream. They opened them up, retrieved the little wooden spoons and dug them into the ice cream, which was too frozen to eat.

Dani leaned forwards. 'Do you want to hear some gossip?'

'I like a bit of gossip.'

'Ross's mum told my mum that you two are going out.'

Sofie greeted this with a disapproving grunt.

'Not only that,' said Dani, 'but she told my mum she really likes you. She says you're a good influence on him.'

Sofie laughed. 'Me? A good influence?'

'Yes.'

'I don't think anyone's ever said that before.'

'Well, I think you are.'

'Thank you.' Sofie prodded her ice cream. It was still frozen solid.

'Now there's one thing I don't get,' said Dani. 'I meant to ask you about this the last two times we met but I keep forgetting.'

'What?'

Dani took a sip of her cappuccino. 'When I was at Tara's party, I asked Ross about you, and he says you told him you didn't fancy him. He was like, "She says I'm not her type."'

Sofie's face turned serious. 'Yeah, I did say that.'

'Is it true?'

She gave a little shrug. 'No.'

'You do fancy him?'

After a moment, Sofie said, 'Yes.'

'More than fancy?'

'Give me a break, Dani.'

'Come on, Sofie. You're my best friend, right? He's my favourite cousin. People used to ask if we were twins. I love you and I love him. You'd be so perfect together. What d'you go and say that for?'

'I don't know. It just came out.'

'Well, don't you think you should let him know...?'

'No. Not now. He needs my friendship. He don't need no pressure. Maybe after his trial. Promise you won't say nothing to him.'

'All right, I promise.'

'And no getting Raj to say it neither. I know you.'

Dani laughed.

*

'Tea for two, please.'

Bee and Robbie were in the café in Edinburgh's Royal Botanic Gardens.

'Anything else with that?'

'A chocolate brownie, please.'

'Other cakes are available, you know,' said Robbie.

'Yeah, but I like chocolate brownies.'

Robbie ordered a flapjack for himself. Once their tray was full, he paid for everything and they found an empty table near the window.

'Oh, I didn't tell you: I heard from Sofie.'

'Oh, right, how is she?'

'She's good. They had the Alpha Course weekend away, and Dominic bagged him a convert. A guy called Bob. Really nice guy, actually. We told you about him: Bob the Builder.'

'So the Alpha Course is now a score draw,' said Robbie. 'God lost Omega Bee and gained Bob the Builder.'

Bee laughed. 'Bob started speaking in tongues half-way through a lecture.'

'Do they still do that?'

'Oh yes, and not just Christians. Apparently there are ceremonies in Japan and Indonesia where they do it too. And some tribal ceremonies in Africa, I think.'

'Presumably, you've never done it?'

'No, but I've seen it a couple of times.'

'Really?'

'Yeah. It's pretty bizarre. Quite powerful in its own way, but definitely bizarre. It's usually recent converts. They stand there going, "Whin bim lim f'tang f'tang olé," and if it sounds a little bit like something in a foreign language, then they say, "A miracle! He can speak Outer Mongolian." Usually it's just nonsense sounds. You know what they say then?'

'What?'

'It's the tongues of angels.'

'Ah, like in the U2 song? "*I Still Haven't Found...*"'

'Yeah. She says Ross's dad showed him a video of Derren Brown doing this show where he posed as a charismatic preacher. Then he converted atheists on the spot and made them fall over without touching them.'

'Oh, I think I've seen that.'

'Now Ross is convinced that all religious experiences are just the result of stage hypnotism.'

Robbie nodded. 'I should think a lot of them are.'

'Yes, but not all of them.'

'Have you seen Anil Seth's TED talk?'

'No?'

'It's brilliant. We can watch it when we get home. I think he's a neuroscientist or something. What he says is we don't perceive reality directly.'

'Like Plato's shadows on the wall.'

'Exactly, but updated for the twenty-first century. I can't remember if it's him or someone else who says our senses give us a user interface on reality. It's good enough for what we need, but it only tells us what we need to know. And we have to interpret it.'

'Okay,' said Bee.

'And then what we think is reality, the picture our brain builds from what we see, hear, touch, smell etcetera, the word he uses is that it's a controlled hallucination. I'll give you an example: when I'm cycling, I really hate it when dogs chase me.'

279

'Me too.'

'So sometimes, I'm riding my bike, minding my own business, and then I'll see something out of the corner of my eye. And because I'm wary of dogs when I'm cycling, I'll see it as a dog. That's a hallucination, right. But it's controlled because I look at it again, and it's just a plastic bag being blown about by the wind.'

Bee was too busy munching her chocolate brownie to speak, but she nodded her assent.

'So, everything we see or hear or feel is a controlled hallucination. And managing that, keeping it properly controlled is a learned skill. We learn it in infancy. And like any skill, sometimes we screw up and it goes all uncontrolled.'

'Just like that?'

'Aye, just like that, without any need for stage hypnotism or what have you.'

Bee finished the last of her brownie.

'Yes, maybe.'

'So,' said Robbie, 'let's say your brain screws up, and you have a bit of an uncontrolled hallucination, then you have to interpret it. If you're already religious or interested in religion, then you might interpret it as a religious experience.'

'Or if you're superstitious, and it happens in a dark, spooky house, you might think it's a ghost.'

'Exactly. And if you're a rationalist, you interpret it as a bit of a funny turn.'

'And wonder if you're going mad.'

Robbie grinned and pointed up with his finger. 'And if you're totally batshit crazy, you think aliens have abducted you and probed your rectum.'

They both laughed.

'That is so weird, isn't it?' said Bee.

Robbie nodded. 'Aye, but they believe it. At least, I assume they do.'

'I'm sure they do.'

They stopped talking for a while and drank some of their tea.

After a moment, Bee said, 'There is one thing that's much more important than all this.'

'What?'

'Are you going to eat all of that flapjack?'

'What? You've just had a whole chocolate brownie.'

'Yeah, but I only had a small lunch. And you did say other cakes are available.'

*

As the week progressed, Ross's mood began to darken again. He wasn't sure why. Perhaps it was because he was missing Sofie. Or maybe the novelty of the lakes and mountains was wearing off. Whatever the reason, the accident and Lizzie Johnson's fate started to reassert themselves. He was also worried about the start of term and going back to college. Everyone would know, and he had already encountered one person who would take pleasure in reminding him of it.

Beyond that, his trial was less than three weeks away. He knew he was very unlikely to be sent to prison, but very unlikely doesn't mean definitely not. It was a possibility that terrified him.

On Thursday, he and Sofie had a chat on WhatsApp.

Ross:	I'm a bit like Crank have you seen it
Sofie:	Don't think so
Ross:	Jason Stratham is injected with this drug right that will kill him if he doesn't keep the adrenaline flowing
	I'm like that I have to keep busy or the accident creeps up on me
Sofie:	Are you keeping busy?
Ross:	Most of the time yeah but we have down time before we go to bed
	Everyone just reads a book or something
Sofie:	Message me if you need to
	I go to bed late
Ross:	Thanx
Sofie:	You can call if you like
	I'm happy to speak
Ross:	Maybe I will
Sofie:	BTW I had a chat with B the other day
	She's in Scotland with her BF
Ross:	Did she say anything about stage hypnotism
Sofie:	Not really
	She just said yeah it could be that, could be something else
Ross:	I think the omega course is over don't you
Sofie:	Yeah.
	What about Alpha
Ross:	Dunno maybe I'll keep going
	I was so close but now I'm not even sure I want to get converted
	But the accident hasn't gone away I need something
Sofie:	👍

Chapter Forty

Ross and his family got home late on Saturday evening. Sunday was spent with his maternal grandparents in Bexhill, along with Dani and her mother. Dani dragooned Ross into joining her, Raj, Sofie and others by the beach on Monday, for the final afternoon of the college summer holidays.

Ross and Sofie cycled down to the seafront together. They parked their bikes near the Wish Tower and set off to find the others. It was a perfect day for sunbathing and possibly even a swim.

As they walked along the promenade, Ross noticed Sid walking towards them. He was wearing shorts and had his T-shirt rolled up in one hand and a cigarette in the other. He was with an equally muscular young man who, like him, was covered in tattoos.

'Uh-oh,' said Ross. 'Our favourite person.'

'Yeah. We're not stopping to chat.'

As they got near, Sofie looked away but Ross smiled and said, 'Hi.'

His companion pointed at Sofie and said, 'Yo, Sofie. Long time no see.'

Sid grinned and said in a very loud voice, 'It's Ross the killer driver!'

Sofie grabbed Ross's arm and put herself between them.

"Fuck off, Sid,' she yelled. 'Bastard.'

Sid's friend laughed. 'She hasn't changed.'

'You can fuck off too, Jake.'

Passers-by stopped to stare at them.

Ross tugged at Sofie. 'Come on, let's go. He's not worth it.'

'At least I ain't killed no-one.'

Sofie raised her hand and stepped towards Sid, but Ross pulled her back.

'Paedophile!' she shouted.

Sid went to as if attack her.

Ross jumped between them.

'Just don't.'

'You know how I know your girlfriend's a little slapper?' said Sid, jabbing his finger at Ross's face. 'Because I fucked her. Bet she didn't tell you that, did she, Mr Killer Driver?'

With that, he turned his back on Ross and Sofie, and he and his friend strode away.

Ross watched them go, all the while holding Sofie's arm to make sure she didn't run after them. The small crowd that had gathered round them slowly dissipated.

He turned round to face Sofie. She had tears in her eyes.

'You okay?'

She nodded. 'I'm sorry. I should have told you.'

'Don't worry about that.' He let go of her arm. 'Let's go down on the beach, find a quiet spot where we can talk.'

They walked down some wooden steps onto the shingle below. There weren't many people on this part of the beach, so they soon found a spot where they could sit and speak without being overheard.

'I'm sorry, Ross. I wanted to tell you, but I didn't feel I could when we were at the hotel.'

'Don't worry, I'm not angry with you. I'm angry with bloody Nigel. He must have told him. You'd have thought you could trust a priest to keep his mouth shut.'

'Yeah.'

'Bloody hell,' said Ross. 'I really thought I could trust him.'

Sofie reached over and gave his hand a squeeze.

He looked at her and smiled, though he was still quivering and could feel the adrenaline rampaging through his veins.

'Do you need a handkerchief?' he asked.

She nodded. He retrieved it from his pocket and passed it to her. She wiped her eyes and blew her nose. 'Sorry. This is getting to be a habit, innit?'

'No worries.'

After a moment she said, 'I was really scared just then. I thought you two were going to get in a fight.'

'I thought *you* were going to hit him.'

She shook her head. 'He wouldn't have hit me back, but he'd happily thump you if you gave him an excuse.'

Ross gave a little laugh. 'I've never had a fight in my life.'

'I wish I could say that.'

They sat and watched the waves for a long time. Then Sofie said, 'God, I hate that bastard.'

'Was it him that got you pregnant?'

She nodded.

'And you slapped him for it?'

She gave a little laugh. 'Yeah.'

'Serves him right. You must have had a shock when you saw him at his mum's hotel.'

'I wouldn't have stayed if I didn't need the money. My dad's really bad at paying maintenance, and my mum's other ex, he moans if she spends any money on me.'

'Do you think Martha knows?'

'Don't know. I mean, she must know he cheats on her. Me and him sometimes spent the whole night at my sister's. But I don't think she knows it was me, or more accurately, she doesn't know one of them was me. I'm sure there's been plenty of others.'

They sat in silence for some time.

Sofie took a deep breath and said, 'I didn't know he was married, not at first anyway. No way would I have gone out with him if I'd known. My sister knew, but she didn't tell me till it was too late. Bitch.'

'Did you love him?'

'Yeah.' After a moment, she said, 'He was my first love. Can you believe it, a scumbag like him? That's how stupid I am.'

'You're not stupid. You were too young and he's a bastard.'

'You sound like Kitty.'

'I didn't know counsellors were allowed to say things like that.'

'Not in as many words, no.' After a moment, she said, 'He was kind to me. I told you about Jake and his mates. They were real bastards, and I was so desperate to fit in, I went along with it. But Sid was kind. I mean, probably he was just trying to get his end away, but he was very sweet sometimes. And he...he could be vulnerable. When he was coming down, he'd get really depressed. When I found out he was married, I was like, "I can't go out with you, you're married," and he was like, "Don't dump me. I'll jump off Beachy Head if you dump me."'

'Did he say that?'

'Yeah.'

'Bloody hell. That's quite manipulative, isn't it?'

'I know. But at the time, I thought he would, you know, because of how low he got when he was coming down. He used to say he'd never really loved Martha, but he couldn't leave her because he loved his kids so much.'

'Did he know you were under age?'

'Oh, yes. On my sixteenth birthday, he was like, "It won't be so much fun now you're legal." Ha bloody ha.' She looked Ross in the eye. 'I hope it don't make you think less of me, thinking about me with him.'

'Sofie, how can you say that?' He paused. He wished he could tell her he loved her. But this wasn't the moment. Right now, she needed him to be her friend. 'I admire you. I really admire the way you've got your life back together.'

'Thank you, Ross. You're very sweet.'

They looked into each other's eyes and smiled.

'You okay to join the others?'

'Depends if it's just Dani and Raj. Give us a sec.'

She took out her mobile and messaged Dani:

Sofie:	Hi babe
Dani:	Where RU
Sofie:	Is it just you and Raj?
Dani:	Nah there's quite a few of us here

'There's other people there,' she told Ross. 'I can't face them at the moment. Do you mind?'

'No.'
'Thanks.'

Sofie: I think I'll give it a miss.
Dani: Wot?
Sofie: I just seen Sid and had a big row with him
Dani: OMG RU OK
Sofie: I'm a bit upset
Dani: Where RU babe I'll come and find U
Sofie: It's OK I'm with Ross and he's looking after me

'Did you notice how blasted he was?' Sofie said after a moment.
'No?'
'God, yeah, completely off his face.'
'I didn't notice.'
'Didn't you see his eyes? Totally dilated. When I knew him, he was never this bad. It was, like, recreational. He'd get coked out or loved up in the evening, but not in the middle of the day.' She shook her head. 'He's completely out of control now.'

Chapter Forty-One

College began the next day. Ross desperately hoped his lessons would keep him busy enough to keep dark thoughts at bay. But the college week was structured as a bridge to university. One third of the timetable was given over to free-study periods when the students would take responsibility for their own learning. Ross was really worried about all the free time this would give him.

When his tutor group reassembled, his tutor Harry Liptrot began by telling them about his summer. His main achievement had been to dig a pond in his garden, and he had also gone for a two-week walking holiday that took him to the Malvern Hills and the Brecon Beacons. He asked the seven students in the group about their summers.

Ross had decided it was better to be open rather than to worry about who knew what. When his turn came, he took a deep breath and said, 'I didn't have a very nice summer. In April, I was involved in a car crash. I caused it when I tried to overtake without looking in my mirror, and this car crashed into the back of me. It flipped over and a Ford Transit smashed into it. The driver died. So I kind of spent my summer dealing with that, and it hasn't been great.'

His tutor was clearly shocked. 'I'm so sorry, Ross. I didn't know.'

None of his classmates seemed surprised.

'Is it true you were arrested?' one of the girls asked.

'Yeah, I've been charged with causing death by careless driving.' He looked at his teacher. 'I have to take next Monday morning off to see my solicitor. Then I'm due to go to court on Monday the seventeenth. I need to take the whole day off for that.'

'Could you go to prison?' his classmate asked.

'Theoretically, yes. But my lawyer says I won't. He says I'll lose my licence and get community service.'

'God, Ross,' said his classmate. 'That's really terrible. Can I give you a hug?'

She got out of her seat and went over to him. He stood up and she hugged him. Then all of his classmates and his tutor followed suit, which reduced Ross and several of them to tears.

He lost count of all the hugs he received that day, mostly from girls (including his ex-girlfriend Mollie) but from several boys too. Sympathy wasn't universal, however. Pete the Prat shouted, 'Watch out, it's Ross! Careful he doesn't crash into you!' every time he saw him. He had a coterie of friends who thought this was very funny.

Ross didn't react. At a certain level, he felt he deserved it.

*

That evening at the Alpha Course, Bob the Builder was still radiant. His eyes shone and his smile lit up the room. Alison had a worried, haggard look about her. 'I should be pleased for him,' she whispered to Sofie. 'He's got what he came here for, the thing he said was always missing in his life.'

'That's good, isn't it?'

'Yes, but he wants to convert me and the children. He's desperate for us to believe too. I mean, I don't have a problem with believing in God. I do believe in God, but all the other stuff that goes with it, I have real problems with that.'

'Bee was a Christian without believing any of it was literally true. She said you don't have to believe it, just respond as if it's true.'

Alison frowned. 'I'm not sure about that, Sofie. I've always been pretty straight, really. I have an opinion and that's that.'

Sofie smiled. 'Same as Ross.'

'How is Ross?'

'He has good days and bad days. Today was good.'

'It's a good job he's got you,' said Alison with a wink.

'We're just friends.'

'I'm sure you are, dear.'

Dinner was home-made pizza. The chat around Ross and Sofie's table was dominated by Bob telling everyone what a difference conversion had made to his life. The last few days had been among the happiest he had ever known. The only times that could compare were his honeymoon and the birth of his children. 'You've got to let God into your lives,' he told Ross and Sofie. 'It'll make such a difference to you.'

Ross wanted to tell him that he had fallen for a stage hypnotist's tricks, but he kept quiet. He had promised Sofie that he wouldn't mention Derren Brown at all.

They sang two hymns as usual. As they did so, Ross reflected that the Holy Spirit may have taught Bob to speak in the tongues of angels, but it hadn't taught him how to sing.

Dominic's theme for the evening was Satan. 'Behind all the goodness in the world we find God, and behind all the evil in our hearts and in the world stands the personification of evil: the Devil. I'm not talking about a red man with a goatee beard and horns. That would be absurd. But I am talking about an active, personal force of evil who's all around us, waiting for us to fall into the traps he sets for us.'

This came as a jolt to Ross, who was astonished that anyone could believe that Satan literally existed. But Dominic reeled off a number of Biblical quotations and references that proved the existence of the Devil and his army of demons: Adam and Eve's serpent, Ezekiel 28, Isaiah's description of the fall of Lucifer and the story of Job. The New Testament showed that Jesus had believed in Satan and had been tempted by him. Saint Paul had warned against him and his army of fallen angels. The Book of Revelations refers to him as a dragon and an ancient serpent.

'Doesn't common sense tell you that Satan is out there? Don't you watch the news every day? All the wars, the terrorism, the senseless killings. The murders, the rapes and the abductions of innocent children. All the lies, the deceit, the corruption and the crime. All the sex scandals, the prostitution and pornography, all the extra-marital sex and abortions, all the drugs, all the suicides at Beachy Head. Satan is out there, tempting us all the time.

'And he wants us to be interested in *him*, not in God. He doesn't want us to come to church or to pray. He prefers us to consult our horoscopes or our Ouija boards. He wants us to watch horror movies or vampire films and become fascinated by him. He wants to tempt us with witchcraft using seemingly innocent tales of the clever magician Harry Potter.'

At this point, Ross and Sofie looked wide-eyed at each other. Both of them loved Harry Potter.

Dominic said Satan's aim is our destruction. He quoted the Bible to show that it was Satan who blinded the eyes of unbelievers. It was Satan who raised doubts in people's minds. 'Does it *really* say that in the Bible? Is that *really* what God wants?'

Ross wondered if Dominic, Pat and the others thought Bee had been doing Satan's work when she sent emails that undermined Dominic's message. No wonder Pat had been so hostile.

Dominic spent some time talking about sin and shame. For a few minutes, this plunged Ross back into crisis mode. He thought Dominic would say that it was Satan that had whispered to him, 'Go on, overtake that car.' But for Ross it wasn't a question of Satan, or even of evil. It was more a question of stupidity, impatience and toxic masculinity.

Dominic was talking about pre-marital sex and how evil it was. Ross didn't understand why Christians had such a thing about this. But, of course, it was wicked because it said so in a book written thousands of years ago, when all sex was unprotected.

Hadn't the world changed a bit since then?

Now Dominic was talking about the weapons that Christians can use to combat Satan: the Belt of Truth, the Breastplate of Righteousness, the Shoes of the Gospel of Peace, the Shield of Faith, the Helmet of Salvation and the Sword of the Spirit.

'The war is already won. Jesus won the final victory on the cross. All that's left are mopping-up operations. The Devil has lost. He has been defeated and he's about to be wiped out completely when Jesus returns in glory to judge the living and the dead. And his kingdom will have no end. We will witness the resurrection of the dead and the life of the world to come.'

*

Ross and Sofie took their coffees outside. They sat on the wall near the pavement.

'What did you think of that?'

'I hated it,' said Ross.

'Me too.'

'I really don't want to come any more.'

Sofie winced. 'I don't know. We said we'd see it through to the end.'

'Well, let's see how the discussion goes. We can make our minds up after that.'

'Okay.'

They tried not to get drawn into the discussion, but it when Pat asked Sofie direct what she thought, it was difficult for her to stay silent. 'I didn't like it, to be honest. I mean, I think I might believe in God, and I believe the Christian message is a good one. But I'm not comfortable with all this stuff about the Holy Spirit and the Devil. I know it says so in the Bible, but I just don't think you should take the Bible so literally.'

'But we do take God's word literally,' said Pat. 'That's the whole point.'

'Sofie,' said Bob. 'Two weeks ago, I would have agreed with you. Even when we drove up for the weekend away, I think I said to you in the car that I was quite sceptical about a lot of the things Dominic and Pat were saying.'

Sofie nodded. 'I remember.'

'But my opinion's completely changed. It was something I really wasn't expecting, but when we were in Northfields Hall, I opened myself up to the Holy Spirit and I felt him pour himself into me. It was one of the most amazing experiences of my life, maybe *the* most amazing. I'm still glowing. I've never known anything like it. It's completely transformed my attitude. I'm not a sceptic at all now.'

Ross glanced at Alison, who was sitting next to her husband looking glum. Sofie, for her part, clearly felt very uncomfortable to find herself the focus of the discussion.

Bob leaned forwards his palms upturned above the table. 'You were there, Sofie. You saw what happened to me. I started speaking a language I've never even heard before. I've got no idea what I was saying, but I couldn't stop it coming out. I felt it, Sofie. I really felt it. I can still feel the afterglow now. It's the most wonderful feeling in the world, and I know what it is. It's the Holy Spirit, Sofie. The Holy Spirit poured itself into me. If you're uncomfortable with the Holy Spirit and the Devil and so forth, then how are you going to explain what happened to me?'

Sofie looked down at the table. Her face had turned red.

By now Dominic was standing next to the table. 'Bob's right. Can't you see how he's changed since Saturday night? You were there, Sofie. We were all there. We saw it with our own eyes. Bob knows what it was: it was the Holy Spirit. What else could it have been?'

'There is another explanation,' said Ross.

Sofie glared at him and gave a little shake of her head.

'What do you mean?' said Dominic.

'When I told my dad what happened, he showed me a video of Derren Brown, on YouTube. Do you know Derren Brown?'

Dominic looked puzzled.

'He's a magician. Channel Four sent him to America a few years ago. He posed as an evangelical preacher. He got this audience full of atheists and he converted them on the spot. Then they interviewed some of them and they were speaking a bit like Bob, saying they'd just had this amazing insight. And then afterwards Derren Brown told them it was just a trick.'

'You can't believe this kind of thing on TV,' said Pat. 'The whole thing was probably a set up.'

'Well, that's the thing,' said Ross. 'My dad showed me this other YouTube video. This guy explained how Derren Brown did it. He said the sequence was heavily edited, but you could see enough to know it was just stage hypnotism.'

'What?' said Bob. 'Are you saying I was hypnotised?'

'You asked what else it could have been.'

Dominic laughed. 'I can assure you that I'm not a hypnotist.'

'No, but maybe the techniques you use are very similar to hypnotism.'

'What? Such as?'

'It's difficult to explain it.'

Sofie joined in: 'The second video explained how Derren Brown got his audience into a suggestive state. To a certain extent, Bob was already in a suggestive state.'

'I was?'

'Yes. Do you remember? When we went walking, you told us how you the idea of the Holy Spirit resonated with you because of experiences you'd had when you were younger.'

Bob nodded.

'So you were already receptive. Then, I'm not saying Dominic did this deliberately, but it could be the effect's the same as hypnotism, there was music and this relaxed you further. And then during his talk, Dominic planted the idea of speaking in tongues in your head, and then it happened.'

Bob shook his head. 'No, that's not what happened.'

Dominic said, 'So if I was hypnotising the audience, how come Bob was the only one who succumbed?'

'Because he was the only one in a receptive state,' said Sofie.

'No, he wasn't,' said Ross. 'Don't you remember? I stood up too, just after Bob stood up. I was in a receptive state. I was expecting the Holy Spirit to pour itself into me at any moment. But when Bob started speaking in tongues, I didn't believe it.'

'What do you mean?' said Bob. 'Did you think I was pretending?'

'No, far from it. But I didn't believe it was the tongues of angels.'

'Well, I can assure you I wasn't pretending,' said Bob.

'I never said you were.'

'I think we can turn this explanation on its head,' said Pat.

Everyone looked at her.

'This is what Dominic's been talking about. Where do you think Derren Brown gets his special powers?'

Sofie and Ross looked at her, puzzled expressions on their faces.

'What do you mean, powers?' asked Sofie.

'The power to hypnotise.'

'Hypnotism isn't a special power,' said Ross. 'It's just a trick, a technique anyone can learn.'

'Is it?' said Pat. 'Are you sure about that? I mean, it's a pretty amazing trick, isn't it? The power to take over another person's mind. Where do you think that comes from? And what does Derren Brown use his powers for? To try and discredit Christianity. Now who do you think would give someone special powers to do that?'

Sofie stared at her in astonishment. 'You think Derren Brown is working for Satan?'

'Yes.'

'That's ridiculous.'

'Is it?' said Dominic. 'That's what my talk was all about.'

'So anyone who disagrees with you is working for Satan?'

'No, I wouldn't put it like that. But I would say that anyone who sets out to undermine Jesus' message is doing the Devil's work.'

Sofie and Ross exchanged glances. Then the two of them stopped arguing and sat out the rest of the meeting without saying a word, waiting desperately for it to end.

*

'They're fascists,' said Sofie as they walked to the bus stop. 'That's what they are. Anyone who doesn't agree with them is working for the enemy. I thought Christianity was all about love and compassion, but these people are just a bunch of fascists.'

Ross grinned. He was glad she was so angry. He didn't think he could sit through another of Dominic's talks without screaming, and now he wouldn't have to.

Sofie still hadn't finished. 'I could go for Bee's version of Christianity, without any of this rubbish about Satan. But Dominic's version? People like him would still burn heretics if they could.'

Ross laughed. 'I don't think he's that bad.'

'But it's the same mentality. Can't you see? If you think, "I'm right, and anyone who thinks differently is evil," then you're only a small step away from wanting to ban them. You can see how the Spanish Inquisition happened. It wasn't an accident. That's where all this crap about Satan leads.'

There were two other people from the Alpha Course at the bus stop, so Sofie ended her rant. They didn't speak again until they were safely seated on the top deck.

'You know who I feel sorry for?' said Sofie.

'Who?'

'Alison, having a fanatical convert for a husband.'

'He'll get over it,' said Ross.

'You think so?'

'Yeah. Did you do *Captain Corelli's Mandolin* for GCSE?'

'I loved that book,' said Sofie. 'But what's it got to do with Bob?'

'When Bob talks about the Holy Spirit, right, it's just like he's fallen in love with it. Don't you think so? His eyes, the way he can't stop smiling.'

Sofie gave a little laugh. 'Yeah, I see what you mean.'

'In *Captain Corelli*, yeah, do you remember that bit when Pelagia's dad realises she's in love with Captain Corelli? He tells her falling in love is just a temporary madness, and it'll wear off.'

'Oh, I remember that bit. It's brilliant.'

'Yeah.'

'We done that in psychology,' said Sofie. 'When you fall in love, your hormones just go bananas. There's one of them dips – it's the one that keeps you sensible, basically. It goes through the floor. And your dopamine and oxytocin go through the roof. But it all wears off after a few months, and that's when you fall out of love.'

'Or, what it said in *Captain Corelli*, if you really are right for each other, you stay in love, but it's a much deeper kind of love.'

'And you think Bob's hormones have gone mad?'

'Too right, but eventually, they'll go back to normal and it'll wear off. Meanwhile, Aston Villa haven't won any of their last five matches, and they've already been knocked out of the EFL cup. You wait, they'll probably miss out on promotion again. He'll soon realise he's been conned and there is no God.'

*

Next day was Wednesday, and both of them had a free period first thing, so after registration, they met in a quiet corner of the student common room.

'I don't want to go back,' said Ross. 'It's just a waste of time.'

Sofie nodded. 'Yeah, I know what you mean.'

'I can't believe I was so close to being converted. It feels like a narrow escape, to be honest. I mean, "Blib bob blib" – what a load of crap.'

'I feel quite different,' said Sofie. 'For me, it's like, I've started out on a journey, and it's been interrupted. And I've seen something I really don't like, yeah, all that speaking in tongues. And Satan, I really hated that. I miss Bee, you know? She was my guide, not Dominic.'

'Why don't you speak to her?'

'Yeah, why not? I've got another free period this afternoon. I'll message her then.'

'Good idea.'

Sofie fixed her eyes on Ross. 'But there is another question, innit?'

'What?'

'You.'

Ross frowned and leaned back a little.

'Come on, Ross. You didn't go there to find Jesus.'

'Oh, that.'

'Yes, that.'

'I hope you're not going to shout at me again.'

She smiled. 'You could go and see Nigel. He's always helpful.'

Ross shook his head.

'What? Because of Sid?'

'Yeah.'

'Are you sure it was Nigel who told him?'

'Who else could it have been?'

'So, what are you going to do?'

Ross shrugged. 'I got my trial a week on Monday. See how I feel after that.'

*

Bee:	Oh, hiya. How are you?
Sofie:	I'm good. You?
Bee:	Yeah, actually, I'm on a train. I'm coming back down to my parents.
Sofie:	Oh right. Look why don't we meet up?
Bee:	That'd be great. Are you free on Saturday? Maybe we could go for a coffee somewhere Saturday afternoon.
Sofie:	Great
Bee:	How's Ross BTW?
Sofie:	He's OK. We've both dropped out of the Alpha Course. We'll tell you all about it on Saturday
Bee:	OK CU then. Give my love to Ross.

*

Ross quickly began to experience the failure of the Alpha Course to deliver redemption as a heavy blow. His college timetable wasn't busy enough to keep him from brooding, and he started to avoid his friends and spend his free periods alone in the college garden or nearby Hampden Park.

The only person he could talk to was Sofie. Their free periods rarely coincided, but after the first lesson on Friday afternoon, both of them were free.

'Shall we go for a walk in Hampden Park?' he asked.

'I was hoping to get my Spanish homework done.'

'Oh, right. I don't really want to study. I'll go by myself.'

'Let me come with you.'

'No, it's all right.'

'Be nice to me and let me come.'

He smiled. 'Go on then.'

They headed for the park, where they spent some time watching the ducks in the enormous pond, and the little children who had come to feed them.

After that, they walked past the playground. It was full of pre-school children with their mothers or grandparents.

'Do you know what I think when I look at them?'

'What?'

'I wonder if Lizzie Johnson ever brought her kids here. I'm sure she must have. She won't be bringing them again, will she?'

'You're back in self-flagellation mode, aren't you?'

'I've never stopped.'

'But it's getting worse, innit?'

'Maybe.'

'You're avoiding everyone, apart from me.'

Ross didn't reply.

'I thought with all your hugs on Tuesday…well, I was hoping…' She turned to face him. 'All your friends accept you, Ross. They're supporting you. They want you to join them and have a good time.'

'It's really difficult to have a good time. I know a family that isn't.'

She touched his arm with her hand. 'You can't keep torturing yourself for ever.'

They crossed the road and walked towards the wooded area.

'I hear you've dropped out of the football team.'

'Yeah. There's no point. If I get community service, I won't be able to play on Saturdays, will I?'

'Oh right. I hadn't thought of that.'

They walked a little further.

'Raj says you've dropped out of table tennis too.'

'Yeah.'

'Why?'

'There's no point.'

'Why?'

'I wouldn't be able to concentrate.'

'You concentrated just fine when you played against me.'

Ross shrugged.

'You really enjoyed it.'

He said nothing.

After a moment, Sofie said, 'Jesus, Ross. You're just sabotaging yourself. I don't know how to help you when you're like this.'

'I'm not asking you to help me.'

She stopped and halted him with her hand. 'Ross, how can you say that? How can you say that to *me*?'

He closed his eyes and hunched his shoulders.

'I'm sorry. I didn't mean it.'

She turned her back on him and brought her hands up to her face. They stood like that for over a minute. Eventually, she turned round to face him. Her face was puffy and her eyes were red.

'Don't push me away, Ross. You need me.'

'Yeah, I know. I'm sorry.'

'You really upset me. I'm going home. I'll message you tomorrow.'

Ross nodded, and Sofie hurried away.

Part Four

Great Tribulation

Chapter Forty-Two

Sofie was leaning forwards on the sofa, her head down, her arms folded tight across her body. Kate sat next to her, leaning forwards too, her body pointing towards her, with her right knee gently touching Sofie's left.

'I just don't know what to do when he's like this.'

'Maybe there's not a lot you can do.'

Sofie nodded. After a moment, she said, 'It's like everyone I love falls apart, you know? My dad, Amy, and now Ross. I don't think I can stand to sit there and watch it happen again. But I don't know how to stop it.'

'You know something I've learned?' said Kate. 'A very bitter lesson.'

'What's that?'

'You can't be responsible for how another person deals with their problems. They have to take responsibility. That's what you did after you got pregnant. You realised you had to change. And you did it: you succeeded.'

'I couldn't have done it without you.'

'Maybe not, but it's you that did it. All I did was help you a bit.'

'You helped me a lot.'

Kate smiled. 'Thank you.'

'It's me that should thank you.'

After a minute, Kate said, 'I thought I could change your dad, but I couldn't, because he didn't want to change. I'm sure part of him wanted to, but the biggest part of him preferred to carry on drinking, and there was nothing I could do. Maybe Ross just wants to be miserable.'

Sofie laughed. 'Wants to be miserable?'

'Yes, exactly that. All you can do is be there for him, and then, if and when he decides to change, that's when you can help him.'

Sofie frowned. After a moment, she looked at Kate. 'Do you think I should get in touch? Make sure he's okay.'

'Thought you told him you'd message him tomorrow?'

'I did.'

'It's up to you. It might not hurt to set some boundaries.'

'You think so?'

'What do I know? I've only got a one-third success rate. I succeeded with you, but I failed with your dad and Amy. And my marriage: that wasn't exactly a roaring success.'

Sofie looked at Kate and smiled. 'I'll let him stew till tomorrow. Treat 'em mean to keep 'em keen and all that.'

*

Sofie didn't message Ross until after Paula, Lydia and Carl had finished breakfast and got dressed.

Sofie:	Hiya
Ross:	Hi
Sofie:	You okay?
Ross:	🙈
	Sorry I upset you yesterday
Sofie:	So you should be
	Sorry I got so cross
Ross:	It was my fault you don't need to apologise
	You babysitting this morning
Sofie:	Yeah. U coming to meet B this afternoon?
Ross:	Can't my mum just announced we're going to dani's for lunch it's her mum's birthday
Sofie:	What about tonight?
Ross:	England v spain
Sofie:	😳
	How about tomorrow?
Ross:	Yeah shall we go for a ride if the weather's good

Sofie replied with a GIF of a grinning Borat saying, 'Yes!'

*

Bee arrived first and got herself a pot of tea and a chocolate brownie. Sofie came a few minutes later, a little sweaty from cycling.

'No Ross?'

'No, he's gone round to his cousin's. He sends his love.'

'That's a shame. Shall I get you something?'

'No, I'll get it. I've got loads of money from my summer job.'

Sofie ordered a cappuccino and a scone. She let Bee have a bit, and had some of her chocolate brownie in exchange.

'So how are you?'

'I'm good thanks.'

'And how's Ross?'

'He's quite down, actually. Apart from anything else, he's very stressed about his trial. It's coming up a week on Monday.'

Sofie gave Bee details of his charges and the likely outcome of the trial.

'Anyway, how are you, Bee?'

'I'm okay. I was very upset, you know, what happened at the Alpha Course.'

'I bet you were. We were very angry with Pat.'

'I went to stay with Robbie, and he took me to meet his parents, who are lovely. I had a great time and I feel good about the future.'

'That's good. A future without religion?'

'Yeah. But I'm in a good place, you know? I'm going to work really hard on my degree, and if I get the right grades, I'll go for a postgrad next year.'

'Brilliant. I'm sure you will. I bet you're a star student.'

Bee smiled. 'Mind you, my mother's giving me a hard time.'

'Why?'

'She wants me to go to church tomorrow, but I've put my foot down and said I'm not going. And I'm not.'

'She'll get over it.'

'You don't know my mother.'

'Really? That bad?'

'Yes. What about you, is your religious quest over?'

'Ross's is. I think speaking in tongues was a turning point for him. I mean, it's just…' Sofie shook her head. 'And then when his dad showed him those videos. Now he's a bit like your mum, but completely the other side. He says religion's all BS.'

Bee laughed. 'And you?'

'I don't know. I'm not sure whether I believe in God or not. It's kind of like, I think there might be something, but I don't know what. And I'm intrigued by *mythos*. But Satan, that really put me off. They're like, if you don't agree with us, you're evil.'

Bee nodded. 'My mum would agree with them.'

'Really?'

'Oh yes. If I told her about my little Omega Course for you two, she'd say I'd been doing the Devil's work.'

'I bet Pat and Dominic would too.'

'I'm sure they would. That's quite offensive, really, isn't it?'

*

On Sunday, Sofie messaged Ross from just outside his house. He got his bike and came out to join her. It was just about warm enough to wear a T-shirt with no pullover. They set off for Normans Bay, an hour's ride away. Their route took them through the town centre and along Seaside, the artery that led east through row after row of houses built in the 1920s and 30s. They knew the road well from all the buses they had taken to St Anselm's for the Alpha Course.

Modern housing developments gradually became more common, and eventually, they left the town behind, cycling along the busy A259 to Pevensey Bay. There, they abandoned the main road for the narrow coast road, which had minimal traffic. It took them through residential streets just a hundred metres or so from the beach. On the right, they mostly passed back gardens and garages, and on the left, a combination of car parks, flat fields and the occasional row of houses. Many of those on the right were art deco bungalows. On the left, there were lots of somewhat dilapidated 1960s houses with flat roofs and wooden cladding on the front that needed attention.

They came to a small kiosk, the first shop they had seen since Pevensey Bay. Here, they stopped to buy Cornetto ice creams, and then wheeled their bikes up some red-brick steps and onto the wide shingle beach. They sat down and opened up their Cornettoes.

'I enjoyed that,' said Sofie. She took the first bite.

'Yeah, me too. Be a bit harder on the way back. The wind'll be against us and then it's uphill once we get past the town centre.'

'We can hack it.'

She looked at Ross and they both smiled.

'You ready for tomorrow?'

'It's not like I have much choice.'

*

At 11 o'clock next morning, exactly a week before his court hearing, Ross found himself seated between his parents in his solicitor's office. The solicitor was going through the advantages and disadvantages of a guilty plea. On the plus side, it would make it more likely that the case would be settled in just one day, without the risk of a long wait for a further hearing. There wouldn't be any need to call witnesses, and Ross himself wouldn't need to testify. The police would simply present their report, and then Ross's solicitor would plead mitigation. And a guilty plea might help reduce the severity of the sentence.

'The big disadvantage,' his solicitor said, 'is if you plead guilty, you'll definitely be found guilty. It's not a small thing for a court of law to say you are guilty of causing someone's death.'

'I am guilty,' said Ross. 'So I'll plead guilty.'

Silence.

Eventually, Ross's father spoke: 'Let's say he pleads not guilty...'

'Dad, I'm guilty. I'm pleading guilty, okay?'

'Just hear me out, right. For the sake of argument. So, let's say, for the sake of argument, Ross were to plead not guilty, what would be the chances of getting him off?'

Ross looked away in disgust.

'Well, it'd be very difficult. First of all, the law's quite specific: if Ross drove without due care and attention, and if that was a cause of Mrs Johnson's death, then he would be found guilty. It doesn't have to be the main cause. It doesn't even have to be a very significant cause. If his careless driving contributed to her death, then, in the eyes of the law, he's guilty.

'So the next question is, can the prosecution prove that he drove carelessly and that this contributed to Mrs Johnson's death? Well, they've got Ross's statement to the officer who arrested him.'

'But you said that doesn't count.'

'I can make a good case for it being inadmissible, yes. But you've seen the police report. They've done a lot of work on the timing, from when Ross decided to overtake to when he pulled out and Mrs Johnson's car hit him. And they've got Ross's statement that he didn't see her until she hit him, and they conclude from their calculations that he couldn't have looked in his mirror. Now, I can argue against this, but, frankly, it would be an uphill struggle.'

300

Ross's father frowned. 'So what you're saying is, if he pleads not guilty, the chances are he'll be found guilty anyway.'

'Yes. And after a much more traumatic trial, and having annoyed the judges.'

'So you're saying that it's in his interests to plead guilty?'

'Yes.'

Ross said nothing, but his heart was racing and tension gripped his body. His father and his lawyer didn't seem to want to allow the fact that he actually was guilty to enter into their calculations.

*

Dominic, Pat, Rodney, Andrea and Tom sat in a circle. All of them slumped in their chairs.

'You shouldn't blame yourself, Pat,' said Dominic. 'It's normal for some participants to drop out during the course.'

'I know. But I worry about Ross.'

'I worry about anyone who turns their back on Jesus,' said Dominic. 'The sad thing is, Ross was so close. When Bob stood up, he stood up too. And then, I don't know what happened.'

'He said Bob speaking in tongues put him off.'

'It's strange. If Bob hadn't spoken when he did, Ross would have done the same thing just a couple of seconds later. I'm sure of it.'

'Maybe it wasn't his time,' said Tom. 'Maybe the Lord wants to call him another day.'

The others all nodded.

'I hope so,' said Dominic. 'In any case, we've got three more sessions. We can pray that they come back.'

'I've got an idea,' said Andrea. 'Why don't you contact that vicar in Old Town? Maybe Ross is still in touch with him.'

'Good idea,' said Dominic. 'I'll send him an email.'

Dominic wrote next morning. Nigel replied to say that Ross and Sofie were no longer working at his mother's hotel now that college had started, but he would have a chat with Ross if he got the chance.

*

On Wednesday evening, Ross received a pre-arranged home visit from a member of the local Youth Offending Team. A tall woman in her 40s, she introduced herself as Joyce Wheen ('Call me Joyce.') and explained that, in the event of a guilty verdict at his hearing, it would be her job to provide the magistrates with an assessment to help them determine an appropriate sentence. She was there to get a picture of the kind of person he was.

Ross's mother sat in on the interview, which took place at the dining table over tea and biscuits. Joyce asked him about his school record, the sports teams he had played in, his GCSE exam results and how his AS-Level exams had gone. She was very interested in his summer job and perked up considerably when his mother mentioned the Alpha Course. She was only interested in his reasons for attending and didn't ask about how he had found it.

'A few more questions. How much driving have you done since the accident?'

'None.'

'Why not?'

Ross shuddered. 'I don't know if I ever want to drive again.'

She nodded. 'Do you smoke?'

Ross wondered why this was relevant, but he didn't feel like arguing. 'No.'

'Do you drink alcohol?'

'Well, if I go to a party, yes.'

'Do you drink a lot?'

He looked at his mother, and they both smiled.

'It has been known.'

'Do you take recreational drugs?'

'No.'

'Have you ever?'

This time, the glance Ross cast at his mother was a little more anxious. 'I tried weed once a couple of years ago, but it's not something I want to get into, so I haven't since.'

'Do your friends take drugs?'

Ross shrugged. 'I suppose some of them are like me. They might have tried something once, but they don't.'

'Do you do a lot of social media?'

'I used to but I haven't since the accident.'

'Why not?'

'What is there to say? "Yay, I haven't killed anyone yet this week."'

'What accounts do you have?'

'Instagram, WhatsApp, Snapchat. I think I've still got Twitter but I've never used it.'

'Could I possibly look at your Instagram account?'

'Yeah, sure.' He took his mobile out of his pocket, opened the Instagram app and handed it to Joyce.

She spent several minutes scrolling. Then she smiled, handed Ross's mobile back to him and sat back in her chair. 'Thank you very much, Ross, for being so open. Is there anything else you'd like to say before I finish?'

'No, can't think of anything.'

'Do either of you have any questions for me?'

Ross shook his head, but his mother had one question: 'What is your report going to say?'

Ms Wheen put her hands together and her elbows on the table. 'I'm afraid the report is for the magistrates, so I can't tell you at this stage. But I think I can tell you this: the magistrates want to know the answers to two questions. Is this person likely to reoffend? Is he or she a danger to society?'

She released her hands into a shrug of sorts, smiled and raised her eyebrows.

*

The rest of the week leading up to his hearing was as bad as anything Ross had endured up to that point. He had difficulty sleeping and woke up in the small hours with recurring dreams about climbing into a house and getting stuck in the window, with a fierce dog barking at him from the garden below.

In his head, he ran through every possible worst-case scenario, from his solicitor making inept attempts to mitigate by slagging off Lizzie Johnson (the police reports indicated that she had broken the speed limit at every opportunity during her fatal homeward journey) to a fearsome cross examination by the prosecutor. He had another recurring dream in which the magistrates wore a black cap before pronouncing sentence.

Once more, the cliffs at Beachy Head started to call to him. Just a quick jump, that's all it would take, and all your problems would be over.

No. No. There was no way he could do that to his parents. Or to Sofie.

His lessons were excruciating, and he couldn't concentrate at all. His free periods hardly ever coincided with Sofie's, and there was nobody else he could bear to be with, so he would slope off to Hampden Park and brood. He even went there once when it was raining and got soaking wet.

On Friday, he and Sofie both finished at 2:30. They were hoping to cycle somewhere, but it was raining, so they went to Ross's house and played table tennis instead. Ross's brother joined them after an hour. He was just a little better than Sofie and very competitive.

On Saturday, his parents drove him to Arundel Castle for the day (the journey there and back took them past the spot where the accident happened), and on Sunday, Dani, Raj and Sofie came round in the afternoon to play table tennis.

Ross's mother opened the door. She greeted Dani and Raj with a hug. To Sofie, she said, 'It's lovely to meet you properly at last. Call me Sandy, and let me give you a hug.'

Sofie caught Ross's eye and grinned as she hugged his mother.

Once Sofie had kicked her trainers off, Ross's mother took her arm and introduced the rest of the family.

'You've met Matt, haven't you?'

Ross's brother looked up from his mobile for long enough to exchange a quick greeting.

'And this is Dave.'

'Hello.'

Ross's father got up and shook her hand, 'Nice to meet you at last, Sofie.'

They spent more than two hours playing table tennis. They only let Ross use his special serve against Raj, who returned it with interest almost every time. Even so, in their one-on-one games, Raj only won three to Ross's four.

If friends and family managed to keep him distracted during the day, the evening was another matter. The accident and his impending hearing washed over him like a fever. His pulse raced, his innards tightened and sweat drenched his body.

On Monday, his nightmare about getting stuck in a window woke him up at 4:30.

The tension seized hold of him at once.

This was it.

Today was the day.

Chapter Forty-Three

Ross arrived with his parents at 10:30. Like his father, he was wearing a suit and tie. They checked in at the courthouse, where their identity was confirmed. After that, they were ushered into a small waiting room, where Ross's solicitor greeted them.

'You ready?' he asked.

Ross nodded. He could hardly speak, his mouth was so dry.

'Do you have any questions before we go in?'

They all shook their heads.

Some 15 excruciating minutes later, a uniformed officer invited them to follow him into the courtroom. It looked like something from an old 1950s movie, with panelled walls, a large royal crest with a lion and unicorn behind the magistrates' benches, and heavy teak furniture. Ross could see that the furniture had been rearranged into a circle of sorts. The official asked him to sit behind a large, polished desk.

His solicitor sat to his right. Beyond him would be three magistrates, with another seat in front of them where the Clerk of the Court would sit. 'He runs the show,' Ross's solicitor had said.

Ross's parents sat to his left. Opposite his solicitor would be the Crown Prosecutor. After a few minutes, a youngish woman with a dark complexion arrived, a bundle of papers in her arms. She smiled at Ross's solicitor and then looked at Ross and his parents and said hello.

Ross was taken aback by this, but he managed to return her greeting.

Opposite Ross's parents were the witness box and a desk with two chairs. The sergeant who had taken Ross's statement came and sat in one of the chairs. Like the Crown Prosecutor, he greeted everyone in the room. Joyce Wheen from the local Youth Offending Team came next.

The public gallery was opposite the magistrates' chairs. Ross looked at it and shuddered. The only people allowed to watch the trial would be Lizzie Johnson's family.

Sure enough, after a couple of minutes, the official who had led Ross to his seat brought in Lizzie Johnson's husband and the elderly couple Ross assumed to be her parents.

The Clerk of the Court came in, a wiry man in his late 50s. He stood to attention behind his chair.

'Please can you all double check that your mobile phones are turned off.'

Ross took his out of his jacket pocket. It was already off.

The clerk spoke again, in a loud voice: 'All rise.'

Everyone stood up, and the three magistrates came in and took their seats. They were all middle-aged, two men and, in the middle, a woman with short, ginger hair.

'Please be seated,' said the Clerk, 'but the defendant should remain standing.'

Ross took a deep breath. He remembered the line from *Rosemary's Baby*: 'This isn't a dream. This is really happening.'

The Clerk continued: 'We are here today for the case of the Crown against Ross James Collins.' He turned to face Ross. 'Ross Collins, you are charged, under Section 2B of the Road Traffic Act, 1988, that on the eleventh of April twenty-eighteen, you did cause the death of Elizabeth Marjorie Johnson by driving without due care and attention. Do you understand the charges against you?'

Ross swallowed. 'Yes, sir.'

'And do you plead guilty or not guilty.'

'Guilty, sir.'

'You may sit.'

Ross sat down, relieved that he had remembered to say the right thing.

The female magistrate asked those present to identify themselves. Ross's solicitor was first.

She passed over Ross: 'We know who you are, don't worry.'

Ross's parents stood up. His mother spoke: 'We're his mum and dad.' Next, the Youth Offending Team member, the investigating officer and the Crown Prosecutor.

'I understand Mrs Johnson's next of kin are here. Would you like to identify yourselves?'

Ross hardly dared to look as Mr Johnson stood up. 'I'm Anthony Johnson. I'm Lizzie's husband, and this is her mum and dad.'

'Thank you,' said the magistrate. 'May I offer you our deepest condolences.'

'Thank you, ma'am.'

She turned to Ross. 'Okay, Ross, what's going to happen is this: Miss Ahmed will ask Sergeant Peters questions, to outline the case against you. After that your solicitor can ask him questions. Your solicitor will then address the court and talk about any mitigating circumstances which he would like us to take into account. We will then hear a report from the Youth Offending Team. After that, you and your parents will be invited to make a short statement if you wish. We will then hear any victim impact statements from Mrs Johnson's family before retiring to consider out verdict and any sentence. Do you understand?'

'Yes ma'am.'

The sergeant was called to the witness box. Under questioning, he explained that the police had interviewed 15 witnesses and conducted a forensic examination of the crash site in order to piece together the events of the 11th of April.

Mrs Johnson worked late that day, leaving Brighton at approximately four o'clock, about half an hour later than she would normally leave. She drove quite fast, because she needed to pick her daughter up from netball at 5:15.

Ross passed his driving test the previous day, and to celebrate, he drove three friends for a day out in Brighton. They spent the day on the beach and the pier and had lunch in the North Laine area. Ross didn't have any alcohol or drugs, and he had a short nap on the beach, which left him feeling quite refreshed for the drive home.

Ross's car left Brighton at approximately 3:45. His car was subsequently observed by six speed cameras. In every case, he was driving well within the speed limit.

The two drivers headed along the Lewis bypass. When they hit the single-carriageway road, Ross got stuck behind a Ford Focus that was travelling at less than 40 miles per hour. For most of the road, the speed limit was 60. They were stuck behind this car for almost six miles. Ross found this very stressful. He saw the long tail of traffic behind him, and he found the fact that he was unable to get past the Ford Focus embarrassing. Also, one of his friends kept nagging him to overtake.

Ross wondered who had fed this line to the police. He guessed that it was Sofie.

The sergeant said he had tried to overtake twice. Both times, he indicated, but then changed his mind. After the Drusillas roundabout, he had a clear opportunity to overtake. The road ahead was straight, and there was nothing coming the other way. Ross indicated right, changed down to third gear and pulled out to overtake. Unfortunately, he forgot to look in his mirror and didn't realise that another car was trying to overtake him.

'Are you certain that he didn't look in his mirror?' the prosecutor asked.

'Yes, Ross said as much to one of our officers at the time, though in fact he hadn't been cautioned. In his statement under caution, he said he didn't see Mrs Johnson's car before it hit him. We calculated the timings, and we believe there's no way he can have looked in his mirror.'

The female magistrate interrupted and spoke to Ross's solicitor. 'Does the defence accept that Ross definitely didn't look in his mirror before indicating or overtaking?'

'Yes, madam.'

'Thank you. Miss Ahmed, please continue.'

Under her questions, the sergeant said Mrs Johnson was behind a Ford Transit van that was behind Ross's car. After the Drusillas roundabout, she indicated, pulled out and began to overtake the Transit van. She would have had time to see Ross's car indicate and it is possible that she may have sped up in an effort to get past him before he pulled out.

When he pulled out, Mrs Johnson's nearside front collided with his offside rear. The police estimated that Ross was travelling at just under 40 miles per hour and Mrs Johnson at around 55. It was a rotary impact collision, which shunted both cars towards the kerb. Ross's car drove up onto the verge, but because Mrs Johnson's car was going faster, it tipped right over. The Ford Transit van behind was unable to stop and crashed right into her car. Mrs

Johnson sustained multiple injuries at this point. She was unconscious when the police arrived and never regained consciousness. She had to be cut out of the car and was taken to the District General Hospital, where she was pronounced dead on arrival.

The magistrate asked if the driver of the Transit van was facing charges.

'No, ma'am. We concluded that he can't be blamed in any way.'

The magistrate thanked Miss Ahmed and asked Ross's solicitor if he had any questions.

He stood up. 'Just a few questions, if I may. Sergeant Peters, what was the first thing Ross said to a police officer at the scene of the accident?'

'Just a moment.' The sergeant looked through his papers. 'Here it is. He said, completely unprompted, "It was my fault. I didn't look in the mirror."'

'Thank you. I'd also like you to consider Mr Nicholas Demant's testimony. He was the driver of the Ford Transit. Mr Demant overheard a conversation between Ross and his friends. Could you tell me the advice that Ross's friend Rajiv Vazerani gave to him?'

The sergeant looked through his notes again. 'This is from Mr Demant's statement: "The driver told his male friend that the accident was his fault because he hadn't looked in his mirror. His friend advised him not to say that to the police."'

'So,' said Ross's solicitor, 'Ross's friend told him not to tell the police that he hadn't looked in his mirror, but Ross told the first officer he saw anyway.'

'Yes.'

'One more thing. Do you remember, after Ross made his statement at the police station? He asked you about Mrs Johnson's children and how old they were.'

'Yes.'

'What happened then?'

'When I told him, he burst into tears.'

'No more questions.'

The sergeant was stood down, and the three magistrates conferred in hushed tones. The clerk stood up and joined them. After a moment, he turned round and said, 'The court will adjourn for ten minutes. All rise.'

Everyone stood up and the magistrates left the room.

They all sat down.

Ross's solicitor turned to speak with him and his parents in hushed tones. 'It's going well. I thought the prosecution were extremely fair. And I know exactly what's happening now. The magistrates are checking the law. They're saying to the clerk, "It wasn't all Ross's fault." And he's saying it doesn't matter, even if he's only partly responsible, he's still guilty. But the fact that they're asking is good news from our point of view. It won't affect the verdict, but it will affect the sentence.'

'That's good,' said Ross's father.

Ross said nothing. He just wanted the whole thing to be over.

Next it was the turn of Ross's solicitor to offer mitigation. He started off with his age, and the fact that he had never been in trouble with the law. He had never had a detention at school and had been selected as a prefect in year 11. His GCSE results had been outstanding, with A grades in more than half of the subjects taken.

As he listened, Ross remembered that he had told Joyce Wheen from the Youth Offending Team that he had had one detention at school. His parents must have forgotten this when they spoke to his solicitor. Or maybe he had made sure they never found out.

'Another factor I would like you to consider is Ross's extreme inexperience. The accident happened just one day after he passed his driving test. He had never overtaken a car on a single-carriageway road before. The police report indicated that he drove within the speed limit throughout his journey. He didn't drive recklessly. He was aware of the build-up of traffic behind him, and felt under pressure to overtake the Ford Focus. But this indicates that before the accident, he was using his mirrors.'

Next, Ross's solicitor turned to his conduct after the accident. 'Ross has faced up to his responsibility in this matter from day one. He told the police that he hadn't looked in his mirror, despite the fact that his friend advised him not to.

'The accident has had a devastating impact on Ross, because he blames himself for Mrs Johnson's death. He has told me that he doesn't intend to drive again for at least ten years. He used to have an active social life, but his parents tell me he's become very withdrawn and now never goes out. Before the accident, he represented his college in its football team and played for the Old Town C Team in the local table-tennis league. Since the accident, he has dropped out of both teams. He used to post regularly on social media but hasn't made a single post since the accident, and he has hardly liked or commented on anyone else's posts either.

'The vicar at St Margaret's Church was so concerned that Ross would spend the whole summer brooding over the accident that he arranged for him to work full-time in an hotel near the seafront in order to keep his mind busy. After the accident, Ross attended counselling, but it didn't help. Apparently he told his counsellor, "I don't deserve to be happy because I've killed someone."

'I think all this demonstrates that Ross is genuinely remorseful about the accident. So much so that, despite the fact that he had never shown much interest in religion, he enrolled on the Alpha Course and attended sessions every week between the tenth of July and the fourth of September.

'I would also like to reveal something about the conversations I have had with Ross. Right from the beginning, he has insisted on pleading guilty. He has refused to listen when I have tried to discuss the possibility of a not-guilty plea. His mantra has always been: "I am guilty, so I'm pleading guilty."

'In summary, I would say that there are serious mitigating factors in this case: Ross's age, his previous good conduct, his inexperience and the way he has fully accepted his responsibility and shown genuine remorse. Ross is not a danger to society, and a custodial sentence would be completely inappropriate. The police investigation reveals that this tragic accident was the result of a unique set of unfortunate factors coming together, among them Ross's inexperience which led him to make a mistake which has had devastating consequences. I ask you to take all these factors into account.'

The solicitor sat down and the magistrates thanked him. They turned to the woman from the Youth Offending Team.

'Ms Wheen. I understand you visited the defendant at home last week. Would you like to present your report to the court?'

Joyce Wheen stood up, opened the file in front of her and read from her notes.

'"I visited Mr Ross Collins at his home on the evening of September the eleventh. I interviewed him in the presence of his mother. I felt that Ross was open and co-operative throughout the interview. He has an excellent school and college record, including excellent GCSE results and an excellent disciplinary record." If I can depart from my written report for a second, I'd like to correct one thing his solicitor said. He did in fact have one detention at school, for throwing a snowball at a prefect.'

Ross glanced at the lead magistrate, who seemed to be smiling at this.

Joyce Wheen returned to her script. '"He was appointed prefect at school and has played for both school and college sports teams as well as a local table-tennis team. There are no issues with drink or drugs and he has never been in trouble with the police before. His form tutors at both school and college speak highly of him, as does the proprietor of the Livingstone Hotel, where he worked over the summer."'

Ross was taken aback by this. He hoped Ms Wheen didn't tell his old school teacher why she was contacting her.

'"It is clear from speaking to Ross that he has been deeply affected by the accident. He has not driven since and I believe he is extremely unlikely to reoffend. I do not believe that a custodial sentence would be appropriate and would recommend a community punishment."'

'Thank you Ms Wheen.'

Ross's heart was racing. He knew what was coming next.

'Ross? Would you like to say anything at this point?'

He stood up. He didn't know where to look. Eventually, he turned to the leading magistrate and took a deep breath.

'I know it must sound pathetic, and I know it's too late. I know that if I'd looked in my mirror, Mrs Johnson would still be alive today. The only thing I can say is that I'm very…' He had to pause and take another breath. '…very, very, very sorry.'

He stopped and sat down. He took several deep breaths to keep himself from crying.

'Mr and Mrs Collins?' said the lead magistrate. 'Would either of you like to say anything?'

Ross's mother put her hand up and the magistrate nodded.

She stood up and briefly touched Ross's shoulder with her hand. 'I know the real victim of this accident is Mrs Johnson and her family, especially her children. My heart goes out to them, it really does. But I'm Ross's mum, and I've seen what it's done to Ross, and it breaks my heart. It really breaks my heart.' She started to cry. It was some time before she regained enough control to speak again. 'All I can say to the court is please have mercy on him.'

She cried again and sat down. Ross's father put his arm around her. Ross hung his head and wiped away his tears.

'Finally,' said the lead magistrate, 'would any of Mrs Johnson's next of kin like to make a victim impact statement?'

Lizzie Johnson's husband indicated that he would like to speak. The uniformed official led him out of the public gallery and back into the court, where he stood in the witness box. He was holding papers in front of him. His hands were shaking, whether with nerves or anger, Ross didn't know.

He was looking right at Ross, who didn't know where to look. Would it be more insolent to make eye contact or to look away? In the end, Ross looked him in the eye for a brief second and then looked down.

'Lizzie was the love of my life.' His voice was very shaky. 'We were introduced by a mutual friend, and right on our first date, I knew she was the one. She was funny. She was sassy. She was kind and thoughtful. I loved her so much. I couldn't believe my luck, to have such a beautiful, wonderful woman love me back. But she did. I knew she did.

'Her mum and dad welcomed me into their family. They were so proud of Lizzie. She was everything you could want in a daughter, and everything you could want in a wife. And for Jude and Adam, she was everything you could want in a mother. She loved our children so much, and they loved her back. She loved making up silly stories for them at bedtime. Her stories were so funny; she'd have the kids in fits of giggles. And she knew how to comfort them when they were sad, or poorly, or if they'd scraped their knee.

'She was a much better cook than me. And she'd take the kids to the library. And it was Lizzie who always arranged our holidays. She'd go online and find the best place to go, the best place to stay. She'd read all the reviews and make sure there was a good kids' club at the camp site.

'She was the heart of our family.' Ross could tell from his voice that he was close to tears. 'I miss her so much. And the children miss her. It's really set them back. I've been trying to fill that void, but it's hard. It's so hard. There are only three of us round a four-sided table. The sofa seems so big and empty when the kids have gone to bed and it's just me, on my own. And for Lizzie's parents too. Their beautiful little girl's gone. They try so hard to support me and the children, but I know it's very difficult for them. They're grieving too.'

Mr Johnson put his papers down on the edge of the witness box and looked at the magistrates.

'I've listened to Sergeant Peters. I've listened to the counsel for the defence, and I've listened to…Ross and his mum.'

Ross looked up and briefly made eye contact with him again.

'I know it was an accident. But a driver owes a duty of care to other road users. And my wife is dead, and she means something. Her life means something. And our family wants this to be reflected in the sentence of the court.'

Chapter Forty-Four

The court was adjourned for 30 minutes. Ross, his parents and his solicitor were led to the same waiting room as before. There was little conversation. Ross felt completely drained. He thought his solicitor's mitigation had swung things in favour of a lighter sentence, but Mr Johnson had been pretty explicit. He wanted justice for his wife, and Ross didn't blame him.

His solicitor continued to insist that a custodial sentence was out of the question, but he said he thought Mr Johnson's comments might lead to a longer period of community service than he was otherwise expecting.

Ross said nothing. He would accept whatever punishment he was given.

When the time came, they returned to the courtroom and rose for the entrance of the magistrates. The clerk asked everyone to be seated but instructed Ross to remain standing.

He could almost hear his heart beating, and he felt sweat trickle down his neck.

The leading magistrate glanced at a sheet of paper in front of her. Then she looked at Ross.

'We have reached our verdict and decided upon the sentence that we will impose. Ross, we have found you guilty of causing death by dangerous driving.'

He nodded.

'There are a number of mitigating factors. Your age, your inexperience, your guilty plea and the genuine remorse that you have shown. There are other mitigating factors too. You didn't drive recklessly or over the speed limit at any stage. You had made two previous attempts to overtake but had been cautious and changed your mind. And you indicated before you pulled out.

'And it must be said that, tragically, Mrs Johnson took a number of risks. She tried to overtake three cars in a single manoeuvre. This isn't illegal, but it's certainly very risky. She also continued to overtake you after you had signalled your intention to pull out. This is, in fact, a breach of the highway code.

'What this means is that, although your carelessness caused the accident, it was not the only cause of the accident. The sentence you will receive will reflect this fact.'

Ross wished she would get on with it.

'Another factor the court must take into consideration, is the devastating consequences of the accident for Mrs Johnson and her family. We have heard the powerful victim impact statement made by Mrs Johnson's husband. We note that he is entirely correct to say that Mrs Johnson's life means something, and this must be reflected in the sentence imposed by this court.

'However, because of your previous good conduct, your age, your inexperience, your guilty plea and the remorse you have shown, a custodial sentence would not be appropriate in this case.'

Ross gave out an audible sigh of relief.

'Your sentence will have three parts. Firstly, you will lose your driving licence for the maximum period of two years. When you regain your driving licence, it will be a provisional licence and you will have to take your test again.'

Ross nodded. He had been expecting this.

'Second, we are going to impose a fine on you. I understand you had a job over the summer holidays?'

Ross blinked. 'Yes.'

'How much was the pay?'

'Erm…ninety-four pounds a week plus tips.'

'How much were your tips?'

'On average about twenty pounds a week.'

'And how many weeks did you work?'

'Erm…I'm not sure. I started on the seventeenth of June and finished on the Thursday before the bank holiday.'

One of the other magistrates got out his mobile phone and spent a moment looking at it. 'Is that Thursday the twenty-third of August?'

Ross hesitated. 'Yes, that sounds right.'

The lead magistrate turned to her colleague. 'How many weeks?'

He counted on his mobile. 'Ten.'

'So ten weeks at one hundred and fourteen pounds a week?'

'Yes.'

'Well, we don't need a calculator for that.'

She glanced at both of her colleagues, who nodded.

'The second part of your sentence is a fine of one thousand, one hundred and forty pounds.'

Ross was stunned. He hadn't expecting them to work it out like that.

'The third part of your sentence is a youth rehabilitation order. You are required to undertake one hundred hours of unpaid work.'

Chapter Forty-Five

Three days after his trial, Ross and his mother had an appointment at the office of the Youth Offending Team, situated in St Matthew's House, an ugly, four-storey concrete building on the main road into town. The receptionist directed them to a small waiting room on the second floor. They were the only people there. Ross wondered if it was a humiliation for his mother to find herself taking him to the social services.

After 10 minutes, Joyce Wheen, the woman who had interviewed him and attended his trial, came in and shook their hands. She showed them into an interview room with soft furnishings and a see-through door, inviting Ross and his mother to sit down. After some formalities, she explained how his youth rehabilitation order would work.

'So, it's a hundred hours. You have to do a minimum of six hours per week, starting next week at the latest. You're at college full time, aren't you?'

'Yes.'

'Do you have a part-time job?'

'No.'

'Basically, you're going to have to do Saturdays. The pick-up time is eight-thirty outside this building. You'll do seven hours a day and you'll be dropped off by five. Don't be late, because they won't wait for you. If you're sick, you must phone in before eight o'clock. Not eight-thirty, eight o'clock. Anything else counts as absent, and absences aren't allowed. This is compulsory. Do you understand?'

'Yes.'

'You get two weeks off at Christmas-New Year, and you're allowed two weeks of holiday. But you have to give us two weeks' notice if you're going away. Anything less counts as absent, and absences aren't allowed. Okay?'

Ross nodded.

'Wear work clothes, something old, because you might get paint on it. You might be working outdoors, so keep an eye on the weather forecast, especially going into the winter. We'll provide tea and coffee, but no food. Bring a packed lunch and snacks and water or a soft drink.'

'Okay.'

'Now, on another matter, from what I understand, the accident has affected you deeply. Is that the case?'

'Yes.'

'Are you having counselling?'

'No.'

'Have you had counselling or are you planning to have any?'

'I had one session at the college, last April. It wasn't for me.'

'I think you need counselling. So, what I'm going to do it this: three of your one hundred hours will be taken up with counselling. There's a lot of pressure on our counselling services, so it probably won't be until the New Year. It might even be after you've finished your ninety-seven hours of unpaid work. It's compulsory, okay?'

Ross nodded. 'Okay.'

He thought he noticed his mother smile.

*

Ross got back to college with 15 minutes to go before his next lesson. He and Sofie went to a quiet corner in the common room.

'How was it?'

'It was okay. Same woman as interviewed me last week, only this time, she was very...' he made three chopping motions with his hand.

'So is it every Saturday like your lawyer said?'

'Yeah. And I have to have three counselling sessions.'

'Really?'

'Yes, as part of my punishment. What a waste of bloody time.'

'It might help.'

'Sofie, I've tried counselling. It didn't help.'

'It helped me a lot.'

'Yeah, but you're you and I'm me. We're not the same.'

Sofie clenched her jaw and pursed her lips. 'I think you should give it a chance.'

'It's not till next year, anyway.'

'No?'

'No. Maybe even after I've finished my community service.'

'Well, think about what I said.'

He gave a slight nod of the head and looked away from her.

*

Ross's father dropped him off outside the concrete building 15 minutes early. He saw two glum-looking teenagers with hoodies sitting on the steps and guessed he would be working with them. He had some sandwiches in his drawstring backpack, along with a bottle of Coke Zero, a packet of crisps and a KitKat. By the time the minibus arrived, they had been joined by three other youths, one of whom Ross thought he recognised from school.

The driver, a tall and powerful-looking man with a shaven head and tattoos on his forearms, opened the side door and they clambered in. Ross sat near the front, where he was joined by one of the others.

The driver read out a list of seven names, one of whom was absent.

'We'll give him till half past, but more fool him if he's late.'

They set off at 8:30 precisely, without participant number seven.

'For those who don't know me, I'm Geoff, and I'm your supervisor today,' said the driver.

'What we doing today, Geoff?'

'Community College gardens,' he replied.

316

This brought loud moans from all the others on the bus.

'We've got sanding and painting the fence, and sanding and painting benches and goalposts. There's also pruning the hedge, and one lucky person will be weeding the flower beds.'

'Boring!' came the reply.

After a few minutes, the youth Ross recognised said, 'Here, Ross. Did you use to go to Devonshire School?'

'Yeah.' Ross turned round. 'So did you, but I can't remember your name.'

'Tommo.'

Ross nodded. They had never been in the same class or friendship group, but their paths had crossed often enough.

'You was always a goody-goody. What you doing here?'

'Traffic offence.'

'Oh, right.'

'What about you?'

Tommo grinned. 'Selling weed. Do you want some?' He then said in a very loud voice, 'Only joking, Geoff. Only joking.'

'I hope so,' said Geoff. 'I'd report you if I caught you.'

Everybody laughed.

As they were getting off the bus, Tommo asked, 'Are you going out with Sofie Manning?'

'No, but she's a friend.'

'I seen you together once, in the town centre.'

'How do you know Sofie?'

Tommo leaned in close and whispered, 'I used to get my supplies off her sister.'

*

They were all given high-visibility orange vests with 'community payback' on the back. Ross ended up sanding and painting the goalposts, alongside a morose youth called Alex, whose heart clearly wasn't in it. It took quite a long time to figure out how to assemble the portable scaffold they would need to stand on when they did the crossbars and the tops of the posts. Geoff had told them not to get on it until he had okayed it, so they started at the bottom of the goalposts.

Eventually, Ross managed to draw Alex out and they discussed Brighton's very poor start to the season. They stopped at 10 for tea and biscuits with the rest of the group. Ross was the only one who didn't have a cigarette or vape. He had been very apprehensive about how the others would treat him, but in fact, they were all friendly and the banter was enjoyable.

An hour later, Geoff came round to see how Ross and Alex were getting on.

'Having a rest, boys?'

'Yeah,' said Ross. 'Our arms are aching from sanding the crossbars.'

Geoff inspected their work. 'Actually, you're doing a fair job.'

He sat with them on the mobile scaffold, gave Alex a cigarette and lit up.

'So, you at college, Ross?'

'Yeah, doing A-Levels.'

'Planning to go to university?'

'Yes.'

'Interesting. You're not my usual clientele. What d'ya do?'

Ross told him about the accident.

'Wow. That's grim. Has it affected you?'

'You could say that.'

'Do you get depressed about it?'

'Yes.'

'Very?'

Ross nodded.

'Still?'

'Yes.'

'Do you beat yourself up?'

'Yeah, I suppose so.'

'That's good. I'm not saying it's good that you're unhappy, but what kind of person would you be if you didn't get depressed about it? It shows you're a decent human being, don't it?'

'I never thought about it that way.'

'How many hours d'ya get?'

'A hundred.'

'Quite a lot. Presumably you lost your licence?'

'Yeah. I have to do my test again.'

'Fair enough. Get fined?'

Ross let out a little laugh. 'One thousand, one hundred and forty pounds.'

'That's a funny amount. Why the one hundred and forty?'

'I had a job in a hotel in the summer. That was every bloody penny I earned, except I forgot to tell them about my statutory holiday pay.'

Geoff laughed. 'Was it a female magistrate with ginger hair?'

'Yes.'

'I know her. She likes to do things like that. There was one case, right, these two German tourists got done for shoplifting. She says, "How much English money you got? How much does it cost to get back to Germany? Right, we'll have the rest, *danke schön* and off you trot."'

The three of them laughed. Geoff and Alex finished their cigarettes, and Geoff said it was time to get back to work.

As Ross picked up his sandpaper, Geoff pointed at him and said, 'What you got to remember, Ross, is this is an appropriate punishment set by a court of law. You're being punished right now. So it's time you stopped punishing yourself, innit?'

*

318

Geoff's words stayed with Ross. Was that really an appropriate punishment? A fine (about which he still felt annoyed), having to retake his driving test and losing his Saturdays for 14 weeks. And that was it? Could he then get on with his life and forget all about it?

But Lizzie Johnson would still be dead. Her children would still have no mother. Her husband would still have lost his wife, and he could see from Sofie's family what the consequences of that might be.

Ross sometimes found himself wishing that Bob the Builder hadn't beaten him to it to start speaking in tongues. His head might be full of nonsense, but at least he would have been saved. He would be able to go to bed at night without seeing that upside-down Renault the instant he closed his eyes. He would be able to look in the mirror without seeing the face of a killer.

Or would he? Would it really have been that simple?

*

'So?' said Dani.

She and Sofie were sitting at the back of their psychology class. The lesson was over and all the other students had gone.

'What?'

'It's after his trial. You don't have to wait for him, you know. You can make the first move.'

'I'm not going to.'

'Why not? You're both besotted with each other. Everyone can see that except you.'

'It's not that simple.'

'Why not?'

Sofie turned to face Dani full on. 'Look, you don't know what I've been through. I had to watch my mother die. It was horrendous. You should have seen her at the end. She was like a stick insect, and she used to bend double with the pain of it. Then I had to watch my dad fall apart. And then my bloody sister pimped me out to her boyfriend's mate, and he turned out to be married. And then he got me pregnant.'

Dani nodded 'Yeah, I know.'

'I can't do it, Dani. I can't tie myself to someone who's falling apart. I can't put myself through that again.'

'You're already tied to him. You love him.'

'It's not the same. If I have an affair with him…'

Dani burst out laughing. 'An affair? You mean a relationship, don't you?'

'Whatever. If I give myself to him, I'll give myself one hundred percent, and I'll expect him to give himself one hundred percent to me. He's not capable of that, not now.'

They sat in silence for a moment.

'I've been badly burned,' said Sofie, 'and I'm not willing to take that risk again.'

'There's always a risk when you fall in love.'

'Yeah, I know that. But he's not doing anything to help himself. Until he does, I'm not going to take that risk.'

*

That Friday, Sofie, Dani and Raj ganged up on Ross and nagged him into joining them at the cinema to watch *Crazy Rich Asians*. During the film, Ross laughed when everyone else laughed and welled up a little when lovers Nick and Rachel got together at the end.

As they left the cinema, he winked at Sofie and Dani, and said to Raj, 'What did you think of that, mate?'

'It was fun, yeah.'

'I'd have thought you'd be hoping the proletariat would storm the scene at some point and line them all up against a wall.'

Dani and Sofie laughed.

Raj shook his head, 'I'm not in favour of the death penalty.'

'Just expropriation?' said Ross.

'Yeah, or failing that, taxing the bastards.'

He and Ross looked at each other and grinned.

Their route to the bus stop took them past Marks and Spencer. Ross noticed a man lying prostrate in the doorway. As they got nearer, he realised that it was Sid. He nudged Sofie and pointed to him.

'Bloody hell,' said Sofie.

'What?' said Dani.

'That's Sid.'

'What, *the* Sid?'

'Yeah.'

Sofie and Ross approached him. Sofie crouched down and shook him gently.

'Sid? You all right?'

'Leave him,' said Dani.

'I can't just leave him.'

'Yes, you can. You don't owe him nothing.'

'Sid?' She shook him again. 'Sid. You okay?'

He half opened his eyes. 'Oh, hello, Sofie.' His words were very slurred.

She helped him to sit up and lean against the shop door.

'What you doing here, Sid?'

'I'm so fucking stoned.'

'Yeah, I can see that.'

'You're such a lovely girl, Sofie. I'm really sorry what happened.'

'Leave it out, Sid. Do you want me to go and get Jake?'

'No,' Sid said out loud. 'Never want to see that bastard again.'

Sofie blinked and glanced up at Ross.

She turned back to Sid. 'Can you walk?'

'I doubt it.'

320

Sofie stood up and stepped towards Ross and Raj. 'We can't just leave him here. His flat's just round the corner. We could take him there.'

Ross and Raj looked at each other and nodded. They pulled him to his feet.

'Oh God, it's you,' said Sid.

'Yeah,' said Ross. 'It's me.'

'And who are you?' he said, looking at Raj.

'I'm his mate.'

'Surprised he's got any.'

'Sid!' said Sofie, 'Don't be so horrible.'

Ross and Raj walked Sid along, his arms round their shoulders as they held him up by the waist. His feet made token walking movements.

'You're such a sweet girl, Sofie.'

'Can you shut up? I'm taking you to your wife. Just keep your mouth shut.'

They walked Sid across the road and up the pedestrianised shopping street, passing cafes, bars, a one-pound shop and assorted charity shops as they headed towards the seafront. His flat came just after the traffic lights and a fish and chip shop that used to be a bank.

'Give us your key.'

Sid took his right arm down from Raj's shoulder, fumbled in his pocket and handed his keys to Sofie.

'You're such a lovely girl, do you know that?'

'Be quiet, will you? We're taking you to your wife.'

'You can do so much better than this jerk,' he said, indicating Ross with his free hand.

'Jesus, Sid. We should have bloody well left you.'

'You'd better stay here with Dani,' said Ross. 'Me and Raj'll take him in.'

Sofie opened the door and passed the keys to Ross. They manoeuvred him into the lift and up to the second floor, where he pointed them to his flat.

Ross knocked on the door, and after a moment, the spy-hole flickered.

'Hi, Martha, it's Ross. I've brought Sid home.'

'I'm in trouble now,' said Sid.

Martha opened the door, an expression of absolute fury on her face. She pointed to the sofa and spat out her words: 'Put him on there.'

They spun him round and gently lowered him.

'Where did you find him?'

'Outside Marks and Spencer.'

'You know, Ross?' growled Sid, 'Shall I tell you something?'

'What?'

'As killers go, you're not that bad.'

Martha placed herself between them.

'Sid, shut your bloody mouth,' she said.

'We better go,' said Ross.

Martha nodded. She showed them to the door. 'Thanks, guys. I'm really sorry about what he said.'

Ross nodded.

Just before she shut the door, Ross asked, 'Who told him? Was it Nigel?'

Martha shook her head.

'So who was it?'

Martha took a deep breath. 'It was his wife. Nigel wasn't happy when he found out. He wasn't happy at all.'

'Oh.'

'Thanks for bringing him home.'

'Yeah, see you.'

'See you.'

'So that's the great Sid?' said Raj, as they got into the lift.

'Yeah, and I tell you what,' said Ross. 'Next time we're bloody well leaving him.'

*

The next two weeks passed with no improvement in Ross's state of mind. In fact, things were getting worse. Suicidal thoughts invaded his head more frequently. Sometimes at night, he would imagine himself driving to Beachy Head, parking, running to the cliff and hurling himself off.

He hated himself for these thoughts, but they didn't go away.

From time to time, Dani and Raj cajoled him into spending time with them, and for a while his spirits seemed to lift, but the next day, he avoided them again, failed to reply to messages and reverted to brooding alone. The only person he didn't avoid was Sofie, but as their free periods only coincided first thing on Wednesday and last thing on Friday, he had plenty of opportunities to keep himself to himself.

Then, 10 days after the encounter with Sid, Sofie received a message on her mobile:

Sandy: Hi Sofie. This is Ross's mum.
        Dani gave me your number. Hope you don't mind
        Can I give you a call?
Sofie: Yes, sure

Ross's mother audio called at once. 'Hi, sorry to disturb you.'

'No worries. Is anything wrong?'

'Nothing urgent, no. But we're very worried about Ross. He just locks himself in his room and he won't speak to us. Dani says you're the only person he'll talk to.'

'To be honest, I'm worried about him too. He won't do anything to try and get a grip. I keep telling him about how much counselling helped me, but he just doesn't want to.'

'I know. He's never been very good at listening to advice.'

'Yeah, I remember Dani said.'

'We were hoping his trial would be a bit cathartic for him, but he seems even worse since.'

'Yeah. He says the victim impact statement really hurt him.'

'That was pretty tough.'

They were silent for a moment, and then Sofie said, 'I think the community service might help a bit. He says he likes the people who run it.'

'I think the person who helps him most is you.'

'That's very kind of you, Sandy, but I'm out of my depth. I really don't know what to do.'

'Maybe we can stay in touch a bit. If there's something we think you should know, we'll tell you, and maybe you do the same for us.'

'Yeah. Good idea.'

'Thanks, Sofie. We'll be in touch.'

'Yeah, okay. Speak to you later. Bye.'

'Bye.'

Ross's mother ended the call. She was sitting in her car on the driveway outside her house. She got out of the car and went back into the house. She motioned to her husband, who followed her to the kitchen. In hushed tones, she reported the conversation to him.

*

Two days later, it was Ross's turn to clean up after dinner. He had cleared the table and was half-way through loading the dishwasher when his mobile pinged.

Sofie:	Hi Ross. Can you call me?
	Something terrible's happened.
Ross:	Gimme 2 minutes
Sofie:	Yeah but be quick

He hurriedly finished loading the dishwasher and turned it on. It took just a few seconds to wipe the worktops and wash his mother's favourite carving knife. He rushed upstairs, shut his bedroom door and, leaning his mobile against a pile of books on his desk, he video called Sofie. When she turned her video on, he saw her eyes were red and her face was puffy.

'Hi, Sofie. What's happened?'

'Hi. Veronika from the hotel just contacted me. She told me about Sid.'

'What?'

'He's dead.'

'Oh my God. What happened?'

'He killed himself.'

Chapter Forty-Six

'Veronika says Martha threw him out because he was taking drugs in front of the kids again. She says he drove up to Beachy Head and threw himself off.'

'Jesus, that's terrible.'

'Yeah.'

Ross blinked. He had imagined doing exactly the same thing often enough, but he would never actually do it. Surely, he wouldn't. Not him.

After a moment, he shook his head and said, 'You okay?'

She shrugged. 'I'm pretty upset, actually. I mean, he was a bastard, he really was. But I remember when I was screwed up, I was a right little bitch. But it's not because I was evil. I was screwed up. You know, because of my mum and everything.'

'Yeah.'

'Sid, he was screwed up too. And all his drugs were supposed to deaden the pain, but they just made everything worse. And he hid it behind all that bloody machismo, so nobody could help him. It's so sad. And those poor kids. They really loved him.'

'It's very sad for them.'

'Yeah. I bet losing them must have pushed him over the edge. Veronika's really upset. She says Martha's in bits, and Mrs Akehurst looks like she's aged ten years overnight.'

'God,' said Ross.

He would remember that next time he thought about suicide. There was no way he could do that to his mother.

'We should send them a card,' said Sofie. 'Maybe flowers too.'

'Yeah.'

'Shall we go to town after college tomorrow?'

'Okay.'

'You'd never do anything like that, would you, Ross?'

'Course I wouldn't.'

'Promise me, no matter how bad it gets, promise me you'd never try to top yourself.'

'Absolutely never.'

*

'He's getting worse, innit?' said Sofie.

Dani nodded. 'Yeah, me and Raj tried to drag him for a coffee yesterday. He wasn't interested.'

It was Monday morning, not yet a week since Sid's death. They were sitting in a corner of the common room, speaking in hushed tones.

Sofie leaned towards Dani. 'I don't know what to do. It's like watching my dad again. He's just sinking.'

'He's not as bad as your dad,' said Dani. 'He's not drinking or anything.'

'No, but what happened with Sid really scares me.'

'He wouldn't do that,' said Dani. 'Not Ross.'

'Yeah, well I never thought Sid would.'

Dani frowned for a moment and then said, 'Why don't you speak to Kitty?'

'How's that gonna work?'

'Well, tell her about the problem.'

'But counselling's totally confidential, innit? She's not allowed to talk about another person with me.'

'Yeah,' said Dani, 'but you got a problem, ain't you? Your problem's that your boyfriend, except he's just your friend, he's all depressed and you don't know how to help him. You're allowed to talk about that.'

Sofie shook her head.

'Well, I tell you what,' said Dani, 'I'll go. I'll tell her I got a problem with my cousin.'

Sofie fixed Dani with her eyes. 'You're blackmailing me, innit?'

Dani smiled the most innocent of smiles. 'Would I do that?'

'Yes, you bloody well would. All right. I'll give it a go.'

*

The next day, she knocked at the door and a petite woman in her 40s with long, permed hair opened it.

'Hi, Sofie.'

'Hi, Kitty.'

'Come in and have a seat.'

The room was small, with a desk under the windowsill, and four soft, blue-green chairs. Sofie sat down and Kitty sat opposite her, placing a folder and some papers on her lap. She put on a delicate pair of gold-framed glasses.

'Do you remember the formalities we did last time? We have to do them again, okay?'

Sofie nodded.

'It's Sofie Manning, date of birth fourteenth of February 2002.'

'That's right.'

'So that makes you seventeen?'

'Yes.'

'Still in Julia Dunnett's tutor group?'

'Yes.'

Kitty took off her glasses and looked at Sofie. 'Okay, before we start, you'll remember that I need to tell you whatever you say will be treated in confidence. I'm not going to gossip to anyone. I won't tell Julia Dunnett or any of your other teachers what you say without your express permission. But I can't promise one hundred percent confidentiality, I'm afraid. If you tell me something I need to share with the Designated Safeguarding Lead, then I have to tell her. You okay with that?'

'Yes, of course.'

'So, you have my email if you need to set up another meeting. I'm here every Tuesday and Thursday in term time. I can't enter into a detailed correspondence, but we can meet as many times as you need.'

'Thank you.'

'So, how can I help?'

'It's my friend, actually. You've met him: Ross Collins. You had a session with him in April.'

'Sofie, I can't talk to you about a session I may or may not have had with another student.'

'Yes, sorry.'

'I can't even confirm whether I've met him.'

'Yes, sorry. I understand.'

'Okay. So, would you like to tell me about the problem that's brought you here?'

'My friend, Ross, he's really depressed. I'm the only person he'll talk to, but I don't know how to help him.'

Kitty said nothing, so Sofie continued. She told her about the accident and the trial.

'I was hoping the trial would give him some kind of closure, but it hasn't. Apparently, the lady who died, her husband made a very powerful victim impact statement. It really shook Ross. Over the last three weeks, he's been even worse than he was before the trial.'

They were silent for a few moments. Kitty said, 'Would you like to say something about how this is affecting you.'

'I'm the only person Ross will speak to, but I don't know what to say to him. He doesn't want to do anything. He refuses to spend time with his friends. He used to play football and table tennis but now he doesn't. In summer, we had a job, and that was really helpful. He was so busy he didn't have much time to mope. But now, at college, we only have about three lessons a day. And most of his free periods, I'm studying, so I can't be there for him. He just stays by himself and gets more and more depressed. I'm really worried about him.'

'Could you say a bit more about your worries?'

'In summer...Do you know the Alpha Course?'

'I know a bit about it, yes.'

'We attended the Alpha Course for about two months, one evening a week. When we were doing the course, it's like there was hope. Maybe he could find redemption in Christianity. Does that make sense?'

'Yes.'

'In the end, he didn't like it. It kind of put him off religion. And now there's nothing. He can't see any hope.'

Silence.

'My ex, the one who got me pregnant, he killed himself last week.'

'I'm sorry to hear that, Sofie.'

'I'm really scared that Ross may end up doing the same.' Her voice cracked as she spoke.

Kitty frowned and put her glasses back on.

'Sofie, if we are dealing with the possibility of suicide, I'm afraid I can't offer you confidentiality. I have to report what you've said to the Designated Safeguarding Lead, Donna Rayfield.'

Sofie nodded. 'That's fine.'

'I'm going to have to take some notes.'

She picked up the pen on top of her papers, and took out a blank sheet of paper.

'Can I confirm your boyfriend's name. It's Ross...'

'Ross Collins.'

'Is he seventeen too?'

'Yes. He's eighteen in December.'

'And which tutor group?'

'Harry Liptrot.'

'You say Ross confides in you?'

'Yes.'

'Is there anyone else he confides in?'

'Not really.'

'What about his parents?'

'He gets on with them, but his mum says I know more than she does.'

'Does he know that you talk to his mum?'

'I don't think so.'

'Does he know you're here?'

'No.'

'Do you plan to tell him?'

Sofie hesitated. 'Probably not.'

'Okay. That's something you have to weigh up. He'll never hear it from our end.'

'Thank you.'

'Has he had or is he having counselling or therapy?'

'He had one session with you.'

Kitty smiled. 'I can't confirm that.'

'Of course. He's doing community service, and as part of that, he has to have three counselling sessions. But he says that's not till next year.'

'Has he seen a doctor?'

'No. He says he isn't depressed. He's just unhappy because he killed someone.'

'Has he spoken about suicide?'

'No.'

'Has he self-harmed?'

'No.'

'Has he spoken about self-harming?'

'No. Well, quite a long time ago, he said he used to think people who self-harm were stupid, but now he understands them.'

'Okay. Right, this is what's going to happen. I'll report to Donna Rayfield, the DSL, today. There'll probably be a case conference tomorrow or Thursday. Donna has to do a risk assessment, and if she thinks there's a need for intervention, then she has to come up with an action plan. She may want to speak with you in the next couple of days. Is that all right?'

'Yes. Thank you very much.'

*

Donna Rayfield interrupted Sofie's Spanish class the following afternoon. She was a chubby woman in her late 50s with short, grey hair.

'Is Sofie Manning here?'

Sofie put up her hand.

'Have you got a few minutes?'

Sofie looked at her teacher, who signalled permission. She grabbed her mobile and her shoulder bag and followed Donna to her office.

'It's about Ross.'

'Yes.'

'I spoke with Kitty last night, and this morning we met with Ross's tutor and some of the safeguarding team. Ross's tutor said he'd noticed he's become very withdrawn of late. Kitty says you're worried that he may end up attempting suicide.'

'Yes.'

'From what I understand, he hasn't spoken about suicide, he hasn't self-harmed and he hasn't spoken about self-harming. Is that correct?'

'Yes.'

'My assessment is that he isn't in immediate danger, but he needs help. Would you agree with that assessment?'

'Yes.'

'That's good. You told Kitty he has to do counselling as part of his community service, but it's not till next year.'

'Yes.'

'I'll call the YOT and ask them to bring it forward. That may help.'

'Thank you very much.'

'His tutor, Harry, will have a word with him tomorrow morning, and we'll take it from there.'

'Thank you.'

'I need to inform his parents. If I do, would you mind if I told them you've expressed worries about him?'

'That would be fine.'

'Which of his parents is he closer to?'

'His mum.'

'Okay. I'll call her. Now, can you do me a favour? If I write a quick summary of our discussion, would you be willing to sign it?'

'Of course.' After a moment, Sofie asked, 'Does that mean you're very worried about him?'

'No, it's just procedure.'

As Donna was writing her summary, Sofie had another question. 'I don't really know how to help Ross any more. I feel like I'm in over my head.'

Donna stopped writing. 'From what Kitty says, Ross feels he can talk to you.'

'Yes.'

'Then just keep listening. Maybe the other thing you can do…when people are depressed, what they really need is other people. But they often don't want it, they just want to be alone.'

'That's Ross.'

'What you should try and do is sometimes give him a little nudge. Don't nag him. Don't make him feel that you're getting at him. Just encourage him to take that next little step. You know, "I'm dying for a coffee. Why don't you come with me?" "Ooh, let's sit with so-and-so." That kind of thing.'

*

The call from Joyce Wheen at the Youth Offending Team came through the next day just after Ross, Sofie, Dani and Raj finished their lunch. He stood up to take the call.

'Hello, can you give me a minute to get outside?'

He walked out of a side exit.

'Hello, I'm free to talk now.'

'Okay, so it's Joyce Wheen from the YOT. Do you remember me?'

'Yes, of course.'

'We've got a space for you with one of our counsellors. It'll be Friday afternoons at three. Do you have classes then?'

'No. I'm free at that time.'

'Good. It'll be here at St Matthew's House. First one tomorrow and then the next two Fridays, three o'clock.'

'Yes. Thank you very much. I'll be there.'

'Good. It's compulsory.'

'Yes, of course.'

They ended the call, and for a moment Ross stood still, staring at his phone. Then he noticed that Sofie had come out to join him.

'What was that?'

'The woman in charge of my community service. She says my counselling starts tomorrow.'

'You going to go?'

'I have to.'

Sofie stepped right up to him and asked, 'How do you feel about that?'

He looked down and sighed. 'I don't know.' He looked at her. 'Maybe this time, I should take it seriously, give it a chance. I mean, I need something, don't I?' He almost said, 'after what happened to Sid' but thought it best not to.

'Really? You're going to give it a chance?'

'Yeah.'

'That's fantastic.'

She reached up to his face with both hands and kissed him on the mouth.

She broke off the kiss and stepped back, a worried look on her face.

'Did you just kiss me?'

'Yeah.'

His heart was beating so fast he could feel it in his ears.

'You can do it again if you like.'

She laughed.

They kissed again, and as their lips and tongues met, his whole body exploded with the bliss of it.

Chapter Forty-Seven

'What's that big grin on your face?'

Sofie and Dani were standing outside their psychology classroom, clutching their books and papers.

'Nothing.'

Dani laughed. 'I don't need to be a genius to work it out. He had a big grin on his face too.'

'We haven't gone public yet.'

'What happened to change your mind?'

'His counselling's been brought forward.'

'What? Because you…?'

'Shush. He don't know about that.'

'You're not going to tell him?'

'I don't know.'

'You should. You shouldn't have secrets, and the longer you leave it, the harder it'll get to tell him.'

'I'll think about it. Have you told Raj?'

'Yeah.'

'Tell him to keep *schtum*.'

Dani nodded.

'He says he's going to take it seriously this time.'

'Good. He should have done that six months ago, without any of this Alpha Course crap.'

*

It rained heavily that evening, which put paid to Ross and Sofie's plans to meet up outdoors. In the end, Ross went round to her house at 8:30, when Kate was putting the little ones to bed. Sofie led him into the dining room.

'She knows about us.'

'What? You told her?'

'She guessed. Same as Dani.'

'Are you being a bit too obvious?'

Sofie grinned. 'Anyway, it means she'll leave us alone in here, except she'll probably want to make herself a cuppa once the little ones have gone down.'

They spent a few minutes kissing, after which Sofie insisted that they behave themselves. She proceeded to tell Ross about her experiences of counselling.

'Don't imagine it'll be easy, because it won't. Everything you say, they'll ask you, "Why did you say that? What do you mean by that?" You'll have to have a very hard look at yourself. When I done it, I cried more than once, especially the first few sessions.'

'But it was worth it?'

'God, yeah. If I had to name the people who've helped me most in my life, I'd put Kitty right up there, along with Kate at joint number one. You know who else I'd put high up on that list?'

'Who?'

'Bee.'

'I was expecting you to say Dani.'

'Yeah, Dani's on there too. But Bee, she's like my spiritual teacher. I think she's brilliant.'

'Not Dominic, then.'

Sofie laughed. 'No bloody way.'

'Funny thing is,' said Ross, 'I would have put Nigel on my list. But in the end, he kind of betrayed me.'

'It's not his fault.'

'Well, he should control his bloody wife.'

Sofie laughed. 'Control his wife? You sexist pig. Don't imagine you'll be controlling me, because you won't. Let's get that straight from the start.'

He laughed. 'I wouldn't dare.'

'Good.'

They both grinned and leaned forwards to exchange a kiss.

*

He got home soon after 10 o'clock, took off his shoes, hung up his jacket and went into the living room, where his parents were watching the BBC news. His brother was kneeling on the floor in his pyjamas and dressing gown, gurning at his mobile and pressing it frantically with his thumbs.

'Hiya.'

'Hi, Ross,' said his mother. 'We've just boiled the kettle if you fancy a cup of decaf.'

'I've just had some tea, thanks. I thought I'd share some news with you.'

'What's that?'

'Me and Sofie are an item.'

His brother was first to react. Without looking up from his mobile, he said, 'Well, duh!'

His father grinned and said, 'Congratulations.'

'Yeah,' said his mother, 'congratulations. I'm really pleased for you. That's the best news I've had all day.'

'Seriously?' said Ross.

'Yes, seriously,' said his mother. 'She's a lovely girl. It's great news.'

'Well, you'd better break it gently to Auntie Zoe.'

*

Ross's counsellor was a hefty man in his late 30s with a thick beard and a gentle northern accent. He introduced himself as Adrian and led Ross into an interview room with soft green chairs and IKEA coffee tables identical to those in the common room at college. He placed a file of papers on one of the coffee tables and sat opposite Ross.

The formalities included a warning that he would prepare a written report for the Youth Offending Team that would remain on Ross's record until six months after the end of his youth rehabilitation programme, after which it would normally be shredded. He also warned him that if he said anything that needed to be reported to the police, it would be.

Adrian asked Ross to describe the accident, which he did quite dispassionately.

'And how has it affected you?'

Ross thought for a moment. 'It's been pretty devastating, to be honest.'

'Could you say a bit more about that?'

Ross explained how, whenever he wasn't busy, his thoughts would almost immediately turn to the accident. 'I have a lot of free time these days, so I have plenty of time to think about it.'

'And what happens when you think about it?'

'Once it starts, I can't stop it.'

Adrian said nothing, so Ross continued. He spoke about Lizzie Johnson and how he spent weeks stalking her on social media. He talked about her family and her husband's victim impact statement.

'How did that make you feel?'

Ross was silent for a long time. 'Awful. I mean, I could see how angry he was, and just how heartbroken. I've ruined his life, haven't I?'

'It's interesting to hear you say that. Can we drill down into it for a moment? You say it's you that's ruined his life.'

'Yes.'

'Not the accident?'

'It's the same thing, isn't it?'

'So, do you feel a hundred percent responsible for the accident?'

After a moment, Ross said, 'People keep telling me it's not a hundred percent.'

'And what do you think about that?'

Ross shrugged. 'Well, yes. But I blame myself.'

'One hundred percent?'

'Yes, I can see where you're going.'

'Where am I going?'

'That I shouldn't blame myself one hundred percent.'

'Okay. I'm sure we'll come back to that. The other thing is, you say you've ruined his life.'

'Yes.'

'How old is he?'

'I don't know. Mid-forties?'

'So he's probably got another thirty or forty years to live. Do you think it's possible, in that time, he might be able to rebuild his life and find happiness again?'

'I hadn't thought about it that way.'

'If there's one thing this job has taught me, it's that people can be amazingly resilient.'

Ross frowned. 'Yeah, but my girlfriend, right, her mum died when she was little, and her dad just hit the bottle. He's a complete alcoholic now.'

'Was that an inevitable result of his wife's death?'

'No.'

'Was it a probable result?'

'I don't know.'

'Do most people become alcoholics if their spouse dies quite young?'

'Probably not, no.'

'So, why did it happen in this case?'

'I don't know. She says he was quite fond of a drink anyway.'

'Any other reasons?'

'Maybe he…I don't know. Maybe he made some poor choices.'

'Okay, so, when you say that you ruined Mr Johnson's life, is there another way you could frame that?'

Ross thought for a moment. 'The accident I caused…'

'You caused?'

They spent several minutes negotiating a more appropriate way of putting it. Eventually, they agreed on: 'My mistake led to an accident which has caused him a great deal of suffering.'

'Yes. I think that's probably quite accurate. And how would you describe your feelings when you think about that?'

'I don't know. I feel guilty. And very sad.'

Adrian asked Ross to say more about what he thought about when the accident dominated his thoughts. He talked about how he replayed it in his head, how he sometimes tried to duck out of responsibility and how he used to feel angry towards the other drivers and towards Raj, for egging him on.

'Is this something you think about a lot?'

'Not really. I blame myself, not other people.'

'So as well as guilt and sadness, there's anger.'

'Yes.'

'How much anger?'

'A lot.'

Directed at who?'

'Myself.'

Adrian was silent again. Ross felt a need to break the silence, so he spoke about his sense of shame. He was ashamed of his incompetence, ashamed of his criminal record, ashamed of the fact that the accident defined him in the eyes of so many people.

'Let's talk about the people who matter most to you. Who are they?'

'Well, my parents, my family. And my girlfriend. My friends.'

'And does the accident define you in their eyes?'

'No.'

'What about the teachers who teach you?'

'Well, I suppose I'm mostly Ross who got grade B or whatever.'

'So, who are the people for whom the accident defines you?'

'People who don't know me, I suppose.'

'And how much do they matter to you?'

'Well, I do care what they think. But they're not the most important people in my life.'

Adrian nodded and pushed his glasses back to the bridge of his nose. 'Okay, so we've talked about guilt, sadness, anger and shame. Let's move onto another question. What is it you need?'

'I don't know. Redemption, I suppose.'

'And how can you find redemption?'

'Geoff, one of my supervisors on the community payback scheme, he says the punishment is a kind of redemption.'

'And does that work for you?'

'Not really. If I'm honest, I quite enjoy the community service. It doesn't really feel like a punishment.'

'Do you think you need to suffer to find redemption?'

'I don't know.' Ross hesitated for several seconds. 'I attended the Alpha Course in the summer. I tried to find redemption that way.'

'Did it help?'

'Sometimes I thought it might, but in the end no. I didn't get converted.'

'How would it have helped if you had been converted?'

'You get your slate wiped clean. That's what they say.'

'What does that mean, to get your slate wiped clean?'

Ross thought for a long time. 'I don't know. I suppose it means God forgives you.'

'Do you feel God has forgiven you?'

'I don't really believe in God.'

'Okay, let's put it this way. Let's imagine you had been converted, would you now still have all these feelings of guilt, sadness, anger and shame? Or would you be more at peace?'

'There was this guy who got converted. It was quite amazing to watch him. It's almost the same as like he'd fallen in love or something. I would have been the same, I'm sure. In fact, I have fallen in love recently, and it's incredible. But I did *Captain Corelli's Mandolin* for my GCSEs. I know falling in love's a kind of madness, and it eventually wears off. I think it would have been the same if I'd been converted. You know, whoosh, hormone rush, and then it all settles down again.'

'So if you'd been converted, do you think you'd have ended up in pretty much the same place as you are now? Or do you think it would be different?'

'Eventually, pretty much the same, really.'

'So let's try and get to bottom of the word redemption. What does it mean? What is it that you need?'

'Forgiveness, I suppose.'

Silence.

'Could you say a bit more about that?'

'Well, there's a lot of people whose forgiveness I need. I mean, Lizzie Johnson's family for a start. Her children, her husband, her parents. Then there's that driver of the Transit van. I bet I traumatised him.'

'Did you traumatise him?'

'Yes, okay, the accident traumatised him.'

'Is it the same thing?'

Ross gave a little shrug. 'Okay, no.'

Adrian smiled. 'Sorry, I interrupted you. You were talking about the people whose forgiveness you need.'

'Well there's my parents. I'd promised not to take the car out of town so soon after passing my test. And my friends – I could've got them killed.'

'Have your parents forgiven you?'

'Yes. Almost instantly. I almost wish they'd given me a good bollocking, but they didn't.'

'What about your friends?'

Ross shook his head. 'They've been really great.'

'What about Lizzie Johnson's family?'

'I'm sure they haven't. I mean, the husband's victim impact statement was pretty clear on that.' Ross remembered what Sofie had told her about the girl she had been horrible to. 'And I don't think I have the right to pester them and ask for their forgiveness. Same with that bloke in the Transit van.'

'I think you're probably right there. So, you've mentioned several people whose forgiveness you need. Is there anyone else?'

Ross was silent for a long time. Eventually he said, almost in a whisper, 'Me. I need to forgive myself.'

'And have you forgiven yourself?'

'Not in the least.'

He closed his eyes and turned away from Adrian. After a moment, the tears started to flow. He cried for a long time. He took out his handkerchief and held it to his face.

Adrian said nothing until he had regained control.

'As you say, your parents and your friends have forgiven you, which is good. And you have no control over whether Lizzie Johnson's family and the other driver forgive you. You're right that you should leave them well alone. But you do have some control over yourself. There are techniques that you can learn that will help you forgive yourself. We call them self-compassion techniques.

'You've done well today. I think you've got to the bottom of your problem. This is a good place to end today's session. Next week, we'll start on the journey of learning to forgive yourself. It's a hard journey. There's no quick fix. It's something you'll need for a very long time. But you've made good progress today and you'll get there.'

'Thank you.'

Chapter Forty-Eight

The weather was dry that evening, so he and Sofie were able to meet outdoors. They hung around the Greenwich Road recreation ground, sitting on the children's swings as they talked. The weather was cold and crisp, and the sky cloudless with a bright, gibbous moon. Ross told Sofie about his counselling session.

'Is that what made you cry? That you haven't forgiven yourself?'

'Not just that.'

'What then?'

'I realised…' He paused for a moment. 'I realised, redemption isn't a thing, is it?'

'How do you mean?'

'All that time, when we were doing the Alpha Course, right, I was desperate for redemption. I was desperate to believe, because I thought, "If I believe, my slate will be wiped clean and I'll get redemption." But it doesn't work like that. It's not, like, "Bam! You are now redeemed." It's…I don't know how to put it.'

'What Kitty said to me was, recovery's like a process, a journey.'

'Yeah. And I've been desperate, I've been so desperate, Sofie, trying to find this thing. And it's not a thing. I've wasted the last six months. I should have listened to you, my mum and dad. Even Nigel, he wanted me to have counselling.'

Sofie put her feet down and brought her swing to a full stop.

Ross did the same.

'You know another thing Kitty said to me? She said mistakes are part of life. The important thing is to learn from them and not make the same old mistakes again and again.'

Ross sighed. 'I've certainly made my share of mistakes.'

'So have I, believe me.'

After a moment, she said, 'There's something I haven't told you.'

'What's that?'

She lifted her feet, and her swing started to oscillate a little. Ross followed suit.

'Well, indirectly, it was me that got your counselling brought forward.'

'Really?'

'Yeah.'

'So, how did you do that?'

'I was very unhappy…You were getting worse and worse, and I didn't know how to help you. So Dani told me to go and see Kitty. So I did, right, and I was telling her about the situation, and I mentioned Sid. Soon as I said the word "suicide", she was like, "Whoosh! Right, we gotta get this sorted." And she set everything in motion, and they ended up bringing your counselling forward.'

'Wow, Sofie, you are amazing.'

'You don't mind?'

'Why would I mind? Look at where I am now. Where would I be if you hadn't done that? Thank you, Sofie. Thank you.'

'I thought you might, you know, think I'd gone behind your back.'

'Come here, let me say thank you properly.'

She got off her swing and stood in front of him. He put his feet down, wrapped his arms around her waist and pulled her towards him. She bent down and they kissed, long and slow.

After a moment, they broke off the kiss. She said, 'You know when you walk me home, you go up Beechwood Avenue, there's that dark alleyway just before we turn off to my house?'

'Yeah?'

'Do you fancy…checking it out?'

He grinned. 'We could, couldn't we?'

They held hands and set off. It took almost 10 minutes to get there. Ross didn't think he had ever walked so far so aroused in all his life. Once safely out of sight, they kissed and caressed, and his hands began to explore her breasts.

After a while, they slowed down and just held onto each other.

Sofie said, 'Is it too soon for the L-word?'

'What? Lesbians?'

She laughed. 'No, you idiot. Love.'

'No, it's not too soon.'

'I love you, Ross.'

'I love you too, Sofie.'

*

The next day, his community payback scheme took him to the forest near Middle Brow, where he and half a dozen others spent the day burning branches and tree trunks in an area that had recently been felled, as part of a project to create a forest glade which would be home to a greater variety of wildlife.

It was hard, physical work, but Ross enjoyed it. It was good to spend the day outside, and he found something satisfying in burning wood, even if it made his hair and clothes stink.

He spent most of Sunday with Sofie and her little siblings. Kate had started a second part-time job in a nursing home on Sundays plus Wednesday and Thursday evenings. This left Sofie with a lot of babysitting commitments when Paula, Lydia and Carl weren't with their father, but she told Ross she adored them, so this wasn't a problem for her at all. Even though he was frustrated at not being able to have Sofie to himself, Ross had lots of fun with the children. He especially enjoyed playing with Lego for the first time in years.

At one point, Sofie leaned into him and whispered, 'You know Raj, right?'

'Yeah?'

'He don't believe in Lego.'

They both laughed, and Sofie ended up having a fit of the giggles.

'What are you laughing at?' said Lydia.

Sofie stopped laughing, wiped the tears from her eyes and said. 'It's a long story. We've got this friend who don't believe in Lego.' She immediately burst out laughing again.

*

The little ones were in bed, and Sofie and Kate were on the sofa together. Sofie unlocked her metal money box. In an envelope at the bottom were three letters she had written but never sent almost exactly a year earlier, when she was having counselling with Kitty.

She took out one letter and handed it to Kate, who read it out loud.

Dear Josie,

I am writing to apologise for being really horrible to you at school. I am very sorry. I am ashamed of what I did to you.

Maybe you know I had problems at home. But that is no excuse. I had no right to take out my problems on you. You are a good person and didn't deserve it.

You do not need to get back to me. I hope this letter does not bring back unhappy memories for you. I just wanted to say sorry.

With warm regards,

Sofie Manning

'It's a nice letter,' said Kate. 'Why didn't you send it?'

'I talked about it with Kitty. In the end, I decided I didn't have the right to disturb her.'

'Yeah. Maybe not.'

'There was another reason.'

'What's that?'

'She might want to get revenge by sticking it on Instagram or something.'

Kate laughed. 'Very sensible.'

'You think so?'

'She doesn't owe you anything, does she?'

'Nothing positive, no.'

'Let's have a look at the other two.'

Sofie handed them to Kate. They were near-identical letters addressed to two teachers she had given a very hard time in her last two years of secondary school. Kate read them silently.

'I liked Mrs Palmer,' she said, 'but several parents told me Mr Chapman wasn't a very good teacher.'

'He was all right.'

'Why now?' Kate asked. 'I mean, these letters have been sitting there for a year. Why send them now?'

'I don't know. It's like, with Ross having counselling, it's kind of brought it all back to me. I want to have closure.'

'What do you expect your teachers to do if you send the letters?'

'I don't know.'

'Do you want them to reply and forgive you?'

'Not really. I just want to apologise so I can put it behind me.'

'Well, I suppose you can be sure they won't stick it on Instagram.'

Sofie smiled.

'I tell you what they might do: they might say to everyone in the staffroom, "Look at this letter I got from Sofie Manning." And then there might be a few other teachers thinking, "How come she hasn't written to me?"'

Sofie laughed. 'I wasn't that bad with everyone else!'

'So why these two?'

'I had Mrs Palmer in tears once. And it was Mr Chapman what got me suspended. He just refused to teach me any more.'

'I remember,' said Kate. 'Believe me, the whole episode is engraved on my heart.'

'How come you never gave up on me?'

Kate put her arm round Sofie's shoulder and gave her a squeeze. 'Because I saw the good in you.'

Sofie closed her eyes and smiled.

After a moment, Kate retrieved her arm. 'Just a thought,' she said, 'if you just want to apologise and you don't want them to feel obliged to reply, you could write the letters out again, but this time don't put our address. That way, you're just saying sorry, end of story.'

'That's a brilliant idea. I'll do that. Thanks, Mum.'

'What about the letter to Josie?'

'I'll just tear it up. I think I have to let that one go.'

Sofie went upstairs, tore up the letter to Josie and put the pieces in the bin. Then she copied her two letters to teachers, minus her address. She went downstairs, put them in envelopes, addressed them to Upperton School and put stamps on. She put on her coat and took the letters to the nearest post box, where she posted them before she had time to change her mind.

*

Next day at college, Ross found it as difficult as ever to concentrate in class. But now it wasn't dark thoughts about the accident that marched into his consciousness and took over. It was Sofie. He couldn't stop thinking about her, all the times she had listened to him, supported him, helped him. He thought about the tough times she had been through, and his admiration for the way she had survived and got her life back together.

Thinking about how her mother had died didn't set off thoughts about the accident and Lizzie Johnson's children. Instead, he thought about how strong Sofie was. He liked that about her. And he thought about her smile, her kiss, her taste, her soft breasts and the way she breathed in sharply when he touched them.

He sought her out at break time, and they sat with friends, a very public couple, holding hands and looking into each other's eyes. In the afternoon, he had a free period and spent most of it playing table tennis with Natalie's boyfriend Declan and two other friends.

On Tuesday, he had two free periods. In the first one, he studied for half an hour and then went into the common room, where he scrolled on his mobile and chatted with friends from time to time.

He devoted his second free period to one of his set texts for English Literature: Pat Barker's novel *Regeneration*, set in a World War One military hospital. All went well until he got to page 19, which told the horrifying story of a patient named Burns, who, when thrown into the air by an explosion, landed on the rotting corpse of a German soldier and got a mouthful of his putrid flesh.

This left Burns severely traumatised, tormented by nightmares that made him wake up retching and vomiting.

The instant Ross read this, the accident snared him, and he couldn't escape it. It pulled him down again, down into his own personal inferno where his demons flayed him with their red-hot whips.

Sofie sought him out at break time and found him in the library, his head in his hands.

'What's happened? You okay?'

'It's back. I've hardly thought about it since we…you know. It's back.'

'It isn't going to suddenly disappear, Ross. You have to find ways to cope with it. It'll fade over time, but it's not going to disappear just like that.'

Ross nodded.

'Come on. Let's go and get a coffee.'

*

After his final lesson, Ross went into the common room to find Sofie. She was sitting with Mollie and two other girls, all of them busy looking at their mobiles. Mollie and the other two greeted Ross with a 'Hi' and a smile. Sofie stood up, gave Ross a quick kiss and said goodbye to the others.

'How you doing?'

'Yeah, I'm okay.'

'Have you seen that email?'

'What email?'

'Mrs Akehurst has invited us to Sid's funeral.'

'Oh, right. Do you want to go?'

Sofie scoffed. 'No! His wife's there, completely devastated, and his ex-mistress turns up. What could possibly go wrong?'

'Yeah.'

'Plus my sister will be there, and Jake, and all his gangsta mates who I never want to see again, ever.'

'Fair enough.'

*

Sofie turned out the light and pulled the door to. 'Goodnight all.'

'Goodnight,' chorused the children.

She went downstairs and into the living room.

'Thanks for doing that, Sofie,' said Kate.

'My pleasure. Except, blooming Lydia, the only story she wants is *Benjamin Bunny*. I must have read it to them about ten times.'

Kate smiled. 'At least it's quite short. Anyway, fancy a cuppa?'

'Ooh, yes please.'

Sofie took out her mobile while Kate made the tea. She caught up with four different conversations, including one with Ross.

When Kate came back, Sofie said, 'It's Sid's funeral tomorrow.'

'Hope you're not thinking of going.'

'No way.'

'Good.'

'You still upset about him?'

'Yeah. Very. I loved him once, you know? I really loved him.'

'He didn't deserve it. He had no right to take advantage of you.'

'I was a willing participant.'

'You were fifteen. How old was he?'

'Twenty-eight.'

Kate shook her head. 'That's disgusting.'

'I know,' said Sofie. 'But I just feel so sorry for his children. They've lost their dad.'

'I guess you know how that feels.'

'Yeah. It made me think, right, would you mind if I contacted my dad?'

'Of course not. Why should I mind?'

'Because you're my real parent now. You're the one who's there for me.'

Kate smiled. 'Well, you're my daughter now, aren't you?'

They looked at each other and smiled.

'Do you think I should adopt you, legally?'

'Oh, yes please. I'd love that.'

'Okay, we'll do it.'

'Thank you.'

They looked at each other for a long time. Both of them had tears in their eyes.

After a moment, Kate took a deep breath and said, 'When it comes to your dad, right, don't expect it to be easy. He's not a bad person, but he can't control his drinking. It controls him. He's not suddenly going to get his act together just because you get in touch.'

'I know.'

'Prepare yourself for a lot of frustration. I mean, you've only just got Ross starting to make progress. Are you sure you want to take on your dad so soon?'

'It's not like he's going to be my latest project. I just want to be in touch.'

Later that evening, she sent her father a text.

Sofie: Hi Dad
Dad: Hi Sofs

*

At his next session, Adrian asked Ross about his week.

'Kind of up and down, you know. I had good days and bad days.'

'What happened on the bad days?'

'Dark thoughts.'

'We talked about your dark thoughts last week, didn't we?'

'Yeah.'

'Were you thinking about the same things as before?'

'There's one thing I didn't tell you.'

'What's that?'

'I've had suicidal thoughts.'

Adrian didn't blink. 'Tell me about them.'

Ross was silent for some time. 'I imagine myself nicking my dad's car, driving up to Beachy Head and jumping off.'

'How often do you think about this?'

'Sort of on and off, ever since the accident. There'll be weeks when I don't think about it at all, and then other times, I think about it quite often.'

'And recently?'

'Not this last week, but before our first session, a bit, yeah.'

'Okay. Can we categorise your suicidal thoughts? If one is a harmless fantasy and ten is a definite plan of action, what number are your suicidal thoughts?'

It took Ross a long time to reply. 'I'd say…two, three at most.'

'Okay. Anything above one is a cause for concern. 'Could you say something about what lies behind these thoughts?'

'It would end the pain.'

'Say more about that.'

'Well, I'd be dead.'

'And that would end the pain?'

Ross looked down. 'My pain, yes.'

'Your pain? Could you say more about that?'

'Well, what I mean is, only my pain. I know this guy who committed suicide, about two or three weeks ago. I know what it did to his family. Apparently, his mum has aged ten years overnight.'

'So, if you did commit suicide, would it end the pain?'

'No. Not for my family. Especially my mum and dad.'

What about your wider family? Are there any other family members you're close to?'

'My auntie, she lives just a couple of miles away. I've got a cousin the same age as me. We grew up together.'

'Do you still have grandparents?'

'Yes, three out of four.'

'How would it affect them?'

'Pretty devastating, I should think.'

'And you have a brother, don't you?'

'Yeah.'

'How old is he?'

'Fourteen.'

'Does he look up to you?'

Ross gave a little laugh. 'I don't know. He doesn't show it.'

Adrian smiled. 'I can imagine that. It doesn't mean he doesn't look up to you.'

'Maybe.'

'How would it affect him if you killed yourself?'

Ross shrugged. 'Not good.'

'How not good? Think of a fourteen-year-old boy, who's just beginning to explore who he might be. And then his big brother kills himself. How big do you think the impact of that would be?'

'I don't know. Pretty catastrophic?'

Adrian nodded. 'How long would it take him to recover?'

'A long time, I should think.'

'A very long time?'

Ross nodded.

'What about your girlfriend?'

'Actually, it was her ex who killed himself.'

'Really?'

'Yeah, he was a lot older than her. He had problems with drugs.'

Adrian was silent for a moment. 'So, think about your girlfriend. Is she the same age as you?'

'Yeah.'

'So, she's seventeen, and her ex-boyfriend kills himself. How would it affect her if her current boyfriend did the same thing?'

Ross took a sharp intake of breath and blew out noisily. 'Wow, yeah. It doesn't bear thinking about.'

'Suicide's a terrible thing, Ross. It causes mayhem in the lives of those left behind. So, if you have these thoughts, even if it's only a two or a three, you need a defence mechanism. Do you have one?'

'Yes.'

'What is it?'

'I think about the people it would hurt.'

'Hurt? Is that word strong enough?'

'Devastate?'

'That's a good word. Can you list these people?'

'My mum, my dad, my brother, my girlfriend, my grandparents, my auntie, my cousin.'

'Okay,' said Adrian. 'What about Lizzie Johnson's family? Would it end their pain?'

'No.'

'Could it have the opposite effect?'

Ross frowned. 'How do you mean?'

'Well, think about Mr Johnson. You said he made a very powerful victim impact statement. So, let's say you committed suicide, how might that make him feel?'

'What? You think he might blame himself?'

'I'm asking you.'

'I hadn't thought about that. Maybe. God, that would be terrible.'

Adrian stroked his beard for a moment. 'It's difficult to quantify pain, isn't it? But I'm going to ask you to. Would the pain all these people would feel, would that be more or less than the pain you feel?'

Ross sighed deeply. 'More. Much more. That's why I'd never do it.'

'Do you think about that when you have suicidal thoughts?'

'Yes.'

'Is that sometimes, occasionally, every time?'

'Every time.'

'That's good. Now, if your suicidal thoughts go above a two or a three, that's a big red flag. You need help.'

Ross nodded.

'Can you think of any practical steps you could take?'

'How do you mean?'

'What method of suicide do you think of?'

'Beachy Head.'

'And how would you get there?'

'I'd take one of my parents' cars.'

'So, if your red flag is flying, what impediment could derail your plans?'

Ross frowned and looked at him for a moment. 'What? Like if I couldn't find the car keys or something?'

'Would that make a difference?'

Ross took a moment to reply. 'It would slow me down. Give me more time to think about it.'

'So, what practical step could you take if your suicidal thoughts are getting above a two or a three?'

'Tell my parents and get them to hide the keys?'

'Yes. Are there any organisations that help people who are suicidal?'

'The Samaritans?'

'Yes. Do you need to wait until it's a ten, or can you contact them as soon as it becomes a four or five?'

'Well, the way you ask the question...But I don't think it would come to that.'

Adrian nodded. 'But if it did, there are things you can do.'

'Yeah.'

'Do you think you're in immediate danger?'

'No.'

'Okay. Now, because you're under eighteen, I'm obliged to report the fact that you have been having suicidal thoughts to the YOT. I'll let them know that you've been having these thoughts, but my assessment is you're not in immediate danger. I'll tell them that it's my judgement that they don't need to do anything now, and I'll get back to them after your third session. I hope you're okay with that.'

Ross shrugged.

'They may contact your parents. In fact, they probably will. And they'll almost certainly contact the Designated Safeguarding Lead at your college.'

'Yeah, whatever.'

'You did the right thing to tell me.'

Ross nodded.

'Okay, now, apart from suicidal thoughts, which you occasionally have, what else happens when you think about the accident?'

'I just replay it in my head. I curse myself for not looking in the mirror. I think about the woman I killed...'

'The woman you killed?'

Ross smiled. 'The woman who died as a result of the accident.'

'Which accident?'

'The accident that happened as a result of my mistake.'

'And was your mistake the only cause of the accident?'

'Yes...Well, no. Not the only cause.'

'What were the other causes?'

'She was taking risks.'

'Any other causes?'

He shrugged.

Adrian said nothing.

'It was the first time I'd ever overtaken anyone.'

'So?'

'So, my inexperience was a cause.'

'Anything else?'

'Maybe I was unlucky.'

'Only maybe?'

'All right then, yes.'

'In what sense?'

'Lots of people have told me they sometimes forget to look in their mirror.'

'And...?'

'They got away with it.'

'How many times out of a hundred do you think people get away with that sort of thing?'

'Probably ninety-nine.'

'Okay. So is it accurate to talk about the woman you killed?'

'No.'

'We talked about this last week. The reason I've gone through it all again is that you're still doing it. I want to drill down into this: the reason why you talk about the woman you killed.'

It was a moment before Ross replied. 'I...I always think, when you do something wrong, you have to take responsibility for it.'

'I agree. But are you one hundred percent responsible for the accident?'

'No.'

'But what percent of responsibility are you taking when you say, "The woman I killed"?'

'One hundred percent.'

'But you know you're not one hundred percent responsible?'

'Yes.'

'And yet you keep taking one hundred percent responsibility?'

'Yeah.'

Adrian said nothing. They sat in silence for almost 20 seconds, though it seemed a lot longer to Ross.

'Maybe...' he said, 'Maybe I'm trying to punish myself.'

'To punish yourself?'

'Yes, for...'

'What were you going to say?'

'For killing her.'

'Is that right?'

Ross shook his head.

They spent several minutes working on this. Adrian elicited exactly what Ross was punishing himself for and then interrogated his replies. They eventually settled on a very long answer: 'I'm punishing myself for making a mistake, partly because of inexperience, which, due to an extremely unfortunate set of circumstances, including risk-taking by another driver, led to an accident in which that driver was killed.'

'Is that different from the woman you killed?'

Ross smiled. 'Yes.'

'Okay,' said Adrian. 'Now, here's a question for you: what is the appropriate punishment for your mistake?'

'Do you know Geoff? I don't know his surname. He's one of the supervisors on community payback.'

'Big guy, shaved head?'

'Yes.'

'Geoff Ridley.'

'He says it's what the court gave me: lost my licence, big fine, a hundred hours of community service.'

'What do you think of that?'

'Maybe he's right.'

'But you're still punishing yourself more?'

'Yes.'

'Could you say something about that?'

The reply was a long time coming. 'I don't know why I do it.'

'Let's look at it another way. Does anybody benefit from you punishing yourself like this?'

'No.'

'Do Elizabeth Johnson's family benefit?'

'No.'

'Do you benefit?'

'No.'

'So, how can you explain it?'

Ross leaned forwards in his chair and looked down. 'I do it because I hate myself for what I did.'

*

Sofie: How was it?
Ross: Pretty intense
Sofie: Was it useful?
Ross: Yeah I have to reframe how I think about it and stop saying I killed her

It was obvious to Ross that Sofie typed and deleted three or four times before she finally sent through her reply:

Sofie: That's good
Ross: And I'm not an evil person and I have to stop treating myself as if I was
Sofie: Nobody thinks you're evil Ross
        I bet even Lizzie Johnson's family don't think that
Ross: Yeah, we talked about that
Sofie: You're a really kind person and that's one of the reasons I love you
Ross: We talked about that too
        You coming round tonight

Sofie: Yeah CU L8er

*

On Saturday afternoon, while Ross was doing his unpaid work, Sofie went into Costa Coffee in the town centre. She quickly spotted her father. He looked older than his 51 years. His grey-black hair was quite long, and he hadn't shaved for several days. His clothes had a crumpled look about them.

'Hi, Sofs.'

'Hi.'

They hugged and exchanged a kiss.

'This is for you.' He handed her a small and very beautiful bunch of scabious, cosmos and assorted leaves. 'From my landlady's garden.'

'Thanks. They're lovely. I'm just going to get a coffee. Do you want anything?'

'I'm okay, thanks.'

Sofie returned a few moments later with her Americano.

'You look beautiful, Sofie.'

'Thank you.'

'It's so good to see you.'

'You too.'

'How's college?'

'It's good. Did I tell you I got three As and a B?'

'Yes, you said.'

'I kind of reinvented myself when I started college. I'm a good girl now. I don't get in trouble, I don't drink, I don't smoke, I don't do drugs. I hang around with the goody-goodies.'

'That's great.'

'I've got a very nice boyfriend, too. You've met him, actually.'

'I have?'

'Yeah. His name's Ross. He used to play table tennis for the Old Town C team.'

'Oh right. We're going to play them in a few weeks.'

'Unfortunately, he's not playing this season.'

'Oh.'

'Maybe I'll bring him next time.'

'That would be good.'

After a moment, Sofie said, 'Dad, Kate wants to adopt me. You'd still be my dad, but I'd have a proper mum again.'

'Is that what you want?'

'Yeah, more than anything.'

'I won't stand in your way.'

'Thanks, Dad. I really appreciate that.'

They looked at each other and smiled. After a moment, her father said, 'Have you seen much of Amy?'

'I was going to ask you the same thing.'

350

He shook his head.

Sofie said, 'I haven't seen her since…since I got pregnant. One of the reasons I got back on the straight and narrow is that I don't see Amy no more.'

Her father nodded. 'It's very sad. We used to be a beautiful family.'

'I know. Maybe we can salvage something from the wreckage. That's what I want to do.'

'Yes. I'd like that.'

*

On Tuesday evening, Sofie came round to Ross's house to play table tennis. After a while, his father and brother joined them, and the four of them spent over an hour playing singles and doubles matches.

Ross's father was the best player of all, but when they played doubles (Ross's father plus Sofie against the two brothers), the two teams were very evenly matched and won five games each. Sofie even returned Ross's demon serve about 20% of the time.

When he walked her home later, they returned to their favourite alley for a little passion. Ross's hands became a little more adventurous, and there was every indication that they were well received.

After 10 minutes, she said, 'I'd better go home soon. My mum will start to worry.'

'That's a shame.'

'What time do your parents leave for work?'

'Soon after eight.'

'What about your brother?'

'About quarter past.'

'We've both got free periods first thing tomorrow. We could be very naughty and skip registration. I could come and spend an hour up in your room.'

'That would be nice.'

She kissed him and they exchanged a long kiss. She broke off and whispered in his ear: 'Have you got any condoms?'

Chapter Forty-Nine

By the time Ross got home, Sofie's question had thrown him into a panic. The first thing he had to do was make sure he actually had the condoms he claimed to have. It took several minutes to find them, in the deepest, darkest recess under his bed. There were two left from his second pack of three.

His second worry was his lack of sexual experience. He had only ever had sexual intercourse four times. He and Mollie had lost their virginity together, and the first time was a bit of a disaster. She found it painful and said afterwards that she had been relieved when he climaxed quickly. The other three times had gone better, but he wouldn't exactly say the earth moved.

Sofie, in contrast, had been with a man almost twice her age. And presumably very experienced. Ross would have to up his game if he was going to compete. It was now 10:55, and he would soon have to take his mobile downstairs for the night. He went down to the dining room and made sure he sat facing the door so neither of his parents could creep up behind him and see what he was doing.

He put in his earphones and googled *how to make love to a woman*, but all that came up were dating websites and a film of that name. He changed it to *how to satisfy a woman in bed* and had more luck, as there were plenty of videos on YouTube. He clicked on one and watched it. The speaker explained that the man should be slow and gentle, consistent in terms of pressure and non-linear as he explored her body. She also stressed the importance of the all-round sensory experience, with clean sheets and a tidy, fresh-smelling room.

'Ah.'

Ross had no idea when his mother had last changed his sheets, and there was nothing he could do about that. But his bedroom was a tip. He needed to tidy it up, and to do so quietly so as not to arouse suspicion.

Panic resumed when he went for his morning shower. Should he shave? Would she find his stubble alluring or scratchy? After much debate, he shaved it off; it was starting to look scraggy in any case. When he got into the shower, he agonised over whether to shave off his pubic hair. But there was no time. His parents and his brother would be banging on the bathroom door before long.

By 8:05, both parents had gone, but his brother was dawdling in the dining room. Ross decided to ignore him. He went to the utility room next to the kitchen and retrieved a cloth and his mother's Dyson Cordless vacuum cleaner. He wet the cloth in the bathroom and quickly dusted all visible surfaces. Just before he finished, he heard the clunk of the door as his brother left.

It took just a couple of minutes to vacuum the floor. Once done, he hurried downstairs, put the vacuum cleaner away, squeezed the cloth and hung it up by the radiator in the utility room. Then he washed and dried his hands and went into the living room.

The doorbell rang almost the instant he sat down. He jumped up and opened it. Sofie was wearing black yoga pants and her dark blue cropped puffer jacket. She had mascara and lip gloss, plus a little foundation on her face. Ross smelt her perfume the instant he opened the door. That was a nice touch.

'Hi.'

'Hi.'

They exchanged a quick kiss and she came in, kicked off her trainers and hung up her puffer jacket. Under it, she had a dark blue denim jacket and a white T-shirt.

'Shall we go upstairs?'

'Yeah.'

He led her up to his room, where she took off her denim jacket and draped it across his chair.

'You'd better close the curtains.'

He closed them, and when he turned round, he saw that she had pulled her bra out from under her T-shirt.

If Ross took the initiative during foreplay, once the last of their clothes had been removed, it was Sofie who reached up under the pillow and retrieved the condom.

'Shall we do it?'

'Yeah.'

'Get on your back.'

It was quite a kerfuffle for her to squeeze her way out from under him. She deftly put the condom on him and pulled him inside her.

'Don't move,' he said, worried that things might come to a premature conclusion. Fortunately, Raj had told him what to do in just such a situation, so he closed his eyes and calculated the 17 times table in his head. By the time he worked out that 17 x 5 = 85, the crisis had passed.

'You okay?'

'Yeah.'

She told him where she wanted his hands. Then she closed her eyes and, as she began that most intimate of dances, Ross stole a quick glance at the clock on his bookshelf.

When their *pas de deux* reached its natural conclusion, Sofie buried her face in his pillow. Ross checked his clock again and saw that he had lasted more than 15 minutes. He smiled broadly and would have puffed out his chest if Sofie hadn't been lying on top of him.

'Wow,' he thought, 'I can really do this.'

Sofie had climaxed twice. He could hardly believe it, not just that her orgasms had happened – two of them! – but also their staggering intensity. Neither his experiences with Mollie nor all the porn he watched had prepared him for that.

He stroked her hair and ran his fingers down her spine.

She lifted her head and kissed him.

'Uh-oh,' she said. 'I've got mascara on your pillow.'

He laughed.

'Sorry.'

'Don't worry about it.'

They disengaged. She pulled his duvet up to cover them and took care of the condom. They lay still for a long time.

Eventually, she raised her head. 'You good?'

'I'm so good. You?'

'Yeah. That was lovely. Thank you.'

'Thank you. Do you know what?'

'What?'

'I've been thinking – all this time, when I was looking for redemption, I was looking in the wrong place. I didn't find it in Alpha, or Omega, or my punishment. I found it in you. I'm not there yet, but I can get there, thanks to you. I can be happy with you, and I can love you like you deserve to be loved.'

She brought her hand to his cheek and kissed him.

'I can love *you* like you deserve to be loved,' she said. 'And you do deserve it. You're a good person.'

*

Adrian greeted Ross with a warm handshake and invited him to sit down.

'How's your week been?'

'Much better, thanks. I've been nagging myself quite a lot, trying not to think negative thoughts.'

'Have you been succeeding?'

Ross gave a so-so gesture. 'Sometimes yes, sometimes no.'

'Any suicidal thoughts?'

'No.'

'What would you do if you had them?'

'I think about all the people it would hurt.'

'Hurt?'

'Devastate.'

'That's the word to use, because it would, all of them.'

'Yeah.'

'Do you feel you're making progress?'

'Definitely.'

'Good. You have to keep working at it. There's no quick fix.'

'Yeah.'

'Let me say something about our situation, Ross. In an ideal world, when you do counselling, it's supposed to take as long as it takes. If it just takes one session, then that's all you do. If it takes ten sessions, it takes ten sessions. See what I mean?'

Ross nodded.

'But that's not our situation. We have three sessions, and this is the third. I have a very full schedule and I don't have the option of continuing to do counselling with you.'

'I understand.'

'So, there's two ways we can go about this. One way is that we take what we did in the first two sessions as done, finished, completed. We say there are five things you need to keep in mind. Can you remember what they are?'

'I think so, yes.'

'Go on, then.'

'I have to stop saying I killed Lizzie Johnson. I made a mistake that was one of the causes of an accident that killed her.'

'Yes. Number two?'

'I haven't ruined her husband and her children's lives. The accident has caused them a lot of pain, but they have agency, and they have every chance of finding a way through it.'

'Like your girlfriend has.'

'Yeah, eventually. But not her dad or her sister.'

Adrian nodded. 'Nobody says it'll be easy for them. Number three?'

'I'm not an evil person. I'm basically a decent person who made a mistake.'

'And mistakes are…?'

'Something you learn from.'

'A very painful lesson in this case.'

'You bet.'

Adrian was silent for a moment. 'And number four?'

'I have people who care about me, who love me.' Ross paused. Tears came to his eyes.

'And are they stupid to love you?'

'No.'

'Why not?'

'Because I love them.'

'And are you worthy of their love?'

Ross nodded. 'Most of the time, yes.'

'And number five?'

'If I have suicidal thoughts, I have to think about all the people whose lives it would devastate.'

'Okay. Now, there's two ways we can proceed. Number one, we can take all that as done, finished, and I give you a very short course in self-compassion techniques, and I introduce you to a couple of mindfulness techniques that can help you. And then, that's it, wham, bam, that's your counselling done. Good luck and off you go.

'But, the problem with this, Ross, is you've suffered a major psychological trauma. A massive trauma. Most people never have anything like this in their whole life. And you've got some big challenges ahead of you. Not just this, coming to terms with this trauma, and that's big enough. And you've still got the inquest to come. That won't be easy. You've got your A-Levels next spring. That's a challenge. When you go to university, it'll be a challenge. You'll probably relish the challenge, and hopefully, you'll have the time of your life. But it's a challenge. And when you have your year in France, same thing. It'll be a very big challenge.

'Other challenges too. Teenage years and your early twenties can be a wonderful time, should be a wonderful time. But they're challenging. You know, affairs of the heart, finding your way in the world, becoming the kind of person you want to be. It's not easy. There will be ups and downs, significant downs. Those downs will happen. And the danger is, if you haven't dealt with this trauma in the right way, got on top of it, learnt to cope with it properly, it might come back and bite you, years down the line. And my worry is that when that happens, you'll have forgotten everything you learnt in our sessions.'

Ross nodded his agreement. 'Yeah, I can see that.'

'So, can you see an alternative strategy that we can adopt?'

'I think so.'

*

The following Thursday, he left home at 8:20 and cycled round to Sofie's house, arriving just as Kate came out with the little ones in their school uniforms.

They greeted Ross, and Lydia ran up to him and gave him a hug. Kate left the front door open so he could go inside.

'Hiya!'

'Oh, hello. I'm in the dining room.'

He closed the door, kicked off his shoes and went through. Sofie was polishing off her scrambled eggs on toast.

'You're early.'

'Yeah,' he said. 'Don't want to be late.'

'You all ready?'

'Yes.'

'Nervous?'

'No. Why? Should I be?'

'No.'

When Sofie had finished her breakfast, she went upstairs to clean her teeth, and then the two of them cycled down to the college. They locked their bikes and retreated to a corner round the back of the building for a cuddle and a quick snog.

Just before nine, they walked round to the main entrance, where they passed the smokers and vapers having a fix before starting their day.

'See you later.'

'Yeah, see you.'

Sofie headed off to her psychology class. Ross went the other way and knocked on one of the doors opposite the library.

It opened and a woman in her 40s with a petite figure and long, permed hair smiled at him.

'Hi. It's Ross, isn't it?'

'Yes, hello.'

'Do come in and have a seat.'

Epilogue

It is April 2019, a year since the accident that cost Lizzie Johnson her life. Ross's recovery has been slow and gradual, and it remains incomplete. He understands now that there is no magic bullet that will bring redemption. He will feel guilt and remorse for the rest of his life. He thinks of the accident as an injury, a pain that is always there but is mostly tolerable, even if it flares up from time to time. He still can't bear to watch movies with car chases. He can play something cartoonish like Sofie's ancient Super Mario Kart, but he avoids racing games with realistic graphics like Gravel or F1. He cycles every day but can't imagine that he will ever drive again.

He is extremely grateful to Adrian and Kitty, his counsellors. He had a total of six sessions with Kitty, and he has managed to internalise several different ways to reframe his negative thoughts. When these don't work and he begins to sink into his abyss of guilt, he has learnt to treat himself as a friend: he asks what he would say to a friend who was troubled by the same negative thoughts. So far, this has always worked, but he knows that if it doesn't, he can reach out to Sofie.

His gratitude to her is boundless, as is his love for her. She is always there for him, and she has always seemed to know when it is the right moment to nudge him to take a step away from self-isolation, inviting him to join their friends in the common room, to go for a coffee, to ask friends round to play on his new Wii or, now that they are both 18, to make the occasional trip the pub. He almost always spends his breaks with other students, and in his free periods, he either studies or skives off to chat or play football or table tennis.

He has hardly posted anything on social media, however, though he did put up a new profile picture on Instagram with him and Sofie together. He is still terrified of Anthony Johnson looking him up and seeing him boast about the great times he is having.

He will have to encounter him again at the inquest in October, by which time he will be at university. Ross is dreading it, but he feels that life will finally get back to normal once this is behind him.

In January, Raj persuaded him to rejoin his table-tennis club, and so far he has a win ratio of 62.5% (much better than Raj, as he points out whenever Raj beats him). One evening, while they were playing table tennis at Ross's house, Raj said, 'You know, I've been meaning to say, I feel really bad about nagging you to overtake that time.'

Ross shrugged. 'I would've tried to overtake anyway. It's not your fault.'

'Yeah, well, I'm sorry.'

'Don't worry about it. New game, your serve.'

Ross hasn't rejoined the college football team, however. Until the second week in February, he had to spend every Saturday doing unpaid community payback work. Ross is full of admiration for Geoff and the other supervisors from the Youth Offending Team, and he regards his community punishment as a positive experience that helped his recovery.

Because he has been unable to play football seriously, Ross has taken up running and joined a club that meets every Wednesday evening. He has already run his first half-marathon and is building himself up to run in the Brighton Marathon next spring. He will use the race to raise money for Orphans in Need, and hopes to do the same in the London Marathon in 2021.

He and Sofie are desperate to make sure they go to the same university, and both of them are working hard to get the A-Level results they need.

*

In December, as they walked past McDonald's while doing their Christmas shopping, Sofie spotted two girls she knew sitting near the window.

'Give us a mo,' she said to Ross. 'I want to speak to them girls.'

Ross waited outside and watched as she went in and walked up to them.

'Hi.'

Her heart was racing.

'Oh, hello.' The tone of the reply indicated that they weren't exactly pleased to see her.

'Do you ever see Josie Bromhall?'

'Yeah. What of it?'

'Can you do me a favour? I was really horrible to her at school, and I'm ashamed of what I done. Can you just tell her I'm sorry. She's a good person, and she didn't deserve it, and I'm sorry. Can you do that for me?'

The two girls looked at each other in evident astonishment. One of them finally said, 'Yes.'

'Thanks. Merry Christmas.'

'You too.'

'What was that all about?' Ross asked as she approached him, a big grin on her face.

She linked arms with him and they walked off. 'Just me having a Tiny Tim moment.'

*

Bee has thrown herself into the final year of her degree. It wouldn't have been in her nature to drift through it. She has been working hard to improve her Hebrew and Ancient Greek and is preparing her applications for a postgrad degree, with a view to a possible career in academia. If that doesn't work out, she has the option of doing a PGCE and becoming an RE teacher. Even though she is an atheist, religion remains her passion.

Her mother seems to have convinced herself that her loss of faith is just a phase she will eventually grow out of. Bee no longer goes to church or leads the prayer before meals when she is at home during university vacations, though she agreed to go to a service on Christmas Eve and quite enjoyed it. Robbie is even allowed to sleep in her bedroom when he stays.

She and Sofie message each other from time to time, and Bee enjoys meeting up with her and Ross when she is in town. Occasionally, they will talk about religion, but mostly their chat is the same as any other friends.

*

Mrs Akehurst has it in her diary to email Ross and Sofie in a few weeks' time to invite them to work for her next summer. What she doesn't know is that they have already asked Bee to put in a good word for them at the language school where she worked. They feel that events since they left the hotel have tainted their relationship with the Akehurst family.

Mrs Akehurst doesn't blame Martha for Sid's death, but she fears that a rift has opened between them. Soon after the funeral, Martha took her children to live near her parents in Liverpool. Mrs Akehurst worries that she has lost her grandchildren as well as her son.

For his part, Nigel was devastated by Sid's suicide. He has spent his working life helping other people and can't believe that he failed to notice his own brother was falling apart. His faith remains strong, but he can't understand why God chose to subject him and his family to such a dreadful test.

*

Dominic is worried about his Alpha Course starting in July. Pat is refusing to help out, saying she is too busy with her baby. Dominic isn't convinced that this is the reason. She was very upset by what happened with Bee and Ross, and he thinks this has hit her confidence. He would regret the loss of such a capable team leader.

Bob has offered to help out, but Dominic has his doubts about him. He and Alison are regular churchgoers, but Dominic has heard that Alison only agreed to go on condition that he stop trying to convert their children. He isn't sure if this is true, but if it is, it shows a distinct lack of fervour on his part. If charity starts at home, so does the saving of souls.

If Dominic is unable to talk Pat back into leading a table, he will have to try and persuade Tom. He is sure he would be good, but not as good as Pat.

*

Looking back, Ross thinks he was an idiot to embark on the Alpha Course, though he doesn't regret it, since he and Sofie might never have fallen in love if they hadn't spent so much time together. Nevertheless, he feels he had a lucky escape: were it not for Bob, he might have been converted and wasted years of his life on something that simply isn't true.

He and Sofie recently read Richard Dawkins' *The God Delusion*. Ross loved it and is now ploughing his way through his father's copy of *The Selfish Gene*. But Sofie hated it. She says Dawkins doesn't understand that religion can be liberal and questioning, that there have always been religious thinkers who treat the Bible as *mythos* and allegory, something that can be explored like poetry, literary fiction or great art to help us understand our place in the cosmos.

She is not sure whether she believes in God, but she certainly doesn't feel that her spiritual journey is over.

Ross, on the other hand, regards all religion as nonsense. He doesn't consider *mythos* to be viable: most believers will always take myths literally, which means that they will be drawn to conservative and intolerant versions of their faith. For him, *logos* is the only form of knowledge worth having.

He and Sofie sometimes have heated debates about religion, *mythos* and *logos*. And after their arguments have gone round and round in the same old circle, they will pause.

Sofie will look Ross in the eye and say, 'I'm right and you're wrong.'

'No, you're not.'

'Yes, I am.'

'Not.'

'Am.'

'Not.'

They will laugh and exchange a kiss, after which they will embrace and remember how much they love each other.

Author's Note

D id you enjoy this book?

If so, I would be grateful if you could take just a moment to do me a HUGE favour and rate this book online at Amazon, or on Goodreads, if you have an account.

As an independent author, I don't have the financial muscle of the big corporations, who take out full-page ads in newspapers and put posters in train stations. But I can have something much more powerful and effective than that: feedback from readers. Honest ratings and reviews will help bring this book to the attention of others.

It only takes a moment to leave a rating (preferably four or five stars!). If you would like to write a review, it can just be a couple of sentences.

*

You may also be interested in my other novels, a trilogy of thrillers set in the final decade of Soviet communism and the period of murderous chaos that followed its collapse.

Available from your favourite online bookstore:

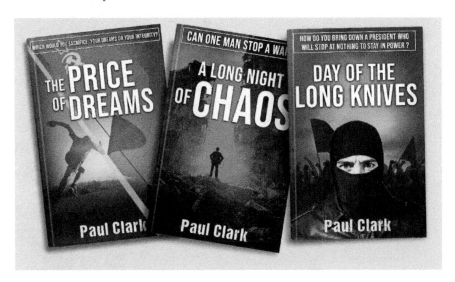

Notes on Further Reading

You can find detailed source notes on both the Alpha Course and the Omega Course on my website: https://paulclark42.com/omega.

The Alpha Course: My Alpha Course and all Dominic's lectures are based on two books by Nicky Gumbel: *Questions of Life: A Practical Introduction to the Christian Faith* and *How to Run the Alpha Course*. I also found Hans Küng's *On Being a Christian* a useful introduction to a more liberal version of mainstream Christianity.

Mythos **and** *Logos*: A defence of a liberal religious outlook through the *mythos-logos* distinction can be found in the works of Karen Armstrong, in particular *A History of God*, and *A Short History of Myth*.

The Old Testament and the Ancient Israelites: These books have had a big impact on my writing: *Who Wrote the Bible* by Richard Elliot Friedman, *The Bible Unearthed* by Israel Finkelstein and Neil Asher Silberman, *The Invention of God* by Thomas Römer, *Introduction to the Bible* by Christine Hayes and *God: An Anatomy* by Francesca Stavrakopoulou.

For an intellectually rigorous Christian perspective on the Bible, see *The Human Faces of God* by Thom Stark or *A History of the Bible* by John Barton.

The New Testament and the Historical Jesus: A very good introduction to the topic is *The Historical Figure of Jesus* by EP Sanders. I would also recommend anything by Bart Ehrman, one of the most eloquent contemporary writers on the historical Jesus. For this book, I have drawn on *How Jesus Became God* and *Did Jesus Exist?*

Other books that have influenced my thinking are: *The First Coming* by Thomas Sheenan, *Christian Origins* by Christopher Rowland. *The Authentic Gospel of Jesus* by Geza Vermes, *A History of Christianity* by Diarmaid MacCulloch and *Introduction to New Testament History and Literature* by Dale B Martin.

Stage Hypnotism and Hallucinations: Derren Brown's *Tricks of the Mind* has a fascinating discussion on hypnotism and the power of suggestion. I have also drawn on *The Demon-Haunted World* by Carl Sagan and *Being You: The New Science of Consciousness* by Anil Seth.

Atheism and Scepticism: If you read just one angry exposition of the New Atheist viewpoint, read the best: Richard Dawkins' *The God Delusion*. It is a devastating hatchet job. For a more charitable view of the impact of

Christianity, see *Dominion: The Making of the Western Mind* by agnostic historian Tom Holland.

Will Storr's *Heretics: Adventures with the Enemies of Science* is a brilliant and humane meditation on the clash between the sceptical outlook and the dogmatic, during the course of which he finds rigid thinking in unexpected places. *The Righteous Mind: Why Good People are Divided by Politics and Religion* by Jonathan Haidt is a more in-depth examination of a similar topic.

Fiction: If you believe that fiction can combine with non-fiction to discuss serious ideas, then I would recommend two philosophical novels without whose brilliant example this book would never have been written: *Zen and the Art of Motorcycle Maintenance* by Robert M Pirsig and *Sophie's World* by Jostein Gaarder.

Appendix One

The Two Versions of Noah's Ark in the Bible

Full source notes are available at https://paulclark42.com/omega/

I have separated out the two versions of Noah's Ark and then show how they are woven together in the Bible.

The Yahwist's Version of Noah's Ark

The LORD saw how great man's wickedness on the earth had become, and that every inclination of the thoughts of his heart was only evil all the time. The LORD was grieved that he had made man on the earth, and his heart was filled with pain. So the LORD said, "I will wipe mankind, whom I have created, from the face of the earth – men and animals, and creatures that move along the ground, and birds of the air – for I am grieved that I have made them." But Noah found favour in the eyes of the LORD.

The LORD then said to Noah, "Go into the ark, you and your whole family, because I have found you righteous in this generation. Take with you seven pairs of every kind of clean animal, a male and its mate, and two of every kind of unclean animal, a male and its mate, and also seven pairs of every kind of bird, male and female, to keep their various kinds alive throughout the earth. Seven days from now I will send rain on the earth for forty days and forty nights, and I will wipe from the face of the earth every living creature I have made."

And Noah did all the LORD had commanded him.

And Noah and his sons and his wife and his sons' wives entered the ark to escape the waters of the flood.

And after the seven days the floodwaters came on the earth.

And rain fell on the earth for forty days and forty nights.

Then the LORD shut him in.

For forty days the flood kept coming on the earth, and as the waters increased they lifted the ark high above the earth. The waters rose and increased greatly on the earth, and the ark floated on the surface of the water. They rose greatly on the earth, and all the high mountains under the entire heavens were covered. The waters rose and covered the mountains to a depth of more than fifteen cubits.

Everything on dry land that had the breath of life in its nostrils died. Every living thing on the face of the earth was wiped out; men and animals and the creatures that move along the ground and the birds of the air were wiped from the earth. Only Noah was left, and those with him in the ark.

And the rain stopped falling from the sky. The water receded steadily from the earth.

After forty days Noah opened the window he had made in the ark

Then he sent out a dove to see if the waters had receded from the surface of the ground. But the dove could find no place to set its feet because there was water over all the surface of the earth; so it returned to Noah in the ark. He waited seven more days and again sent out the dove from the ark. When the dove returned to him in the evening, there in its beak was a freshly plucked olive leaf! Then Noah knew the water had receded from the earth. He waited seven more days and sent the dove out again, but this time it did not return to him.

Noah then removed the covering from the ark and saw the surface of the ground was dry.

Then Noah built an alter to the LORD and, taking some of all the clean animals and clean birds, he sacrificed burnt offerings on it. The LORD smelled the pleasing aroma and said in his heart: "Never again will I curse the ground because of man, even though every inclination of his heart is evil from childhood. And never again will I destroy all living creatures as I have done.

"As long as the earth endures,
seedtime and harvest,
cold and heat,
summer and winter,
day and night
will never cease."

The Priestly Writer's Version of Noah's Ark

This is the account of Noah.

Noah was a righteous man, blameless among the people of his time, and he walked with God. Noah had three sons: Shem, Ham and Japheth.

Now the earth was evil in God's sight and was full of violence. God saw how corrupt the earth had become, for all the people on the earth had corrupted their ways. So God said to Noah, "I am going to put an end to all people, for the earth is filled with violence because of them. I am surely going to destroy both them and the earth. So make yourself an ark of cypress wood; make rooms in it and coat it in pitch inside and out. This is how you are to build it: The ark is to be 450 feet long, 75 feet wide and 45 feet high. Make a roof for it and finish the ark to within 18 inches of the top. Put a door in the side of the ark and make lower, middle and upper decks. I am going to bring floodwaters on the earth to destroy all life under the heavens, every creature that has the breath of life in it. Everything on earth will perish. But I will establish my covenant with you, and you will enter the ark – you and your sons and your wife and your sons' wives with you. You are to bring into the ark two of every living creature, male and female, to keep them alive with you. Two of every kind of bird, of every kind of animal and of every kind of creature that moves along the ground will come to you to be kept alive. You are to take every kind of food that is to be eaten and store it away as food for you and for them."

Noah did everything just as God commanded him.

Noah was six hundred years old when the floodwaters came on the earth.

Pairs of clean and unclean animals, of birds and all creatures that move along the ground, male and female, came to Noah and entered the ark, as God had commanded Noah.

In the six hundredth year of Noah's life, on the seventeenth day of the seventh month – on that day all the springs of the great deep burst forth, and the floodgates of the heavens were opened.

On that very day Noah and his sons, Shem, Ham and Japheth, together with his wife and the wives of his three sons, entered the ark. They had with them every animal according to its kind, all livestock according to their kinds, every creature that moves along the ground according to its kind and every bird according to its kind, everything with wings. Pairs of all creatures that have the breath of life in them came to Noah and entered the ark. The animals going in were male and female of every living thing, as God had commanded Noah.

Every living thing that moved on the earth perished – birds, livestock, wild animals, all the creatures that swarm over the earth, and all mankind.

And the waters flooded the earth for a hundred and fifty days.

But God remembered Noah and all the wild animals and the livestock that were with him in the ark, and he sent a wind over the earth, and the waters receded. Now the springs of the deep and the floodgates of the heavens had been closed.

At the end of the hundred and fifty days the water had gone down and on the seventeenth day of the seventh month the ark came to rest on the mountains of Ararat. The waters continued to recede until the tenth month, and on the first day of the tenth month the tops of the mountains became visible.

And he sent out a raven, and it kept flying back and forth until the water had dried up from the earth.

By the first day of the first month of Noah's six hundred and first year, the water had dried up from the earth.

By the twenty-seventh day of the second month the earth was completely dry.

Then God said to Noah, "Come out of the ark, you and your wife and your sons and their wives. Bring out every kind of living creature that is with you – the birds, the animals, and all the creatures that move along the ground – so they can multiply on the earth and be fruitful and increase in number upon it."

So Noah came out, together with his sons and his wife and his sons' wives. All the animals and all the creatures that move along the ground and all the birds – everything that moves upon the earth – came out of the ark, one kind after another.

Noah's Ark in The Bible

The story of Noah begins in Genesis Chapter 6, Verse 5

I have put the Yahwist's version in *Italics* and the Priestly Writer's Version in **Bold**.

5 The LORD saw how great man's wickedness on the earth had become, and that every inclination of the thoughts of his heart was only evil all the time. 6 The LORD was grieved that he had made man on the earth, and his heart was filled with pain. 7 So the LORD said, "I will wipe mankind, whom I have created, from the face of the earth – men and animals, and creatures that move along the ground, and birds of the air – for I am grieved that I have made them." 8 But Noah found favour in the eyes of the LORD.

9 This is the account of Noah.

Noah was a righteous man, blameless among the people of his time, and he walked with God. 10 Noah had three sons: Shem, Ham and Japheth.

11 Now the earth was evil in God's sight and was full of violence. 12 God saw how corrupt the earth had become, for all the people on the earth had corrupted their ways. 13 So God said to Noah, "I am going to put an end to all people, for the earth is filled with violence because of them. I am surely going to destroy both them and the earth. 14 So make yourself an ark of cypress wood; make rooms in it and coat it in pitch inside and out. 15 This is how you are to build it: The ark is to be 450 feet long, 75 feet wide and 45 feet high. 16 Make a roof for it and finish the ark to within 18 inches of the top. Put a door in the side of the ark and make lower, middle and upper decks. 17 I am going to bring floodwaters on the earth to destroy all life under the heavens, every creature that has the breath of life in it. Everything on earth will perish. 18 But I will establish my covenant with you, and you will enter the ark – you and your sons and your wife and your sons' wives with you. 19 You are to bring into the ark two of every living creature, male and female, to keep them alive with you. 20 Two of every kind of bird, of every kind of animal and of every kind of creature that moves along the ground will come to you to be kept alive. 21 You are to take every kind of food that is to be eaten and store it away as food for you and for them."

22 Noah did everything just as God commanded him.

Chapter 7

1 The LORD then said to Noah, "Go into the ark, you and your whole family, because I have found you righteous in this generation. 2 Take with you seven pairs of every kind of clean animal, a male and its mate, and two of every kind of unclean animal, a male and its mate, ³ *and also seven pairs of every kind of bird, male and female, to keep their various kinds alive throughout the earth.* ⁴ *Seven days from now I will send rain on the earth for forty days and forty nights, and I will wipe from the face of the earth every living creature I have made."*

⁵ *And Noah did all the L*ORD *had commanded him.*

⁶ **Noah was six hundred years old when the floodwaters came on the earth.**

⁷ *And Noah and his sons and his wife and his sons' wives entered the ark to escape the waters of the flood.*

⁸ **Pairs of clean and unclean animals, of birds and all creatures that move along the ground,** ⁹ **male and female, came to Noah and entered the ark, as God had commanded Noah.**

¹⁰ *And after the seven days the floodwaters came on the earth.*

¹¹ **In the six hundredth year of Noah's life, on the seventeenth day of the seventh month – on that day all the springs of the great deep burst forth, and the floodgates of the heavens were opened.**

¹² *And rain fell on the earth for forty days and forty nights.*

¹³ **On that very day Noah and his sons, Shem, Ham and Japheth, together with his wife and the wives of his three sons, entered the ark.** ¹⁴ **They had with them every animal according to its kind, all livestock according to their kinds, every creature that moves along the ground according to its kind and every bird according to its kind, everything with wings.** ¹⁵ **Pairs of all creatures that have the breath of life in them came to Noah and entered the ark.** ¹⁶ **The animals going in were male and female of every living thing, as God had commanded Noah.**

*Then the L*ORD *shut him in.*

¹⁷ *For forty days the flood kept coming on the earth, and as the waters increased they lifted the ark high above the earth.* ¹⁸ *The waters rose and increased greatly on the earth, and the ark floated on the surface of the water.* ¹⁹ *They rose greatly on the earth, and all the high mountains under the entire heavens were covered.* ²⁰ *The waters rose and covered the mountains to a depth of more than fifteen cubits.*

²¹ **Every living thing that moved on the earth perished – birds, livestock, wild animals, all the creatures that swarm over the earth, and all mankind.**

²² *Everything on dry land that had the breath of life in its nostrils died.* ²³ *Every living thing on the face of the earth was wiped out; men and animals and the creatures that move along the ground and the birds of the air were wiped from the earth. Only Noah was left, and those with him in the ark.*

²⁴ **And the waters flooded the earth for a hundred and fifty days.**

Chapter 8

¹ **But God remembered Noah and all the wild animals and the livestock that were with him in the ark, and he sent a wind over the earth, and the waters receded.** ² **Now the springs of the deep and the floodgates of the heavens had been closed,**

and the rain stopped falling from the sky. ³ *The water receded steadily from the earth.*

At the end of the hundred and fifty days the water had gone down ⁴ **and on the seventeenth day of the seventh month the ark came to rest on the mountains of Ararat.** ⁵ **The waters continued to recede until the tenth month, and on the first day of the tenth month the tops of the mountains became visible.**

⁶ *After forty days Noah opened the window he had made in the ark*

⁷ **and he sent out a raven, and it kept flying back and forth until the water had dried up from the earth.**

⁸ *Then he sent out a dove to see if the waters had receded from the surface of the ground.* ⁹ *But the dove could find no place to set its feet because there was water over all the surface of the earth; so it returned to Noah in the ark.* ¹⁰ *He waited seven more days and again sent out the dove from the ark.* ¹¹ *When the dove returned to him in the evening, there in its beak was a freshly plucked olive leaf! Then Noah knew the water had receded from the earth.* ¹² *He waited seven more days and sent the dove out again, but this time it did not return to him.*

¹³ **By the first day of the first month of Noah's six hundred and first year, the water had dried up from the earth.**

Noah then removed the covering from the ark and saw the surface of the ground was dry.

¹⁴ **By the twenty-seventh day of the second month the earth was completely dry.**

¹⁵ **Then God said to Noah,** ¹⁶ **"Come out of the ark, you and your wife and your sons and their wives.** ¹⁷ **Bring out every kind of living creature that is with you – the birds, the animals, and all the creatures that move along the ground – so they can multiply on the earth and be fruitful and increase in number upon it."**

¹⁸ **So Noah came out, together with his sons and his wife and his sons' wives.** ¹⁹ **All the animals and all the creatures that move along the ground and all the birds – everything that moves upon the earth – came out of the ark, one kind after another.**

²⁰ *Then Noah built an alter to the L*ord *and, taking some of all the clean animals and clean birds, he sacrificed burnt offerings on it.* ²¹ *The L*ord

smelled the pleasing aroma and said in his heart: "Never again will I curse the ground because of man, even though every inclination of his heart is evil from childhood. And never again will I destroy all living creatures as I have done.

²² "As long as the earth endures,
seedtime and harvest,
cold and heat,
summer and winter,
day and night
will never cease."

Appendix Two

Part Two of Bee's Email About the Resurrection

Full source notes are available at https://paulclark42.com/omega/

2. JESUS' APPEARANCES AFTER THE RESURRECTION

Do these provide extraordinary evidence to back up the extraordinary claim of the resurrection? Read on for the case against.

The earliest document we have about the resurrection is in Paul's First Letter to the Corinthians, which was written about 25 years after the crucifixion. Paul says Jesus died and was raised on the third day. After that he appeared first to Peter, then to the 12, then to five hundred Christians at the same time and finally to Paul himself.

Paul uses the Greek verb horao for all these different appearances. The Septuagint (the Greek translation of Jewish scriptures) often uses the same verb to describe appearances of God or angels. The verb doesn't mean these people "saw" Jesus, rather it means Jesus "appeared" to them or "showed himself".

Appearing can be done in different ways, as a vision or as a voice or simply as a presence. In Paul's case, for example, it was as a blinding light and Jesus' voice asking "Saul, Saul, why do you persecute me?" (Acts 9:3-9).

In a similar vein, the Bible has many instances of God appearing to other people in lots of different ways:

Abram heard God's voice.

Jacob wrestled with God.

Isaiah saw God seated on a throne with six-winged seraphim angels flying above him calling out his praises.

Jeremiah said God reached out and touched his mouth with his hand, literally putting words into his mouth.

Ezekiel saw an approaching thunderstorm which revealed four creatures each of which had four faces and four wings. Then, above them, he saw God.

Others inside and outside the Bible have encountered intermediaries such as Jesus or angels:

Moses saw an angel in a burning bush. Then after he approached, God spoke to him from within the bush.

The Prophet Mohamed was in a cave when he heard a voice coming from all directions, even from inside himself. Then he saw the Angel Gabriel, who began to reveal the verses of the Koran to him. Later, when Mohamed went outside, he looked up and saw Gabriel, who was so enormous that he filled the sky.

Joseph Smith saw flesh and bone visions of God and Jesus when he was just 14. Later he was visited by the Angel Moroni, who gave him the golden plates that were to be the source of the Book of Mormon.

When **Sun Myun Moon** was a teenager, Jesus came to him while he was praying on top of a mountain and commanded him to complete the unfinished task of establishing God's Kingdom of Heaven on earth.

Other traditions have similar experiences, but the idiom may be different:

Zoroaster emerged from ritual bathing in a river to find himself bathed in pure light with the words of God resounding in his head.

Gautama Buddha found enlightenment after 49 days of continuous meditation. He experienced it as like awakening from a dream to find a new awareness of the true nature of the cosmos.

Bhagwan Shree Rajneesh went into a garden at night, and through the luminosity of a maulshree tree, God caused him to experience the benediction of the universe.

These are the religious experiences of prophets and religious leaders, but history is littered with countless thousands of others, from Joan of Arc's voices that told her to drive out the English to Emanuel Swedenborg's vision of God advising him not to eat too much.

My argument is that all these different religious experiences are basically the same thing. I am not accusing any of these people of making it up (though obviously there are religious charlatans who fake such things).

So what do these different experiences mean? Are they all genuine insights into the divine, or only some of them? If only some of them, how can you distinguish between those that are real and those that are not? I suppose you could say, "My god's better than your god; the visions in my religion are genuine, and those in your religion aren't." There are plenty of people who think like this, but I don't think it gets us anywhere.

It's more fruitful to approach the question of these religious experiences via psychology and an examination of altered states of consciousness like trances and hallucinations. These things are a part of being human, just like sleep and dreaming. They aren't evidence of cosmic forces any more than they're evidence of insanity or the use of narcotics; they're simply things that happen to a surprisingly large number of people.

For example, one study of widows and widowers revealed that up to 14% have a visual hallucination of their dead spouse. Almost as many will hear their voice, and nearly half will experience an awareness of their presence at some stage. Other research indicates that 20% of people have an out-of-body hallucination some time in their life, and these can have a purely physical explanation.

A lot of research has been done into hallucinations. They happen when our ability to distinguish between internal and external stimuli breaks down (internal stimuli: thoughts, dreams, memory and imagination; external stimuli: sights, sounds, smells, tastes and sensations). Thus, for example, a widow, so used to seeing her husband or hearing his voice, can briefly fail to distinguish between a memory or a dream of him and the real thing.

Psychologists have also examined the related phenomenon of trances, which often lead to hallucinations. And how do you induce a trance? Music, chanting, dance, prayer, focused attention, meditation. These things are all part of the everyday practice of organised religion, so can it be a surprise that so many hallucinations happen during prayer and religious services?

There can be medical causes too. Aldous Huxley believed LSD was a short-cut to religious experience. A strong dose of ketamine will induce an out-of-body experience. People who suffer from sleep paralysis can be unable to distinguish between dreams and reality. And we know there's a correlation between temporal lobe epilepsy and religious hallucination.

So, let's go back to where I started – Jesus' appearances to his followers as documented 25 years after his death in 1 Corinthians 15:2-8. The first person he appeared to was Peter. Here was a man in a profound state of crisis. His leader, who he believed to be God's Messiah, had just been arrested and killed in the most horrendous and shameful manner imaginable. And remember how low Peter had stooped to save himself: he had denied that he had anything to do with Jesus, allegedly not once but three times.

How susceptible would Peter have been to religious hallucination, particularly if he had responded to his crisis with fasting and prayer? After he reported his experience of the risen Jesus, some other followers of Jesus went on to have their own hallucinatory experiences. In some cases, these may have been visions, in other cases voices or a general awareness of Jesus still being with them. Still others may have felt compelled to make similar claims without actually having the experiences.

Tales grow in the telling, and some 45 years after the crucifixion, the authors of Matthew and Luke would write the accounts of Christ's appearances that we still have today. By now, the different stories of people's religious experiences had been combined with the tale of the empty tomb. The variety of hallucinatory experiences had now become flesh-and-blood appearances of the resurrected Jesus.

Can I prove that this interpretation of Jesus' appearances is right?

No.

But if we ignore the "Jesus didn't die on the cross" school of thought, we're basically left with two competing explanations for the resurrection of Jesus. One is this kind of "rational-scientific" explanation, which sees his appearances as imperfectly recorded tales of the hallucinations experienced by some of his followers. The other explanation claims that it happened pretty much as it says in the Bible.

Apply Occam's Razor to these two versions of the truth: whenever you are confronted by two explanations for the same phenomenon, always go for the simplest one.

Ladies and gentlemen of the jury: I put it to you that the "rational-scientific" explanation is the simplest. And, therefore, these appearances most certainly don't constitute extraordinary evidence that can support the extraordinary claim at the heart of mainstream Christianity: the resurrection of Jesus Christ.

Appendix Three

How the Bible Came to be Written Part One

Full source notes are available at https://paulclark42.com/omega/

Hi Sofie,

This is just like being at university, except I haven't got my books and I usually work in the library so I don't get distracted. Here goes. The title of my assignment is "How the Bible Came to be Written" but I will only be looking at the Old Testament.

THE OLD TESTAMENT

You cannot understand who wrote the Old Testament if you do not know the story of the Ancient Israelites and how they became the Jews, so I am going to have to tell you that story and then the story of how the Bible came to be written.

But let's begin with a brief summary. The Old Testament starts with the creation, then Adam and Eve, Cain and Abel, Noah's Ark and the Tower of Babel. After that, it goes on to the Patriarchs, the founding fathers of the Israelite nation: Abraham, Isaac and Jacob and Joseph and his brothers. Next comes Moses and the Exodus from Egypt and Joshua and the conquest of the Promised Land.

This is followed by the Judges and the various kings, including David and Solomon. Things go downhill after that: The kingdom splits in two, and within four hundred years, the Kingdom of Israel is annihilated. Just 130 years later, the Kingdom of Judah suffers the same fate, Solomon's Temple is destroyed and a large part of the population get carted off to exile in Babylon.

This is the "historical" core of the Old Testament.

OK, let's go back to the first bit, the ancient myths, from the creation to Noah's Ark and the Tower of Babel. Sophisticated Jews and Christians have long known that you should not take these bits any more literally than we would take the stories of Zeus, Prometheus and what have you. They are myths, brilliant myths, but no more than that.

THE PATRIARCHS

But the Biblical accounts of the Patriarchs and Moses were different. Until quite recently, these were taken more or less at face value, with or without the supernatural bits, according to taste. Historians thought there really was a man called Abram who travelled from Mesopotamia to the Holy Land, made a covenant with God and became Abraham. Same thing with Isaac, Jacob, Joseph and Moses. They believed these people really did exist.

Archaeologists tried very hard to find evidence to back these stories up, but without success. Indeed, as time has gone on, the clash between the archaeological evidence and the Bible has become more and more glaring.

Let's take a famous example from the story of Abram/Abraham. It is generally accepted that the Bible has him making his journey sometime around 2100 BCE.

Trouble is, the Bible mentions the camels he used. But the archaeological evidence is very clear: although camels were domesticated for food before Abram's time, they were not used as beasts of burden until at least a thousand years later. So the appearance of camels in the story of Abram is anachronistic, a bit like seeing a wristwatch in a movie about Henry VIII.

What this and other anachronisms show is that the stories of the Patriarchs were written much later, probably in the 7th or 8th Century BCE, and they are in no sense an accurate guide to what really happened.

I will come back to the Patriarchs and where their stories come from later, but first let's have a look at Moses.

MOSES AND THE EXODUS

The Bible tells how the Egyptians enslaved the Israelites until Moses led them to freedom. Presumably you know about how the plagues forced the Pharaoh to let the Israelites go. They reach the borders of Canaan, the Promised Land, but they are too frightened to proceed further. This infuriates God, who punishes them by making them remain at Kadesh Barnea for the next 38 years.

When archaeologists descended on the region in the 19th and early 20th centuries, they had some success in backing this story up. They managed to locate many of the places in the Biblical account, such as Kadesh Barnea and the city of Pi-Ramesses, which the Bible says was built by Israelite slaves.

Once they learnt to read hieroglyphics, historians built up a very detailed year-by-year account of Egyptian history. Among other things, they found Egyptian sources that told the intriguing story of the Hyksos, a Semitic people whose story seemed to mirror the Israelite Exodus. The Hyksos settled in Egypt in large numbers, much like Jacob and his sons. They established themselves as rulers of northern Egypt (a bit like Joseph?), but eventually the Egyptians rose up and drove them out.

So is this the Exodus story from the Egyptian point of view? On the face of it, it looks very similar. But when you try to date the Exodus, you run into trouble. The Bible's chronology puts the Exodus sometime between 1491 and 1440 BCE. Unfortunately, this does not chime with the Hyksos, who were driven out of Egypt a hundred years earlier.

Nor does it chime with the city of Pi-Ramesses, built by Ramesses the Great, who became Pharoah in 1279 BCE. So if the Bible is correct about Israelite slaves building Pi-Ramesses, then the Exodus took place at least two hundred years after dates given by the Bible, and three hundred years after the Hyksos.

Historians have found a brief record of a military campaign the Egyptians waged against the Hebrews in the year 1207 BCE. This is the first ever historical record of the Israelites, and it places them inside the Promised Land.

So, if the Bible is correct and the Israelites built Pi-Ramesses, the Exodus can only have happened between 1279 and 1207 BCE. Which does not fit the dates given by the Bible. In any case, at that time, Egypt controlled both Sinai and Canaan. So even if Moses and the Israelites had made it across the Red Sea, they would have run into powerful Egyptian armies on the other side.

Also, Egyptologists can find no evidence whatsoever for the departure of 600,000 Israelite men and their families from Egypt – more than a quarter of the total population. But that is what the Bible claims.

What is more, archaeologists have scoured the Sinai without finding a single trace of the wanderings of the Israelites. At Kadesh-Barnea, for example, where they are supposed to have stayed for 38 years, there is no archaeological evidence of them whatsoever.

So which do we go with? The details in the Bible? The Bible's dates? Or the archaeological evidence?

Almost all historians think there is probably a kernel of truth in the story of the Exodus: some of the ancestors of some of the Israelites must have settled in Egypt for a time and then either left or been driven out. Perhaps there is a connection with the Hyksos. Maybe there really were leaders called Moses and Aaron, but we will probably never know because the true story is lost in the mists of time.

Whatever the case, we should not take the Biblical account of the Exodus any more literally than the tales of King Arthur and the Knights of the Round Table. The Exodus is a national myth of the Israelites and the Jews, just as King Arthur is a national myth of the English and the Welsh. We are talking about *mythos* here, not history.

THE FIRST ISRAELITES

The story of the conquest of Canaan is told in the Book of Joshua, and it is one of the most horrific parts of the Old Testament. It is at best a tale of ethnic cleansing, and at worst genocide. If Joshua were alive today, he would deserve to end his days in the hands of the International War Crimes Court at The Hague.

But – yes, by now you have probably guessed – the Biblical story does not chime with the findings of historians and archaeologists.

The first generations of archaeologists thought it did. They discovered evidence of fire and the destruction of city walls at Jericho and assumed they had found traces of the Biblical story of the fall of that city. No such luck. We now know that there were no walls around Jericho or any other Canaanite city in the 1200s BCE. The Egyptians would not have allowed it.

So, what is the real story? Who were the Israelites and where were they from?

As I said, the Israelites did not invade Canaan in the 1200s BCE. Nobody did.

But somebody did invade in the following century, and it was not the Israelites. These invaders were the "Sea Peoples" from the north, possibly from Greece. Among them were some of ancient Israel's greatest enemies: the Philistines.

The 1100s BCE was a time of massive disruption in the eastern Mediterranean. Archaeologists call it the Bronze Age Collapse. Before this time, two powerful empires flourished, the Hittites in the north and the Egyptians in the south. To the north-west, Mycenaean Greece prospered too, and there were extensive trade links between these three civilisations.

Then everything fell apart and nobody really knows why. Populations fell, cities were destroyed, cultivation ceased and trade routes were disrupted. Mycenaean Greece and the Hittite Empire disintegrated, and Egypt seems to have survived by the skin of its teeth. And in the western highlands of Canaan, a new settled community seems to have emerged: the Ancient Israelites.

To understand how that happened, you need to know something about the relationship between settled farming communities and pastoralists who move around with their sheep and goats. Farming communities and pastoralists have a mutually beneficial relationship. Pastoralists get grain from settled farmers, and farmers get milk, cheese and meat from pastoralists.

So a pattern emerges. In the most fertile land, you have settled farming, and in the more marginal lands, you have pastoralists and their flocks.

But what happens if you have war and the destruction of the farming communities in the fertile lands? If that happens, the pastoralist way of life in the marginal areas becomes unsustainable because there is no grain for them to eat. So some of the pastoralists settle down and become farmers.

If the more fertile lands become productive again, then this can lead to the abandonment of the settlements in the marginal areas as it becomes more profitable to revert to pastoralism.

Archaeologists know that this happened several times in the western highlands of Canaan. In their book *The Bible Unearthed*, Israel Finkelstein and Neil Asher Silberman say the third wave of settlement after 1150 BCE was the largest and most permanent. And archaeologists have discovered one crucial difference: in these new settled communities, there is no evidence of the presence of pigs. A taboo against the eating of pork had taken hold, which we associate with the Ancient Israelites, who seem to have arrived as a distinct settled community.

They have not invaded Canaan or arrived as a wave of immigrants. Invasions and mass migrations leave tell-tale signs in the archaeological record: different ways of making pottery, houses built differently, weapons and tools made to a different design, that sort of thing. There is none of that here. The Israelites are themselves Canaanites, and they have emerged from within Canaanite society. I have already mentioned a brief record of them, presumably as pastoralists, when they were attacked by the Egyptians in the year 1207. But now the Israelites have settled, and they can begin the long process of creating a civilisation complex enough to produce written documentation and eventually put its myths and its history in writing.

YAHWEH

Another interesting thing is that at first, the Israelites did not worship Yahweh. Archaeologists can guess which gods a community worshipped by the names they gave people and places. With the Israelites, the clue is in the name they gave themselves: Isra**EL**. They worshipped the same gods as the rest of Canaan, a pantheon headed by a god called El.

There is strong evidence to suggest that Yahweh did not arrive among the Israelites until around 1000 BCE, possibly brought by a tribe that migrated north into Canaan. Yahweh was a god of storms and war, and he was now incorporated into the pantheons of several nations in the region.

It is likely that Yahweh became a royal or national god of the Israelites under one of their early kings, possibly David. The Bible describes the process in the Song of Moses, a very ancient poem inserted into Deuteronomy, "When **the Most High** gave the nations their inheritance, when he separated the sons of man, he set the boundaries of the peoples according to the number of **the sons of Israel**. For **the LORD's** portion is his people; Jacob is the allotment of his inheritance."

Unfortunately, this translation obscures as much as it reveals. Today, many scholars think that it should really say this: "When **El** gave the nations their inheritance, when he separated the sons of man, he set the boundaries of the peoples according to the number of **the gods**. For **Yahweh's** portion is his people; Jacob is the allotment of his inheritance."

It was not a case of God selecting the Israelites as his chosen people. It was El, the king of the gods, who allocated the Israelites to Yahweh.

THE BIBLE STORIES

OK – let's get back to the Bible, in particular the stories of the Patriarchs. Where did all these stories come from? Who were Abraham, Isaac, Jacob and his sons? Who were Moses, Aaron and Joshua? Did they exist? And if they didn't, why did their stories become so important to the Israelites?

Perhaps the best answer to this question comes from anthropology. In pre-literate societies, if one community wishes to form an alliance with another, they have to find a way to bind themselves together. The best way to do this is to create blood ties with a marriage between the children of leading families. Another good way of creating blood ties is to invent them. Elders from the two communities sit down together and tell each other stories about their ancestors. And then, lo and behold, they "discover" that if you go far enough back, it turns out that the two communities have a common ancestor.

And so it was that over time, the various communities that united under the Israelite banner wove their different ancestor myths into a single narrative that brought together Abram, Isaac, Jacob and the people who became his sons, plus Moses, Aaron, Joshua and something about an Exodus from Egypt. Out of many different local legends belonging to different tribes and clans, a single ancestor myth was born that was strong enough to bind together the scattered Israelite communities.

Two other things seem to have united the Israelites: one was a taboo against pork, and the other was the circumcision of male babies (as opposed to teenagers), though it is possible this was only practised in the south. In terms of religion, the Israelites worshipped the same gods as their neighbours, apart from the fact that they had adopted Yahweh as a royal or national god.

ISRAEL AND JUDAH

There were always two very different communities of Ancient Israelites. To the north, the land was more productive and had better communications, and so up to 90% of Israelite settlements were in this area, which would eventually become the Kingdom of Israel.

To the south, in what would become the Kingdom of Judah, the land was harder to farm and had worse communications. Judah was Israel's poor, backward and under-developed sibling. Even the biggest settlements, such as Hebron and Jerusalem, were no more than villages.

According to the Bible, around 1025 BCE, confronted by the growing menace of the Philistines, Israel and Judah united, first under the Saul and later under David, who is a pivotal figure, uniquely favoured by Yahweh, who promised that his descendants would continue to rule forever.

The Bible tells how, under David, the Israelites became a regional superpower and subjugated all the neighbouring countries. This continued under his son, Solomon, under whom the first great Temple in Jerusalem was built. The Bible says the unified kingdom became so wealthy that "King Solomon was greater in riches...than all the other kings of the earth." (1 Kings 10:23).

Hmmm...maybe not.

Archaeologists have long since learnt to spot the tell-tale signs of the development of powerful states: you need large-scale settlements and evidence of international trade and the creation of a rich and powerful elite with a taste for luxury goods and major building projects. The archaeological record shows no traces of these things during the era of David and Solomon. Judah remained a sparsely-populated backwater and Israel was a society of small and medium-sized settlements.

But over the next century, Israel's population grew, and it began to export olives and grapes. This eventually led to the formation of a wealthy elite and a literate culture. Israel expanded into the plains of Canaan, southern Syria and what is now Jordan, ruling over a multi-ethnic kingdom that was strong enough to hold its own against medium-sized rivals.

THE CULT OF YAHWEH

What follows is based on fairly recent ideas that aren't accepted by all scholars, but I think it is the best reading of both the archaeological evidence and the evidence that can be gleaned from the Bible.

In Israel, Yahweh was often worshipped as a fertility god and was strongly associated with the Exodus. There is also evidence of two new factors: one is conflict within Yahwism between those who worshipped Yahweh as a statue of a bull and those who did not (we see echoes of this conflict in the story of Moses, Aaron and the golden calf). The other is an intransigent Yahwism that wanted to suppress the worship of the Canaanite bull god Baal.

In Judah, Yahweh's statues tended to depict him more as a kingly figure, one to whom human sacrifices were sometimes made in times of crisis. He was frequently worshipped alongside his wife, the mother goddess Asherah. Over time, the royal god Yahweh began to take over the functions of other gods, both El, the king of the gods, and Shemesh, the sun god (similar things happened in other countries in the region).

I'm going to finish here. In the next part, I'll talk about how Yahweh changed from a pagan god to the transcendent one only God of Judaism and Christianity. I'll try to send it tomorrow.

With love,

Omega Bee xx

Appendix Four

How the Bible Came to be Written Part Two

Full source notes are available at https://paulclark42.com/omega/

Dear Sofie,

Okay – the final part of my assignment. I'm going to begin with a potted history, because these are really key events.

- 930 BCE: the Israelites split into two kingdoms: Israel and Judah (not all historians accept that they were ever united).

- 722 BCE: the Assyrians invade Israel and wipe it off the map, deporting much of the population (the lost tribes of Israel).

- 701 BCE: the Assyrians attack Judah. They devastate the country but fail to capture Jerusalem.

- 605 BCE: Babylon, the new superpower in the north, invades Judah, loots Jerusalem and carries off much of the ruling elite.

- 586 BCE: Babylon invades again, destroys Solomon's Temple and effectively ends Judah's existence as a separate kingdom. Many of those who are not deported flee to Egypt.

  This period is known as the Exile.

- 539 BCE: Cyrus the Great of Persia conquers Babylon and allows the Jews (as the remnants of the Judahites were now known) to return home and rebuild their Temple in Jerusalem.

- 332 BCE: Alexander the Great overthrows the Persians and ushers in the Hellenistic era. During the second century BCE, the Jews successfully rebel against the Greeks and regain a precarious independence, which is eventually snuffed out by the Romans.

E: THE ELOHIST'S TEXT

So let's come to the first of the great texts hidden in the Bible: E, which may or may not have been a single text. Julius Wellhausen's documentary hypothesis dated E to the ninth century BCE, but these days most scholars date it a hundred years later, probably not long before the destruction of the Kingdom of Israel in 722 BCE. It cannot be later than that because E reflects the concerns of Israel and shows no interest in Judah.

After the fall of Israel, a mass of refugees flooded into Judah. The resulting population explosion triggered an economic and social revolution. Jerusalem grew 15-fold and many other villages expanded into towns. What had been an isolated rural backwater began to integrate itself into the regional economy and became a centre of the trade between Arabia and Assyria.

Archaeologists now find for the first time evidence of a wealthy Judahite elite that was strong enough to wield what had been a collection of clans into a centralised state.

And with this social, economic and political revolution came a religious revolution.

Both the Bible and archaeological sources agree that the Judahites worshipped a variety of gods. But now, following the calamity of the destruction of Israel, intransigent Yahwists sparked off a great national-religious movement that called for the unification of all Israelites and the worship of Yahweh and no other god. This Yahweh-only faction was something new and different with no real parallels in the other countries of the region, apart from briefly in Egypt some 600 years earlier.

J: THE YAHWIST'S TEXT

Scholars are divided about when the second great hidden text of the Bible was written, the Yahweh-only manifesto we know as J. Julius Wellhausen thought J came first and was written in the tenth century BCE, around the time of the construction of Solomon's Temple in Jerusalem.

Now most scholars date it much later, some as early as the ninth century but I tend to favour the view that it belongs in the sixth century, after the Assyrian siege of Jerusalem in 701 BCE. The failure of the Assyrians to capture Jerusalem may have convinced the Temple priests there that their city really was special: Jerusalem survived because Yahweh lived there, which meant it was the only place where Jews should make sacrifices to him.

D: THE DEUTERONOMIST'S TEXT

After the siege of Jerusalem, Judah was reduced once more to the status of an Assyrian vassal, and the Yahweh-only faction lost much of its influence. It did not regain it until 640 BCE, when an 8-year-old named Josiah came to the throne. The Bible tells of temple restorations early in his reign that led to the discovery of an ancient book of the law.

More than 200 years ago, scholars concluded that this was an early version of the Book of Deuteronomy (the D text), which suggests that it must have been written early in Josiah's reign as a "pious fraud", a forgery purporting to date from the time of Moses. This is probably still the majority view among scholars, but I think it may be wrong.

Some modern scholars say we should not take the finding of a long-lost book literally. It is a common trope that also appears in Hittite, Egyptian and Greek texts. According to these scholars, the D text did not come until much later, when it was written as a response to the catastrophic Babylonian invasions.

384

THE BABYLONIAN EXILE

When Babylon rebelled against Assyrian rule, Egypt intervened on Assyria's side. But in 605 BCE, the Babylonians inflicted a crushing defeat on the Egyptian army. The Egyptians fled homewards and the Babylonians chased after them, laying waste to Judah as they did so. They besieged Jerusalem, and when the city surrendered, they looted the Temple and carried the king and all the city's nobles, priests and craftsmen into captivity.

The Babylonians placed a new king, Zadekiah, on the Judahite throne, expecting him to be docile. But Zadekiah rebelled, and in doing so, he doomed himself and his people. In the year 587 the Babylonian army marched back into Judah, laid siege to Jerusalem and rampaged through the countryside bringing fire, destruction and death.

In desperation, Zadekiah and his army broke out of the city and fled east. But the Babylonians captured him near Jericho. The Bible tells us the exemplary punishment they meted out to him: "They killed the sons of Zadekiah before his eyes. Then they put out his eyes, bound him with bronze shackles and took him to Babylon."

After another round of slaughter and destruction, the Babylonians appointed a tame governor to rule over what was left. But even then, resistance continued, and the governor and his Babylonian advisors were assassinated. At this, a massive wave of Judahite refugees fled to Egypt.

The catastrophe was total. Jerusalem was in ruins, the Temple, supposedly the only place where Yahweh could be worshipped, had been destroyed. Every single city in Judah had been burned to the ground. The royal family, the nobility and the priesthood had either been deported or killed or had fled, and much of the countryside had been depopulated.

How could the survivors account for such a calamity?

The traditional explanation would be that Marduk, the Babylonian national god, was stronger than Yahweh, and that was all there was to it.

But some Yahweh-only ideologues put forward an alternative explanation. The destruction of Israel and Judah had not come about because Yahweh was weak. Far from it: Yahweh himself had visited this devastation upon his own people, as a punishment for breaking their covenant in which they promised to worship only him. Yahweh had used the Assyrians and Babylonians to punish Israel and Judah for worshipping other gods.

One faction, possibly centred around the prophet Jeremiah, produced a history of the Israelites that put this explanation in writing. This is the Deuteronomistic History, a collection of books that goes from Deuteronomy (D, more or less) through the books of Joshua, Judges, 1 Samuel, 2 Samuel, 1 Kings and 2 Kings.

These books tell the story of the Israelites, from their wanderings in the desert under Moses through the invasion of the Promised Land, the rule of the

Judges and the first kings, the division into two kingdoms and their eventual fall.

But this is not history as we understand it today. It is *mythos*, history as religious propaganda. It is the story of the Israelites' covenant with Yahweh, their promise to worship only him and his promise in return to favour them as his chosen people. And it is the story of the failure of the Israelites to live up to their side of the bargain. Time and time again, they rush off to worship other gods, often with the blessing and encouragement of their kings.

Every leader is judged good or wicked to the extent that he follows the Yahweh-only, Jerusalem-only, no-mixing-with-foreigners rules. The bigoted, the narrow-minded and the fanatical are hailed as good; the liberal, the cosmopolitan, the pragmatic and the tolerant are condemned as wicked.

This is the dark secret at the heart of the Judeo-Christian tradition. The authors of these key holy texts were not the good guys. They were not pragmatists or gentle liberals. They were not cautious conservatives or far-sighted reformers.

They were fanatics. They were the Robespierre, the Lenin, the Ayatollah Khomeini of their day, fierce ideologues for whom toleration and diversity were dirty words.

[Please note, Bee eventually deleted the last three paragraphs above.]

THE RETURN

And then, in 539 BCE, there came a dramatic reversal of fortune. The Babylonian Empire collapsed in the face of invasion from Persia. Cyrus the Great became ruler of a vast empire that stretched from the borders of India to the frontiers of Greece and Egypt.

He needed collaborators to govern his new territories for him, and he sent Jewish exiles in Babylon to rule Jerusalem and the surrounding area. (From this point, historians speak of Jews, rather than Israelites or Judahites.)

Cyrus allowed the Jews to restore their Temple. The Jewish returnees refused the offer of help from the surviving Israelite communities in Samaria, thereby creating the distinction between Jew and Samaritan that has lasted to this day. Their leaders also made sure that Deuteronomistic law was strictly enforced. Among other things, they compelled those Jews who had taken foreign wives to divorce them, enforcing the distinction between those who were Jews and those who were not.

P: THE PRIESTLY WRITER'S TEXT

Some scholars insist that P was written before the Exile, but the majority place it during or after the restoration of the Temple. P is enormous, much bigger than J and E, and completely different in style.

The Priestly Writer knew all about J and E. He was not writing a text to complement them but to replace them. He did not like J and E's idea of Yahweh as a merciful god. In his view Yahweh is not merciful; he is just. If you

386

commit a sin, you should not rely on Yahweh's mercy; you should go to the Temple in Jerusalem and make an appropriate sacrifice. Only then would he forgive you.

THE MONOTHEISTIC REVOLUTION

But the Jewish religion was changing. The Deuteronomistic History claimed that it was Yahweh himself who had used the Babylonians to punish Judah. This indicated that Yahweh was a very powerful god indeed, one whose power extended over other nations.

This was the gateway to a massive revolution in Jewish theology, the development of monotheism, the idea that there is just one God, a perfect being who is who is all-knowing and all-powerful. Monotheism is not just polytheism minus all the other gods. It is something new and completely different.

So, let's look at some of the most important differences between monotheism and polytheism.

Polytheistic religions have mythology, the story of how the gods came to be. In the Bible, all this has disappeared. There is no origin story of God. He just is.

Polytheistic gods need names to distinguish them from each other. God doesn't. And so within Judaism there developed the doctrine that God's name must never be pronounced. Most Christian Bibles dispense with his name altogether, replacing "Yahweh" with "the LORD".

Polytheistic gods have a body. God does not. The Old Testament is peppered with references to God's face, head, hands, feet, torso and even (smoothed out by copyists and translators) his genitals. Jews and Christians learned to read all these references to his body allegorically, but we should not forget that they were originally written to be taken literally.

And if God no longer has a body, then he must not be portrayed in a statue. Overt references to statues of Yahweh disappeared from the Jews' holy texts. However, this did not stop their enemies recording the capture of Jerusalem Temple statues on the stone steles that commemorated their victories.

Polytheistic gods are not particularly nice. They are vain and prone to spiteful and vindictive behaviour if you do not show them due respect. God, on the other hand, is a perfect being.

Here, Jews and Christians have a real problem, because, in the words of Richard Dawkins, the God of the Old Testament is "jealous and proud of it; a petty, unjust, unforgiving control-freak; a vindictive, bloodthirsty ethnic cleanser; a misogynistic, homophobic, racist, infanticidal, genocidal, filicidal, pestilential, megalomaniacal, sadomasochistic, capriciously malevolent bully."

In other words, he behaves like a typical polytheistic god.

Unfortunately, the worst kind of Jew and Christian see this version of God as an example to follow. But for thousands of years, the best Jews and Christians have seen this aspect of the Bible as purely allegorical, as *mythos*, not something to be taken literally at all. And certainly not something to be imitated.

The most intellectually rigorous Jews and Christians see this aspect of the Old Testament for what it is, a remnant of its polytheistic origins.

Monotheism has a big problem with evil. Why does an all-powerful and perfectly good God allow terrible things to happen? Polytheism has no such problem. The gods can be horrible, and in any case, their powers are limited.

One explanation for evil and suffering is to say that God is not evil but just. He allows terrible things to happen to us because he is punishing us for our sins. But, as Ecclesiastes (the best book in the Bible by far) points out: "In this meaningless life of mine I have seen both of these: the righteous perishing in their righteousness, and the wicked living long in their wickedness." There is often precious little sign of divine justice here on earth.

And so the idea of divine justice in the afterlife develops. The deserving shall enjoy everlasting bliss in Heaven while the wicked simply perish (what the first Christians probably believed) or suffer eternal torment in Hell (later Christian doctrine).

Another solution to the problem of evil is to give God an antagonist. Satan is a very minor character in most of the Old Testament. He is a provocateur, a member of the council of the gods who acts on Yahweh's behalf. But, perhaps influenced by Zoroastrianism during the Persian era, he evolves into God's enemy, eventually becoming almost his equal in terms of power, and he is projected back into the early texts so that, for Christians, the snake in the Garden of Eden becomes a manifestation of Satan.

But Satan cannot be God's equal, which means that, ultimately, God must triumph over him. This leads to eschatology, a belief in end times and a final, devastating war between good and evil that culminates in the arrival of the Kingdom of Heaven on earth.

Among some Jews, such eschatological beliefs combined with a yearning for liberation from their foreign overlords. The end times would not only entail the defeat of Satan but also the return of a Davidic king anointed by God to lead the Jews to ultimate victory over the Gentile nations.

The Hebrew word for this anointed king is, of course, Messiah.

RELIGIOUS TEXTS

At this point, I need to say something about religious texts. Until the use of paper spread beyond China around a thousand years ago, texts that were not carved into stone or clay were written on papyrus or parchment. The problem with papyrus and parchment is that, under normal circumstances, they only remain legible for a few decades, which means the texts have to be copied out laboriously by hand two or three times every century.

This means that texts only survive because somebody powerful or wealthy is prepared to invest in their survival. Texts that are no longer considered important will disappear. It also means that texts may be edited every time they are copied. It is possible to add, delete or make small changes. Where a text is considered sacred, scribes will feel obliged to preserve it, even parts they do not like. But they may also want to add or to improve what looks like a botched job by the previous generation of scribes: "Why does it say that? Surely they didn't mean that. They must have meant this."

EDITING J, E, P AND D TOGETHER

The redactor(s) who stitched J, E, P and D together to form the Pentateuch were monotheists. Hence the decision to leave out any mythology about the origins of Yahweh. But many of the sacred texts they used to create the first books of the Bible had been written by polytheists.

There is some debate about exactly when the Pentateuch was compiled. Some place it very early in the Persian era. Others put it much later, around 400-350 BCE, and still others suggest that it was compiled during the Hellenistic period, perhaps in the late 300s or early 200s.

The Pentateuch was adopted by both Jews and Samaritans, who came to believe that it had been written by Moses himself. The D text more or less survives as a separate book, but the J, E and P texts had nobody to copy them before they became illegible, so they disappeared as separate texts. They would not be seen again for over two thousand years, when painstaking detective work by generations of scholars uncovered them.

So that is how the Old Testament came to be. It must be said that this is one version of the story, the one that I believe to be true. There is a lot in the above that some scholars would disagree with, and some of them could put forward very good reasons why this version is wrong. But I could cite equally strong counter-arguments, and we could publish journals and hold conferences in which all these things were debated at length.

Well, in fact of course, these scholarly journals and conferences already exist, and their debates continue. I suppose they generate as much heat as light. But that is the way of the academic world. It keeps people in stimulating jobs and it gives students interesting things to study, so I shouldn't complain.

I do not think it detracts from the Bible. It just means you should read the Bible as what it is. It is *mythos*, and as such, it can teach you a lot and broaden your horizons. Just don't take it literally, because if you do, you might become like Dominic, a decent man whose faith lifts him up and makes him a better person, apart from the reactionary ideas that infect his mind because he finds them in the Bible.

Don't let what I have said get in the way of your own spiritual journey. There are plenty of devout Christians who would agree with everything I have written in my "Omega Course" and it does not stop them being Christians. So please, please, please, don't let me stop you. I have seen for myself what a wonderful thing religious faith can be and it would be something I would regret forever if I prevented you from experiencing it for yourself.

I am going to sign off now. I have enjoyed writing for you, because it has helped me clarify a lot of things in my own mind. It has helped me realise something I haven't been able to face up to before.

I now know that I really have lost my faith. I am not a Christian any more. I am an atheist.

There it is; I have said it. I am an atheist. It is not something I want to be, heavens no. It means I have wasted two years of my life studying a subject I don't believe in. I am two thirds of the way through a degree that feels a bit embarrassing, and I have spent all these years dreaming of a career I no longer want.

With love and affection,

Omega Bee xx

The Author

Paul Clark was born in the Forest of Dean in south-west England, the son of atheist teachers, and grew up in Coventry and Manchester. He graduated in modern history and became a teacher of English as a foreign language.

He has lived in Italy and Thailand and has worked with people from more than 80 countries. He lives with his wife in Sussex. They have two grown-up children. This is his fourth novel.

His author website is https://paulclark42.com and you can also follow Paul.Clark.Author on Facebook or on Twitter @paulclark42GB. He would love to hear your feedback.

Printed in Great Britain
by Amazon

38029154R00223